J. M. MANYANGA

AORATOSIA

— PART I —

INVISIBLE WITHIN

Big Brains
PUBLISHING LLC

Published by Big Brains Publishing LLC
www.bigbrainspublishing.com

FIRST EDITION, April 2021
Library of Congress Control Number: 2021904719

Paperback ISBN: 978-1-7367883-0-1
e-Book ISBN: 978-1-7367883-1-8

For June, Aunt Deb, Sharon, and Earnest. For your timeless inspiration.

ACKNOWLEDGMENTS

I'm grateful for the continued support from my family; I couldn't have written this book without them.

I'm also grateful for my first readers—Debbie Bosch and Barbara Johnson. You guys rock!

Thanks to Morgan Manyanga for cover art.

Lastly, I'm grateful for countless people who continue to inspire me every day, intentionally or by chance.

FORTHCOMING BOOKS

AORATOSIA, Part II: The Beginning of the End
The City of Gold.

AORATOSIA

PART I
INVISIBLE WITHIN

CHAPTER ONE

Stratford, Oklahoma

Springtime! Spring was just another season!

Max's phone buzzed. It was Aunt Dori. Max pressed the phone to his ear, steadying the bicycle handle with his left hand.

"Where are you?" Aunt Dori said.

"I am almost there," Max said.

"Hurry up; we are waiting for you!" Alonna said into Aunt Dori's phone.

"Have you ordered yet?" Max said.

"Not yet," Alonna said. "Too many compatriots."

"Typical Sundays," he said.

"What would you like? Same stuff?"

"You know it."

"Of course."

"Thanks, babe. See you in a bit."

Max turned north off Main Street onto Jan Drive, skipped two blocks, and turned right onto Crestpoint towards Hayday Pigstand, perched in the middle of a peach and wheat farm. The tarmac felt crisp from snow-melting salt grain residue. The early spring breeze beamed with freshness from the peach trees recuperating from the unusually long inclement winter. The parking lot was packed. Max locked his bicycle at the bike rack on the west side and headed for the main entrance. The streets were filled with droves of people—bikers, drivers, runners, and restaurant patrons. It seemed that everyone had forgotten the virus pandemic from a few months earlier.

Max took out the small maroon leather casing from his pocket. It was still there! He smiled. He carefully opened the box and was relieved to find the diamond engagement ring still wedged in the white foam. Max gently slipped the box back into the pocket of his gray blazer, brimming with anticipation. He whistled, relishing those extra hours he had worked saving money for the ring. He had done it. Finally. He moon-walked on the pavement, unable to hold back the anticipation of Alonna saying yes.

Max Folksay grew up and still lived in Stratford, a small Oklahoma farming town between Pauls Valley and Shawnee. Stratford seemed self-sustaining, laid-back, and immune from the economic depressions and market crashes. Stratford was well known for its peaches, thus was better known as Peach Country. Family and community kept the small town strong. Husbands loved their wives and the wives loved their husbands. The community milieu was essential—family, friends, church, and a tapestry of shared core values passed down over generations. These kept the community healthy. To Max, life was a routine: go to school, eat, pray, go to church on Sunday, and the occasional movie and Friday night high-school football game or rodeo. Everything seemed naturally programmed and operated by rote.

After recently graduating from North Central University, like most of his classmates Max was ambivalent about what he wanted to do with his life. Spending time with family and friends was special. Still, he was increasingly becoming disenchanted with everything he had known these past seven years. Max wanted more, so much so that everything around him felt like drudgery. He had outgrown Stratford life. He craved to be elsewhere. He wanted to travel; he wanted to visit the Pyramids; he wanted to see the Alps. Each passing day felt like an opportunity plucked away. He felt his valuable time was running out. He was an outlier anyway—in class, in restaurants, at church, on the streets. He wanted more. It was early April. The thought of being a graduate, the feeling of job hunting and endless waiting for graduate-school responses made those few months overwhelming. *Maybe I should have freaking applied to more schools,* Max would say as he sulked over his predicament.

The responsibility of his burgeoning adulthood frightened him. Time crawled by with days filled with emptiness. But the project kept him alive and optimistic. With nothing much to do, he spent a lot of time working on his project. The project insulated him from constant boredom and meaninglessness that continually weighed on his consciousness. It provided an escape from Stratford. It galvanized him and made everything new and exciting each day, even the little things. It gave him a purpose. Maybe fate had offered him another path which he would soon find out. A project that had so captivated him. Sometimes he caught himself thinking about how ridiculous it he was to keep working on it when no perceivable reward would come out of it. But like an innate force pulling him in, he stuck with it, again and again, until it was all he thought about. Slowly it started taking shape and form. By then, it possessed him—an obsession! An algorithm. Mere nonsense! Only he felt it taking shape. He understood it, he protected it—like his baby! He lived with it through all things.

Max strolled past the "All-Natural Food" sign etched above the door—one reason he liked to eat there, apart from it being arguably the most underrated barbecue spot in the country. He gently slapped the sign, as was his habit. The place was packed, with people waiting in line for tables along the doorway, most fiddling with their cellphones. Max breathed in the smoky barbecue aroma and squinted through the elegantly dressed diners for familiar faces. The peach-scented Oriental chandeliers spread throughout the room an exotic yet charismatic atmosphere over pale blue décor ringed with a beautiful frieze, half of it adorned with images of trophy holders of the restaurant-sponsored, annual hot barbecue rib-eating contest. The warm setting infiltrated his soul. He breathed deeply. Home sweet home! A handful of acquaintances greeted him as he made his way through.

Aunt Dori beckoned Max over. Max acknowledged the maître d' and squeezed through the patrons lining the entryway. He proceeded to the table where everyone was sitting. And more. There were plenty of people sitting at the table, and Max scrutinized them as he approached. Four tables had been joined to make one. *Oh crap! So many people.*

Hayday Pigstand was a mid-size restaurant outside of Stratford's town limits, surrounded by lush wheat fields and peach orchards on all sides. It was the place to eat on a Sunday afternoon after church. It was the place where church folks, especially the elderly, liked to hang out and share church gossip over barbecued ribs, brisket, and mounds of home-cooked garlic curly French fries—a staple in Stratford, and Hayday's signature dish. Max could barely remember the last time he had skipped a barbecue meal on a Sunday. He ate the barbecued ribs despite the unpleasant stomach discomfort that always followed. It was a lifestyle. It was because of Aunt Dori. With her ailing body, she spent most days housebound, and Max was her devoted companion everywhere she went.

Max was surprised to see Alonna's parents, Mr. and Mrs. Price, at the table. With them were Max's cousins, Aunt Dori's daughters Natalie and Erica, and their four children. There were also a few members of the First Baptist Church and an older gentleman he did not recognize. Max smiled at Aunt Dori, knowing this was her doing. She smiled back. He knew she was the best at pulling together the town, and he hoped whatever the celebration was for today, she had not posted it on her blog. It was her habit to surprise him from time to time. A multiple-sclerosis patient, she spent most of her days in bed and on social media, which allowed her to post anything new that passed her way. Max did not enjoy her social media postings about him at first but had gradually become used to it. She was proud of him, and he knew it, so he let her do what pleased her. He greeted everyone.

"So this is Max?" the unfamiliar man sitting across the table immediately said. "Like what Titus always described you."

The man wore a nice grayish-green suit. Max tried to recall if he had seen this man before. Max looked at Aunt Dori for any cues, but she only smiled back.

"I hope it was good things," Max said, with a half-smile.

"Bold and confident," the man said. "Your uncle considered you his protégé, you know."

Max stood mute for a few seconds before thanking the man. He had seen this man somewhere.

The man extended his hand. "I'm Reverend Kay Mhornsi."

Max's pupils opened wider, and he kept his grip on the man's rough hands. "Wait, the air force chaplain?"

"That's right."

Max had seen the man giving a sermon on TV during President Blanchard's inauguration at the US Capitol. Reverend Kay was a well-known pastor across America. His church in Houston was comprised of tens of thousands of people. Reverend Kay Mhornsi was an intriguing figure. Besides being a pastor, he was an air force chaplain and had been an aviation attorney for almost three decades. Max wondered how he managed to juggle business, law, science, and religion simultaneously.

Max said, "Uncle Titus talked about you a lot."

"We were good friends."

"I know. How you served together in the Gulf, and some of the adventures you went through together."

"Yup. Those were the good old times."

"Nice to meet you, sir!" Max said.

"You too, Mr. Folksay," he said.

"So, what brought you to town?"

"I'm preaching tonight."

"Oh?" Max said, raising his brow.

"The pastor is on vacation, and he asked Brother Kay to lead the evening service," Aunt Dori said.

"That's great."

"That's what happens when you retire. You get all the time you need," Reverend Kay said.

They laughed.

"I was headed this way anyway to survey a site, so it worked fine."

"Where?"

"Durham in the Oklahoma Panhandle."

"Durham?" David said. "There is nothing there. Last I been there, there was only one grocery store, one church, and one electronic and auto repair shop. But them people are the kindest I've ever met."

"I agree," Virginia, David's wife, said.

"For business?" Mr. Price said.

"Yes, I am surveying a site to build a new rocket launch site. Business is booming for my clients."

"Why Durham?"

"From my research, it is quiet and isolated. The land is cheap. And the land is flat."

"I'd think you would need access to the sea to build a spaceport," Mr. Price said.

"Typically yes, but Oklahoma gave my clients some excellent incentives because they understand that the site will boost the community and state's economy. Plus we get to utilize most of the solid structures from abandoned air force practice bases there."

Alonna was sitting next to Aunt Dori. Since Max and Alonna had started dating, Max had been to her parents' house a handful of times, mainly during the weekends when Alonna was able to leave the dormitories. The Prices were a modest family, despite being affluent. Max was fond of Alonna's mother, Mrs. Price, but her dad, not as much. Mrs. Price was a teacher at the local kindergarten. Fueled by her beautiful, large, cheerful blue eyes that squinted when she shared her infectious smile, Mrs. Price possessed a contagious outgoing personality that was warming to anyone. Max usually saw this in flashes in Alonna's behavior. Her husband, on the contrary, was different. Mr. Price was the town's most prominent attorney and owned the Price Law Firm. Mr. Price, a hometown hero, was famous for shutting down a multinational fracking and natural gas company that was polluting the town and winning the city the largest lawsuit ever filed against major companies. Unlike Mrs. Price, his austere outlook always made Max nervous when around him. Max respected him. He liked to play chess, which was the only place Max felt a connection with him. Mr. Price was impressed by Max's abilities in the game. Most of the time, he asked lots of questions—what Max wanted to do, his plans, him and Alonna—a subject Max didn't want to think of at the time. Mr. Price made it clear that he was looking for someone with a carefully crafted life for his daughter, his one child. He would kill anyone for his daughter. That was clear.

"Come sit here, Max," Mrs. Price said, a perpetual smile tracing across her face. She reached out for a hug. She signaled her husband to scoot over to create space for another chair. He complied.

"Oh, O.K.!" Max said. He knew that he had no choice but to spend the whole lunch stuck between Alonna's parents.

Mr. Price drew up another chair for Max.

"Thank you, sir," Max said.

"You're welcome," Mr. Price said.

Max wiped away the tiny rivets of sweat clustered on his forehead.

"Man, it's getting warm out there," he said, sitting down.

"That's Oklahoma," Aunt Dori said. "You never know what each day's gonna be; one minute it's warm, the next minute it's raining or sleeting."

"Them weather forecast boys play it safe by using percentages," David Golden said from across the table, in his charismatic Western twang. "They say 10 percent chance of rain, and if it rains, then it's O.K., and if it doesn't, it still is fine—it was a 10 percent prediction anyways."

Everyone laughed.

"So, how're you doing, Max?" Mrs. Price said, nudging Max's back.

"I'm doing fine. How're you?"

"I'm doing pretty well."

"Great."

Pat, another member of Aunt Dori's Sunday school class, smiled. "It's always a great day when you spend a day without calling the doctor. Oh, that reminds me, honey: Your appointment with the doctor is tomorrow at 11:00 a.m."

Her husband winced. "Yup. Thanks, honey! What would I do without you?"

Light laughter broke again.

"How're you doing, Pops?" Max said.

"I'm still vertical!" David Golden said. Everyone laughed.

David Golden was also a member of Aunt Dori's Sunday school class and owned a ranch in Wynnewood, a small town about 30 miles south of Stratford. He owned a hay ranch, and Max often worked there during the summers helping with the cattle, horses, and repairing the fence. David taught Max how to ride a horse. He treated Max like his grandson, and Max called him Grandpa. Despite being in his late 60s, he was strong as steel, and Max envied his strength. Although five years David's senior, his lovely wife Virginia still looked beautiful. Virginia baked the best cinnamon rolls Max had ever eaten. After undergoing multiple spine surgeries, she spent most of the day in the house and hardly worked outside. Her only job was to cook breakfast, it seemed. For all the summers Max worked there, they ate lunch every day at the local café in Colgate, Oklahoma. Max liked the fried catfish and zucchini there.

The waiter brought the drinks.

"Have you heard anything yet from graduate school?" Mrs. Price said.

"Not yet," Max said.

Those words flew out of his mouth unconsciously. Max was sick of that question. Since graduating in December, he had learned of countless ways to answer that question.

"Why is it taking so long?" Charlie, Pat's husband, said. "I'd think you should know by now."

"I don't," Max muttered, sipping his water, already thinking of a way to circumvent the subject.

"Did anyone feel the earthquake last night?" Max digressed.

"I did," Virginia said.

"That was crazy," Charlie said.

"We have never had one that strong before in Oklahoma," Pat said.

"A lot of things are happening now we have never had before," Aunt Dori said.

"Signs of the end times!"

"Who knows?"

"Max, I have something for you," Reverend Kay said. He handed a thick orange envelope to Max.

"What is it?" Max said.

"Open it."

Max's hands were slightly shaking, trying to open the thick paper. He finally used the steak knife. He looked at Aunt Dori's face looking for clues. She kept smiling. *I hope she hasn't told anyone*, Max thought.

Everyone was quiet, all looking at Max. Max retrieved the papers from the envelope.

"Is this for real?" Max said, his eyes wide open and his heart beating with excitement.

"Yes, it is!" Reverend Kay said.

"Are you serious?"

"Yup. I saw your name, and I decided to come break the news to you myself."

"How is this even possible?" Max said. "I applied for this six months ago, and I had already forgotten about it. I was starting to think I'd not get in."

"Congratulations, Mr. Folksay. You're one of the only four candidates for the Big Brains America Internship Summer Program at the Federal Institute of Science and Technology!"

"Thank you!" Max said, wiping a tear that was escaping his left eye.

"You're welcome."

"I can't believe this. I never thought I'd be accepted!"

"Now you are," Aunt Dori said.

Max handed the acceptance letter to Aunt Dori, who showed it to the others at the table.

"Did you know about this, Aunt Dori?"

"Yes. That's why I invited my Sunday-school classmates to celebrate before you leave."

"Oh, man. I knew something was up!"

"Congratulations, Max!" voices roared around the table.

On cue, the waiter rushed to the table with a tres leches cake slice with a glittery golden cardboard "Congratulations" sign perched on it.

Max smiled and thanked everyone and continued reading the papers that came with the acceptance letter.

"I'm proud of you, Max," Alonna said at last. She did not flinch, and even managed an enigmatic smile. That's how Alonna was—a natural introvert and challenging to predict. Max often wondered exactly why he loved her so much, but the more he thought about it, the more he realized he loved everything about Alonna.

Max looked at Alonna and managed to choke out a thank you. Her full rosy lips moved swiftly with the words. He gazed at her as if for the first time, even though she was sitting right across from him, realizing how beautiful she was. The blue eyeshadow gave her a consummate radiant hue that enhanced her brown eyes. It perfectly complemented the plain sky-blue sleeveless silk dress she wore. The dress moderately hugged her toned arms and played off her naturally curly red hair spreading over her beautiful bosom, revealing the silver necklace with a blue-green heart-shaped gemstone attached to its lower end. His gift to her.

Even though Max had been avoiding staring at her, her appearance made it a difficult task. He noticed she often stole glances at him, making brief eye contact. He wanted her. He wanted to kiss her. *Did she always do that to tease him?* Max wondered. She had a way with clothes, which made anything she wore look chic. The presence of her parents and church elders made the whole encounter awkward.

"So, Max," Mr. Price said. "When are you leaving for Texas?"

"Yes, when are you leaving?" Pat said.

"Tonight, it seems," Max said, perusing the forms.

"Gosh, that's abrupt!" Mrs. Price said.

"I didn't know it was this sudden."

Reverend Kay looked on, then said, "If you accept the scholarship, you may sign the forms."

Are you kidding me? Max thought, smiling both in confusion and excitement. Being awarded the Big Brains America Scholarship was like winning a championship. How could he decline such an offer? It was the most prestigious program in the nation. Only four candidates were selected nationwide. There was no way he would turn this down, plus this would give him much-needed time away from Stratford. He looked at Aunt Dori; she nodded, smiling.

"Yes, sir! I accept the offer," Max said. Aunt Dori was smiling too.

"Very well, then."

Max signed the forms.

"Your itinerary and plane tickets are in the package," Reverend Kay said. "Do you have a suit?"

"Yes, the one I am wearing."

"Come on," Reverend Kay said. "For the program, you need one or two nice suits and a real tuxedo."

"This is the only one I've got."

"No worries."

Reverend Kay retrieved a billfold from his blazer and handed Max a red credit card.

"Pass by the mall today and get two nice suits," he said. "Give this to the manager. He should be able to take care of it."

"But sir, if those are expensive suits?"

"I know. Don't worry about it. Let Uncle Sam worry about that."

Everyone laughed.

"Thank you."

"Max, it's afternoon," Aunt Dori said.

"I guess I'd better get going then soon."

"When did he say he is leaving?" Charlie asked from across the table.

"Tonight, he says," Charlie's wife, Pat, said.

"Max has a softer voice," Charlie said. "It's hard to hear what he says sometimes."

Charles was 78 years old and having hearing problems, so Pat always repeated things for him. He was a deacon at First Baptist Church. He was also an adjunct professor at North Central University. Max had gone to a few basketball games with him and his wife. They were nice folks. He had worked in the oil refinery industry after working for a cancer research pharmaceutical company in Kentucky. Like Charlie, most of the people at the table were older people, and Max hated his futile efforts to say things twice every time he spoke. Apart from Aunt Dori and Alonna, Charlie was probably the only other person on the table interested in science.

"So what program will you be doing during your internship?" Charlie said, leaning forward.

Max finished sipping on his water.

"Cancer research," he said.

"Any specific area?"

"Cancer stem cells. But I'm also interested in neuroscience, so I might be able to get some experience there too."

"That sounds interesting," Pat said. "I read researchers are getting close to finding the cure."

"Yes, it's promising," Max said.

"What therapeutic methods will you be using?" Charlie said.

"I'm not sure yet," Max said. "Probably immunotherapy. It's been hot for a while now. I guess I'll find out when I get there. The field is always changing."

"I hope you find the cure," Mrs. Price said.

"Soon, I hope!" Max said.

Charlie smirked. "Sure you will," he said, with apparent sarcasm. "Researchers have been saying that for more than a century now, and they got nothing."

Max smiled, trying hard to contain his words. He was used to these discouraging remarks: at school, sports, everywhere. The sad thing was the prejudice coming from older people. Their deliberate bias was preconceived. There was no need to pretend their bigotry did not exist. He had developed a shell to subvert these degrading stereotypes in his way. He was different, and there was nothing wrong with being different. He stood out, as Aunt Dori had often told him when he was a teenager. Charlie was one of those perpetually pissed-off old men.

Max wanted to yell "Screw you!" but instead he nodded, smiled, and said, "That's good, then. At least we don't have to start from scratch. I like the challenge."

"That's right. Even Newton knew that standing on the shoulders of giants allowed him to discover gravity," Aunt Dori said, sensing the looming tension.

Charlie's mouth quirked. "Well, maybe."

"Doesn't Ecclesiastes say, 'There is nothing new under the sun,' honey?" Pat said.

"I'm sure someone will find it at the right time."

"Well said," David Golden said. "Is that what you are planning to do in graduate school?"

"Probably," Max said. "Honestly, I'm not sure what I want to do anymore."

"Don't tell me," Mrs. Price said. "I still remember those days." She stared blankly at the table, her countenance and mind carried back in time. "We called it graduate transition fever back in the day," she said. "But you will be over it soon."

"I might go into neuroscience."

"That's way over my head," David Golden said. Everyone laughed.

"He wants to find a cure for M.S.!" Aunt Dori said. "I believe he will find it. Hopefully, I will be alive then."

Alonna rubbed Aunt Dori's back.

"He will," Mrs. Price said. "I know you'll be great in anything you choose to do."

"Thank you," Max said.

The waitress finally brought lunch. With hands held together around the table, Charlie prayed for the food and for many blessings, health, and politics. He concluded by praying for Max's new path as he pursued God's plan for his life.

Immediately after the prayer, the conversation shifted to small talk —about the foolish politicians, the new young pastor at church, right-wing conspiracies, *Jeopardy*, and new pain medication. Max concentrated on devouring the succulent barbecued ribs and mounds of curly fries accompanied with green beans and sweet corn on the cob. Max appreciated that peaceful moment to enjoy the food. They talked about one thing and another, but Max was off, far away, dreaming of his proposal. He knew this was the right moment to propose to Alonna, with everyone there. He looked around the table, and everyone was laughing and smiling.

Max felt the small case in his blazer pocket. It was about time. His armpits were soaked. *It's the hot ribs,* he thought, trying to subdue his nervousness. Fortunately, nobody at the table seemed to pay much attention to him. Max glanced at his watch and excused himself for the restroom.

"You're already done?" Mrs. Price said jokingly.

Max nodded, swallowing the tiny bits of food still in his mouth.

"I wasn't gossiping," he said laconically. Everyone laughed.

The people at the table always treated Max like a young boy, despite his being 22 years old.

"He is a growing boy," Pat said. "He needs to eat like that."

"That's a lesson you learn when you are old, retired, and spend most of the time with your wife. Right, Pat?" Charlie said, rubbing his wife's back teasingly. Everyone giggled.

"Don't listen to him, Max; men gossip a lot too," Pat ribbed back with a smile.

"Unless you find one of them rich girls," David Golden said, winking at his wife Virginia. He wiped his thick white mustache with a paper towel before taking a swig of the sweet tea.

Virginia glared at him. "Don't listen to these guys. Marry for love."

"As I did," David said. "Now I spend all my time on a ranch."

Virginia rolled her eyes. "And whose fault is it? Look where I am."

Everyone laughed.

Being among these people every Sunday after church lunch was always the best part of Max's weekly routine. They say wisdom increases with age, and he sure did enjoy some of the encouragement and love these people gave him. They shared fascinating stories, mostly from their heydays. Even though he was the only younger person in the group on most Sundays, he loved their discussions. All this had made him take everything lightly, knowing that the seemingly-so-important issues may not be so important. This pack valued the mundane things about life—the rain, a good night's sleep, a successful hand surgery, a visit from a grandchild, or letting out the loudest fart to joke about it. None of the men at the table took things seriously, except for their deeply-seated conservatism which seemed somewhat contrived, and they formed their own tribe for the sole purpose of bashing the other side. Like-minded! Max would tread on shells so as not to argue with them on some trivial issues.

MAX PULLED out his chair and left for the restroom.

In the restroom, Max realized he had not planned any strategy to propose to Alonna. His heart was pounding in his chest, his head was light on his shoulders, his ears blocked from all the sounds everyone was making. A nervous flutter ran across his body. Max felt the case in his pocket. *Maybe I'm too hasty about this,* he thought.

He stared into the mirror for a long time contemplating how he would proceed. He felt excited and frightened all at once. *Damn! Movies lied. This thing does take guts.* A second thought struck the back of his mind urging him to postpone the proposal for a later date, in private. But he never backed down from a challenge, ever; doing so meant failure to him. Today was the perfect moment; maybe proposing wasn't expected to be planned, it was supposed to be spontaneous, a mere impulse when no one knew it was coming. It turned out that it required guts to pull it off. The thought comforted him. He silently cheered himself up. Alonna loved him, and he loved Alonna, so there was no reason to be nervous. They had grown so much since their first encounter on a mission trip in Papua New Guinea. *Dang it, there is no day I'm going to be ready for this. I will do it,* he thought.

Max returned to the table, with no one paying much attention. He went to Alonna's chair and kissed her on the forehead. He knelt on one knee. That immediately drew attention from everyone in the restaurant. Everybody was startled and abruptly stopped what they were doing. Alonna moved her chair to face Max, her eyes wide open. She covered her face with both hands. She suddenly knew what was coming.

"Alonna Price," Max said, holding her hands and stammering for words. "I love you!"

"I love you too, Max!" Alonna said. She was trembling. Tears soaked her eyes. "What's going on?"

Everyone in the restaurant was quiet, and everything seemed still except for Alonna and Max. Everyone had stopped eating. Max ignored her question. He kissed her hand again.

"Max, you are sweating!" Alonna said.

"I am?" he said.

"Yes. You are!"

"And you're crying," he said.

"I am. I—I don't know why," she said.

Max wiped the tears from Alonna's eyes with his thumbs and dried his hands with his handkerchief.

"I need to tell you something," Max said, taking large breaths of air.

"O.K."

"Alonna, you are the most competitive and hardworking person I have ever met," he said. "You inspire me to strive for higher as I pursue my dreams. You are the most honest and direct person, which frightens me sometimes, but challenges me to be a trustworthy man."

Max paused.

"You are a kind-hearted and loving woman. Thank you for being Aunt Dori's best friend even though she requires so much attention and is a pain sometimes."

Max smiled at Aunt Dori, and Aunt Dori winked back. She was crying too.

"And most importantly of all, I want you to know that you're the picture of a godly woman, which I cherish very much, and I am always challenged to ask the Lord to direct my ways like you do. I am always amazed at how much you know. You teach me that even though I don't know my future, I can still press on joyfully knowing that God will comfort me.

"I love what you and your family stand for—your mom and dad are the best people in the world.

"Thank you for all that you are, for the things you have taught me and the things you will teach me in our lives together in the future. Thank you for being the puzzle that I'm gladly willing to solve every day." Max sighed.

Alonna was crying even more, with hands clasped.

"So, Alonna Price," he paused, gazing into her eyes. "Will you marry me?" He opened the leather box and extended it to Alonna.

"Yes!" she said exuberantly. "I will marry you, Max Folksay!" She embraced Max.

Almost every woman in the restaurant was crying. The crowd rose, cheering and applauding, all chairs turned to Max and Alonna.

Max slid the ring on Alonna's finger, his hands trembling. Alonna helped him to stand up.

"It's beautiful!" Alonna said, tightly embracing Max.

They kissed and hugged, feeling each other's thudding hearts against their firmly pressed bosoms.

The restaurant crew quickly responded. The waiters brought a large bouquet of assorted red and pink roses with a bunch of red and purple balloons. Confetti sleeted all over the table. The song "A

Hundred More Years" floated through the restaurant from the speakers above. The song suited the moment; Max wanted to freeze that moment forever. Everyone congratulated the pair. Alonna's mom hugged Max and said she was proud of him; her dad shook Max's hand firmly and congratulated him. Reverend Kay commended them in a jovial mood: "This day keeps getting better and better!"

Aunt Dori was a genius; maybe she had planned this all along. A peach pie slathered with ice cream was served to conclude the celebration.

More people came to congratulate the pair on their way out. Max was ecstatic. He wanted this moment to last forever, like the song said. She was his fiancée, and soon she would be his wife, and he felt even more in love with her. The thought of leaving her for Houston made him sick. *It was definitely worth the wait,* he thought. He was thankful to God. Moreover, he was proud of Aunt Dori for setting up the whole thing. Max walked over and hugged Aunt Dori.

Holding back tears, she said, "I'm proud of you, Max! I wish Titus were here. You know what he would've loved the most?"

"What?"

"The man you have become. A few years ago, you were a skinny kid. Just seeing how much you have grown. He would be proud of you. Doing the right thing, that Titus and I never got to do."

"Thank you." Max rubbed Aunt Dori's back.

Alonna's phone rang. She excused herself from the table into the hallway close to the exit. Through the glass, it looked as if she was arguing or having a misunderstanding with someone. When she got back, she had a capricious smile.

"Is everything O.K., baby?" Mrs. Price said.

"Yes, everything is fine, Mom," she said. "A call from the mayor."

"Our mayor?"

"Yes. I've been selected to participate in the annual Rodeo Festival!"

"That's awesome, babe. Congrats!" Max said, pecking Alonna's cheek.

"Thank you!"

"When is it?"

"In June."

"Great!"

"You'd better be there," Alonna said, staring affectionately at Max.

"I will."

Later that day, Alonna offered to drive Max to Will Rogers International Airport.

"Thank you for agreeing to look after Aunt Dori," Max said, as they cruised onto I-40 West.

"My pleasure," she said. "I'm practicing being a nurse anyway, so I'm still doing my job."

"I hope Aunt Dori will behave."

"Trust me, she will."

"She likes to let out her pestering alter ego occasionally."

"We'll see. I think we'll be fine."

"I love you."

"I love you."

They passed Midwest City into Oklahoma City.

"How is your project going? Are you still doing it?" Alonna said.

"It's going fine," he said. "I haven't done much lately. Hopefully, in Houston I will be able to pursue it more."

"Keep me posted."

They talked about many other things: their plans, Aunt Dori, their families, and their future careers. They told each other how they missed each other and discussed their upcoming mission trip to Papua New Guinea in a few months, the place where they had first met. At 6:15 they arrived at the airport. They stood outside the car and kissed. Max felt his nose succumbing to the lavender-rich perfume on Alonna's body. She smelled wonderful.

"Please don't go," she said.

Max held her body more tightly.

"I have to go," he said. "Thanks for supporting me on this; I'll make it up to you, Alonna. I promise."

"I know," she said, sobbing. "But I'll miss you."

Max could feel some of her tears soaking the side of his neck.

"I will miss you more!" Max said, starting to get emotional. He softly rubbed her back. Her hands clutched around his neck.

She released him and looked him straight in the eyes with her teary eyes filled with love, and squeezed Max's hands, not wanting to let Max go.

"I have a request," she said.

"What is it?" Max said.

Alonna looked down for a while, then smiled at Max.

"Call me three times a day?"

"Of course, babe," Max said. "I will, maybe ten times."

He kissed her again.

"You'd better," she said, still not wanting to let go.

"I promise," Max said, letting go of her hands. "See you soon."

She turned and walked away, not wanting to look back. Max waved when she started the car. She waved back briefly and drove off. For a split second, he was in a dilemma, unable to decide whether he should go to Houston or whether he should stay. He knew the answer and knew what Alonna wanted of him.

It was 6:35 p.m. Max hurried to check in his luggage and hurried to Gate Four where the last group of passengers was boarding. The flight attendant made the final announcement. Max rushed through the jet bridge. He was ready for Texas.

He did not know what to expect, but he knew time would tell. It is interesting how fast time moves by, and yet time controls our lives. It is time that allows us to do some things, and it is time that makes us dream of the beautiful experiences. And it is only time that tells whether we achieve those dreams as well as allowing us to forget those experiences we wish we might never remember. For Max, time was moving quickly, very quickly that day.

CHAPTER TWO

Federal Institute of Science and Technology (FIST)

Dr. Yates had finished the last phone call. Even with an endowment worth millions of dollars, he always dreaded making those calls. The viral pandemic had nearly derailed this year's meeting. But the program depended on the donations, and it was his job to persuade the donors. It depended on the membership fees and the new ideas. Fortunately, the government was starting to loosen the lockdown and travel restrictions as the newly approved vaccine was now being distributed across the country.

Dr. Yates removed his reading glasses. He looked, satisfied, at the two piles of abstracts and proposals, one for Big Brains America and one for Project ASHE. As the science and technology advisor to the president, he had to review these and update President Blanchard. It was a lot of work, but then he was a pro now. A Ph.D. in Biophysics, with hundreds of high-impact publications, he was used to this much work. He was resigned to the notion that being an academic required working 24/7. Hell, especially if you were a superstar scientist like he was.

A notification beeped from his computer calendar. *Crap!* Dr. Yates thought. He texted President Blanchard. It was nice having the leader of the free world on speed dial, anytime, anywhere—a perk for being an advisor to the president.

He picked up one application that had particularly struck him, thinking of Titus, his longtime friend. This was more than a coincidence. He recalled his promise to Titus that felt a little like nepotism. But the kid deserved it. Heck, nepotism was alive and well, though masquerading in other forms. Everyone did it. Even presidents openly did, unapologetically turning their administration into their own family business, landing jobs for the spouse, daughters, sons, in-laws, mistresses, former lovers, business partners, Russians, Chinese—all holding influential positions they couldn't care less about if it were not for the money and business opportunities that often came with these positions. Who cared, as long as it replenished their coffers?

He checked the time. It was almost 3:00 p.m. Dr. Yates had to be at the airport. He called the valet and headed for the elevator. He guzzled the superfood enzyme cocktail from his lunch bag. He winced. It tasted like crap. So much for the price of being healthy, right? That's what they said anyway. Didn't even know if the stuff worked or not.

He locked the door and went downstairs.

CHAPTER THREE

Will Rogers International Airport, Oklahoma City

MAX SKIMMED through the stubby scrapbook he had received from Aunt Dori as a present, passing through layers of newspaper clips, letter stickers, glitter, travel tickets, and excerpts cut from magazines. Some of his award certificates from college were carefully stacked in the plastic pocket on the scrapbook's front. Aunt Dori had put a lot of effort saving all his experiences into this memory collage. Max often wondered why she cared so much about collecting all these experiences. But it was dawning on him—she did it for moments like these. Aunt Dori wanted him to paste and keep all the memories of his adventures in Houston and the future. "You can show it to your kids someday," she would say.

Max flipped the page. There was a photo of him with Uncle Titus and Aunt Dori on the front porch swing of their ranch house. In bold lettering "The Journey Begins" stood at the top center against the white page. Both Uncle Titus and Aunt Dori had their hands on Max's shoulders while they sat on the old swing. Max was smiling, exposing the gap between his front teeth. He looked sluggish. *Sixteen. Man, I was so skinny, my head too big.* Max shrugged at the self-observance. Good! Thoughts raced through his mind. *The jet lag. Red Lobster. Ugh! The fried crusty shrimp for the first time! The Peach Festival carnival. Jamboree.*

He was smiling now; much had changed since then. He was more assimilated into the lifestyle—"Americanized," as Aunt Dori would put it. He now gobbled down the fried food that once disgusted him. Max smiled and pressed the picture where it was detaching from the page. Uncle Titus stood with a smirk, dressed in a white t-shirt with some dark stains on it, as if someone had forced him into the picture. Max's eyes rested on Aunt Dori—the woman who had shaped who he was as a young man today. Aunt Dori was wearing an elegant striped yellow and white dress. She had a warm, beautiful smile—the familiar smile Max had known for as long as he could remember: a reflection of her modest lifestyle, not having much, yet still generous. He loved Aunt Dori and Uncle Titus. They deserved it. Who would open their homes to a poor homeless boy from another continent? Only love. Faith that tomorrow will be brighter and things will align for good— his true heroes.

The smile had not faded an inch. Dorinda Folksay was 65 years old. She had multiple sclerosis. She had been Max's guardian as long as he could remember, literally his mom. She had two children, six grand-children, and eight great-grandchildren. She always bragged about having the opportunity to mingle with three of the next generations in the Folksay family line. Her husband, Uncle Titus, had died two years earlier at age 76 of lung cancer and pneumonia, and Aunt Dori was living on her pension because most of her husband's savings had been depleted by countless doctor visits. They had been married for 45 years. She was half Native American and half Caucasian. She was proud of her Native American heritage and identified herself as such. As a retired nurse, she had her own savings to live on. Still, the accruing needs from her debilitating condition were draining away those savings.

Her body was succumbing slowly. The disease had painfully limited her lifestyle—no dancing, no walking, no driving, no shop-ping. Yet she was never a curmudgeon; in fact, the disease seemed to make her wiser and more graceful with each passing day. She was an optimist, always seeing the positive side of life. She was not the sort of person who lamented her sickness. She often joked, saying she never complained, but rather, explained. Of course this was whenever she felt her needs were too pressing, and it made everyone around her laugh. Few people felt sorry for her. "M.S. is a gift," she would say as part of a response to the question of why she never complained.

It seemed from the onset she had decided what was important to her was making others happy. Her positive outlook had probably kept her out of nursing-home care, which she solemnly despised. The number of activities she could handle were becoming fewer and fewer each day. A few years earlier, she had been able to do anything, but now, even the most mundane tasks seemed herculean. But one thing remained: She never stopped smiling and fighting. She was far from being an invalid.

For Aunt Dori, every day was a good day. Her can-do-anything attitude was an archetype and had not faded. Despite being bedridden for most of every day, she learned other skills to train her atrophied hands as the doctor suggested: She sewed, typed, and occasionally gave virtual science lectures at the local community college. Aunt Dori always found time to do good things and took pride in spoiling her great-grandchildren. Sadly, neither daughter visited often; she was grateful for having Max to look after her.

Aunt Dori attended First Baptist Church regularly, where she was a deaconess. She strove to teach Max to walk in the right way with the Lord, frequently reminding him of God's plan in everyone's life. She believed God allowed the M.S. to happen to her so she could influence other lives for the better. Max, however, found that difficult to believe. He was amazed at how, despite her ailment, she managed well to make others happy. She was an inspiration to Max. Max barely remembered ever being chided by Aunt Dori. Max loved both his aunt and uncle, but of the two, he preferred Aunt Dori. She was the most considerate and caring. Of the two, Titus was the stricter and had a mercurial character; he would spend time lecturing Max about how to do what he thought was right. Yet Max also enjoyed the intellectual discussions with Uncle Titus, gleaning as much information as he could.

Even with a somewhat unclear future back then, Max loved creating: He wanted to dream, travel, and use his creative imagination to change the world. Aunt Dori encouraged him when he explained things to her, even though she did not understand most of his work.

She thought it was an enjoyable hobby for Max. "At least you're not doing drugs," she would say. "Plus, it gives me a break from watching TV all day." But she still wanted him to graduate, have a job and earn money. He had promised Uncle Titus he would graduate.

Max shook himself from his reverie, catching the scrapbook almost slipping from his hands. He collected himself and straightened up, realizing he had dozed off. He flipped to the next page. On the next page was Alonna. She was standing next to Max beside Aunt Dori's bed, smiling. He looked at the photo for a few seconds and found his thoughts drawn to the day he decided to marry Alonna. He and Aunt Dori were seated at lunch.

"How's your girlfriend?" Aunt Dori had said, looking straight into Max's eyes.

"She's great," Max said. "We're going to the basketball game with the tickets you bought me."

"That sounds like fun. I hope it will be a good game and you have a good time."

"I'm sure it'll be."

"She is a beautiful girl," she said, sneaking glances below her glasses. "I bet you know that, don't you?"

"She is."

Aunt Dori laughed. "Oh, Max dear. Do you want to marry her?"

"Well—I don't know."

"They're a great family, Max. I don't want you playing around with that girl if you're not sure," she said, in a way that showed sincerity.

"I won't," Max said, rubbing her left hand while she continued eating cottage cheese.

Aunt Dori still believed in soulmates. Max wondered whether such a thing existed anymore.

"I'll ask her to marry me soon."

Aunt Dori's face shone.

"Are you serious?"

"Yes, I am. I'll ask Alonna to marry me next month. I have the ring," Max said, bringing out the tiny box with the engagement ring.

"It's beautiful!" she said. "I'm excited to hear that."

"Thank you."

"You're doing the right thing. We're not very good examples," Aunt Dori said quietly. She and Titus had married without their parents' consent because of an unplanned pregnancy, which made things complicated. They had eloped to Southeast Oklahoma, where a preacher in Wapanucka married them. Their parents only learned months later when Dorinda's tummy started protruding. They joked about this moment occasionally.

"And please don't tell anyone about this, O.K.?" Max said.

"I won't tell anyone," Aunt Dori said, smiling.

Max looked at his phone. "Alonna's here."

"You'd better hurry. Don't keep her waiting."

"You're right. I gotta go."

Max smiled and kissed Aunt Dori goodbye.

"Be safe! Have a good time."

"Thanks."

"Let me know when you plan to propose," Aunt Dori said as Max left the room.

"I will."

THE PILOT ANNOUNCED that the plane was about to start descending. Max was perturbed upon realizing he had been staring at the same page for almost five minutes and retained nothing. His memory raced all over the place, and he found it difficult to focus, even on the simple task of looking through a scrapbook. He became conscious of how uncomfortable the airplane seats were, how much they made his back stiff. The inside of the airplane felt too cold. Max glanced to his left and right, realizing how much he did not like being sandwiched between two strangers. He preferred the pandemic days when everyone sat six feet apart. The man on his left was snoring, head facing up and mouth wide open. On his right was a younger girl, who seemed to have everything under control. She had earbuds on with her head bouncing. Max guessed she was listening to hip-hop. The girl ignored the flight attendant's announcement to buckle up and prepare for landing until Max signaled it to her. The girl grinned at Max before fastening her seat belt, then quickly looked away.

A few moments later, the flight attendant gave permission to turn on electronics. Reflexively, Max reached into his pocket to check the time on his smartphone, even though he had a wristwatch. He checked again, frustrated he had not absorbed what time it was the first time. The plane had arrived early at the Houston International Airport. He had a lot of expectations for the big city. He was glad that he had plans for the fall. He knew he was going to spend time solving the algorithm. His algorithm.

Max grabbed a pulled pork sandwich and a cappuccino at the McDonald's and sat in the waiting area. He watched droves of people walking briskly along the terminal, most of them focused on their smartphones. He eavesdropped on the couple sitting next to him, who seemed to be bored with each other.

"Why do they call this natural water?" the husband asked after a sip.

"Because it's natural," the wife said bluntly.

The husband laughed mockingly, then said, "How can it be natural when you have supplemented minerals and enhancements?"

The wife rolled her eyes.

"Water should be tasteless and natural," the man continued emphatically.

The woman nodded and said, "Baby. But it is still—."

Kak kak kak! The sound from the janitor's cart clouded the rest of the conversation. Soon after, Max turned around and saw a man approaching. He continued watching the man as he approached. The man was wearing cargo safari khaki shorts and a blue t-shirt with flip-flops. He walked deliberately, with his short, sturdy frame swaying from side to side. A ring of white and gray hair formed a horseshoe on his scalp. He was probably in his mid-60s. Max dumped the remaining sandwich into the trash bin and headed towards the man, who was smiling.

"Maxwell?" the man said.

"Yes, sir," Max said. "Maxwell Folksay."

The man putt out his hand.

"Tony Yates!" he said.

"Oh. Dr. Yates?" Max said, shaking his firm grip.

"Yes. Call me Doc."

"I'm thrilled to finally meet you, sir."

"My pleasure to meet you too, Max," Dr. Yates said. "I'm glad you made it."

"Glad to be here finally!"

Besides being the science advisor to the president of the United States, Tony Yates was a renowned Nobel Laureate biophysicist and professor at the FIST, the Federal Institute of Science and Technology. He was the chairman of NASA's Planetary Division and had led the development of the first probe teleporter to Mars by Spartan Enterprises, an aerospace company of which he was executive chairman. Dr. Yates held numerous patents. He was also the coordinator of the prestigious Big Brains America summer program at the FIST. Max could not believe he was actually talking to Dr. Yates.

"How is your aunt?" Dr. Yates said, running his left palm across his bare scalp.

"Um, she's doing fine," Max said. "How do you know about my aunt?"

"I try to read all of my students' applications and personal statements to better know how to serve them. I thought your story was quite sincere. You mentioned her a lot in yours."

"I did, didn't I?"

"You did."

"She's doing great," Max said. "At least that what she would say anyway."

"She's a smart woman."

They laughed.

"Is this all your stuff?" Dr. Yates said.

"Yes. That's all of it."

"Great," Dr. Yates picked up one of Max's bags. "I'm parked in the west wing garage."

Max nodded. They exited the terminal towards a grayish Mercedes sedan.

"Congratulations for getting accepted," he smiled, revealing his crooked teeth.

"Thank you, sir," Max said pridefully. "I am looking forward to the new experience."

"I am sure you will be fine," Dr. Yates said. "You have a unique story, which makes me believe you will succeed."

"Thank you," Max said.

Dr. Yates slammed the trunk and unlocked the doors.

"Great. I think we can beat rush hour traffic."

"I hope so."

They sat quietly as the vehicle exited the airport garage.

CHAPTER FOUR

FIST

MAX AND DR. YATES arrived at the Federal Institute of Science and Technology around 5:30 p.m. The campus was bustling with people ready to go home, hurrying to beat Houston's nightmarish rush-hour traffic. Everyone was in suits and ties, jostling, with cheerful faces. They were met with "how do you do, how are you sir, how's it going," as if everyone knew each other. Everyone strode purposefully with great energy. Everything at FIST was permeated with professionalism. With the brand-new gray suit and the leather attaché case he carried, Max blended in right away.

"Wow, this is nice. Is it a requirement to wear suits?" Max said.

"No. It used to be, but now it's a tradition. It's what makes FIST unique from other institutions. If you don't, you don't fit in."

"I kinda like this. Why does everyone greet everyone?"

Dr. Yates smiled. "Not everyone does, but most of the people. It is purpose—as you'll see when you know everyone here has a special gift or one even better than yours. Knowing you're among the best changes the way you see everyone. After all, we all are. So why not cherish each other?"

Max pondered the point for a while, nodding.

"That explains why everyone is nicer."

"To some extent. Respect. Freedom of expression is a core value for our system, but it's never taught or required. The students develop a sense of being."

"That's a great way to put it."

"It is a hassle sometimes, but we progress."

Dr. Yates waved at the group of students gathered on the lawn next to the water fountain. "It's the way to live. If everyone could understand that, things would be different."

Max nodded silently, looking out through the cracked window.

"This is beautiful!"

"Thank you. I really enjoy it here."

They passed the lush lilac-bloomed jacaranda trees abutting the covered entryway to the staff parking lot. The shed flowers produced a lavender-blue carpet along the alley. Songs of hundreds and hundreds of small birds and bees clustered in the trees collecting nectar before the nightfall filled the air. A tingling sweet fragrance of fresh jacaranda flowers wafted through the window.

"Let's drop your stuff at my office and see the campus nurse; then I will take you to your apartment."

"O.K."

The Science and Math Department's front wooden doors led into the atrium where a giant brass pendulum swung on the center hinged at the ceiling five floors up, with 24 sticks placed strategically in a circle. The pendulum knocked one down every hour. The area was ornamented with two large aquariums on opposite sides and glass cabinets of stuffed birds, snakes, and rodents. They proceeded into the Epictetus hallway, on the left of the main entrance.

"Our department is divided into seven sections, each named after Stoic philosophers," Dr. Yates said.

"Oh?" Max said, looking and turning around. Epictetus, Aurelius, Seneca, Apollonius. The seven different hallways all merged into the atrium—the names carved into the wall above the door frames.

"Was this intentional?"

"Yes. That's what we stand for. We believe each and every one here can change the world."

Max nodded at the seemingly pretentious statement. But Dr. Yates was sincere.

"The other sections are upstairs, which I will show you."

Dr. Yates' lab spanned half of the whole second floor. His office was a few doors southward, into the Epictetus hallway, and reflected a busy life. A framed Ph.D. degree from MIT, and a photograph of him and President Blanchard after receiving the Presidential Medal of Freedom at the White House were mounted on the wall. A few golf trophies sat on the windowsill. Above the credenza behind his desk were a Nobel Prize in biophysics plaque, numerous group photos of his lab personnel, and a family photo beside his computer. There were other certificates laid out under the window for his community achievements and involvements. On the left side of his desk was a shelf full of books on subjects ranging from astronomy to zoology, with the majority being physics. A classical Galilean telescope stood adjacent to the window facing outside.

Dr. Yates' lips quirked, noticing Max's fascination. "I still prefer the old way of things. I like reading on paper most of the time. I like my anachronism; it allows me to see things differently, and it works for me. You can call me old-fashioned."

"Not at all! I do that too. I like the feel of the paper in my hands."

"I do too!"

"That's a nice collection you have here," Max said.

"Thanks. A few things to remember the victories!"

"That's a lot."

"It is," Dr. Yates said, pausing mid-sentence and scratched his forehead as if to retrieve something deep down his mind. "But it's all stuff."

Max remained still, unsure of the right response. He wondered how such a busy man managed to conflate all these different endeavors.

"What matters is taking action that will change the lives of everyone for many years when I'm gone, not only myself," Dr. Yates said.

Max nodded. "I see. Is that why you decided to be a scientist?"

"No. I mean, yes, when I think of it. But back then it was for the stipend," he laughed. "I wasn't sure at your age. With time, it kind of grew on me, and I realized I could affect more lives than I could ever imagine with my work. And here I am."

"I feel the same too sometimes."

"It's normal."

Dr. Yates scribbled on a yellow notepad.

"All right, let's go and get you set up."

They exited the office, passing through the Rufus courtyard, gleaming with green plants and exotic flowers. Students were scattered across the lawn in small groups of twos, threes, or fours, and greeted Dr. Yates cheerfully. They walked past the oval into the student services building. A security guard stood on the inside of the door and motioned Max to stop at the security checkpoint. The guard smiled at Dr. Yates.

"How're you, Doc?" the man said.

"Well, George. Yourself?"

"Doing great, sir. Thank you."

Dr. Yates sat down on one of the couches in the anteroom.

"I'll wait for you here."

"O.K.," Max said.

The guard shifted his focus to Max. He scrutinized Max's identification card for a few moments.

"Sorry, young man. But we gotta do this with all the shooting that's going on at campuses."

"I understand."

"Hands up, sir," he said. "Do you have anything in your pockets?"

"No."

"Any metal plates in your body?"

"No."

"Great."

He ran a scanning bar on Max's back and front sides, which beeped loudly.

He still ran his hands through the pockets.

"Your necklace, sir?"

"Oh, my bad. I totally forgot I had this on."

"That's all right; it happens to the best of us."

He reran the scanning bar. This time there was no beeping.

"You may step forward now. Follow the corridor and turn on the first door to your left."

"Thank you."

"I miss the good old days when we didn't have to go through all these procedures on orientation day," Dr. Yates said.

"Don't say it," the guard said. "Those were the good times."

"Yup, times change."

Max followed the corridor into a blue-colored room, where an automated voice instructed him to stand on the footpads at the center of the room, marked "Stand Here." A thick beam of white light radiated down, then up, repeatedly across Max's body from head to toe. After a few minutes, an automated female voice uttered, "Profile complete," and Max proceeded to the door with the blinking exit sign. He emerged on the other side of a glass door and waited in the small room. A woman in pink scrubs entered the room, carrying a clipboard.

"It wasn't too bad, was it?" the woman said with an easy smile.

"No. Not at all. I barely felt a thing."

"Great. Some of the students are shaken by the light when they leave the room."

He swung his arms in the air, yawning.

"I'm Jaimie, the campus nurse," she said, offering her hand.

"Max. Nice to meet you," Max said, clasping her hand warmly. He eyed the lanyard hanging around her neck over the pink scrubs.

"About your scan, Max. I have good news and interesting news."

"What is it?"

"On a positive note, your overall health looks fine, and everything is normal." She wrote on the clipboard.

"That's great!"

"However, your genomic profile indicates some weird pattern. Interestingly your pattern matches none of the polymorphisms and DNA sequences linked to any diseases in our database."

"What does that mean?"

"I can't tell exactly. It's probably nothing serious, maybe a missense mutation which might not cause any disease."

"Thank goodness."

"Have you ever had any unusual feelings—any pain, fever, or similar?"

"No."

"Headaches, confusion?"

"No."

"Great. Sorry for all these questions, but we have to follow protocol in case the machine misses something."

"You're fine."

They remained quiet as the nurse scribbled on the blue forms on the clipboard. Max scrutinized her. She was likable and cheerful, a great nurse. She talked and held herself ebulliently. The large, eye-catching pearly-blue earrings she was wearing dangled like miniature African tambourines as she walked and talked. The earrings made her head seem small. Apart from the snowy white hair and a few wrinkles around her eyes, she looked like someone in her 30s. She was dressed too youthfully for her age. She had moderate makeup, desirable for a nurse.

"So, Max, where are you from?"

"Oklahoma."

She tensed. "Oklahoma! I hate anything Sooner."

"Really? Why? Football?"

"My family are die-hard Longhorns fans, and I simply cannot stand O.U. fans."

Max smirked. "That's too bad. But I feel your pain."

They laughed.

"We are almost done. I'll draw some blood for lab work." Jaimie smiled and placed the clipboard in the drawer next to the examination chair Max was sitting on.

She put on a pair of blue nitrile gloves, took a needle and a box from the cabinet, and assembled the apparatus effortlessly.

Max outstretched his right hand. The nurse swabbed Max's inner elbow with alcohol directly above Max's protruding median cubital vein before performing the venipuncture. She did it effortlessly, all the while talking.

"You have nice veins," she said, drilling the shiny hollow needle into the vein. Max watched blood drain into the test tube.

"Thank you."

"We will have the results in a week."

"O.K."

She covered the spot with a Band-Aid.

"Now, one last thing. I'm going to inject this."

Max flinched.

"It won't be painful, I promise," the nurse said.

Max shrugged. "I trust you. What is this for?"

"It's a soluble silicon isotope that allows our system to monitor your health better as long as you're on campus and as long as you're the responsibility of FIST."

"I've never heard of it."

"It's new. FIST is one of the first institutions to use it."

"Is it safe?"

"Don't worry. The isotope dissolves in your gut and is deposited into draining lymph nodes where we can monitor immune cell fluctuations."

"That's convenient."

"It is," she said. "Since the approval this year, we have saved many people from our campus before they got worse from diseases or spread them to others."

"That's awesome."

"I know. And you can pair it with any smartwatch or fitness tracker once you scan the barcode on each tablet."

"I see. Is it a one-time thing?"

"Unfortunately, no. You have to get one every year. It's like a prophylactic vaccine. The isotope half-life is 12 months."

"Oh, O.K."

"This won't take long. You will feel a slight pinch that will go away."

"All right," Max said.

She disinfected the shoulder area with an alcohol swab, then injected the liquid. Max felt the brief pinch and winced quietly. The nurse covered the area with a Band-Aid.

"All right, Mr. Folksay. You're all done," she said.

"Thank you very much!"

"You're very welcome," she said. "Welcome to FIST."

"Thanks. Have an awesome day."

"You too, Max. Thank you!"

Max strolled past the wooden door into the lounge where Dr. Yates was drinking coffee, absorbed in the TV, and George the guard stood by.

"Done?" Dr. Yates said.

"Yes," said Max.

"How was it?"

"It was not too bad. Most of the stuff is new to me."

"What was new?"

"The flashlight scanning and the isotope. I've never seen that before."

"Oh, we forgot to get you your brochure."

"What brochure?"

"Your health orientation brochure contains all the information about the services. I had one in my office."

"Oh, O.K."

"Hopefully, the mandatory bill will be passed."

"They have a bill for a mandatory health pre-orientation?"

"Not health orientation per se, but it requires all citizens to have the chip implanted. They can detect any disease threats anytime, and it also helps catch criminals faster. I'm sure in a couple of years the technology will be available to all hospitals across the country."

"Who are they?" Max said.

"The Secret Service," Doc said, sipping his coffee, followed by a half-grimace. "At birth, they can tag you with a code that allows them to monitor your body on their database in case of any diseases happening."

"That would be nice, wouldn't it?"

"There is a bill underway right now to ensure that everyone born in the US is in the Secret Service database," he said. "One of the interns developed it three years ago. The bill has been gaining some traction since last year's virus outbreaks. I'm sure they will pass it, which should make things easier."

"Possibly," Max said.

"There are even rumors they can track our thoughts and emotions too, to prevent domestic violence and any act of terrorism. But who knows what they are capable of?"

"Really?" Max said. "That sounds like an outright invasion of privacy. I feel this crap is taking away our freedom. They will end up controlling us."

"That's the issue with A.I.," Dr. Yates said. "That's why the petition took longer to be passed since last year."

"I don't have an issue with it. But makes you wonder how much is too far."

"I know," Dr. Yates said. "But they have been doing this stuff forever, back during the wiretaps. This is just another level of snitching our data."

"That's not right."

"Sooner or later we'll be categorizing people on the genetic makeup for status."

"Who knows? Just when you think the world is getting better," George interjected. "I hope it doesn't end up being another form of discrimination. Seems like we're going round and round in circles."

"You're probably right," Dr. Yates said. "There are still debates. In a continuously moving world, this technology is for the greater overall good for everyone and an advancement against the terrorism that has tortured our nation. For instance, the chip can alert your health care provider of any impending health conditions like a heart attack before they happen, instead of reacting after the event."

"That makes sense."

George, who had been quiet for a while writing some stuff on a pad, pitched in looking at the live news streaming on the anteroom TV. "Man, this humanoid thing is getting really interesting!"

"What is it?"

"A team of anthropologists has landed on the small stretch of beach in the Amazon."

"They finally did it?" Dr. Yates said.

"That's unbelievable," Max said. "Who in their right mind would go there? Maybe those humanoids don't even exist."

"That's what they want to find out," Dr. Yates said. "After the recent outbreaks, everyone is afraid of everything."

"But still—"

"What about that?" George cut in, stopping Max from finishing his statement.

The video showed a Chicago woman cuddling her infant affectionately. It was sweet, but the unusual baby had four hands, two heads, and two feet. The chyron "Minotaur baby vexes surgeons! Is he human too?" ran below the video.

A panelist of pundits weighed in on the issue. Doctors and scientists could not figure out the cause, and the family had refused to abort the pregnancy. At first, doctors thought they were conjoined twins, but that had now changed. New data had surfaced that the parents recently traveled to the Amazon for vacation. One of the hosts downplayed the issue as a contrived conspiracy to divert the public from more crucial things.

They debated whether this might be an epidemic. There were also speculations that the mother drank water contaminated with a chemical that affected her infant's development. Usually that would have served as enough evidence.

The whole humanoid-sightings issue brought to life speculations about a long-dreaded quasi-alien attack and invasion of Earth. The media were preying on the anxious and panicked. Speculations said that maybe the child was another stage in the grand scheme of biological evolution. The public response was polarized. Some were in support, but others were downright dismissive of the issue. Jokesters said the woman was a witch, hence should be burnt at the stake. There was a cult-like interest in the topic. *Are we barbarians?* Max wondered.

"There has been speculation that it's an infection, with some dwellers along the Amazon allegedly claiming they have seen humanoids like this before. Folklore or tales," one pundit put it.

George looked up. "It's interesting, because the Greeks knew people like this a long time ago."

Dr. Yates nodded. "We do know from developmental studies that infecting rodents with certain parasites can cause abnormal limbs to form, and sometimes more than normal limbs. So this isn't far-fetched."

"Maybe."

"Some critics ascribe this to the pernicious effects of increased consumption of genetically modified foods, chemicals, climate, and all the stuff that we've been putting into our bodies for generations. All the cosmetics, dietary supplements; man, it's absurd," said George.

"Maybe the next stage of human evolution."

"The big bodies, yes. But up here, I think we are going back in time," George said, tapping the side of his head with a finger.

They laughed.

"We've heard the talk for a long time. Usually, these changes come little by little. All of a sudden, you start having mysterious birth defects, epidemics, and now mutant humanoids," Max said.

"Might be, but nothing is really new. Every generation in the history of the world has experienced problems they thought were insurmountable. But humans always prevail."

An anonymous video had surfaced on the Internet showing a giant humanoid-looking creature with multiple hands and feet, and an over-sized head, tearing apart a group of workers from a timber-felling company in the Amazon jungle before disappearing into the forest. There were speculations that it had been a space alien. Others argued that these humanoids were members of an isolated tribe who had been infected and had never received any modern medicine. No one knew for sure. The press estimated 50,000 humanoids in the depths of the Amazon basin, but no one knew where this number came from.

"Why is the video coming in now?" Max said.

"It's a hot topic now. Probably no one would have listened back then," George said.

"I'm sure the company annoyed the creatures. In some way, I think it's a good way of saving the forest. No one would dare go cut their trees now. Some argue it's the spirits of the forest. Some debated whether the US should be involved in the investigations or leave it to the International Wildlife Agency and the Brazilian government."

This breaking news had sparked renewed interest in some anthro-pologists who had gone missing six months earlier in the Amazon basin, and still hadn't been found. They were investigating these supposed tribal creatures. The United Nations had declared the Amazon a temporary world-restricted area.

"Why would anyone in their right mind go there?" Max said.

"It's human nature. We are drawn to adventure," Dr. Yates said. Dr. Yates gazed on. "I understand. Who wouldn't go? As for the anthropologists, anyone in their shoes would jump at an opportunity like this. It's an opportunity of a lifetime. They get to carve their names in anthropology books."

Dr. Yates finished his coffee and discarded the cup.

"Are you ready?" he said, standing up. "Let's get you settled in."

"I am."

They left the building.

They walked past a rally against the bill to fund the Advanced Space Habitation and Exploration project, Project ASHE. What a coincidence: Today was Earth Day. Some of the signs denounced the project and claimed humans should take care of Earth first. A petition against Project ASHE had garnered over a hundred thousand signatures, enough to force Congress to seriously look into the issue.

The protestors chanted and waved signs echoing the same sentiment for Earth's moribund state. They blamed global issues such as virus outbreaks, extreme weather, corruption, stockpiling of bioweapons, and increasing wars as the fate of our own making, as well as local issues such as exorbitant taxes on the poor, social justice, monopolies feeding off instability, and power-grabbing politicians disregarding those who put them in office.

CHAPTER FIVE

FIST

DR. YATES' lab was one of the most prominent labs at FIST. There were 16 people in the lab—three technicians, five postdocs, and the rest students. Days flew by, and Max was immersed in his studies and research. He sometimes felt he had missed the first quarter of his life. He wanted to change the world and felt the tremendous urge and potential in his veins. But those days at FIST flew by. Max enjoyed the weekly seminars. He was learning a lot from these. The best part is they were offered for free. He often wondered why more people didn't attend them. He gave a presentation about bioengineering, won the second-place presentation prize, and worked on the final draft of his research paper, for submission. The flexible internship hours gave Max plenty of time to concentrate on his research.

Dr. Yates inspired Max. Max admired his remarkable acumen. He was the quintessential scientist Max hoped to be—sharp, astute, successful, outgoing, at the same time down-to-earth. With a world-wide reputation, an endless list of achievements, and an outstanding scientific career, Dr. Yates was a pearl of great value among other scientists, someone others strived to emulate. Yet he remained grounded and carefree. You would expect someone of his remarkable scientific career and achievements to be somewhat pompous, corrupted by the respect he got from those around him, but quite the contrary, Doc was a downright simple person. Despite his busy schedule, he still found time to get involved in the community. He seemed to always lighten up everyone's day with his constant wisecracking. Often, his charisma overshadowed the air of dignity you would expect to linger around someone of his reputation. He spoke of science with rigor, and valued proactiveness from anyone in the lab.

Dr. Yates and Max had discovered various things in common: their passion for science, golf, ping-pong, trivial discussions on issues that many people avoided, and their love of Chinese food. He often invited Max and a few other friends for Chinese buffet at the local Chinese restaurant. They became friends through these interactions. They had a humorous rivalry between mentor and student, always competing in golf and ping-pong. Max had not played golf before, but he had grown fond of the game over the past 30 days at FIST. He liked the networking. On occasion, they would be joined by Dr. Yates' circle of friends—physicians, lawyers, professors, entrepreneurs. A regular was Dr. Stevens, who was the chief medical examiner at the Texas Medical Center.

One Thursday during their late afternoon round of golf at the Country Club, Dr. Yates' daughter arrived in running shorts with earplugs stuck in her ears. The astrobiologist. Max recognized her from the pictures framed in Doc's office. She was gorgeous, and Max could not resist looking at the colorful flower tattoo that emerged from the cleavage of her t-shirt.

"Hey, Doc," she said, hugging Dr. Yates.

"Hey, sweetheart," Dr. Yates said. "This is Max, one of my interns."

She removed one earplug, took a deep breath, and said, "Hi, Max. I'm Yvette."

Max removed his glove and extended his hand formally.

"Nice to meet you."

"Nice to meet you too, Max," she said, shaking Max's hand.

The warm sweat from her silky-soft palms soaked Max's hand.

"Yvette; that's a unique name!" Max said.

She smiled. "Oh, thank you."

Max was convinced she was a confident woman, mildly defiant, smart but reticent. She was also athletic and had an attractive body. Yvette probably had a stable white-collar job that allowed her to get whatever she wanted. He guessed she was between 20 and 23 years old.

"Dad, Dr. Stan called at the house," Yvette said. Dr. Stan was the animal research department chair at FIST.

"What did he want?"

"He didn't say. He asked for you to call him back as soon as possible."

"O.K., thanks."

Dr. Yates removed the right glove and checked his phone.

"Three missed calls! He knows I don't pick up my phone when I'm playing golf."

Dr. Yates phoned Stan while driving the cart down the trail towards a stray golf ball. Max and Yvette strolled side by side down the hill to the next hole.

"Looks like you and Dad get along really well," Yvette said.

Max said with a smile, "I'm the one getting schooled all the time."

They laughed.

"I've heard that story before. My dad is very passionate about golf. He won't let anyone beat him."

"He is. But I'm getting there," Max said.

"Good. He needs someone to beat him."

They laughed.

"Why do you call him Doc?"

"Everyone calls him that. When I asked him, he said McKomic started it, and it stuck. He likes it."

"Your dad is a cool guy."

Yvette smiled. "Yes, he is!"

"So, do you run often?"

"I try to. As a scientist, I don't have a rigid schedule, so I do whenever I have time."

"Cool. It's always good to stay in shape."

"Running is my favorite pastime. I like it. I have a marathon coming up."

"Really?"

"In two weeks."

"So how do you feel about the race?"

"I'm ready for it!"

"That's awesome. I'm sure you'll win it."

Max and Yvette laughed. "Definitely!" Yvette said.

"You need a running partner."

Yvette giggled. "I know. None of my friends care about running."

"Maybe I should join you on your runs some days."

She shrugged her shoulders. "That would be—that would be awesome!"

"I run very fast, though."

"I can tell, but there is only one way to find out."

"I'm serious."

"We'll see about that."

They laughed.

"What about you? How do you spend most of your limited free time?"

"He told you, didn't he?" Max said, smiling.

"Of course. He tells me everything."

"I can say the same for you. Being an astrobiologist probably takes long hours?"

"Some, but not for me."

"Apart from the lab, I spent most of my time thinking."

"That's a new one!"

They reached the hole. Doc was teeing up his shot on the ninth hole.

"Everything good, Dad?"

"Yes, everything is good. Let's finish this round and head out. I've to go see Stan at four."

"Sounds good."

"We definitely should have done only nine holes; 18 is too much."

"I'm already tired and hungry," Max said. "We should have brought bug spray too."

"Let's finish this hole and call it a day. I've got to see what Stan wants in a bit."

"Sounds good to me."

"All right, let's see what'cha got!"

"You asked for it."

Yvette stretched her hand to shake Max's.

"All right. It was nice meeting you, Max!"

"It was nice meeting you too! Let me know next time when you need some company on a run."

"I will. I definitely could use some company and motivation."

Max nodded.

"All right then, I'll leave you boys to it."

Yvette plugged in her earphones and disappeared behind the cypress-tree grove adjacent to the running trail.

"She is a nice girl, you know," Doc said.

"Yes, she is. Where does she work?"

"FIST, astrobiology."

"That's great. Is she an intern too?"

"She is among the Special Investigations Department group studying the Amazon humanoids."

Doc swung the club. He paused to observe the trajectory of the ball.

"Good shot!" Max said.

"Your turn."

Max teed the golf ball.

Doc opened a beverage from the ice chest in the cart while they drove the golf cart. "I think she's still mad that I wouldn't let her go on the team to the Amazon."

"Was she supposed to go?"

"She wanted to. And I personally removed her name."

"She doesn't know you did it, does she?"

"She knew it; she straight off asked me why I had removed her name, and I told her."

Max laughed. "Sounds like you know each other very well. You should have let her go if that's what she wants."

"There's not much evidence of what's out there."

"She is grown up now."

"I guess I must face the facts, huh?" Doc said. "Time moves fast. I can't believe she is almost 25."

"Yup."

"She is a winner like her mother." His face paled.

"How is your wife?"

"She died of breast cancer four years ago."

"I'm so sorry to hear that."

"Yvette was so devastated that she dropped out of college and started doing drugs. I tried getting her help, but she kept doing it. She has been through tough times. Drugs, unwanted pregnancy, but she overcame it and went back to school. And here she is, aiming higher."

"The little baby in your office frames?"

"That's Yvette when she was a little girl."

As Doc went on, Max felt sorry for Yvette.

Max struck the golf ball and parred on the third hit.

"Good game, son," Doc said.

"I think you let me win this one."

"Maybe. You're getting better."

"I can't seem to get my swing right to where I want it."

"Remember, it's in your mind. With practice, you might be beating me soon."

They laughed and rode the golf cart across the green field. Doc's roadster was parked in front of the reception. Doc dropped Max off at his apartment and proceeded to the FIST animal research center.

CHAPTER SIX

Yates' Lab, FIST

THE AROMA of coffee awakened Max. He immediately knew that it was Doc. Max shook himself and wiped off his eyes to find Doc standing in front of the whiteboard on the other end of the empty laboratory. He was still a bit jazzed. Doc pretended not to notice Max's alarmed expression. Doc had his favorite coffee mug in his hand—the one with Yvette's baby picture on one side and a constellation of stars above the inscription "Everything's there in a cup" on the other. Doc was a coffee-drinking machine. Hardly was there a time during the day when he was without a coffee mug—everywhere, any time of the day —in class, in the lab, except when golfing. He seemed to live on coffee, and his students had tagged him with an "Everything's there in a cup" moniker.

It suddenly struck Max that his biweekly research report was due that morning. Despite the stress it brought him, Max loved to postpone his homework until the last minute. He was late in submitting his biweekly report and knew Doc was going to ask him. Max feigned that he hadn't noticed Doc and approached the board to erase it.

"Oh! Good morning, Doc. Sorry, I didn't know you were already here."

"Good morning, Max," Doc said, wittingly. "Seems like you have been busy. What's all this?"

"Working on some stuff."

"I see."

"I'm sorry sir, I must go. I don't want to be late for journal club," Max said, erasing the whiteboard and picking up his briefcase.

"That's fine," Doc said. "Did you sleep here?"

Max paused. "I missed the train, and it was pouring last night, so I couldn't ride my bike home, so I decided to stay."

"Did you ask any of the other students?"

"I did, but none of them could offer me a ride."

"Even Zac?"

"Zac said he was going on a date with his girlfriend."

"Oh, next time, you should call me if you need a ride."

"I will. Thank you!"

"I know you have been spending many nights here."

"You know? For how long?" Max said, trying to hide his embarrassment.

"About a month now," Doc said. "I knew."

"How?"

"The janitor told me. He was worried you were having a breakdown."

"He did? Oh, man."

"Yvette was worried about you."

"Then why didn't you say so?"

Doc sipped his coffee.

"There was no need to. You were not doing drugs or disturbing anything. I saw no use in confronting you."

"I'm sorry about that."

"Don't be. Do you want to explain to me all this stuff?"

Max placed the whiteboard eraser back into its holder.

"I can," Max said hesitantly.

Doc placed his briefcase on the desk. He walked over to the microwave and set his coffee to warm up, all the time glancing at his wristwatch.

"Ten minutes," he mumbled. "I don't have a lot of time. Can you tell me quickly what this is about?"

Max looked over questioningly.

"Also, I sneaked a peek into your files, and I think you are doing fascinating work," Doc said.

Max looked down, not sure what to say.

"I'd like to hear about your work."

"You want to hear my work?" Max said. *A Nobel laureate!*

"I'm all ears."

"How much time do you have?"

"I've a few minutes. I'm sure that's enough for you to sell me your story."

Max dropped his backpack on the desk.

"Last night was crazy. It was one of those defining moments. I missed the train, had no ride home; I was frustrated and then decided to crash in the lab. When it felt like everything was going to dumps, I had my eureka moment."

Doc gazed at him patiently. "Go on."

"I solved the algorithm!"

"What algorithm?"

"Remember at the golf club, I asked you once what you would think if there was another Earth?"

"Uh-huh, I remember."

"It's there!" Max said. "This algorithm explains all of it."

"That doesn't make sense."

"It doesn't, but that's the point. You can't always understand everything."

"What do you mean, another Earth?"

"Well, a planet resembling Earth."

"O.K., go on."

"There is a planet out there identical to Earth or somewhat like Earth; well, hypothetically."

"How do you mean?"

Max sketched on the board. "That's Earth, and that's Aoratosia," Max said. He joined the two planets with lines and added a 30-degree angle. "We have always thought of Earth as a single planet. As it turns out, a long time ago, Earth had a twin sister. Man, how did I even miss this all along?"

"Miss what?"

"The angle." Max scribbled on the board. "I spent so much time trying to find a way to explain the way things are, but it wouldn't work. It turned out the asteroid hit Earth's sister planet at a 30-degree angle."

Doc said, "O.K., back off a little. Why 30 degrees?"

"I assumed for the planet to take its trajectory, it had to be under zero gravity. That's the only angle that could explain my theory," Max said.

"I see. Thirty degrees," Doc said.

Max smiled broadly, yet his body shook. He flipped to the other side of the whiteboard and started sketching.

"I've been working on this theory and equation for three years," Max said. "I started working backward with 'What if the Earth had a sister planet?' And from the endpoint, I was able to calculate the initial conditions that would lead to a scenario like this."

Doc half-nodded expectantly.

"I know this will sound bizarre, but all the ideas morphed into the equation that you saw on the board."

Doc nodded.

Max scribbled the equation on the board.

"This is Earth's twin sister Planet X, which I called Aoratosia."

"How did you come up with the idea of a Planet X?"

"I dreamt of it."

"Dreamt?"

"It was just in my head."

Doc ran the equation through his own mind.

"So Earth and Planet X were binary planets?"

"Yes."

"There have been several binary planet hypotheses over the years in the field—Earth and moon, Pluto and Chiron. But nothing has come out of it. What's special about your theory?"

"It proposes Earth and Aoratosia orbited around the same axis, at a point between the two planets. Unlike with the moon and Earth where the moon rotates around Earth."

"So identical mass and very close to each other?"

"Yes. But Earth's mass is three times that of Aoratosia and close enough for life to possibly migrate between the two planets."

"If Aoratosia was smaller, wouldn't the planet rotate around Earth's axis?"

"Under normal physical laws, yes. Yet Aoratosia exerted a higher magnetic force, which compounded with its gravitational pull allowed the two planets to be close enough with the axis between them."

"Just to play along, Aoratosia could be one of the Jupiter-mass planets or an exoplanet that ran astray. There are thousands of asteroids orbiting Jupiter, right?"

"That's a good point. I thought about that. But that couldn't explain these drawings or the planet's position."

Doc nodded. "I see your point. It still needs more work. And the feasibility may be questionable. Needs some work to refine it visually if we are going to convince anyone."

"I agree."

"You can use that extra space in the physics lab if you need it."

"Thank you very much, Doc. I appreciate it."

"No problem. That's my job. We need more young people like you here."

Right then, Doc's secretary walked in.

"Sir, your meeting with the group is in ten minutes," she said.

"All right, Mavis. Tell them it's canceled, and I am busy," he said, hanging his coat on a stool.

"O.K." Mavis smiled and left the room.

"So what caused the separation?"

"I speculate it's an asteroid." Max used his marker to highlight the path. "We have several comets with eccentric orbits that might have hit the Earth and Aoratosia at some point—Halley's Comet, for instance."

"I see."

"I played around with different scenarios. This is the one most likely. After the hit, the flare splatter matches the position of Earth's deserts today. Also, I mapped the retrograde motion of the continents after all forces, which helped me create a vector that would represent the continental shift after initial impact and that agrees with what's recorded."

"What about Earth resistance and all that stuff?"

"It's all accounted for." Max handed Doc a notepad.

Doc was quiet for a long time, looking through the page. He seemed amused. In more ways than one, Max reminded him of his younger self—stubborn, relentless, and anti-conformist. He liked the kid.

"This is amazing, son! How did you even come up with such an idea?"

Max tried his best to rationalize his thinking, then said, "It simply happened. For some reason I believed it would work."

"There's always inspiration."

"It wasn't an 'aha' moment. I worked on it for three years. Maybe I drew inspiration from my dreams. I was curious, I guess. I always wanted to know why things worked the way they do. I believe all existence is intertwined everywhere, waiting to be found."

"That's brilliant," Doc said. He had already forgotten his coffee in the microwave.

"I have always been fascinated by relativity, space-time fabric, time travel, and all that stuff as long as I can remember. I always had a hard time wrapping my mind around the whole thing. We spent so much time and effort fantasizing about things that we never pursue, about building time machines, and all that science fiction stuff."

"Everyone does."

"Then suddenly, during my junior year in college, I felt like a cloud had been lifted off my mind, an epiphany of some sort. I was attempting to write an essay for a contest on the complexity of the universe for my philosophy class and got hooked on it. That essay rekindled the fascination I had as a kid reading my uncle's books, and all he did. I've never stopped researching since then."

"How do you mean?"

"I realized we all have a time machine within us; in fact, my brain is one," Max shook, skipping through the details, motioning with his hands. "Time is basically this purely intellectual concept that we have invented; we have made it real in our own minds. In retrospect, I thought, why not create something, use my time machine, and allow it to flow. I was having these dreams, insomnia, and becoming more creative, sketching what I dreamt. I figured the bits and pieces of sporadic events happening to me had to have meaning. They had to connect somehow. I changed from being an art major to a physics major that same semester, which sounded stupid at the time. Sometimes a dream would excite me so much that I would wake up in the middle of the night excited about some visual concept. Eventually, I was able to connect the nuggets into this algorithm."

Doc nodded continuously without saying a word. Max pulled a pile of scratch papers from his satchel. He handed some to Doc, now sitting on the desk adjacent to the whiteboard.

"There's some big truth there," Doc said, skimming over the papers. "This is fantastic!"

"Thank you," Max said with an appreciative smile.

"Why haven't you told anyone of this?"

"No one really buys into theoretical physics that much. Plus, most of my friends think it's too outlandish, especially without any evidence."

"To hell with them," Doc said. "Come on, when you described the motion and stuff, it all makes sense."

"You think so?"

"Of course, I'm thrilled by this!"

A smile traced on Max's face, excitedly confused. "Thank you."

"I'm glad you're proactive. Almost all great ideas start as theories."

Max nodded.

"That's what our advanced program, BBA, is all about," Doc continued. "Very few of us can tap into that source, that core within each of us that drives us to do what we want, that gives us the creativity to achieve the extraordinary, most of which sometimes seems foolish to many."

Max nodded, feeling a surge of uplifting energy.

"This is amazing! I read it, and I understood half of it. If you had told me earlier, we could have given you enough resources to make your job easier. That's the kind of minds we're looking for in the program."

Max bit his lower lip, staring Doc straight in the eyes. After a few moments of silence, he said, "I feel like I want a vocation, not a career."

Doc's face was beaming, and the corners of his mouth quirked. He took out his phone and dialed.

"Mavis, cancel my 9:30 meeting."

"All right. Is everything O.K., sir?" Mavis said.

"Yes, it's fine. Tell them an important issue came up. I'm busy."

"I'll let them know."

"Thank you."

Doc gulped the remaining coffee and picked up his briefcase.

"This is brilliant. In fact, it's the best thing I've heard in a long time. Our organization is filled with brats who fear to dream anything above their heads. I'm sure this will fix them right."

Max remained silent, still not believing his stroke of luck. Doc was ecstatic.

"You know what made this country great? Curiosity! Most seem to have relegated that virtue back to the goddamned good old days. Sometimes I feel like we're kind of hypnotized, romanticizing about the great old inventors. We need that today. That's what the planet needs. It's what BBA was created for."

Doc couldn't stand still. His excitement was like a child's, lips shaking. For someone who had been on much bigger stages in science, you would imagine he would be used to it. He flung his sport coat on.

"Come with me. I want to show you something," Doc said.

Max followed Doc to the elevator.

CHAPTER SEVEN

BBA (Big Brains America) Hub, FIST

THEY DESCENDED TO THE BASEMENT.

"What is this place?"

"We are behind the library."

"I have never been to this part of the campus."

"You haven't been to our beautiful library?"

"No, not really," Max said. "Meant to, but never got to it."

"That's understandable," Doc said. "It's restricted access. And FIST is a huge campus. This was the old building before the new addition at the front."

Doc opened the electric main's control box and scanned his iris on a projected green laser. An automated female voice muttered: "Access granted."

"What is this?" Max said, startled.

"Wait for it," Doc said. "You will see in a bit."

Instantaneously, the wooden floor below them shifted apart, leaving them standing on carefully aligned horizontal iron beams shaped like a sled. Max adjusted his balance, clinging to the metal pillar on the center of the sled, flabbergasted.

"What's going on?" Max said, almost jumping off.

"Relax, it's a lift."

"An elevator hidden in the floor?"

"That's right," Doc said, stepping onto the sled. "Hop on."

Max was still dumbfounded. He stood next to Doc.

"Where are we going?"

"You'll see!"

The sled chime startled Max. The hinges crackled, and the whole floor section suddenly gave way, and they slowly sank into the floor about a single floor height, emerging into a dark circular room. The level above them closed.

The lights automatically switched on.

"Welcome, Professor Yates," an automated voice said.

The glass door opened to an LED platform, engraved with the letters "BBA," that stood at the center of a huge room where about 30 workers were busy on the floor.

"Welcome to the Big Brains America hub," Doc said. "We call it the vault. This is where all the secret missions of the BBA are kept. Used to be a situation room during the world war disaster and Cold War."

They passed two men dressed in white coats who cheerfully greeted Doc and smiled at Max. They skipped past a clan of engineers, glued to their computer screens, who waved at Doc.

The floor was covered with shiny ceramic tiles. There were hundreds of pictures plastered on all four walls: portraits of Albert Einstein, Edison, Oppenheimer, Galileo, Newton on one wall, and even Mother Teresa, William Shakespeare, Napoleon, Alexander the Great, Mohandas Gandhi, and tens of others in lustrous frames. Seemed like everything about BBA was enshrined here.

"Whoa!" Max said, turning around in a circle.

"It's quite an experience, isn't it?"

"What is this place?" Max said.

"Welcome to our Wall of Fame," Doc said, with his arms spread open. "This is the BBA lab for young people with special abilities. By that, I mean exceptional brain abilities, not superpowers. Most of them come from our FIST programs."

"This is beyond belief!"

"I know," he said. "The engineers wanted that effect."

"Who are all these people?"

"Anyone ever recruited into the Big Brains America Program or anyone who stood for anything this organization stands for."

"Einstein was part of BBA?"

"No. The program was started after World War Two. His ideas were core to our establishment nonetheless."

"But Galileo, Newton. That was a long time ago."

"Yes, the west wall is for honorable mentions, great minds who would have been part of the program if it was available. You could call it a posthumous honor."

"Wow!"

He walked over to the wall covered with huge screens. Everything in the room shone bright and untouched.

"Aren't these multiplex computers only used by the Intelligence Agency?"

"Supposedly," Doc said.

"What do you mean?"

"We're the Secret Service."

Max nodded and did not pursue the issue further.

"Do you know what's common among all these people?"

"Creating?" Max said.

"That, of course," Doc said. "The main one is they were all once regarded as insane by Flat-Earthers but eventually venerated."

Max nodded.

Doc continued. "What I'm trying to say is they were like you."

Max gazed on. "They did great work."

"Not bad," he said. "They lived their lives. We are still benefiting from what they produced today: philosophy, science, medicine, technology, you name it."

"Does every BBA enrollee end in here?"

"No, not everyone. Very few ever make it into these frames. I call them the Classe d'Elite."

Max continued to scrutinize the wall.

"Can you guess why I brought you here?"

"To see the greats?"

"I come here sometimes for some inspiration," he said. "You can feel the energy in this room. All these faces, these people represent the mission of BBA and everything we want to accomplish. To change the world."

Max nodded. He could feel the energy in the room, designed like a shrine, probably to elicit that very emotion: an uplifting feeling. He was not sure what to think. It sounded weird for a great scientist like Doc to have a need to feel inspired.

"You see, most of us wander through life being corralled by fear and clutter shoved down our throat from external expectations. We think within the same wavelength—the hopelessness wavelength. Only a tiny percentage of the population thinks above that wavelength. The founders believed it was our job to nourish these people for the betterment of the public if our species would have a chance to live infinitely. We hoped to create an environment where minds can create things together. To foster collaboration. We still believe nothing can be done alone, but within the right environment and people, anything can be done.

"Most of our potential is invisible within," Doc continued. "We believe that the success of our programs is in bringing great minds from all areas. You see, people with the same goal usually intersect somehow. The mind attracts what's in unison with it. You will find out."

Max nodded.

"I know it sounds poetic, but it's really not that simple. As much as we know we should work together, it's hard for people to acknowledge that. Seems like with each passing minute we are increasingly craving individualism. Not that there is anything wrong with that, but here people learn to push to their strength and rely on others to compensate for their weaknesses. There is power in collaboration."

A group of scientists in white lab coats passed by in haste. They waved at Doc.

Max remained quiet and then said, "So that's how Big Brains America came to be?"

"Sort of!" Doc said.

"How?"

"It was a group of powerful people who wanted to make a change. To forge a new world order."

"Like a cult?"

"No. In the beginning it was a few individuals, but in the 1930s, after World War One, fearing the end of the world and to safeguard their investments, several Wall Street millionaires and the government decided to start a program for such people they named Classe d'Elite. I don't know why they chose a French name. Probably one of the big founders was of French descent, from New Orleans. But after a few letdowns by France, Americans did not want anything to do with the French, let alone a French name for one of the greatest innovations in the development of humankind. So they changed it to Big Brains America. BBA is an underground movement, an offshoot to bring together the brightest minds from all over the world to America: space-faring, science, technology, philosophy, faith, you name it."

"That's interesting."

"It is," Doc said.

"So they recruited people immediately after?"

"That was the goal. But the program didn't start then. It dragged on for 16 years."

"Why?"

"Bureaucracy. Control. Some of the major donors wanted to own the program, but the advisory board refused. Eventually, they relented, and the board has run the program ever since. Well, until 1945, when everyone was scared of the atomic bomb apocalypse after World War Two. That's when it really kicked off."

"I see."

"The goal was to develop a weapon that would end all wars on Earth, to create permanent world peace. A weapon that would guarantee a safer future for the planet. What better weapon than a collection of minds, a 'megamind'? That's how BBA came to be—a crucible of the modern world."

"By the federal government?"

"No, it was private. It's still private. There were some very powerful people whom the war was disrupting, and some of them wanted to change the world. You can't rely on the state for everything. They had to take matters into their own hands."

"That's interesting."

"The program flourished, bankrolled by many charitable donations from millionaires, and eventually developed into an institution."

"So that's how the university was founded?"

"Right. They named it FIST. BBA was a shadow, FIST a coverup. The university did recruit some of the best talents in the world. It's like the training ground for great minds, and a few people end up being members of BBA."

"Wow!"

"What do you think made the USA the greatest nation in the world?" Doc said. "Why were we the first to land a man on the moon?"

Max nodded and said nothing.

"The Manhattan Project. The atomic bomb. It was all BBA. Unfortunately, peace is a temporary achievement which has to be sought after constantly. Let's put it this way: We maintain balance in the background. As time went by with economic troubles and other difficulties, BBA's function has shifted and focused on other horizons, such as space habitation, the moon, Mars, and stuff like that."

Max nodded.

"That was the main goal. However, over the years, the program has evolved to be part of the CIA and now includes a DNA sequence database for all US-born children. The goal is to screen every child born and pick the ones with the right sequence. If the chip is allowed in all states across the US, we can reach that goal."

"That's invasion of privacy."

"You're right. But it happens all the time. You have youth programs that sieve out the wheat from the chaff. And look at it as a superpower. The job of BBA is to tame those superpowers for the betterment of mankind. That's why the government invested all the money to build FIST in the first place. Of course, only a few end up here."

Max stared blankly at the rugged BBA seal carved on the center of the room.

"You all right, son?"

"I feel as if I have seen a badge like this before. Trying to remember where I've seen it," he continued, looking at the seal.

Doc glanced at the badge and strolled forward. "It's a small world we live in, son," Doc said in Max's direction, but seemingly to himself. He laughed. "I hope this is it."

Max nodded, confused.

"As you can tell," Doc said. "I don't show this room to anyone except for my favorite students. I believe you have a great future, Mr. Folksay. For this country and for yourself."

"Thank you."

"The program has gone downhill in recent years. There haven't been any breakthroughs. Right when we think everything there is to discover has been discovered, there is your idea—boom!"

He walked back and forth. After years in the doldrums, Doc hoped this was a chance of a lifetime for BBA, that could rekindle the Promethean character that once defined BBA and had been lacking in recent decades.

Max was in awe.

"It takes special talents to get in here," Doc said, sitting on the stool close by. "I'm sure you will work here someday. I believe that."

"I see."

"It's always like that."

"How?"

"Every generation, there is one person or a group of people that bring about something utterly new, off the charts, that shapes the course of generations to come. This may be it. This is great stuff."

"Am I part of the elite?"

"I don't know the answer to your question, Mr. Folksay. I'm no psychic. You're the only one who will answer that. You see, when we read applications, we can see beyond the application. You wrote about cancer research, but applied to FIST so you could be closer to NASA. Space travel fascinates you. I knew that, and I let it manifest itself. Nothing can stop a person who believes in himself. We can tell who is sincere or lying—you lied."

"I didn't—"

"In fact, you have lied for a long time. Even when I came here, you were going to lie. The question is, why do you lie to yourself instead of opening yourself to your greatness? You were born for this."

Max avoided eye contact with Doc.

"There is always a hidden message in every sentence or statement. Our machines can detect that in every application. On the positive side, your ability to lie for a long time makes you an ideal candidate for our program. It's like a covenant to keep humanity flourishing: combining like-minded people."

"Really?"

"Of course."

"So who's in charge of BBA?"

"That's classified. No one knows. I guess we all do."

"I don't understand."

"You will, one day," Doc said. "No one person runs the program. We all do!"

"How do you mean 'we'?"

"Myself, the other board members, the students. We all run it. Everyone runs it."

"Oh, like other board members?"

"You can call it that."

"Do you have meetings?"

"Yes, we do. We have actually never met each other. But when I see one, I know. We talk in codes."

"How does it work when you don't know each other?"

"It works. That's how national security works."

Max nodded. "That's odd. So you don't know who runs it?"

"Let's say I have a rough idea," he said. "After your tenure, you receive a badge and a 300-page graduation guideline outlining all the do's and don'ts. The way it's set up, you never know who's in it."

"Who appointed you?"

"The board."

"The board owns it and funds the scholarships for all the candidates?"

"No," he said. "No one knows. Maybe the government or some wealthy person. Money is donated to the trust fund. It's complicated. You'll learn over time."

"Why are you telling me this?" Max said.

"Because I know you will keep it a secret. That's the beginning of your training."

"Training?"

"Yes."

"Have you presented this idea of yours to anyone?"

"To a few of my friends."

"What did they say?"

Max laughed. "They think it's nuts; some think I got the idea from a science-fiction story."

"And what do you think?"

"I know it exists. Otherwise, why would I be spending countless sleepless hours trying to solve it? I can't help it."

"I like that enthusiasm. You will need that if this is going to take off," Doc said.

He paused for a moment.

"Now I think you are onto something. I think you might consider focusing on refining your model and being able to defend it in a few sentences. It makes sense to me, but maybe not so to the ones with the money. You need to convince people who know nothing about physics. If you can do that, then you'll be ready."

Max nodded.

"Like I said, you can use any of the software and equipment in the department if you need any."

"Thank you."

"You need to put these ideas out there. Ideas in secret are just that: ideas! Well, for the most part, especially in this profession. You want your peers to critique you."

Doc's phone rang again. It was Mavis.

"Excuse me, I've got to take this," Doc said. Doc talked briefly, while pacing.

"It was the president," he told Max. "Duty calls! Think about what we've talked about."

They stepped onto the sled, and it screeched upward.

"Tell you what, there is a Project ASHE meeting coming up in a couple of weeks. It's not about space *per se*, but everyone will be talking about it due to the anticipated budget cuts. Many top government officials and aerospace company representatives will be there, even the president. Maybe you can present there?"

"I don't—"

"Think about it," Doc said as the lift reached the top floor. "Send me an email if you have any questions. Actually, I might have the pamphlet about the meeting."

He reached into his briefcase, retrieved a pamphlet, and handed it to Max.

"Everything is in there."

"Thank you."

"The main topic there will be the humanoids and solar storms," Doc said.

"Solar storms?"

"That's the main reason Project ASHE was created by NASA."

"How do you mean?"

"A solar storm narrowly missed Earth a few years ago and nearly shut down the global economy for the whole week: no electricity, no oil, no food, no satellite TV, no flying."

"I remember hearing about that," Max said.

"We estimate a bigger storm is likely in the next few years."

"That's wild!"

"It is. I'm always intrigued walking around meeting people oblivious of how the world can end any time."

"I know. We take things for granted."

Doc continued. "All the time worried about who's Black, who's Caucasian, all that tribalism bullshit. But nature doesn't select. In one stroke, everything we know will disappear from existence. There's nothing you can do about the sun or space weather. We can have the best conservation, take care of the planet, but a solar storm can wipe everything away. The best solution is to find a habitable planet farther away from the sun."

Max nodded.

"It's the only meeting where anyone gets to discuss their wildest imaginations, no matter how ridiculous they may sound. Selected applicants for Project ASHE grants will be there. It's a good place to network. Perfect for you," Doc said, with a half-smile.

"The president will be there?"

"Yes," Doc said. "Blanchard loves science. She has vowed to

increase the funding for medical and life sciences research. She recently ratified the space amendment bill, which we hope will increase the budget allocation for Project ASHE."

"Nice."

"Do you think you can make it? It would be good for your résumé."

"I think so."

"Think more," he said. "An opportunity like this comes once in a lifetime. I'm sure the committee will love it."

"You sound so certain."

"I've been in many of these meetings, and know a good idea when I see it. I haven't seen anything as exciting as this in a long time. We have to find a proper way to put your theory out there. Your project gives me hope. Come to the meeting. Your proposition is perfect."

"That would be great!" Max said.

"Great? That would be enormous! You've no idea what this will do to the department and Project ASHE."

Three times Doc checked his calendar without saying a word and then finally spoke. "Tell you what: I'll see what I can do. Keep at it."

He picked up the sketches and asked to keep a copy.

"I have another copy," Max said.

Doc smiled. "All right. I'm out. And I need that report today."

Max grinned. "I will send it later today."

Max left the library through the wooden doors onto the pavement towards the cafeteria. He was still felt flustered. The information was coming so fast. It was true. Not conspiracy theories, after all—the Junta world order or stuff like that. In plain sight. He smiled as he passed a group of students. They were so naïve, he thought. No one would guess that in the heart of Houston, below all the hustle and bustle, was one of the most influential underground organizations ever created. The organization that had probably made today what it was: a better day.

He could not wait to tell Aunt Dori and Alonna about his project. But first, he had to finish his biweekly report.

Max brooded over the BBA badge letters. He vividly remembered seeing the emblem somewhere. He could not recall where.

CHAPTER EIGHT

Yates' Lab, FIST

A FEW WEEKS later Max had finished recording the last measurements from his experiments for the day when his phone rang. It was Doc. It was unusual for Doc to call, particularly at night, so this had to be important. Usually he would email Max if he wanted anything done in the lab. Doc routinely spent most of his time globetrotting—attending conferences and giving lectures in various institutions worldwide. A perk for being one of the best scientists in the world and an advisor to the president of the United States. He had recently returned from a humanoid conference in Geneva, Switzerland. Max was excited to hear about the conference.

Max had been waiting impatiently for Doc's return to share his development on the algorithm. Even for the few days that Doc was in the lab, he was locked in his office writing grants or answering phone calls. However, he emerged once in a while on his brief coffee breaks or lab meetings. That's when most would chat with him. He seemed to enjoy his scarcity, which was probably his secret to success. Fortunately, most of the lab's daily operation was run by the two post-docs.

Max pressed the phone to his ear with his shoulder while he finished packing his things.

"Are you still in the lab?" Doc said.

"Yes."

"Good. I need you to bring me something I forgot."

"Sure. What is it?"

"An important folder in my office."

"All right. I can drop it at your house on my way home."

Doc was quiet for a few seconds before answering.

"I'm not at home. I am at a meeting in Austin."

"Austin?" Max said.

"Yes. And I really need that folder!"

Max pondered the request for a moment. "That's, like, over two hours away."

"I know. This is urgent."

"I'm supposed to be in Oklahoma for the weekend. My flight is in an hour!"

"Sorry, son. Can you reschedule?"

"I can try."

"Even if you can't, the department will pay for your refund."

"Awesome."

"In fact, let me call Mavis after this; she will take care of that."

Doc dialed his phone.

Max frowned. He was scheduled to be in Oklahoma that night for the weekend. Deep down, he wanted to refuse. But again, he did not want to turn down the opportunity.

He mumbled, "I don't have a car. How am I supposed to get there?"

"Use my car in the parking garage."

"Your car is here?" Max smiled. He had always wanted to drive that Corvette.

"Yes, I will call the security guard right away to give you my spare keys."

"O.K."

"Thanks, son. I'll make it up to you!"

"No problem."

"Are you by yourself?"

"Yes."

"Good. Go into my office and open the safe box behind the book-shelf on the west wall. The door should be unlocked."

"I'm heading there now."

Max ran through the corridor and turned left into Doc's office.

"I'm in."

"O.K., there should be a hex key in the top drawer corner."

Max slid out the drawer and moved the papers out of the way. The key was snug in the left corner.

"Got it," Max said.

"Use that to remove the screws and slide the bookshelf to the left."

Max carefully loosened the screws and slid the shelf to the left. The shelf on the wall growled, separating into two and bulging inwards, leaving an empty space between.

"Is this a safe?"

"Yes. Listen carefully for the next part to open it."

"I'm ready."

"Enter '6447#227#', then pull the lever down immediately after the beep."

The safe door beeped and swung open.

"It's open."

"There is a small light switch on the bottom."

"Got it. It's on."

"Great. Right in front of you, do you see the Project ASHE shelf?"

There was a bold sticker labeled Project ASHE attached to the lower interior of the shelf. There were green, yellow, black, and red folders nicely filed side by side.

"Yes, I see it."

"There should be a red folder named Project ASHE farther left. Do you see it?"

Max peeked into some of the files as he unloaded the shelves looking for the red folder. There were files of all the missions Big Brains America had embarked on and some future missions, including Antarctica and the Amazon basin.

"Yes, I think I found it," Max said. "Is it the one labelled Project ASHE?"

"Perfect! That's the one."

There was no red folder in the safe, but there was one on the table with a thick blue seal printed with "Project ASHE 2100."

"It was on your table."

"Goodness gracious! I must have left it there."

"I believe so," Max said. "Is this all I need to bring?"

"That's it."

"Sounds good. I'm on my way," Max said. "Where am I going again?"

"Science Park," he said. "It's northeast of Austin. I texted you the address. Be quick. The meeting will end in a few hours."

"Leaving right now."

"Keep the file safe; our lives depend on it."

"I'll be there as soon as possible."

"Thank you."

"You're welcome!"

The line died. Max took a sneak peek into the file and skimmed through the pages. Project ASHE was an offshoot of NASA's planetary division, established to speed up the scouring of the Milky Way galaxy for habitable planets. Project ASHE had been in planning for centuries. The enormous red folder contained all the detailed reports on missions, projects, and research NASA and the US Air Force had done related to the Moon, Mars, and other attempts to reach planets in our solar system, and some of the future strategies. *Our lives depend on it!* Doc's voice echoed in Max's head. Losing this would jeopardize all the missions. Copies of Max's algorithm were stapled in. Reading on, Max understood why Doc was so captivated with his algorithm. He could not believe the Doc had inadvertently forgotten the folder. This was all his planning. He placed the folder into his backpack, locked the room, and ran down the stairs to the parking garage.

MAX EXITED THE PARKING GARAGE, drove down the alley, turned onto University Boulevard, and drove two blocks onto Main Street towards downtown. The Corvette roared past convivial bistros lining the streets on either side, with bright lights and people dining on the patios.

The aroma from a roadside pizza shop evoked nostalgia in Max's mind. He was already missing Oklahoma and his favorite chicken enchiladas—the ones Aunt Dori always made. Max gulped a painful mouthful of saliva. Aunt Dori made the best chicken enchiladas: She was the best cook ever. Max sighed, imagining what he would miss if he was not going home for the weekend.

It was 6:30 p.m. Alonna's rodeo performance was set for 8:00 p.m. Max had been looking forward to seeing Alonna and Aunt Dori. He saw Alonna on her horse at the starting line, performing all the maneuvers, jumping over obstacles; the bright lights, her blue and pink helmet on, and hair tied into a ponytail. In his mind, she finally takes off her helmet and bows before the spectators, looks through the stands, and notices Max is not there. Max checked his phone. He hesitated to call Alonna to tell her about the sudden change of plans. She would be upset with him for not being there. He decided to call her after her games. He texted her: "I'll be late. Good luck!"

Streams of streetlights raced past him, producing a streak that reminded him of how things were connected. The racing street somehow reminded him of how chaotic the universe was, yet well-connected like strings. Sometimes he was surprised by how much inspiration he found in the little things. *Undoubtedly there was a higher purpose for me being tangled in the midst of all this*, Max thought. The only thing he was worried about was getting hit by some drivers in Houston who seem not to follow the driving rules or be concerned about wrecking someone's car.

Our lives depend on it, Max murmured. He whispered Doc's words. The statement kept whirling in his mind. He looked at the satchel lying on the passenger seat. He pressed his hand over it to make sure the folder was still in the bag. Max turned on the stereo and browsed through the stations.

He passed the highway overpass where a few panhandlers held signs. At the stoplight, he handed a five-dollar bill to one of the men. The man smiled and said, "May your wishes be granted, sir." Max thanked him. He felt good for giving; he hoped the guy wasn't a scammer. "Nice necklace," the man also said. "Oh, thank you," Max said. Max rolled up his window and felt the necklace.

He skipped a few blocks and floored the gas pedal onto the freeway towards Austin. The roadster rumbled. He felt oneness with the car as he shifted the gears up and sped off. Max chuckled and shouted, thinking about how much he loved driving manual-transmission cars. He turned off the stereo and turned cruise control on. He needed quiet time to focus. To relax. The eight-lane Texas highway provided exactly that.

CHAPTER NINE

Science Park, Houston

SCIENCE PARK WAS an extension of the FIST. Though a good one-and-a-half hour drive southeast of Austin, the small facility boasted the renowned genetics and immunology labs. It also contained state-of-the-art facilities and conference centers. In addition to being nestled in the middle a pine forest, the facility was near the Tahlequah river, making it an attractive venue. It offered several activities for everyone. No wonder Doc had chosen this as the venue for the Project ASHE meeting.

The roadster shrieked onto the gravel road towards Science Park. Max wrenched the steering wheel into the gravel with a screech, barely missing the signpost that stood at the sharp edge of the embankment. "Crap!! That was too fast!" he yelled, catching himself. The gravel road meandered through the pine-tree plantation that rose on either side towards Science Park.

In two minutes, lights from the Science Park complex glimmered through the spaces among the pine trees. Max felt exhausted. Or maybe he was simply anxious. Soon he stopped at the main gate. A silhouetted figure strode towards the entrance from the hut-shaped security house. It was the armed security guard. There was one at the window and another standing inside watching.

"Hello, sir. May I see your I.D.?" the guard said.

"Yes," Max replied.

Max handed his I.D. to the guard, who stared at him inquisitively. The guard scrutinized Max's license for a moment, stealing occasional glances at Max and the monitor in front of him, evidently comparing the two. Satisfied, he scanned the I.D. and handed it back. Max started the car.

"Hold up," the guard said. Max was surprised. The guard's voice was not aggressive. He watched while the guard spoke into the radio. After a few moments, the metal barrier opened.

"Sorry about that," the man said. "You can go ahead, Mr. Folksay. There should be an empty spot in front of the conference room."

Max thanked the man and passed through.

It was 8:00 p.m. when Max parked. The lot was full of expensive cars, and Max felt as if he belonged here.

A figure approached him. It was Doc.

"You made it," Doc said, with his usual cheerful grin. "Come on in!"

Max handed him the folder and followed him down the hallway into the small auditorium past two guards with their earpieces strapped on.

The room was filled with boisterous laughter, which faded as soon as Max and Doc entered. All heads turned in unison towards Max. Max quickly assessed the room. There were about 30 people, all clad in tuxedos and suits. *Age, about 60 years average. Most probably spent more time playing golf and were less concerned about hitting the gym.* He checked through the cardboard labels placed in front of each seat. The audience included tech giants, physicists, a few Nobel laureates, and reporters. The room was designed in a hollow elliptical shape with seats descending to a long rectangular wooden table.

Max ignored his own rolled-up sleeves and followed Doc down the carpeted stairs to two vacant chairs at the table. Everyone at the table nodded at Max. The table was lined with wineglasses and water bottles, with a projector connection on one end and a hologram console on the other. A wooden podium stood erect at the front corner of the room next to a large projector screen.

"Gentlemen, Max Folksay!" Doc said. He directed Max to a vacant chair opposite Doc.

Max shivered.

Max noticed President Blanchard's live virtual feed on the screen in front of the room. She was sitting at the Resolute Desk in the Oval Office.

There were several other notable individuals. In front, at the end of the table, was billionaire entrepreneur Cordell McKomic, propped on his elbows and staring at some papers.

McKomic was the founder and CEO of Spartan Enterprises, a private multidimensional conglomerate specializing in aerospace, food production, renewable energy, artificial intelligence, technology, and education. The company also owned the first-ever hypersonic intercontinental network of shuttles.

Though relatively a novice, McKomic was revolutionizing and dominating the aerospace industry. In a short time frame, he accomplished more than any of the other well-established companies, redefining the industry. McKomic's knack and grit for going after outrageous propositions had garnered him an almost cult-like following of McKomicists all over the world. His goal was to teleport the first manned flight to Mars.

Max noticed a few prominent right- and left-wing politicians in the audience, some fierce rivals of President Blanchard's reforms and policies. The president always tried to make this a bipartisan endeavor.

Among them was the outspoken Senator Maurice Bloeg, the Texan presidential hopeful, on the other live screen. He sat leaning heavily on the leatherette chair back-rest, his paunch hanging over his belt. His blond hair and long sideburns, like a Victorian gentleman's, hugged his puffy face—a distinct look that had inspired a famous comic-strip character, Lord Bloeg, in culottes and a derby hat, with a walking cane, in the series "Lord Bloeg: Tales of Olde English Politics." The fictitious character exploited Bloeg's idiosyncrasies and how he might act in a Victorian royal court, satirizing Senator Bloeg's words and actions during his presidential campaign.

Bloeg was a devious narcissist, notorious for his reckless humor and his outspoken vilification and rancor against Mexican and Muslim immigrants. To many, he was pompous—a glorified version of a radical capitalist. He had survived two attempted assassinations five years earlier. That incident re-branded him as a hero and catapulted his political career, popular especially among the diehard reactionaries. To some, he was a true patriot, with several inherited oil businesses.

Bloeg had long been widely opposed to the advanced space exploration legislation, which allocated more funding to private aerospace companies. He and his band of Luddites who opposed space exploration had acidly often referred to McKomic as a confused schoolboy, an aficionado of fantasies that did nothing to benefit Earth except inflate McKomic's ego.

Doc passed the black folder to McKomic. They hunched over and whispered for a few seconds.

"Glad you're here, Max." A voice came from his left.

"Oh, Reverend Kay! How are you?"

"I'm good, son. How're you?"

"I'm great."

They shook hands.

Reverend Kay patted Max on the shoulder and sat next to him.

Max observed the place cards that were carefully tented in front of each individual, identifying their name and role. Among the groups represented were NASA, the departments of Defense, Education, Commerce, Health, Environmental Protection, and Special Investigations. The first page of the glossy program gave a brief history of Project ASHE, followed by the presenters' profiles.

Reverend Kay brought the room to order.

"Man, I'm enjoying these discussions and squabbles. Don't you all agree?" Reverend Kay said.

Heads nodded.

"Ladies and gentlemen, thank you for your patience," Reverend Kay said. "Today is an important day indeed. Moving on to our last presentation, we will get an update on the issue we have been waiting for—the humanoids issue. So without wasting time, help me welcome Doctors Stan and Wattenberg."

Wattenberg was the chairman of the Special Investigations Department, SID. Dr. Stan was the chair at the FIST Animal Research Center.

"Yes. Let's do this," President Blanchard said with a big smile.

The audience applauded as Stan and Wattenberg walked to the podium.

"Thank you, Reverend," Wattenberg said. "Ladies and gentlemen, on behalf of SID, thank you for giving me this opportunity to address this contentious issue. I hope you'll be lenient in roasting me today, hopefully less than my predecessors."

The room broke into laughter. Wattenberg's eyeglasses barely hung on the tip of his nose such that they moved with his nose when he spoke. When reading, he looked downwards instead of bending his neck.

"I will let my colleague go first, then I will close," Wattenberg said.

After a few formalities, Stan broached the humanoid issue. He cleared his throat again. "I shall try to be brief."

Stan gave a quick run-through on the updates about Jeff, the child humanoid born in Chicago. He showed that after only six weeks, the humanoid had grown into a full-sized human adult, already running and walking like most men. Power tests showed exceptional strength. Sequencing results showed a genome similar to humans, but with astronomical levels of growth hormones in his system, which explained why at three months old, he already weighed 150 pounds.

"We also observed that he is exceptionally intelligent when he focuses," Stan said.

Stan showed a video of Jeff doing crossword puzzles and numbers. A wave of interest spread across the room.

"Our defense can use this. Think of all the possibilities," Bloeg said. "Imagine what we can be if we can harness the power within this creature. If we can only harness the genetics, we can manipulate it and develop our own super soldiers."

Stan flinched.

Senator Bloeg sat straight up in his seat. "Imagine what we could do. How many lives we could save. We could clone and create more of him and unleash the beasts everywhere. We can create an invincible army."

"I understand, but, sir, Jeff is only a kid."

"With superpowers."

"Maybe. Doesn't make a difference."

"We really don't know what else he can do yet."

"Let's not leap from a springboard here," Stan said. "It's too early to conclude anything. We still need more time to do more tests before we conclude anything."

"Why wait so long?" Bloeg said, with a smirk. "I think you have enough data to convince me."

Stan looked at President Blanchard before responding. The president remained patiently quiet and nodded.

"We can't abuse him," Stan said. "He's protected by the law like any of us—human or animal protection. The process is tedious to even get approval to do his blood work. We have to get permission from the parents and protection agencies."

"Any aggression?" President Blanchard said.

"No, unless annoyed."

"How's his acumen?"

"That's where the issue is—he is strong, but his brain is still much like a toddler who is learning to speak and knows only his parents."

"He looks like he doesn't feel anything."

"Not really. He does. See this."

Stan played a slow-motion video showing the two parents walking outside the plastic barrier, causing the humanoid to jump from his seat and stare at his parents. He zoomed in to show the affectionate lines on Jeff's face. When the mom put her hand on the wall, he put out his too. She was sobbing, and the baby humanoid was crying too. It was heartwarming.

"Could that be because the parents are frequent visitors, so he is attached to them from association?" Doc said.

"Maybe, but the parents come only twice a month. He is not even friendly to the different caretakers who feed him every day.

"We could use that to our advantage; children can be controlled into doing what the parents want," said Bloeg.

"Children can also do the opposite too."

"With that power we can be invincible," Bloeg said.

"True, which makes this a risky endeavor."

"Excuse me." A voice came from the back of the conference room.

Everyone turned towards the shadowy back corner of the room.

"Who are you?" Reverend Kay said.

The young woman straightened herself and smiled at Reverend Kay. "Alex. Alex Hunter. I'm with the Houston Tribune."

"O.K. Go on."

Alex looked up at Wattenberg and Stan. "I noticed you haven't talked about the Amazon humanoids."

Wattenberg cleared his throat. "It has been four months since we started searching for the Amazon humanoids, but nothing was conclusive yet."

"Mr. Wattenberg, is your department aware of this?" Alex said. "I'm sure you've all seen the video that's circulating around the Internet."

Alex played a new video of the humanoid decimating the timber workers. She showed a grotesque video of a giant altered mutant humanoid with double heads, arms, and legs, tearing a man in two pieces, its red eyes and mouths dripping with blood. A few people cringed. She let the lurid images replay several times, obviously to stir the desired emotion.

Wattenberg's face turned slightly red. "How did you get this?"

"I have my sources."

"Answer her question, Wattenberg," Reverend Kay said. "Did your department know of this?"

"Yes. We heard rumors."

"What did you do about it?" Reverend Kay said.

"They were rumors. We let them slide," he said. "There was no use in frightening the masses."

"Many gaps in this theory," Stan said. "The problem is we cannot tell if it's legendary or actually exists."

"I have proof," Alex said.

"That is preposterous. We don't know if the footage is authentic!"

Alex nodded. "My other question was, do you have any comment about the missing scientists?" she said, her gaze towards the president.

"No, not really," Stan said. "I think our team is doing a good job looking for them. It will take time."

"Do you think they are still alive?"

"It's hard to tell. We'll keep at it to uncover the truth."

"What do you say about this footage? This is the last video we have of Professor Scrivner and his team."

Alex played a video of the anthropologists leaving a rocky dock in a skiff on the Amazon riverbank with one of the shirtless guides rowing. They passed a few indigenous people fishing with reeds and string. In another shot, the crew mimicked a troop of Samango monkeys chattering in the trees. The team looked cheerful and in good spirits. The gondola moored at the bank, where they quickly unloaded their equipment, and their guide led them into the forest.

"Where did you get this?"

"I've my sources," she said.

"How?"

"I happened to be on a trip in the area and decided to change my vacation into work."

"And the video."

"From a lumber employee for a tree-felling company. Took the video with his phone. He kept it in case the company refused to pay for his medication. He is still torn between exposing the company since they never reported the issue or honoring his friends who disappeared. Told him I was a reporter, and for some reason, he trusted me with the video."

"So what's your point?"

"What if the humanoids are from somewhere in space?"

Laughter swept the room. All heads turned towards Alex.

"Have you considered the possibility that the humanoid, what do you call him, Jeff, might be from somewhere else?"

"By physical laws that don't make sense."

"If these creatures can enter our planet and establish themselves without us seeing them, they can be capable of doing anything. Hypothetically, they could be trying to establish a relationship with us. Maybe Jeff is the one who can be that bridge."

More perplexed eyes.

"They could be our enemy then," Wattenberg said.

"If they wanted to destroy Earth, they could have," Alex said. "Jeff is very intelligent. Not a monster."

"It is a monster," Bloeg said.

"Of course. We're all afraid of things we don't understand. What if this is a matter of our own creation? When we're afraid, we find reasons. We're creating this thing as a monster," the reporter said, stepping down from the obscured back chairs as if to make sure everyone saw her.

There was silence.

"Can I ask you a few more questions?" she said.

Wattenberg shrugged.

"I assure you none of this will be in the newspaper."

Laughter arose.

"O.K. Go ahead."

"Do you believe our scientists are still alive?"

"I—I can't say for sure."

"We must do something," she said. "We can't sit around idly."

"I've been saying that forever," Bloeg cut in.

President Blanchard, sensing the indirect jab at her, smirked.

Alex continued, "We all know that there is only one question lingering in the minds of the American public and the rest of the world. It's been over four months since the expected return date for the scientists, and they did not have supplies for that long. Speculation is that they have all been killed. The Brazilian government's search party and our choppers have tried circling the area to no avail. The question remains, what are we going to do about it? I think that's what every soul out there wants to know."

Wattenberg sighed loudly.

"Those are unfounded presumptions. We have not seen any suspicious activity from the perimeter on our surveillance."

"Nonetheless, there's a public outcry we cannot ignore. Something has to be done."

Wattenberg remained mute.

"Don't you think the longer we remain idle, it's only going to cause the situations to fester? Better act now than later."

"There is so much at stake here," Wattenberg said. "Any efforts to disturb the forest have been met with opposition from environmental agencies."

Alex said, "Evidence suggests the humanoids are multiplying. Therefore, it stands to reason that once the forest can't support them, they'll seek other areas occupied by humans, and by then, it might be too late. Have you thought about what will happen when the forest can't support them anymore? It will be chaos. They'll start coming for people, and by then, it will be too late."

"I think you're jumping ahead."

"For my last question, do you have any possible solutions and propositions for my previous question?" Alex said.

"We have considered several hypothetical options to ameliorate that situation. Our lab could develop a contagious viral toxin that should infect only the humanoids and can be dumped in the Amazon. The domino effect will do the rest while we sit and watch. The virus kills within minutes of inhalation and can survive for only 30 minutes, so there is less chance of spreading."

Someone in the audience shouted, "Isolate and destroy!"

There was brief laughter.

"Our satellite surveillance is in place. No suspicious activities yet," Wattenberg said. "But the highlighted areas are possible sites of humanoids."

Wattenberg showed a map of the Amazon basin on the PowerPoint, with streaks of red and blue arrows.

"If we must, we wipe out most of these areas," he said.

A stream of bold red arrows webbed across the map.

"Here is the Amazon basin and the circumference we can contain."

"Are you implying that we intend to kill the entire population?" one of the women, Dr. Fountain, said.

"You might say that."

"That is the most ridiculous thing I have heard in a long time," she said.

Everyone laughed.

"We're being pushed to act," Wattenberg said. "We can't forget the incumbent."

"There are uncontacted tribes in the forest. The United Nations is never going to allow us in."

"To hell with the U.N. Wipe them out for the greater good," Bloeg said.

"C'mon. Listen to yourself."

"Maurice," President Blanchard said, "I've made tough decisions in my life, but this one frightens me the most. I propose we use a softer, more humane approach towards the humanoids. We need to know these beings, understand their lives, study them; then and only then can we decide on the proper action. Right now, we're all speculating. Have they harmed any of our people? No. I know we're all angry because the search party did not find the missing scientists, but that does not mean they are dead. I advise we continue monitoring them and keep our people safe."

President Blanchard spoke eloquently. Her words were deliberate and precise. She liked to be articulate, each word seemingly carefully calculated, which gave everything she said an air of respect and elegance. Everyone listened.

The president said, "I have dealt with many critical issues of national security, but I have to admit, Maurice, that your idea gives me chills. The more I try to imagine the consequences, the more it frightens me. It has never worked for those who have ever tried to do it like that. We have tried that before. It didn't work as anticipated."

Many heads nodded. Her sentiment echoed through the room.

"We cannot do that," the president said, adding thoughtfully, "I admire your concern, Maurice, but to me this seems more specious in all considerations. Imagine all the tribes, the heritage, the indigenous people, the wildlife, and so much more will be wiped out due to some ill-advised onslaught. Why? Fear? We have never been moved by fear. Now, I know some of my predecessors may have acted out of fear, but what happened? As the president, as leaders, even though we live in a democracy, we've to rely on our own discernment to run the country. The truth is the same people who push you now will be the same people who will roast you when something goes haywire. We've seen that happen too many times. Despondency and hasty decisions never work!

"And what's next? Then all our efforts for a peaceful studying and resolution will be in vain. I understand it's considered normal to give iron for iron, but if we miscalculate our moves by following a total destruction plan, we run the risk of jeopardizing the lives of our courageous scientists by making hasty decisions," the president said. "What if they're alive? Then our invasion would probably kill them. We're not doing anything until we have solid proof and a clear plan of action."

Wattenberg shrugged. "Again, this is a preposterous proposition, only a last resort."

"I know," President Blanchard said. "I had to speak up."

Reverend Kay wisecracked, "Man, this is intense. Yet I'm enjoying every minute of it. I'm glad no one has challenged anyone to a duel."

Everyone laughed and applauded Stan and Wattenberg.

"I hope by the end of all this fun, we will have good action plans for the year," Reverend Kay said. "Let's take a ten-minute break. We'll resume at 10:15. What do you say?"

The audience agreed.

Everyone filed toward the break room. Max never drank coffee after the noon hour, but he got a mug anyway. Doc was standing across the room with a group of other men. He signaled to Max to come over. "Max, I'd like for you to meet Cordell," he said.

"Oh, Mr. McKomic. I'm happy to meet you!"

"Me too, Max. I'm excited to finally meet you! Doc has told me a lot of impressive things about you. Keep up the good work!" McKomic smiled, under his piercing gaze.

Max beamed. "Thank you. I'm a big fan of your work."

"I'm glad to hear that. Maybe one day you will join us at Spartan Enterprises."

They laughed.

"I'd be honored, sir."

"You can call me Cordell."

"O.K."

Right then, McKomic was pulled away by two other older gentlemen.

"Sorry, I must talk to these gents," McKomic said. "I'll see you around."

Max took out a notepad. "Is there a way I can contact your organization? An email address?"

"You look me up. I'm everywhere online. I will find a way to connect with you."

"I will."

McKomic shook Max's hand and left. Max filled himself another cup of coffee and added several teaspoons of creamer. That's all he wanted—more and more sugar and fat.

A few moments later Reverend Kay entered the room and poured coffee. "Quite a presentation, huh?" he said to Max.

"Yes, it was."

"How's your work with Yates going?"

"It's going well. Exciting."

"I know you will succeed, son," Reverend Kay said. He tapped Max on the shoulder and left the room

Max did not feel like drinking coffee. After another sip, he dumped the coffee. He exited through the glass door where he leaned on the parapet overlooking a ring of glimmering lights around a fountain. He yawned and stretched his arms and back. The clock was leaping towards 10:15 p.m. He was ambivalent, not sure about what was happening around him. He wanted to be in Oklahoma, but at the same time, he did not want to miss any of the discussions. He knew there and then that he was not going to Oklahoma that night.

The beautiful red and blue lights danced under the sprinkled streams of water from the fountain like a sign of reassurance to Max that everything was going to be fine. Max contemplated the lights for five minutes—how the waves formed and dispersed chaotically before fading. *Life!* he thought. Everything was all connected.

He had many questions for Doc.

CHAPTER TEN

Science Park

At 10:15 p.m. the seats were filled and the tables were cluttered.

Reverend Kay sat up front. His countenance—cheek marks, furrowed forehead, and hooded eyes revealed keen interest. Reverend Kay stood up and called the meeting to order.

"Ladies and gentlemen," he said. "Anyone have anything to add to the last session before we move on?"

The room remained quiet. Curiously, Max, who had returned to his seat, raised his hand timidly.

"All right then, we will move on," Reverend Kay said. He apparently had not seen Max's hand.

"The young man raised his hand," Dr. Fountain said, pointing at Max from the opposite side of the table.

"Oh. Yes, Mr. Folksay," Reverend Kay said, lowering the edge of his glasses and peering down at Max. "I didn't see you there. Sorry about that. I'm getting old."

Light laughter filled the room.

"Would you like to say a word?"

"Yes, sir."

"Go ahead."

Max glanced at Doc. Doc never flinched. Everyone stared at Max, at his seemingly glued lips.

"The kid is only 22!" Wattenberg whispered loudly. "What does he know about national security?"

"He is here, isn't he?" Dr. Fountain said.

"Go on, Mr. Folksay," Reverend Kay said. "Among all of us, Mr. Folksay is the youngest and most objective, without corporate or political ties or obligations. Wouldn't you, if this was a court, want the decision made by those with no strings attached or bias to the cause or case? Let Max be the jury."

Everyone nodded.

"Go on, Mr. Folksay," Reverend Kay said.

Max gulped saliva and winced. His head felt light and close to popping away from his shoulders and rolling under the table. He again looked at Doc and rose from the chair. He breathed deeply until he regained his composure.

Finally, in a shaking voice, Max said, "I think we're going nowhere with this discussion. There certainly are other better ways to spend our energy and focus than what we are discussing right now."

"Son, get to your point," Wattenberg said coldly.

McKomic stared at him.

"All right," Max cleared his throat. "Think about it—our principal goal should be to ameliorate the lives of our citizens, not exterminate life. It's inevitable that if we dispatch this virus, we might be calling for the extinction of our species; billions and billions of people, some very close to us, will die. Besides, don't you think the world would be boring with less diversity? I don't see our getting anywhere with this."

"So what are you suggesting, Max?" Doc said.

Max turned to face President Blanchard on the live feed screen.

"I agree with the president," he said. This was followed by chuckles from the audience. "Let's give it more time; learn about the mutants. I also agree with the journalist. I don't know much about national security or world security, but what I do know is there is not enough verifiable evidence to prove that these mutants have done harm. Let's not forget that underneath, they might be like any of us. Let's not allow our fear of the unknown to distort our reason. Personally, I don't see them as a threat. They might be helpful if we can get to know them."

Several heads nodded. Max felt assured that his message had penetrated at least some of the minds of the in the room.

"That's all I wanted to say. Thank you," Max said and sat down.

"Thank you, Mr. Folksay," Reverend Kay said. "The council will take your well-thought opinions into account."

"Anyone else? Finance, Environment, Public Service—nothing?" Reverend Kay said, scanning through the audience.

Not one hand went up. Reverend Kay closed the folder he held open. "All right then, if there are no more questions, I think we can wrap this session up. Oh, I almost forgot. McKomic, can you give us a brief update about your project? How is it going?"

"Good. Last year, we completed all our missions and orders to the space station and teleported twice to the moon. With a substantial net profit, we still have our sights set to farther habitable planets in our solar system, and we're not stopping. I can't stress enough the need for prompt action as we expect another solar storm in a few years. This can only be achieved with sustained government funding until Spartan Enterprises can convince people of space travel. We hit a temporary hiatus, and things have slowed down a bit. With enough funding, we can launch for Mars in a few months. Right now, the project is surviving solely on donations from our major investors and a few others who believe in what we are doing."

There were grins in the audience.

"I don't need to reiterate the Saucepan project in Kaligari. I went into detail about that at the last meeting. We've made very significant strides since then and since my last presentation. The story remains the same—we're getting closer to landing humans on Mars, and to do that, the project needs financial assistance."

"When?" Reverend Kay said.

"End of this year, if not earlier."

The audience murmured.

"Is the concept ready?"

"Almost ready. We're hoping to launch very soon."

"That's promising," Reverend Kay said.

"Well, based on our projections. Hopefully, we are not over-promising."

Bloeg glared at McKomic. "Do what? Send bunny rabbits again? We know what happened when you tried that before. You still want to risk more lives?"

McKomic paused. "We have come a long way since then."

Bloeg shook his head.

"This project is more important now than ever," McKomic said. "Recent data from the NASA solar orbiter predict a much stronger solar storm coming our way in the next few years. And we all know what happened during the last one."

"But we know Mars is uninhabitable," Bloeg said.

McKomic looked at Doc and said, "We have a better destination this time. Far more important than Mars."

McKomic glanced at Max, then Doc.

"Max will tell you about it," Doc jumped in.

All faces seemed startled. Max looked at Doc.

"Go on," Doc said.

"Max," McKomic said. "Doc tells me you have a fantastic theory. You mind sharing it with us?"

Max was startled. He looked up at Doc, who seemed calm. Doc smiled at Max.

"Let's see. We have about 20 minutes if you can be quick," Reverend Kay said, checking his gold wristwatch.

Max shivered.

"Yes, he can," Doc said, with unwavering certainty.

"Oh, all right," Max felt in his pockets and was glad to find the flash drive still there. He took the tablet from his briefcase and approached the podium. He inserted the thumb drive into the computer, immediately pulling up diagrams that had been left open onto the projector.

Max began by explaining how he had discovered the algorithm, describing his deduction methods while the whole room listened. Next, he played the voice-over 3D video on the bubble hologram. He felt proud after having spent many hours developing the video.

Max could see the disbelief in the expressions of most of the scientists. He could see their disapproving looks, reminiscent of that snobbish skepticism associated with academia. How dare he? He knew most of them would consider what he had said insane. Nevertheless, he was adamant about his idea. He had thought it through. Lived it. He had spent hours and hours preparing for the presentation with answers to possible questions. And he was going to show it—an opportunity of a lifetime. There would be no better audience than this.

"Any questions?" Max said as a conclusion.

Reverend Kay cleared his throat and said, "We have time for three questions."

A dozen hands shot up immediately. Expected.

"Good presentation, but—I mean," Dr. Fountain said. "We wouldn't plan a mission to a sister planet because there is no sister planet. Not as far as I know. We've flirted with the idea for decades, but it's all bogus science fiction. Dreams! We've been searching for one for decades, and zero has been found. I wouldn't guess something can pop up from nothing either. Is this some kind of pseudo-science?"

"You're right. I know this is strange to most of you. I can go over my deductions again if that helps. It's simple."

"It is too simple," Dr. Fountain cut in.

"Yes, it is. It's easier to convince people that there are thousands of planets billions of light years away. It's harder to convince anyone that there is a planet next door that they have overlooked for years. Common sense is hard sometimes. Because it's simple. Just because we can't see or understand it yet doesn't mean it doesn't exist."

Dr. Fountain said, "It's hard to believe that our universe is that calculable. We've been looking eons for these things."

"Exactly," Max said. "That's my point. There are so many simple things that govern our universe—gravity, energy and so on. We are so inclined to dwell on the unexplainable or phenomena that can take millions of years to explain.

"The universe has left us cues we can use to study and understand our existence, if only we are careful enough to look. We have cosmic waves, microwave radiation, temperature fluctuations. All these make it easier."

"We have proved there's nothing," someone said from the terrace.

The room was filled with murmurs and some nervous laughter.

Max smiled. "I wouldn't say nothing. We know that a vacuum has particles and energy in it, which basically is something in nothing. Since by definition a vacuum is a place of nothingness."

Dr. Robyn puckered her face. "But space is not a vacuum!"

"You're right. In fact, many studies have shown that we can have something in nothingness. What we call a vacuum is not really an empty space, but merely a space packed with latent particles and forces. That's true. There are patches of vacuums scattered through space which give rise to black holes, loopholes, antimatter, and stuff like that." Max smiled. "Anyway, that's not why I'm here. Sorry for the digression."

Everyone laughed. Dr. Robyn's face seemed to concede the point.

"All right, Max, let's get to the nitty-gritty," Reverend Kay said.

"That's my point," Max said. "We are habituated to our way of thinking. But I will show you otherwise."

Max projected little 3D holographic bubble models around the room. He played through the simulation, explaining the different projection concepts.

"Don't you think the planet is one of Jupiter's moons?" a man in the stands said.

"No, that's the planet embedded in Jupiter's magnetosphere."

"Let's not jump to conclusions here. How can you be so sure?"

"As I explained in my presentation, the position of the planet does not agree with Jupiter's moons."

Max clicked through the slides.

"By meta-analysis, I can predict the likely scenario, retrospectively from a predicted point. Fortunately, we have gravity, cosmic and microwave radiation records, periods and planetary angles, and Jupiter's magnetism. Using all these as vantage points, I was able to extrapolate the probability of the planet's existence. The projection doesn't match any of Jupiter's moons."

"Jupiter has no solid surface," Dr. Fountain said.

"That's true," Max said. "We all know Jupiter is a gas planet. But this planet is embedded in Jupiter's magnetosphere, not within Jupiter or Jupiter's surface."

Max adjusted the bubble model across the conference table, showing all the known planetary systems. "The position of the planet makes it very difficult to view using our current telescopes, which is why we have never seen it before."

Max could tell that most of the people in the room were confused.

"I am not going to bore you with all the details since we're almost out of time, but the take-home message is there is a possibility for an Earth sister planet at Jupiter."

"What caused the separation?"

"At this point, it is challenging to pinpoint the exact cause. As with most events in our universe, we can only speculate what happened, when, and what will happen. For example, we know the entropy of our universe is increasing. This may induce ripples in space-time across the universe which might disrupt orbits, galaxies, polar bodies, and planets."

"Still—how did you estimate the age of the planet?"

"Most of science is deduction, really. Making connections from what's already out there. I believe nature has given us all the reference material we need. We can infer the planet's geography and chemical composition based on what we know about Earth and how matter works. Relationships of matter to masses and gravitation."

"That doesn't make it correct," Dr. Fountain said.

"You're right. But that doesn't make it not correct either," Max said. The audience erupted with comments and questions.

"I don't buy it," one man from the stands said loudly.

Max smiled in his direction.

"Let me ask you a question. How long have we known our universe?"

"A couple millennia," the man said.

"Correct. Not too long ago. That time frame is nothing in the grand scheme of things. There is a ton of stuff we don't know or understand; we're only starting to peel the surface towards understanding the universe."

Everyone remained quiet.

"The algorithm can be supported by many things we have today. Plate tectonics, deserts, et cetera."

"That's impossible," the man said.

Max looked at the man who had asked the question.

"Why do you think it's impossible?"

"We could have found that out way back," the man said.

"I think some of that is in part from our reluctance as scientists to change," Max said. "We like to stay in our comfort zones. For instance, someone suggested a theory for plate tectonics many years ago, and everyone has been believing that for centuries. Remember this was a theory. Have you ever asked yourself about the possibility that the Earth continent separation was a result of something else?"

The man's lips twitched.

"I made my deductions from there," Max said. "As you can see from the simulation. I was able to make simulations of the possible cause of the Earth's plate tectonic movements that resulted in our continents. Using asymmetry calculations, I hypothesized that Earth was coalesced with another planet at one point and then separated by a larger force, possibly a celestial body."

A motion sketch appeared on the bubble hologram.

"This violent detachment would have resulted in a mega tremor that initiated plate tectonic movements that resulted in the separation of Gondwanaland, which led to the formation of the continents we have today. Their distance and momentum all agree with the algorithm parameters."

"How did Earth and this other planet coalesce in the first place?" he said. "That would be a disaster."

"I can't say," Max said. "Gravity is certainly a possibility when you have two masses, but again, we all know nothing is impossible in nature. Our universe is so complex."

"How can you prove that?"

"I can't, but there are people who can," Max said, glancing in the direction of Doc, McKomic, and the NASA director. "We can use aster-oseismology and cosmic radiation to theoretically trace and estimate the retrograde path of the planet."

"If it exists?"

"Yes."

"Why did the separation happen at the time?" he said.

"I can say by chance," Max said. "You see, Jupiter travels in an elliptical path around the sun, like the Earth, and the path is constantly changing. My calculations show that a meteorite that hit the planets caused the separation when Jupiter and Earth were closest to each other. The force exerted by the hit was enough to overcome gravitational attraction between Earth and what I call Aoratosia, which caused the two bodies to separate, and Aoratosia careened towards Jupiter."

"Why an asteroid hit?"

"There is evidence everywhere of comets that could likely hit Earth. It's possible such an event occurred previously also," Max said.

"How can you explain that?"

"After the hit, debris and shards from the impact blasted into orbit and fell back on Aoratosia, and some fell on Earth, scorching large chunks of life."

"How do you mean?"

Max played the simulation.

"This is a representation of all the deserts on Earth today, and here is another simulation of what happened after the impact. After the impact here, these arrows show the possible paths the debris might have taken when scattered throughout space. You can see the congruency from the point of impact. It maps perfectly."

"Why exactly those points?" the man said, stroking his chin.

"Nature, sir," Max said. "That, I can't explain. It's random. There are so many variables: time, space, speed, pressure, and so on. But from calculating the power of the debris' strikes and possible trajectories, this evidence provides the highest probability. At such an angle, you can see the trajectories. All lead to the exact positions of deserts we have today. Same fragment particles. All this takes into account the distance the planets moved after the hit."

Dr. Fountain cocked her head.

"A direct meteorite hit would have smashed both planets to shreds," she said in a way that conveyed this was a fact.

"That's true," Max said. "As I discussed earlier with Doc, this was not a direct hit. Instead, Aoratosia was grazed at an angle with enough angular momentum to dislodge her from orbit and spiral into space against Earth's gravitational pull, as we assumed in our model."

"That kind of makes sense. That would explain why it did not destroy Earth and her twin sister," she said. "But that doesn't explain why Earth did not shift from its axis. According to the second law of thermodynamics, that energy from the hit should have distributed to Earth as well."

Everyone was watching Max.

'That's an excellent point," Max said. "The are several scenarios to explain that, but at this point I'm leaning towards the hypothesis that after the hit, Earth reoriented herself. Through this process, the plate tectonic movement occurred as Earth balanced her internal mass distribution."

Dr. Fountain nodded.

"I'm sure if we can find Aoratosia, half of it might be inhabitable from the point of impact of the asteroid, and there may be tons of uranium clouds and deposits," Max said.

"Doesn't that suggest that we should have areas of dense uranium on Earth?" she said.

"We have traces."

"That's a promising hypothesis," she said.

"I constructed many different situations that might have caused the separation without destroying the two planets. I also used different simulations of the forces required to cause each shift. The only plausible simulation was that, by chance, the asteroid hit only Aoratosia at about 30 degrees farthest from the Earth, causing Earth to detach with minimal aftermath. The cataclysmic strike caused the planets to separate and created seismic waves powerful enough to cause plate tectonic movements that resulted in continents we have today.

"Since Jupiter's magnetic field is two and a half times greater than the Earth's, it was able to attract Aoratosia over some time. Compound effect of gravity and magnetic force."

"How?" Dr. Fountain said.

"Serendipitously. Randomly. The hit could have happened when Jupiter was in its closest orbit to Earth, allowing it to attract Aoratosia. This is rare. I couldn't find anywhere any recorded instances like that."

"Is there a possibility the planet could have been somewhere else instead of Jupiter?" the man said. "I cannot wrap my mind around the concept of it randomly nudging into Jupiter."

"It's possible, but this happened by chance, if I can say. Like most natural phenomena."

Some of his listeners looked as if they remained unconvinced.

"Look at it this way," Max said. "We can launch massive rockets from Earth into other planets' orbits with the right speed and trajectories. What makes you think nature cannot do the same?"

"Even if that's right, the intense pressure in Jupiter's core would have crushed the planet."

"That's right," Max said. "However, the impulse exerted by the asteroid hit was enough to nudge Aoratosia into Jupiter's magnetosphere."

Max showed another simulation.

"I simulated the path Aoratosia might have taken to reach Jupiter. By the time it reached Jupiter, its speed had been significantly reduced, allowing it to be suspended in the magnetosphere. I created an algorithm to explain the path taken by the planet as it flew into Jupiter's magnetosphere in its orbit, as you can see from the simulation on the right, taking into account several factors like gravity.

"I used the distance and time it took for our continents to reach their current position to locate the ideal point of impact that might have caused a separation like we can notice today, and was able to trace the motion to here, taking oceanic resistance into account."

"How?"

"I used a retrospective approach. I basically used the force needed to cause Earth's tectonics to separate Gondwanaland and all the different continents at a specific point in the Sahara desert. With that force and Earth's gravity, we can solve the external mass that exerted the force on Earth. If it was a direct asteroid hit, it would smash Earth to smithereens. That's how I came up with the hypothesis that the force experienced on Earth might not be a direct hit but transferred from another planet of equal mass."

"Sahara desert?"

"Yes."

"How so?"

"This disrupted the gravitation and congruency here. Factoring in a 30-degree point of impact, the planet would be there. And accounting for its rotation in its orbit, Aoratosia should be on the far side, beneath Jupiter's plasmasphere, which makes it even more difficult to see with our telescopes."

Max projected the simulation on a screen.

"The hit created a recoil on Aoratosia that pushed it out of orbit, and somehow it finally was nudged into Jupiter. Algorithm shows this."

Max switched the simulation. "Taking all these parameters in perspective, I was able to determine its path after the hit and how much force it would require to stay in its current position."

Dr. Robyn nodded. "That doesn't explain why the planet stopped in a gas cloud," she said.

"I don't know the answer to that yet. It would make sense for the planet to keep moving unless there was some interaction. The only rationale that makes sense for me so far is to assume Aoratosia has its own magnetosphere interacting with Jupiter's magnetic field, gravity and electrostatic forces, which allowed Aoratosia to eventually find harbor in Jupiter's ionosphere. Maybe that is Aoratosia's permanent position, or the perturbation might still be going on gradually."

"That's interesting," McKomic said. "So we might be talking of a giant magnetic-electric chamber?"

"Yes, sir!"

"If that's so, do you think there is life there?" Reverend Kay, who had been silent, said.

"Maybe," Max said. "Being Earth's sister planet, I'd guess so. As of right now, I don't have proof there is life. That will require sophisticated equipment."

"NASA might be able to help with that," President Blanchard said, leaning forward in her chair.

"Are you saying there is a possibility this planet, Aoratosia, has life?"

"I can't say exactly, ladies and gentlemen," Max said. "But my thinking tells me there is life."

"What makes you think that?" Bloeg shot in.

"I have faith, sir," Max said. "I am convinced that this planet is there and very similar to Earth, possibly habitable. It all makes sense in my mind. If we can develop ways to locate and identify Aoratosia, we might be able to go there."

The audience laughed.

"Let's not get ahead of ourselves here," Dr. Fountain said. "That's too fast."

Senator Bloeg snorted. "This is ridiculous. I can't believe we are all buying into these asinine Planet X theories."

A brief outburst of discussion erupted in the room.

Reverend Kay, who had been quiet for a while, said, "This sounds difficult for of us to grasp, but again, everything is a puzzle. The universe, life, our existence. It's all numbers, and, well, complicated. I think it's an interesting proposition, nevertheless. Imagine if there are civilized beings there; what would they be doing?"

"Probably minding their own business!" Senator Bloeg said with a sardonic laugh. The room filled with laughter.

"C'mon. Just for the fun of it. Imagine."

A reluctant smile crept across Bloeg's face. "Why would we?" he said. "On Earth, we disregard life that is two blocks from us. Take a look at the homelessness, strife, and the recent virus pandemic. Instead of focusing on our planet's issues, we're wasting time and resources looking into the unknown—something that might not even exist. Exoplanets, Kepler planets, habitable zones in the hundreds—to what end? All that is bull crap! We're always focusing on the faraway when we can't even take care of our own borders! Get things straight here on Earth first, then go from there."

Bloeg stopped, his labored breathing echoing across the room.

"Exploration is part of progress," McKomic said.

Bloeg got defensive. "Progress? Have we received any signals? No. It's entirely speculation. And you expect grown men and women to buy into that. Come on, give me a break. We can't win on many fronts at once. We've got to focus."

The room grew quieter. Everyone knew the two had a feud, a

history of conflict. Sensing the growing tension, Reverend Kay immediately stepped in to mollify the situation.

"I think both of you are right," Reverend Kay said, his hands steepled. "At the same time, we can't always wait for conditions to be perfect for us to act. If we'd waited for the perfect time, we probably would have never landed on the moon."

Max smiled and nodded.

Bloeg furrowed his forehead disdainfully.

It seemed the room was now divided—Doc, McKomic, and Max against Senator Bloeg and the rest. Reverend Kay and the president were neutral.

"That's how science works, anyway," Reverend Kay said. "From my limited scientific background, I know that every breakthrough sounded stupid before its time. There's nothing worthwhile that came through without resistance. And that is O.K. That is part of progress and the human experience too! We should look at this report with no biases attached if we are going to get value out of this session.

"History is littered with breakthroughs that started as theories and speculation. I've come to respect that sometimes these theories, as strange as they may seem, and mind-boggling beyond my intellectual estimate, that don't mean they are wrong. Max might be spot-on here."

"I'll be damned." Bloeg's face was turning slightly red.

"Max," Dr. Fountain said. "Setting all this aside, after an asteroid hit, the ground would be boiling and incredibly hot, water sources would have boiled out, and the sky filled with dust and without any light to support life, so how can there be life?"

Everyone looked at Max.

Max rubbed his chin. "There is only one way to find out."

"Which is?"

"We've got to go there."

The room was filled with incredulous laughter. Everyone, including the president, was surprised by Max's certitude about moving forward with his idea. But it was evident that many in attendance were beginning to be swayed by his presentation.

"Let's say we decide to give this Aoratosia a try. What would it take?" President Blanchard said, looking at Doc.

Doc smiled, crossed his legs and rubbed his chin. "Our willingness to do it!"

"What do you mean?"

"I think we can do it if we really want to do it. Of course, no human in the history of space exploration has ever been able to go that far. We have only succeeded in sending robots and rodents, but not humans. I'm confident we can do it; we have the expertise and resources to pull it off."

"How will all this help us?" Dr. Fountain said, her face now showing stolid indifference.

"This may be our modern El Dorado," Doc said. "Imagine all the possibilities. If the planet is indeed Earth's sister—there will possibly be minerals and plenty of natural resources that we need here on Earth, which can change history.

"Look at it this way: If there are no inhabitants, then we can set up a human colony there; and if there are inhabitants, then we can forge relationships, countless possibilities for interplanetary trading, outposts. I know it's far-fetched, but it's exciting."

"And if there are beings more advanced than we?"

"Then we try to forge an alliance. They may be peaceful people like us. My point is to show that this is a great opportunity for the nation and our world. Discovering this new planet will prove our superiority as a scientific power in quests that have been sought after for centuries. Besides, I am sure taxpayers will be delighted to give their money to support our invasion of a new Earth sister planet due to the increasing danger of solar storms. There hasn't been anything as exciting as this in decades."

"I'd think if there was anyone out there, we could have detected signals or the like."

"Yeah," McKomic said. "The idea has always been us scouring space waiting for other supposed life forms to send electromagnetic or radio signals to us, or whatever signal they use to communicate. Why not go there or send our signals first? It's never smart to be always on the defensive. I'm all for making the first meaningful move."

Everyone listened attentively.

"It will definitely seal the president's second term re-election,"

Reverend Kay whispered, catching himself mid-sentence. No one commented.

"Then we have to do this before the Russians get hold of this information," McKomic said.

Everyone agreed.

"Even if it exists, how do we get there?" Bloeg said. "Say we find this planet. How're we going to get there?" Bloeg twiddled his thumbs.

"There's always a way," Doc said. "First things first; let's I.D. the planet, then worry about transportation later."

"This is a waste of money," Bloeg said. "You got funding before, and what came of it?"

"We teleported rabbits and microbes to Mars," McKomic said, defiantly.

"And what's the benefit of that? We are going to spend more billions of dollars on another science experiment."

"This is not an experiment."

"Or turn the planet into a wasteland. That's what we do. Everything we interfere with eventually goes to crap. Can't you see how much change we can impart on Earth by using all that money on meaningful change here at home? Racial justice, social justice, stimulus relief."

McKomic ignored the question. He had heard this criticism before from so-called ethicists who viewed space exploration as nonsensical. He didn't care.

"It's happening," he said with a firm and uncharacteristic cockiness in his tone. "I said we're sending people, not we're going to try to send people. With enough funding, we can expedite the whole process to a few weeks. We already have prototypes in our facilities in Kaligari."

"Send toys again?" Bloeg said bluntly, with a sneer.

"Nope. People!" McKomic said, affecting the same brusqueness. He was losing patience with Bloeg.

Everyone turned their heads in astonishment.

"I can't believe I'm hearing this," Bloeg said.

"You heard me right! We're sending people on the teleporter," McKomic said, with the same bluntness he had honed from countless Senate hearings over his growing enterprise.

"That's ridiculous," Bloeg said. His face flashed with anger. "That's beyond a reasonable doubt."

"I've heard that before. Reasonable doubt? What is that? Just because something is beyond our mental comprehension doesn't mean it can't be done! There is always an acceptable risk to any pioneering. We will be glad to provide our designs to the space commission for review," McKomic said.

"Thank you, McKomic," President Blanchard said. "I look forward to hearing from the commission."

There were faint smiles across the table. They seemed all of a sudden to be buying into McKomic's chutzpah, which on most occasions even baffled his fierce competitors. Why wouldn't they? McKomic had done almost impossible things before, which gave no reason for those in the room to doubt that he would deliver on his word. This had prompted a prominent technology magazine to dub him one of the leading entrepreneurs of the century. Buoyed by an unprecedented track record, he had earned their utmost respect. Everyone knew when he said he was going to send humans, he was going to do it. The man was born for a time like this. He had balls of steel. After all, he did not give a damn what everyone else thought of his plans, and he often openly showed it with a biting sense of humor. To him, it was a done deal from the outset. He had the track record to prove it.

McKomic did not simply want to revamp interest in spacefaring; he wanted to transcend anything done before him. He had done so. He had sent rabbits to Mars and back, a feat deemed impossible a few years earlier. When he spoke, his air of self-confidence, as if by some supernatural power, seemed to hypnotize his listeners, or even his critics, into buying into his grandiose ideas. He had an aura about him that persuaded others to believe he could—heck, they could—do anything! He could sell the picture.

Well, except for Senator Bloeg, who would not give in. The senator shook his head. "That's ludicrous! What happened the last three times?"

"Didn't go as planned, but eventually worked."

"Yes, but—"

"Considering what we were able to accomplish with meager funds and resources, I say we did a fine job. How much more do you think we can achieve with adequate resources?"

"Easier said than done!"

"Of course. Everything is."

"What's your plan?"

"Send humans. Nothing new, only an extension of Project ASHE."

"How?"

"We have the capabilities at Spartan Enterprises now. I'm not going to reiterate all the details, otherwise we will be here all night. If you recall, last year I presented about our Saucepan energy collider and several space transportation options. You are welcome to stop by our headquarters and see all these things for yourself."

"That will take forever!"

"We can do it within a few weeks," he said.

"Impossible!"

"No, my team has been designing a capsule that can teleport humans. We will need a few tweaks before it's ready."

The president looked at Doc. "Tony, what do you think?"

The president respected Doc, as did most people, for his prudence. She was not afraid to admit it. She trusted his judgment on this issue. All eyes focused on Doc, as though he was about to deliver a historic verdict.

"I think we should do it, even if we fail. I know it will be expensive, but I see it as an opportunity, whether we find this sister planet or not. I say we go for it."

McKomic interjected: "Senator Bloeg, tell me of a time when every-thing and everyone was in agreement. There is always going to be someone in need or something else to do instead of this or that. That doesn't mean we allow ourselves to be paralyzed by fear. We need to hear the naysayers, they fuel us to progress. Otherwise, our race will become stale and go extinct. Through this resistance, that's how we achieve meaningful things, and hopefully along the way, with every success, we can convert the naysayers into believers and doers. Heck, we could all be in the Stone Age if none of our ancestors decided to invent metal. Trust me, I'm sure better opportunities will come out of this. Only by aspiring to reach what the human spirit can do can we overcome our problems. Not by succumbing to them. That inspiration to go beyond is what will make Earth better, not how we limit ourselves. Yes, take care of the planet, but at the same time, let's not forget there is a vast universe still to be explored. There's so much more to discover."

President Blanchard nodded. "Well said. All right, you'll get all the equipment you need. This is a collaborative effort. You will have full control of the mission!"

"Yes, Madam President!" Doc said.

President Blanchard cleared her throat.

"Does everyone agree Spartan Enterprises should take control of this assignment?" Reverend Kay said.

There were yeses and nods from most of the people in the room.

McKomic's phone rang. He answered, smiled, and handed the phone to Doc.

Doc listened intently. He looked up at President Blanchard and said, "Great, we'll do it!"

"Doc, care to share with us?"

"Madam President, there have been some important developments," Doc said. "Our team at Spartan Enterprise has confirmed Max's algorithm."

"Does that mean the planet is there?"

"No, Madam President. But it tells us the calculations are correct. And there is a higher probability the planet exists, with 99 percent confidence."

President Blanchard nodded. "What else?"

"They said it may be possible to locate the planet."

"May?" Wattenberg said.

The President glared at Wattenberg.

"Do you trust them?" The President said.

"Yes, I do," Doc said.

"Great. Then let's do it."

"This is absurd," Bloeg said. "Giving one single company that much power is nuts. If they succeed, the space amendment bill gives them control of half of the endeavor's profits."

"There's nothing wrong with that. It's an incentive to drive space exploration."

McKomic looked at Bloeg. "I'm not claiming ownership on any of this," McKomic said. "I think we all know that my company is the one most capable of pulling the mission through. Plus, I have no desire to own a planet. I do it for the thrill of making the world better and propelling us forward. If I wanted that much wealth, why would I open-source Spartan Enterprise technologies?"

He continued, "I'd rather see my fellow American competitor succeed than giving the glory to the Chinese or Russians."

Joslyn Carrillo, the founder of Beyond, a rival aerospace company, said, "I'm here to help if needed. This will be an American victory, but you take the reins. Reach out if you need anything."

Several other private company leaders offered help to McKomic.

"Very well," the president said. "I have budget negotiations with Congress the day after tomorrow. I hope by end of the day tomorrow you give me a good reason to convince them not to scrap Project ASHE."

Project ASHE had been stymied by budget cuts from anti-space-faring bureaucrats. The space amendment bill was a framework to support technology and space exploration. Recently the House Subcommittee on Space was planning to review the bill, and a possible slash in the already meager appropriations for project ASHE was imminent.

"We'll get it done," McKomic said.

"As sweet as this idea sounds, I'm sure it's going to raise hell in Washington," Bloeg said.

"I know," the president said. "That's why I need all the tangible evidence, facts for Congress to chew on. If you can pull this off before the meeting, you will get all the funds you need."

"It's going to be a challenge, but do-able," Doc said.

"Yes, it will be," she said. "It's all about the numbers. If anyone can pull this off, it's you. Get me the numbers and let me do the rest."

"We will," McKomic said.

Max finally returned to his seat. The audience applauded.

"I say we follow Mr. Folksay's discovery," Reverend Kay said. "I have never heard anything more convincing than this."

Everyone in the room echoed, "Second."

The Reverend called for a vote. Everyone raised their hands.

"O.K. then," the president said, looking at McKomic. "You have 24 hours to find this planet. I need the evidence tomorrow. You'll have full control and access to some of our space satellites if needed."

"Thank you."

Reverend Kay rose to the podium.

"Thank you, Madam President," he said. "I'm glad we all are leaving this place in one piece. No punches thrown."

The crowd murmured.

"I want to remind everyone that this is what these meetings are for —to gnash teeth, clash, yell, and respect one another in the end," Reverend Kay said. "After all, what happens at Science Park stays at Science Park. We respect each other for it. That's liberty and freedom. That's America. Let's not forget that we do this for our country."

The audience clapped.

He paused for a moment. "Honestly, I'm always fascinated by all the ideas that always come out of this meeting every year. Don't we all agree? I know I do. For the common good, despite all our different backgrounds and differences in one aspect or another."

He paused.

"Let's thank all our presenters."

A round of applause rose.

Reverend Kay adjourned the meeting.

The virtual feed ended.

Everyone congratulated Max, who could not believe his luck. "Welcome to the team, Max Folksay!" McKomic said. "We'd better get going to Houston. We have a long day waiting for us."

He extended his hand and shook Max's hand, threads of biceps showing under his short-sleeved dress shirt.

Doc turned towards Max.

"You did well, son," Doc said.

"Thank you! How did you—?"

"Get the proof?"

Max, astonished, remained quiet.

Doc patted him on the shoulder. "I sent your work to one of my contacts at NASA last week before I left for Switzerland. I knew it would require some solid proof to convince the committee."

"So the data from the phone is real?"

"Of course. I wouldn't risk playing tricks with the president."

"How come you didn't tell me earlier?"

"I like to be spontaneous," he said. "I knew you'd do great. Come on, let's go. We must hurry."

"What about your car?"

"Don't worry. One of the guards will bring it."

"Sounds good." Max strode behind McKomic and Doc towards a triad of high-gloss black SUVs that were already running.

"Activate TITAN 27!" McKomic said to the driver standing next to the open car door.

"Yes, sir!" the driver said.

CHAPTER ELEVEN

Science Park

THE THREE SUVs were parked a few yards on the east side of the conference room farthest from the Science Park entrance. The engines were already running. The driver, also McKomic's bodyguard, a powerfully built man, maybe in his late 20s, stood beside the middle SUV with the rear doors flung open. McKomic, Max, and Doc hopped into the car and sat facing each other. The thick bulletproof doors immediately slammed shut with a solid thud as soon as everyone jumped in. The back was spacious enough for six passengers to fit comfortably.

The inside of the SUV was dim, in sync with the voluptuously violet velvety leather seats. The seats reminded Max of his favorite childhood animal blanket Aunt Dori had bought him on her trip to Zimbabwe. There were all kinds of electronics around to provide an office-like environment suitable for working while on the road.

"Sir, TITAN 27 is activated," a voice from the overhead speakers said, emanating from the concealed driver's section of the car, as the vehicle rolled onto the interstate.

"Thanks, John," McKomic said.

"Yes, sir," the voice said.

"What is Titan 27?" Max said.

"It's a code name for the secure mobile software that allows me to access communication and use any information without being tracked or hacked in the car," McKomic said, removing an iPad from the leather pockets behind the front seat. One of the perks of being a billionaire.

Max nodded. *What else was in this car?* he thought. It was normal to see McKomic in public with his bodyguards. Despite being outspoken and one of the greatest tech entrepreneurs of the generation, the guy had enemies. It kept him highly alert at all times. He knew that no matter how much good he did for the world, how much of a saint he thought he was, some communist psychopath out there was looking to put his sorry billionaire's ass into the great beyond for no reason other than envy. He could never let his guard down. Sometimes he missed the old days when he toiled day and night to start his business, back when no one knew him or cared that he existed. Now he had to have tight security at all times. He preferred to travel in black SUVs rumored to be armored with the highest ballistic-resistant materials. On the road, the supercar was disguised by two other identical black SUVs. The guy had a few billion dollars to spend!

John's only job was to drive McKomic around wherever he went. He spent every day studying the car and the surroundings to ensure they knew all the maneuvers for emergency situations. To say the least, he lived in the vehicle.

"Alert the Austin police to pave the way for us," McKomic said. "We need to get to Houston in no time."

"Yes, sir," the voice from the speakers said.

McKomic looked up from the iPad. "Another perk," he said. "The city needs you and does everything to keep you."

"True," Doc said. "Your companies bring so much money to the city."

The radio squawked before McKomic could respond.

"All units en route, sir," the voice said again.

"Great," McKomic said. "Let's burn some rubber!"

"Yes, sir! We're moving. Make sure you are securely seated."

John hit the accelerator, and the double seat belts automatically fastened, startling Max before he realized what was going on. They trailed behind one SUV, and another followed as they snaked out of Science Park.

An automated voice emerged: "Please remain seated. Do not remove the seat belt!" The voice repeated the statement three times before dying. Both McKomic and Doc shook their heads, evidently annoyed. They were used to hearing the voice.

"Man, I didn't think Blanchard was going to agree to this so fast," McKomic said.

"I was surprised," Doc said.

"Now we have to prove the algorithm is not merely a theory."

"We can do it."

"I know. I still can't believe the other guys pulled for me."

"They liked your work," Doc said.

"They want you to succeed," McKomic said.

"I have a feeling the other big companies grudgingly agreed for us to have the mission."

"You're right. They are hoping you will fail and discredit yourself," Doc said.

"Probably! But we'll show them otherwise," McKomic said with a defiant smirk.

"And that kid. That kid is quite the young warrior!" Doc said.

"Which one?"

"That one—Hunter," Doc said, squinting as if retrieving a memory.

"Oh, yes. Alex Hunter," McKomic said. "The kid is quite a package. I just had my guys check her out. Clean profile. Twenty-two years old. Columbia graduate. Double majored in engineering and sociology. Magna cum laude. Nothing high profile. Started working for the *Tribune* a few weeks ago. Already some of her stories are causing waves. I could tell she has some special instincts."

"I'd kill to have the kid on my team," Doc said.

"Too late," said McKomic. "I already have a team working on snatching her from the *Tribune* before Bloeg or someone else does. She'll be on our team tomorrow."

Doc and McKomic let out a victory laugh.

"Smart move! You learned well," Doc said.

"I had a good teacher," McKomic smiled at Doc, slapping him on the shoulder.

"A little reckless, but at least she sticks to what she believes."

"Still wonder how she managed to convince her boss to let her come to the meeting. Many older reporters would die to come to this meeting. She was the only media member at the meeting."

"What makes you think she asked her boss? She's hungry to make an impact at that young age. I could tell. It's hard to find that nowadays."

"We will get her. The kid is good, so you can't deny her. She's the right fit for our company."

"True."

There was a brief silence while Doc checked his cellphone.

"That was a bold spiel you gave in there," Max said to McKomic.

"I appreciate it!" McKomic said. "That's how everything works. You have to go beast mode if you're going to scoop a contract. Otherwise the competition will trample all over you."

Max nodded with a grin.

The car accelerated and sped onto the highway. Max turned the fan on and reclined the seat, yawning and feeling the cool air ruffle across his skin. Max tried to think, but his mind would not let him. He felt exhausted. His only desire was to be in Stratford. The cabin was quiet.

Two computer screens flipped down from the car roof when McKomic pressed a button. One screen was tuned to the national news channel, discussing the recent developments in the new coronavirus strain outbreak and the Soviet bioweapon summit. On the other screen, McKomic was sending an encrypted message, typing on his wireless keyboard.

A few moments later, they were greeted by an ambulance siren. The motorcade slowed down, navigating past the accident. Three officers stood on the pavement talking to a man who looked agitated, covered in a blanket and shaking his head. Another ambulance left the scene. On the far side, a tow truck was pulling the wreckage out of a drainage ditch and up the 30-foot embankment. The wrecked car now looked more like a round metal ball. An 18-wheeler was thrust upside down, its food contents splattered all over the pavement. The SUVs crawled past the wreckage and accelerated again.

"I wonder when this carelessness will end," Doc said, looking out the window at the wreck as the motorcade passed by.

McKomic shook his head and said, "It's not even summer yet."

His face said it all. The years leading to today had witnessed the most accidents per year recorded by the US Traffic and Road Agency. Despite increasing accidents, many citizens were filing petitions to increase the maximum speed limit on interstate highways. Their argument was that self-driving cars were now so improved that the speed limits of a century ago should be raised or eliminated altogether. The petition was still under congressional review.

"I hope Congress overturns the petition," Doc said.

"I sure hope so," McKomic said.

The police sirens interrupted Max's thoughts. The SUVs pulled to the outer lane and slowed down as the police crew buzzed by. He watched three motorcycles and two police cars whiz past the SUVs with their colorful lights flickering in the night. A SWAT truck trailed behind the other two motorcycles behind the SUV and an ambulance.

"I'm guessing that's our escort?" Doc said.

"Yes," McKomic said, without looking away from the tablet. He pushed the intercom. "I want the tech team at the central station when we get there," McKomic said.

John's voice responded from the other side. "Copy that, sir."

Meanwhile, Max leaned comfortably on the seat headrest and closed his eyes. He wanted to think. The sudden turn of events had overridden his need for sleep. He wanted to take it all in. He was trying to digest what had happened, how he had changed from being an ordinary, curious intern to being a real participant in Project ASHE. He wanted to let it go, but his mind would not cooperate. He had always hated sleeping in trains, cars, and planes, but this morning he wanted to. He silently prayed to God for some sleep—a brief respite from all that lay before him. A retrospective thought excited him: at least Uncle Titus had not worked in vain—and he knew Titus would be very proud of him. He wanted to share the news with Alonna and Aunt Dori. Then he remembered Alonna. *Oh, Alonna!*

"Damn it!" he murmured. His body jerked a bit, and he stole a glance around to see if anyone had noticed it. He was supposed to be in Stratford for her barrel race and goat-tying competition at the Annual Peach Festival rodeo. He had not called her yet, and he knew she was waiting for him. Of all people, she expected him to be present. He knew how important this event was to her and how she wanted him to be there. She had reminded him every day for the past few weeks and he had promised to be there no matter what. *How will I convince her to believe me—when I could not even keep a simple promise? She would think my work was more important than she.* During their early days of dating, they had vowed to be there at each other's special events—graduation, birthdays, and all. Max knew some of these promises were impractical, but he did it anyway. *Love.* He had promised he would try. He pictured Alonna in front of the arena before the barrel race, looking for Max's face in the crowd after her performance. If the event did not go so well, she would undoubtedly pin the blame on him. All he wanted was to be in Oklahoma. Max knew he had seriously messed up.

"Call her!" Doc said, interrupting Max's thoughts. Doc had been observing Max fidgeting.

Max silently ran his hands fervently through his pockets and looked all over and under the seat. He mumbled, "Crap!"

"Don't have your phone?" Doc said.

"I can't find my phone!"

"You might have left it in my car."

"Oh. I left my jacket in the car."

"You can get it when we get to headquarters."

"I gotta call my fiancée. I'm supposed to be in Stratford right now."

"Do you have to, right now?" McKomic said.

"Yes. I have to."

"You can call her when we get to Houston."

"I can't! I promised I'd be at her rodeo performance and I'm not there. I haven't even told her that I wasn't coming. I'm sure she's worried."

"Why didn't you tell her?"

"I didn't know this abrupt meeting was going to last forever," Max said. "I thought I was going to drop the folder and leave. I guess—"

McKomic handed a shiny silver box phone to Max. "Here, use my phone. It is secure."

Max looked perplexed, holding the rotary dial phone. "It's encrypted?"

"Yup."

"I didn't know these phones still existed."

"Now you do. I like to collect. I thought the phone would be a nice piece of equipment for my calls in the car."

"At least it keeps you busy the whole time trying to dial the numbers."

They laughed.

"It's the chassis that's classic. The electronics are higher tech than any phones today. Customized for me. Maybe the only phone that no hacker can crack."

"I don't even know how this thing works."

"Dial and crank."

Max dialed the phone number and cranked the silver ring several times. Each time the phone produced a crackling sound. After completing the process, he put the receiver on his ear and waited.

"Where should I tell her I am?" Max said, covering the mouthpiece with his hand, even though no one was on the other end of the call.

"Make up a story," Doc said. "Say a work situation has come up, and you have to stay the whole weekend here. You have lied before, haven't you?"

Max frowned. "I have. But not to my fiancée. Well, maybe not for important things," Max said.

"You'll be fine."

"I'm sure she will gladly accept that work is more important," Max said sarcastically.

"Even if she doesn't, this is bigger than her rodeo event," McKomic said. "At least you told her."

Max waited.

"We aren't supposed to be making any outside contact," McKomic said.

"Why?" Max said.

"If any of this gets out there, your girlfriend might be in danger. You understand what this means."

Max nodded. "But it's going to be reported anyway, right?"

"It will, and you saw the reporter there, but the media can only speculate until the project is confirmed. Everything has to follow protocol."

Max nodded and gestured them to be quiet.

The phone rang and rang six times. Max's mind churned, imagining what he was going to tell Alonna. Maybe she was already asleep. Then a voice answered—Alonna's. The voice Max yearned to hear every day answered on the other end.

"Hello!"

"Hey babe, it's Max."

"Max?"

"Yes, it's me."

"Max, why are you using a private call?"

"I'm using my friend's phone. Mine is out of power."

"Oh, O.K. Are you O.K.?"

"I'm fine. Did I wake you up?"

"No, not at all," she said. "I'm still up doing homework."

"I called to say I'm sorry for not making it to your rodeo."

"That's fine. I assumed something must have come up."

"Worked late today."

"Did you see my texts?"

"No, not yet. I haven't checked my phone. How did the rodeo go?"

"It went great. I won. People loved it."

"Congrats, baby. I knew you would. Lots of people?"

"Plenty of people showed up. Many church folks. Except for one."

"I'll make it up to you soon. I'm glad it went well."

"You'd better."

"My bad. I should have called."

"It's O.K. The food was epic, though."

"Oh, man. I know."

"How was your day?"

"Great. Busy. Adventurous. I will tell you about it when I see you this weekend."

"Sounds good. You need a break once in a while," Alonna said.

"I know, but summer is almost over, and I should be back to normal soon."

"I hope so."

"By the way, it was yesterday, not today," she said, laughing.

Max checked his wristwatch. "Man, I'm kinda out of step with time these days."

"Are you O.K.?" she said. "Your voice sounds different."

"I'm tired and sleepy."

"Worked late today?"

"Had to take care of a few things."

"That's cool. I know your schedule is unpredictable, and you get super busy."

"It was crazy!"

"So you are coming home this weekend?"

"I'm planning to—probably tomorrow."

"Great. I'll be here. Be safe."

"Thanks. You too! I love you." Max said.

"I love you, too."

"See you soon," Max said, all the while thinking that was not going to happen.

"See you. Make sure you get some rest," Alonna said.

"I will."

"Bye," Alonna said, and the phone hung up.

Max listened to the crackling sound as the connection died and kept the receiver on his ear for a few moments. He was still surprised how the conversation had gone.

"Not as bad as you thought, huh?" Doc said.

"She was very calm."

"Women like men who communicate," he said. "They understand."

"I can't wait to go home."

"You will, soon," said McKomic, who had been absorbed in the tablet he was typing on. He turned off the computers as they entered the Houston city limits.

HOUSTON'S STREETS WERE DESERTED, except for a few homeless individuals who loitered around and some sleeping on the public benches and under trees. The SUV arrived at the Spartan Enterprises headquarters central station at 1:30 a.m. There were armed security guards at the gate.

"It's 1:30," McKomic said. "Good ride, John."

"My pleasure, sir," John said.

"We are one hour ahead of the normal traveling time."

John scanned his I.D. and the gates opened. The SUVs cruised past two guards, whom McKomic waved to, and descended into a basement parking lot. Max, Doc, and McKomic were dropped off in front of a large brown metal door. John stayed in the car and wished them good night. Max opened the brown metal door and held it for Doc and McKomic. He followed them into the southward tunnel. There were inspirational quotations glued to the sides of the tunnel. Some of the banners read: "Big Dreams Start Here"; "Believe"; "Anything is possible"; "To predict the future you must create it. -A. Lincoln."

The tunnel led to an open reception area for visitors and tours of Spartan Enterprises headquarters. They were greeted by a larger-than-life replica of a metalloid man-machine carrying the globe on his shoulders, who said, "Welcome to Spartan Enterprises."

There were four elevators, two on each side of the hallway. After a few seconds, they reached the tenth floor. The elevator dinged, opening into a corridor that led through the atrium into the Aurelius Hall. They turned right and entered a large elliptical room with "McGill Conference Room" inscribed above the entrance.

The conference room was abuzz with people of all ages—most in their 20s with a few older than that—all dressed in different kinds of attire, mostly casual clothing. Everyone hushed as soon as McKomic entered the room. Some were standing and others sitting. Most had coffee mugs, and the aroma filled the whole room. Max and the others occupied the empty seats near the front. McKomic wasted no time in addressing his colleagues.

"Thank you all for showing up on such short notice," McKomic said. "There have been some interesting developments on Project ASHE, and the president has requested results by 5:00 p.m. today before her meeting with the Congress at 8:00 p.m. It's a good opportunity for us to secure funding and expand our services."

Everyone remained silent with curious faces. There were a few smiles. They were used to McKomic bouncing around random ideas often and wondered what unheard-of idea it was this time. They waited expectantly.

McKomic briefed the group on the findings. He concluded by outlining assignments for each group on the whiteboard at the front of the room. Among the group were engineers, microbiologists, anthropologists, geneticists, and physicists.

"The other aerospace companies let us have this mission because they expect us to fail," McKomic said. "We're not going to let that happen. And we'll show them what we're really made of!"

"When do we have to have the results?" one guy said.

"In less than 18 hours."

"That's a short time," one of the senior scientists, in blue and white slacks, said.

McKomic glared at him. The man's lips twitched defensively.

"Failure is not an option," McKomic said. "We'll do it. At least we will do all we can. There is a chance we might be right, and that's all I need."

The man acquiesced, nodding and staring blankly at McKomic. He dared not say another word lest he get fired on the spot, an act for which McKomic was notorious.

"We will ramp up our time and energy to meet the deadline. We will work like hell if that's what it takes," he said. "And you all know I will be here with you."

McKomic surveyed the faces in the room, looking for emotion. His stare seemed to pierce everyone in the room. No one answered or dared say anything.

"Can't you see this is an opportunity of a lifetime? How many people get to be part of discovering a habitable planet?" Doc said to them.

"This is our bonanza!" McKomic said. "Hell yeah, we need that contract! This has been our goal from the beginning, hasn't it? Now is the time. So let's get to work and make this happen! Any questions?"

No one dared to respond. McKomic was known for his contretemps with Spartan engineers, often because of his micromanagement and sky-high expectations.

Instead, everyone nodded and a few applauded. As if by some extraordinary alchemy, McKomic had managed to rally this group of doubters into believers within a few minutes. It seemed the team had waited for this forever, especially the majority of the employees who were recent graduates, many former and current FIST recruits— hungry for adventure. His radical and revolutionary ideas thrilled them, though he at times seemed to push too hard. They loved being there. Everyone wanted to leave a mark. Without commenting, they dispersed to their various workstations in the building.

Max admired McKomic. McKomic exuded natural confidence that baffled everyone. After his few precepts, his total self-belief gave them an impetus. This was a done deal. They fed on his confidence. They believed it. There was no turning back after he made a commitment. Max liked that.

McKomic summoned one of the men in the room.

"Geoffrey," he said. "You'll work with Max. I will be there shortly."

Geoffrey looked at Max and said, "Yes, sir," which he followed with a belch.

"I'll contact NASA and make sure we get everything we need," McKomic said, before exiting for his office.

Geoffrey nodded and shook Max's hand firmly.

Geoffrey wore loosely fitting plain faded denim jeans and an over-sized, loud, rainbow-colored plaid t-shirt tucked in on the left side, barely concealing a stress gut. He had conspicuously large-framed glasses and a beard that was starting to show some shades of gray. From the outset, despite his unkempt appearance, Geoffrey seemed both carefree and smart. He was the stereotypical chubby dude who talks too much and loudly.

"Geoffrey Foster," he said. "Chief Central Core Engineer."

"Max Folksay. Nice to meet you, Dr. Foster," Max said.

"Pleasure to meet you," Geoffrey said. "Not a doctor yet. Neither am I planning to be soon, and please call me Geoffrey."

"Oh, all right."

Geoffrey led the way into a wide corridor.

"Where are you from again?" Geoffrey said.

"Stratford. It's in Oklahoma."

"I've never heard of that name."

"It's a tiny town."

"Anything famous from there?"

"Hmm. Maybe peaches? Where are you from?"

"Washington."

"Cool. I was there a few months ago. Visiting with my family."

"Why did you decide to come all the way down here?"

"Maybe a change of scenery. All the fun is here. I grew up in Oregon, and it rains a bunch up there."

"But Washington has the museums and tourist attractions."

"Wait—I think we are talking about two different things. Did you go to D.C.?"

"So you meant Seattle?"

"Yup."

"Oh. That makes sense. The rain and stuff."

"Funny we were all talking about two different places the whole time."

They laughed.

"I'm glad we figured it out," Geoffrey said laughing. "That'll definitely help in here. Actually, I've been to D.C. a few times myself. Real nice."

They entered into the corridor and passed a few workers hurrying by. Geoffrey exchanged greetings with a group of employees whom they passed in the hallway. They took the skywalk to the other wing of the complex.

"Props for the good work, man," Geoffrey said.

"Thanks. I appreciate it."

"I am very impressed. Everyone in my department was talking about your findings, and we have been working on it since Doc forwarded us your notes earlier, and everyone is excited. Kind of gives some purpose to everything we've been doing here."

Max smiled. "Your proof came just in time."

"There might be a possibility for a physics Nobel Prize! Heck, you could get a Ph.D. for this!"

Max laughed. He did this only for fun. Regardless, Geoffrey's speculations seemed far-fetched.

"That would be surreal, man," Max said.

"It's possible."

Max scrutinized everything on the way. He did not know what to think of what Geoffrey had said. Strangely enough, Max felt confused. He had never had such praise from strangers, successful strangers, apart from his family and friends. It seemed real now.

"I can't believe that I'm actually talking to you," Geoffrey went on, his face beaming.

"I appreciate that," Max said, hoping Geoffrey would move on to the next topic.

The corridor led to a double wooden door. Geoffrey flung the doors open and stood at the entrance; his arms spread out pompously.

"Welcome to my haven!" Geoffrey said.

Max looked on in awe. "Wow!"

"This is where I live and breathe, baby," Geoffrey said, with a swagger in his step.

CHAPTER TWELVE

Spartan Enterprises HQ

THE DOORS LED to a large hall that spanned the entire floor, with workstations and cubicles partitioned by thin transparent glass. Contemporary furniture and modern art and sculptures erected throughout the space made the floor look more like a playground than a working area. The Spartan Enterprises logo was everywhere: bobbleheads, mouse pads, posters, screen savers. The room oozed innovation—computers, multiplexers, diplexers, laptops, keyboards, probes, projectors, whiteboards, papers—anything ideal for designing, creating, measuring, and developing. Keyboards click-clacked throughout the room. A large glass table stood at the center of the room with four micro-projectors attached on each of the table's four sides. A massive wall-size screen covered the front wall. There were positive vibrations all around. People in the room were all busy and took only brief notice of Geoffrey and Max.

Max said, "Is it always this busy?"

"Mostly," Geoffrey said. He paused and belched again, mid-sentence. "We like to work at work and party later. But our work is play, anyway. That's how we roll here."

Max ignored the irritation he was feeling from Geoffrey's continual burping.

"Wow," Max said.

"Pete!" Geoffrey said. "I want you and your team to establish contact with NASA and see if we can get access to their satellites in orbit. Get any updates from McKomic."

Pete, an engineer, was Geoffrey's second-in-command.

"Yes, sir! Who do we say authorized the access?" Pete said.

"Tell them it's the POTUS. If anyone insists, transfer them to McKomic's office."

"Yes, sir," Pete said and disappeared behind the video console to his workstation.

"Max, we'll work together to put together a model for your algorithm," Geoffrey said.

"O.K."

Geoffrey pressed the intercom and said, "Everyone, remember we have 17 hours to get this thing done. So whatever you're doing, stop it and focus on this job right now. I want all hands on deck."

Max sat in the chair next to Geoffrey. Geoffrey inserted Max's flash drive into the monitor and saved all the data before altering anything. The swiftness with which he approached his work impressed Max. Geoffrey worked effortlessly on the keyboard, displaying his coordination and computer panache. After a few strokes, a planetary 3D hologram appeared on the glass table. He used a joystick to zoom the picture to Jupiter, then entered Max's algorithm. A simulation of Aoratosia, nestled in Jupiter's magnetospheric ring, appeared. Geoffrey ordered one of his colleagues to adjust the contrast while he reentered the formula. He talked, all the while crunching keys on the keyboard.

He paused for a second and gobbled a handful of peanuts from a big jar open behind his monitor.

That's why! Max thought. *All the annoying belching.*

"That's a lot of peanuts," Max said.

"I know it's a lot," Geoffrey belched again. He excused himself and hurried to the break room. He returned a minute later.

"Sorry, I had to go get a drink. I get so occupied sometimes that I forget to drink water. I'm guessing you have noticed all the belching."

Max nodded. "How many peanuts do you eat?"

"Here—a lot," Geoffrey said, without shifting his concentration off the screen over the dozen lines of code he had just written. "I don't know, but a lot. The peanut is special, you know."

"It is."

"It saves me when I don't have time to go to lunch on days like today. Don't worry; if you hang around long enough, you'll get it. Not that it's bad. It's a habit, I guess."

"I still think that's—"

"Weird?"

"A little."

"I've heard that before."

A picture appeared on the monitor.

"Got it," Geoffrey said, elated. Max rolled his chair closer to the screen to have a better view.

Geoffrey paused. "Do you believe in serendipity?"

"It depends. Why?"

"I was looking at these images when I received the file with your model from Doc. Let me show you something," Geoffrey said, opening a separate folder. "Would you believe if I tell you that some work found in the Dead Sea Scrolls and manuscripts explained the possibility of Earth having a twin sister planet? And some recently discovered Mesopotamian or Egyptian stone tablets in the British Museum show Earth conjoined to some blurry dot on the side."

"I didn't know that," Max said.

"Me neither. I only found that out after some digging," Geoffrey said. "You don't believe it, do you?"

"It's an interesting theory, and I can see ancient humans being fascinated by the Earth-moon connection."

"What if it were not a theory?"

"I don't know," Max said, in a somewhat indifferent tone.

"It's possible. I've seen impossible things over my few years."

"I guess so."

"Look at it this way. Every ancient culture seemed to have genius. The Mayans, Egyptians, Mesopotamians. Dude—they created amazing things, some still baffling us even today. Some of those cultures toyed with the idea of another Earth—whether in the stars or deep underground."

Max nodded. "That's true."

"Let me show you this," Geoffrey said.

He swiped the screen with his hand, and a scribbled manuscript appeared on the video console on the wall. "This is an engraving retrieved from the trove the Nazis buried. It dates back as far as the era of the earliest known writings."

Max moved closer to the screen. "How did you even get these files?" Max said. "They're some of the most treasured national documents."

"Dumpster diving."

"What's that?"

Geoffrey rolled his eyes counterclockwise at Max and said, "On the web playing around, and please do not ask me to explain."

Max laughed. "I think I know the answer."

"I'm sure you heard on the news about two years ago when a buried Nazi train was recovered in Poland."

"I remember hearing about it."

Geoffrey smiled. "I was part of the volunteer team tasked to secure and authenticate the trove for refurbishment, which I know will take forever to complete. At the operation site, we found many demolished artifacts. We were called after the valuables had been secured. Anyway, I came across this artifact and took several pictures. I don't know why the curator allowed me to see it. It was some of the many I took, but when Doc gave me your notes a few days ago, these pictures came to mind. I thought they might be some connection."

"Cool."

"I took these images while we were doing the tests. I don't even know why I kept them. A hunch, maybe. But I remembered when McKomic sent me your algorithm. The images seem strange, so I went back and looked. Here's what I found."

He opened an image showing what looked like snippets of weathered marble.

"What is that?"

"Wait for it."

Geoffrey skipped past many files to the one which showed engravings on a reconstituted marble tablet. He sequentially pieced it together like a jigsaw puzzle until the complete picture of a worn-out stone tablet came into view.

"What's that?"

"That's why I've been eating peanuts too much," Geoffrey said, laughing. "I had to solve this puzzle. I like to finish what I start. What do you see?"

"A carving?"

"Correct; that's what everyone thinks. But watch what happens. When I examined the image further, it showed a multispectral image."

"I can see a layer underneath."

Geoffrey punched a series of keys. The image morphed into two multispectral layers of carvings—the one underneath stained violet.

"What's that?"

"Something peculiar."

"What's special?"

"That is what's fascinating to me. Further refining of the erased images shows this."

"A planetary system?"

"Yes!"

"That's our planetary system."

"Yup."

"I wonder what happened."

"I believe it's from the ruins of a tenth-century monastery somewhere in Poland. The papacy had a lot of bureaucracy back then; the genius probably got hanged for it, and then they put something on top. The carving dates back to the fifth century B.C."

"Interesting."

"Many people believe the markings are from weathering. What's funny is that historians and archaeologists believed for centuries that this was because of natural wear and tear over long periods. What's sad is that we have relegated all these to dusty museums. No one cares about the fine print on all these documents anymore."

"So we have two sources that suggest Aoratosia exists then?"

Geoffrey nodded. "Yes."

"So you're saying the artist intentionally included this dot on the cosmic diagram?" Max said.

"Exactly," Geoffrey said. "There's no other explanation. Look at those of Copernicus, Ptolemy, and Kepler's models—they don't have the dot."

"I also found this item on the dark web," Geoffrey said. Geoffrey opened another page showing a worn-out page with faded sketches.

"You use the dark web?"

"People sell all kinds of crap down there."

The page opened.

"What are we seeing?"

"Notes purported to be from Da Vinci's missing collection of papers."

"How can they know?"

"Based on the direction of his handwriting. He wrote from right to left, which agrees with his other works in the codices."

"Everyone did that in those days."

"True, but Da Vinci had a unique way of doing that no known scholars of that era could emulate."

"That's still controversial. I would take that with a grain of salt."

"Agreed."

"How did they know Earth had a twin?" Max said. "They were here a couple hundreds of years ago. How can they know what happened thousands of years ago?"

"Nobody knows."

"Why would a scientist hide that?"

"Heresy, man," Geoffrey said. "Whoever it was, was insulting the papacy. The Catholics wanted the person's head. Maybe he didn't want to make that worse. Or it could be that he didn't have enough painting material, or he intentionally created something that few people could understand."

"I probably would've done the same."

"He didn't want to upset the entire set of dogma and belief about our existence. That would have been a disaster in his days. It's too bad we lost the rest of his work," Geoffrey said. "Maybe the dude had already explained some things we are still trying to find!"

"Probably," Max said. "That would have made our job so much easier!"

McKomic and Doc had entered the room.

"Listening to Geoffrey's preposterous theories?" McKomic said, with a glint of humor in his eyes.

"History never lies," Geoffrey said.

"Since when did you become an aesthete?" Doc interjected, giving Geoffrey a friendly slap on the left shoulder.

Geoffrey grinned. "As long as I can remember!"

"Like your unfounded claim that the Bermuda Triangle exists, when it's not even listed on the most dangerous waters on Earth," McKomic said. "You watch too much paranoia TV, son."

McKomic and Doc laughed.

"What can I say? I never tell people to buy into my loony ideas!" Geoffrey said.

"Instinct, son," McKomic said. "It always turns out right—at least 80 percent of the time."

"Less than 30 percent of the time!" Geoffrey said.

McKomic chuckled, ignoring the jab directed at him. "That's where most of our success comes from, remember. The rest is noise and a waste of time."

Geoffrey laughed. "No comments."

"Your obsession with semantics will drive you nuts one of these days," McKomic said.

"Thank you."

"Not sure I meant that as a compliment."

"I'm determined to take that as one. Someone's got to keep the seeker's baton aflame, right?"

"Here we go again. We're not going into alchemy again," McKomic said.

"It's magic!"

"O.K. Whatever it is!"

Everyone laughed. Max laughed too, barely catching on to the humorous jabs. At first, Max had thought Geoffrey was an academic snob, but realized Geoffrey was a confident freak who enjoyed playing with computers, his mind, books, numbers, theories. Geoffrey knew plenty of everything—physics, engineering, history, metaphysics, biology, art—which all contributed to his unusual personality.

"What do you have here?" McKomic said, his tone more businesslike.

"I was showing Max these images." Geoffrey opened the image on the big screen and scrolled down through the list. "Look. Using spectral imaging, it gives a unique pattern," Geoffrey said, scrolling down the images.

"Like a daguerreotype?" Doc said.

"Yes! That's the word I was looking for."

"Why is that important?" Doc said.

"There's a pattern of some sort!" Max said.

"Someone covered the painting with another one," said Doc.

Geoffrey smiled. "That's right. I experimented with it, refining and tracing the patterns, and this is what I came up with."

Geoffrey pulled up another image onto the screen. "Look closely while I adjust the lighting."

"A sketch?"

"Yes, but not an ordinary sketch."

"Are those planets?" Doc said, adjusting his glasses.

"I think it's a planetary sketch."

"O.K., but how does that help us?"

"I still don't get why would someone hide their work?"

"Wrong question. We should be asking who did the work."

"This could be anyone. Even people like Copernicus sat on their work for 30 years, scared to publish it. Maybe the same artist didn't want any backlash and persecution from the Catholic church."

Doc said, "Remember, Copernicus didn't believe in elliptical orbits in the beginning. Maybe he didn't think his model was correct, and he covered it himself to engrave the Earth-centered universe."

"That was the mainstream dogma back then."

"Radical enough to challenge the belief that Earth was the center of the universe. Saying Earth had a twin sister would be downright heresy and treason."

"Where did you get these images?" Doc said.

"It's from that recovered Nazi ghost train in the Polish mountains."

"I recall that."

"That's exciting, but with too many assumptions here," McKomic said. "Let's go to work, find this planet, and go there first. Don't care if some dead person thought about it first."

Doc stepped back. "Sorry for sidetracking here, but I met this fellow four years ago who claimed he had a trove of ancient Jewish antiquities," he recalled. "He said he was going to meet Popovich."

"And?"

"He talked a bit about Galileo's manuscripts and sketches, but I paid little attention. I'm thinking he was telling the truth. Merely passing out a random thought that struck my mind."

"Where was this?"

"On my vacation on a train from Paris to Budapest with my wife. This guy came up, and after learning I was a physicist he started telling me about his independent studies on cosmology dating back to the Greeks and earliest excavations from the Egyptian pyramids and other Mesopotamian cultures."

"Did he say where he was from?"

"He probably did," he said. "But the guy was taking too much, evidently had too much bourbon, and I was in no mood to listen to his nonsense. I wanted to have a memorable time with my wife, who was dying of cancer. I ended up asking the train staff to transfer him to another booth."

"Did he have anything?"

Doc thought hard for a while. "He showed me vintage sketches of what he claimed could have been from the first century," he said. "I don't remember exactly."

"You think that had to do with this?" Max said.

Doc stared blankly for a moment. "I am not sure, but the guy seemed dead serious," he said. "I should have paid more attention to his ramblings."

"Even if that's true," Max said, "where would someone get first-century drawings in this world? They didn't have paper then."

"The Nazis robbed plenty of the world's precious art," Geoffrey said. "Maybe he was a descendant of a prominent Nazi general who had left him a fortune of artifacts buried in his backyard."

They laughed.

"Possibly."

"How can the antiques survive that long?" McKomic said.

"Art always finds a way," Geoffrey said.

A notification beeped on the computer screen. Geoffrey opened the small icon.

"Something has come up!" he said.

"What is that?" Doc said. "Your chat buddies?"

"Sort of," he said. "We like to call it a 'jamboree of wizards.' They are my eyes out there in the world. That's how I keep track of what's going on out there. That may be an answer to our questions."

"As long as you don't compromise us."

"Come on, I'm the king of all programmers. Partners in crime, but we don't know where and who the other one is. That's how we play the game. I can see what all of you do on your computers if I want to."

"Is that even legal?"

"I didn't say I'd do it," Geoffrey said.

"You just did."

"I thought I said I can."

Three large images appeared on the screen. Geoffrey paused and zoomed them. "This is interesting!"

Everyone looked, transfixed, at the screen.

"Have you ever had a thought that pops into your mind when you hear new information? That's what happened when I received Max's work," Geoffrey said.

"Nice paintings," Doc said.

"Look closely," Geoffrey said, zooming in on the image. He juxta-posed the picture with the other lithographs. "I compared the original painting with the only two existing lithographs."

"Do you see any differences between the three images?"

"They look the same to me. This one is just old."

"They are copies of each other, right?"

"Right. But you can see the differences between the original and the replicas."

"It shows nothing to me," McKomic said.

"That's what everyone said on the recovery team. But I still think it's more than that—the shape and stuff. I've been working on these for a long time. Using 3D mapping and modeling software, I reconstructed the missing pieces. It looks like this."

Geoffrey displayed another image, illuminated with black light.

"See the difference?"

"Right," Max said. "I can see the dots are intentionally drawn but highlighted so that the naked eye cannot see that."

"Here is what's interesting."

"More conspiracies?" McKomic said.

Geoffrey ignored McKomic's question. "Funny thing is, there are only three of them in the world, all from different sellers on the dark web."

"People buy art from the dark web?" Doc said.

"You can't believe what people buy and sell. The main question is who is buying."

"Who?" McKomic said.

"Billionaire Popovich!" Geoffrey said, looking at McKomic.

"The Russian?"

"Yeah. Already bought two replicas for an unspecified amount and has placed a bid on the original one for $100 million to support a charity in Poland."

"That bastard!" McKomic said. "What does he want with this one?"

"Why does that matter?" Doc said.

"Charity for Poland? Nothing is ever free!" McKomic said.

"But why would someone buy three paintings for that ridiculous amount? Replicas? It doesn't make sense."

"Billionaires like splurging on splashy things, probably showing off."

"Still."

"Or he is simply a fanatical art collector," Doc said.

"Why would anyone buy three identical paintings for such an insane amount like that? Three of them! My gut tells me he knows something."

"Apart from meddling in US politics and voting, the guy has no history of collecting expensive art. That makes it even more strange and suspicious."

"Either he is an art aficionado, or he knows their value."

"My gut tells me there's more," Geoffrey said. "Look what he said earlier during his campaign for the presidency. He was into finding another Earth."

"I see your point," Doc said. "Considering that US-Russian relations are in a tailspin, I wouldn't rule out anything," Doc said.

"Yeah," McKomic said. "The guy has been known to support unconventional causes and space travel. He knows more than he's telling."

Doc said, "You think it has to do with planetary search?"

"I know so," McKomic said.

"I still think he is showing off."

"I doubt it. He might as well know what we know now. This is the guy who has been trying to steal my European cargo contracts to the space station."

"This is like a gold mine. For sure, people will piss on each other when the news gets out and the rush starts. I want eyes on him!" McKomic said. "His every move. Call our office in Moscow to see if they can glean some info on him. When is the bidding ending?" McKomic said.

"In a few hours!" Geoffrey said.

"Great!" McKomic said. "Place a bid. We bid double the amount he offers."

That was an order to Geoffrey, who set about it.

"Cordell, that's a lot of money for one painting!" Doc said.

"That will buy us some time," he said. "While he figures his next move, we keep working on this. Hopefully, we can finish our work before then."

"Are you sure?"

"Cancel the bid an hour before the time limit expires."

Everyone remained quiet. They knew the amount of work ahead, and most of all, McKomic's boldness and faith perplexed them.

"How long do you think it is going to take?" McKomic said.

"I'm not sure," Geoffrey said. "Probably a few hours if we work nonstop."

"All right, let's do it!"

"Everyone, you heard the man. Let's find this Aoratosia!" Geoffrey said.

Employees rushed to their workstations.

NEW IMAGES APPEARED on the 3D bubble hologram.

Geoffrey sat straight in his chair, stretched his fingers, and rolled the chair next to the central 3D hologram.

"Based on the algorithm, the planet should be here," he said, pointing with a laser pointer.

"Aoratosia," Max said.

"I like that name," Geoffrey said. "We have a narrow launch window, though."

"How narrow?" Doc asked.

"Our calculations show that Jupiter will be closest to Earth in about two months."

"Which means we should do everything in two months," McKomic said.

"Yes! But might take double that time unless we crank up production."

"We can do it," McKomic said. "We have to find out how. Good thing is we already have prototypes in the shop for the teleporter. Oh, on that note, the teleporter energy should be at its peak around that time."

"Then we have to push this through," Geoffrey said.

"Yup."

"Great, let's see if we can identify the planet."

Geoffrey went back to work.

"Pete, do we have control of Spartan 007S?" McKomic said.

"Yes, sir!" Pete shouted from the next station, which was also lined with multiplexers.

"What is Spartan 007S?" Max asked.

"It's a badass telescope, the most powerful telescope ever built in the history of space telescopes. It's a next-generation infrared space telescope that Spartan Enterprises developed as part of project ASHE, which orbits around Mars," Doc said. "It has a longer lifespan than anything we have developed before. We can also view farther than any other space telescope before her," Doc added. "It monitors and traces any signs of life in our galaxy and beyond: sound waves, atmospheric distortions."

"Interesting," Max said.

There was a brief silence. Geoffrey called out. "The formula shows the right position of Aoratosia on the model with 99 percent confidence," Geoffrey said.

"I'd say that's pretty good," said Doc.

"That's all I need to hear," McKomic said.

"My team is programming the coordinates onto Spartan 007S processor, but so far the planet's position makes it difficult to view, with all the surrounding thick magnetic field tubes refracting light."

"Any thought why?"

"We are predicting all the magnetic fields make the environment dynamic."

"Is there anything we can do?" McKomic said.

"We are working on it," Geoffrey said. "We are writing a new program for controlling the telescope lenses. The lens can be adjusted remotely."

"Is that do-able within the hour?" McKomic said.

"Yes. That might allow us to get a better image of Aoratosia."

"How soon?"

"I think a couple hours. Since we are standing on our toes right now, we don't have that much time."

"I need tangible evidence to send to POTUS," Doc said.

"We can reprogram the route for Spartan 007S in orbit."

"It would take months for it to reach the area where we can view Aoratosia. We don't have that much time either," Doc said.

"There's one satellite with power enough to do what we want," Geoffrey said.

Everyone looked at Geoffrey.

"The Defense Space Monitoring Satellite!" Geoffrey said.

"That might work actually," McKomic said.

"How's that gonna work?" Max said.

"The Department of Defense recently added a section on the satellite to study deep space," McKomic said, and smiled. "We actually designed the space monitoring system for the D.O.D. a couple years back."

"How?"

"I can't tell you. It's classified."

"It's impossible to even get close to the satellite," Doc said.

McKomic nodded. "Yeah, that will be impossible."

"We should at least give it a shot," Doc said. "Geoffrey, what did you have in mind?"

"We can connect the satellite in tandem with our Spartan 007S Mars telescope, which will allow us to observe and map Jupiter better," Geoffrey said, using the laser pointer on the bubble model.

"You think that will work?" Doc said. "That has never been done before."

"I think so," Geoffrey said. "I can't say for certain! It's a challenge."

"We can work with the D.O.D engineers to expedite the process."

"O.K.," Doc said. "I can convince the president, but we need a compelling reason for the president and the commanders to even consider doing it."

"That can allow us to study Aoratosia's atmosphere correctly."

"Are you sure we can do this?" Doc said.

"We can try it."

"How do you propose we do that?"

Geoffrey punched more keys and modified the model.

"I can program the satellite to rotate back to its original position after."

"How long is that going to take?"

"I'd guess somewhere between 25 minutes to an hour. Depends on how difficult it is to see what we want to see."

"Can you do it in 25 minutes?" McKomic said.

"We can try."

"I'll take that as a yes."

Geoffrey nodded, not looking at McKomic.

"There is another problem, though," Doc said. "Even if it works, people in D.C. will not give us control of the satellite. The satellite and others in that constellation also serve as telecommunication and radar security for the entire country and three-quarters of the globe. Interrupting it would cause havoc."

"I can imagine," McKomic said. "We have to be careful it doesn't disrupt mainstream media."

"It shouldn't," Geoffrey said.

"And our astronauts on the space station?" said Doc.

"They should be fine. We'll alert them."

"Are you sure about this?"

"I don't know, Doc," McKomic said. "But we don't have another better way. It's your call."

"O.K.," Doc said. "If we do this, I'll have to get permission from the White House."

"Agreed. But how're we going to do that when the satellite runs a large portion of the country's defense?"

"I'll be right back," Max said, and ran from the room before anyone could react.

"Where are you going?" Doc said, but Max was already out.

Max came back within a few seconds, carrying a copy of the *Houston Tribune*. Max cleared his throat and slammed the newspaper face up on the table.

"There's our solution!"

Everyone stood silent with inquisitive faces.

"Is there a story in there about last night's meeting?"

"There is not," McKomic said, knowingly, and Max realized McKomic had had that leak taken care of.

"The Olympics opening ceremony is this morning," Max said, pointing at the headline announcing the upcoming opening ceremonies in huge bold letters. "We can do it then."

"How does that have to do with us?" Doc said.

"Everything," Max said. "This is the perfect time to shift the satellite. There's a very slim probability of a terrorist attack during the Olympics. It's a time to celebrate life—the Olympic values."

"The Palestinians did otherwise to the Israeli athletes during the Olympics!" Geoffrey said.

"That was a long time ago. We're not saying nothing will happen, but it's less likely than any other time. Can you think of any other time when the world is most united?"

"Max has a good point!"

"Let's try to convince the POTUS," McKomic said. "In the meantime, keep working on it to see what you can find."

"Are you sure this will work?" Doc said. "I want to be certain before we focus all our energy on this method."

"This is the best shot we have," Geoffrey said, still punching keys on the computer.

"Let's go with it, then," McKomic said.

"Great. I will notify the president right away," Doc said. "No one leaves this building, and we will monitor all calls."

"She'll be reluctant to do this," Geoffrey said.

"I know, but she will take a look at it," McKomic said. "Every political leader yearns for immortality. Kennedy dreamt of putting a man on the moon, and he did. Blanchard would not want to miss out on a chance to add to her legacy."

Doc left the control room and strolled towards his office.

The call with the president was brief. Doc returned to the control room after a while.

"Good news?" McKomic said.

"To some extent," he said. "The president thought it wise for her to meet with other advisors before deciding. She will get back to us. From what I could tell, she is willing to push this through as quickly as possible before the Russians get a chance to act on it."

"Great! I hope she does," McKomic said.

Max checked his phone. It was 3:30 a.m. Everyone was still there, busy as if no one cared about going home. Max realized that was how Spartan Enterprises worked. That's how McKomic worked. Unlike most government companies, Spartan Enterprises had a unique way of accomplishing things. Everyone was going to stay there until they solved the algorithm.

A few minutes later, Chad, McKomic's personal chauffeur, entered the control room with a cart full of assorted food. Everyone in the hall was familiar with him. He brought in food on the many occasions when they worked overtime to meet a deadline rush. He dropped a dinner box on the table beside Geoffrey.

"Thank you, Chad. I can smell my favorite strips. Yum!" Geoffrey said, without even taking his eyes off the computer.

"You're welcome! And for you, sir?"

"What do you have?"

"Pasta and marinated chicken strips," Geoffrey cut in before Chad could reply. "You can't go wrong with that."

Chad said, "O.K.?"

"Yes. I'll take that," Max said.

At 4:00 a.m., Max went to the break room. Everyone retired to the HQ guest rooms. Some slept on the couches in the break room. The last metro train to FIST was long gone, and Max curled on the small couch in the lounge across from the McGill conference room. He wasn't the least bit sleepy. He tossed and turned, his brain on fire with anticipation.

CHAPTER THIRTEEN

Spartan Enterprises HQ

MAX WAS AWAKENED a few hours later by the tantalizing scent of perfume. He wiped his eyes and noticed someone standing across the room looking outside the huge glass panel facing the clock tower.

"Hey!" Max said, outstretching his arms. His shoulder joints crackled, and he felt some stiffness as he yawned. It was Yvette Yates.

Yvette turned around to face Max.

"Good morning," she said, smiling.

"Please tell me you just came in," Max said.

"About two minutes ago, I think," she said.

"I'd be damned."

Yvette chuckled infectiously. Her dimples flattered her face. The gray suit she was wearing complemented her svelte figure. *Not bad for a Saturday morning,* Max thought. She looked vibrant and confident, and Max struggled to keep his eyes away from her.

"I should've taken a picture of that," she said, emulating Max's wide-open mouth. "That was a candid moment. Your mouth was wide open."

"Had a long day yesterday." Max yawned out the sentence. "I wasn't snoring, right?"

Yvette rolled her eyes, exposing the green eyeshadow which lent her light-brown eyes a divine greenish appearance. An impish grin traced across her face.

"Nope," she said, chuckling to herself. "You sleep like a little baby."

"I'll take that as a compliment," Max stretched his neck sideways. "Damn, my neck is killing me," he said, squeezing his neck with his hand.

"That's what happens when you curl on a small couch like that."

"I knew that was a bad idea."

"Let me show you what to do," Yvette said, approaching Max.

She squeezed, stretched, tweaked, and turned Max's neck quickly, then messaged the nape of his neck. Max shrieked.

"That worked," Max said. "I feel better already. How did you do that?"

"Magic touch," she said. "You need to know the few pressure points on the neck muscles."

"What are you? A physical therapist?"

"No, but I know the human body."

"Really? You should be," Max said. "How do you know all that stuff?"

"The Internet."

They laughed.

"What can I say? It works."

Yvette walked to the shelf across the lounge sink close to the window.

"Coffee? I bought my dad some coffee on my way to work and I have one extra."

"I definitely could use one right now."

Max watched Yvette at the window.

"Black or with cream?"

"With cream," Max said. "I don't drink dark coffee."

"Neither do I," Yvette said, handing Max one of the paper cups from a rack of four that was sitting on the countertop.

"Good timing. I appreciate it."

"No problem."

Max took a gulp.

"Dark frosted mocha latte?" Max said.

"Yes."

"You're a psychic."

"Maybe I am. Why?"

"This is my favorite."

Yvette giggled. "I'm glad you like it!"

"I love it."

"So do I."

"Especially the original Kenyan blend, from the shop down on the intersection between Main and Houston Avenue."

"I usually go there to do my assignments," Yvette said.

"I go there often. How come we have never met there?"

"Maybe you were hiding from me."

"I doubt that," Max said, taking another sip.

"It's Max, right?"

"You got it. Yvette?"

She nodded.

"We met at the golf club last month," Max said.

"Yes, we did," she said. "I thought you forgot."

"I don't forget that easily."

"You never know with guys. Been waiting for that promised run since."

"Oh, crap. Sorry about that," Max said. "Things have been hectic this past month."

"It's O.K."

"How was your marathon?"

"Great," she said. "I finished fifth."

"That's impressive. Congrats."

"Thank you," she said.

Max joined Yvette at the glass wall where she was standing.

"Beautiful day, isn't it?" Max said, sipping his coffee and looking through the glass panel towards the eastern horizon.

It was 7:00 a.m. Max and Yvette looked outside through the window. The air in the building made Max sick; he was eager to get some fresh air outside. He had had enough of this already. The rising sun was beginning to kiss the Houston skyline, bursting forth with a roseate glow, streaming through the huge glass panels and casting a bright, warm streak into the break room. It was a good day.

"It is," Yvette said. "My dad used to bring me with him to his office when I was little. I used to stand at this window where I could see almost all of Houston and it makes me feel that I could do anything— that anything was possible."

"Yes," Max said. He put his hands in his jeans pockets and looked outside into the endless space. *Anything is possible*, Max thought, the words meaning so much more now.

They stood there looking outside the window in silence, watching the sun emerge over the eastern buildings.

"Oh, by the way, you look great. What's the occasion? Seems kinda early to be dressed up for a Saturday."

"Thanks. I got a notification to be here by 7:30 this morning."

"I see. So you don't sleep much in your department either," Max said.

"Sometimes, but rarely."

"I decided to come early to check on Doc since he didn't come home last night. Sometimes he never eats; I have to force him to."

"That's kind of you," Max said. "I thought I saw him leave yesterday?"

"Nope, he didn't. That's why he has that long couch in his office."

Max laughed. "I had a feeling."

"What about you?" she said. "Why were you curled up on that small couch?"

"It's a long story. I'm sure the same reason your dad's here."

"Cool," she said. "Let me go check if he is in there."

"O.K."

"See you in a bit," Yvette said, disappearing into the corridor.

"See you," Max said.

"Good morning," Geoffrey said. He entered the room as Yvette was disappearing into the hallway. He was carrying a six-pack of coffee and was kind of disappointed to find Max drinking one already.

"What's up, Geoffrey?"

"Hey, Max. Another good day about to launch."

"Super excited," Max said.

Geoffrey placed the coffee on the small coffee table and plopped on the couch.

"You know that's Doc's daughter, right?" Geoffrey said.

"I know," Max said.

"Making sure you're aware, because the man will kill you."

They laughed.

"I'm sure the consequences won't be very desirable," Max said. Max smelled his armpits. "I wish I could change these clothes. There are starting to feel uncomfortable."

"Formal clothes can suck sometimes. Some manly stench doesn't hurt," Geoffrey said. "Joe can go and get you some clothes at your apartment if you like. He does that for me all the time when I don't go home."

Joe was the receptionist's assistant. Already in his 60s, he sat at the front desk and cleaned and replenished the break rooms and did random assignments when needed.

Max thought for a while and went to Joe.

"I can go if you need, sir," Joe said, in a cheerful countenance, with his Thai accent.

"Thanks, Joe. I think I can survive a few more hours. I don't think we'll be here for the whole day."

"I wouldn't bet on that," Geoffrey said.

"Are you sure?" Joe said.

"I am. I appreciate it," Max said.

"No problem. Let me know if you need anything. There are showers down on the third floor at the health club, if you need one."

"I will. Thanks, Joe."

Joe left the room.

Max washed his face at the sink, dabbed it dry with a paper towel and slathered on some hand lotion, and joined Geoffrey in the lounge.

He noticed a commotion on the pavement adjacent to the entrance, a few yards from the main gate. Both Geoffrey and Max got off the couch to investigate. It was unusual for a Saturday morning. There were cameras, reporters, news vans, speakers.

"What's going on down there?" Max said.

"It's the media, man," Geoffrey said. "They need details. Have you checked the local news lately?"

"No, why?" Max said. "What's going on?"

Geoffrey pulled a newspaper from his strap bag and gave it to Max.

"Some lunatic posted images of the flashy police motorcade last night," Geoffrey said, pointing at the front-page photo of the black SUVs with a police entourage. "They probably think the president is here."

"They're wrong," Max said. "It was us."

"They don't know that."

"Do you think someone leaked the project?"

"I doubt that. It's the media, man. Obviously, they would descend like hungry hawks at anything involving President Blanchard."

"Why's that?"

"She's from Houston. Down here, she is a hometown hero," Geoffrey said. "She's done a lot for the city. Especially little girls."

"Oh. I see."

It made sense. President Margaux Blanchard was a Houston native who had attended Rice University. Her parents and grandparents still lived in Houston. Since her inauguration as POTUS, people in Texas, especially in Houston, treated her like a hero. Little girls envied her, as did most parents who took her position to encourage their little ones that anything was possible, that they could be president one day. She was the epitome of what any woman could be—or anyone for that matter. They could say "Me, too." Whenever she was in Houston, which seldom happened, the paparazzi's cars and vans congested her affluent Sugarland neighborhood in hopes of having a glimpse of her. On the night of her inauguration, many of the pubs and restaurants in Houston and some parts of Texas had offered free beer as long as one brought a friend to buy an extra. There were posters and graffiti everywhere, showing the city's pride in their product—the President of the United States.

News crews and vans lined up outside Spartan Enterprises HQ, including reporters from the four major TV networks, with a few from the local stations. Everyone was curious about what the president would be doing at Spartan Enterprises. Speculations from the media made it even more interesting as they brought up theories of what the president was up to, all the more stirring the public interest and sentiment.

"That's why I'll never be a politician," Max said.

"Me too, man," Geoffrey said. "I don't know how these people do it, the paparazzi, fans, and all that stuff. Everyone wants a piece of you."

"That's the reason why I didn't go to medical school. I can't handle talking to many people very well," Geoffrey said.

"Same here. I can worry about bacteria, cell lines, and rodents, and some machines, and a few sane people but not multitudes," Max said, more as reassurance for his choice. "I easily get fed up with people, all the drama and pestering. I enjoy the peacefulness of the lab."

Max sat on the couch and skimmed through the morning newspaper.

Soon McKomic entered the room, shared a few pleasantries, and left quickly to disperse the media. He returned about 15 minutes later. The front of the building was empty again except for a few Spartan Enterprises employees jogging on the trails below.

CHAPTER FOURTEEN

Spartan Enterprises HQ

By 7:29 A.M., everyone was gathered around the glass table in the control room: Max, Geoffrey, Reverend Kay, Yvette, the rest of the other department directors, and Geoffrey's IT and engineering team. Geoffrey sat close to the screen, with the receiver switch in his hand, impatiently waiting for the seemingly long-anticipated call. The whole room stared at the blank screen where the president's image would pop up anytime now.

At precisely 8:00, the receiver beeped, showing an encrypted incoming video call.

"The president is on air," Geoffrey said.

Doc did a visual check of the room, then gave a thumbs-up to Geoffrey.

"Let her through," Doc said.

Geoffrey tossed off his fidget spinner and clicked the receiver. President Blanchard appeared on the screen.

"Good morning, everyone," President Blanchard said.

"Good morning, Madam President," Doc said. Everyone greeted the president.

There were ten other people in the Oval Office with her, most of whom were in their late 50s and 60s, including the Speaker of the

House and the Senate Majority Leader. Several defense generals were tuning in from the Pentagon, and they all nodded as the president spoke. The room was furnished in white, with a large reddish-brown polished wooden mahogany square table with the presidential seal in the middle. The group sat lined on either side of the table. There were paintings of former presidents on the wall behind President Blanchard, including Washington, Lincoln, and Kennedy.

The president smiled. "We did it. McKomic, we finished a long and intense discussion about your proposition. The council is prepared to allocate $50 billion towards Project ASHE."

There was mild applause from everyone in the room. The crew with the president nodded.

"However, there are a few conditions to be met. First, this is dependent on your ability to supply the relevant evidence today. And second, on your ability to finish the satellite shift in only 15 to 20 minutes; 30 won't work. Is that do-able?"

At this point no one said a word, or flinched, or smiled. McKomic looked at Doc and around the room, trying to interpret their disgruntled faces. They all seemed noncommittal.

"That should work," he said. "Everything is set."

"Super! NASA will be working closely with you. The Air Force has also agreed to work with you if need be. So I'm authorizing this mission in front of you all."

The president scanned her right hand, and the computer platform opened into a hollow section. A blurry screen appeared where she entered a long password using all ten fingers in a scrambled particular pattern. The sides of the raised platform around the keyboard created an optical illusion by distorting the screen shape and hand movements, which vexed anyone trying to trace what she was typing. When she finished, a voice said, "Permission granted."

"All right, you are in," the president said.

Geoffrey nodded.

"Thank you, Madam President," Doc said.

"Thank me when this is all over," she said. "I look forward to hearing from you as soon as possible."

"Certainly will, as soon as we have information," Doc said.

The screen went blank. Immediately, McKomic reviewed the assignments for each team, and everyone dispersed.

"Time is not on our side," McKomic said. "Our main goal is to take multiple snapshots of the planet from different angles, as many as possible once she's in view. Then we can analyze all the data later. Doc, anything else?"

"No, not really," Doc said. "Everyone, stick to your assignments and everything will go smoothly."

Geoffrey was beaming. Ritually, he warmed up his fingers by snapping them backward before turning on the bubble hologram model on the central table. The 3D projection blinked and cast a blue light before showing live footage from Spartan 007S. The defense satellite appeared on the farther right above the model.

"Let the party begin!" he said, rolling his chair to the keyboard. He punched a lot of keys. It did not make sense, but he did it with unflappable ease. He probably was the only human who could do that.

Everyone waited, looking at the bubble projection at the center table. McKomic and Doc stood silently behind them, looking on. The TV across the room was showing the Olympic Games opening ceremony. Hundreds of thousands of happy spectators and athletes clamored. The camera sped through the crowds who were cheering. Millions of others were watching at home.

"This had better work," McKomic said.

"It will," Geoffrey said. "Max, I need you on this joystick."

"I haven't used these before," Max said, hesitantly.

"I know," he said. "Approach it like a video game."

"O.K."

"Yvette, I want you on the other one. Your job is to rotate the bubble when I say so and tell me the distance and degrees from the target when I ask. Understood?"

"O.K.," Yvette said.

Geoffrey struck more keys.

"Rotation initiated," an automated voice from the monitor said. A giant digital clock displaying 15 minutes started ticking down on the screen.

The satellite rotated counterclockwise. Geoffrey sat tapping his

149

forefinger on the table. He took off his sweater and wiped off some sweat droplets on his brow with the back of his hand.

"All right, Max, let's go," he said. "Right, right, right. More, more. Yvette, snap that."

"Got it," Yvette said.

"Good," he said. "Now easy, easy. Almost there."

"Fifteen seconds to 90 degrees southwest," Yvette said.

"C'mon, Max," Geoffrey said.

"Almost," Max said, bending his body as he maneuvered the joystick to traverse Spartan 007S. Sweat beaded on his forehead.

"Almost there." Yvette continued the degree countdown.

The back and forth continued as the satellite shifted and slowly aligned with the Spartan 007S telescope.

The satellite finally came to a halt. Jupiter was now in view on the bubble screen.

"Rotation complete," the mechanical voice said.

"We did it," Max said.

"Yvette, zoom into that," Geoffrey said.

She motioned her hands apart on the bubble hologram.

"There she is," Geoffrey said. "We got her!"

Geoffrey wiped his brow again with his shirt.

Everyone's face was bright and relaxed. Max sighed. He enjoyed the synergizing feeling of working with Geoffrey and his crew. Geoffrey was exhilarated by his expertise and proud of the intense attention everyone was paying to his work, as if for the first time in his life since starting work, he felt he mattered, and he wanted to make the best of the moment to display his abilities. Geoffrey leaped at the prospect of finding the new planet.

"Return phase begins in ten minutes," the programmed voice said, reminding everyone that there was nothing to celebrate yet.

McKomic radioed NASA to get an update and said the Spartan 007S was ready. A live broadcast was connected straight from the telescope to the huge bubble image. Geoffrey swiped his hands to rotate the image on the bubble. A small dark sphere was nestled in Jupiter's magnetosphere. Geoffrey carefully plucked it up from the bubble and carefully placed it next to Jupiter's image for analysis. He punched a chain of commands on his keyboard and the diminutive image expanded. He zoomed in on the sphere using several hand motions. As he continued to zoom, the sphere started to show subtle red, blue, green, yellow, gray, and brown color contours, morphing into a planet resembling a satellite image of Earth.

"That's Aoratosia," Geoffrey said.

"The planet's orientation is strange," Max said.

"What do you mean?" Yvette said.

"It's slightly off its spin axis," Geoffrey said.

"I see that too," Doc said. "What does that mean?"

"For one, that would imply varying cycles of night and day," McKomic said.

"Precisely," Geoffrey said.

"What if it's just one of the thousands of asteroids orbiting close to Jupiter?" Doc said.

"It can't be," Geoffrey said.

"How are you so sure?"

"Because the Earth Similarity Index is high," Geoffrey said.

"Point zero eight nine? No way!" Max said, looking at the statistics screen.

"What is it?" Doc said.

"The planet has an Earth Similarity Index of 0.89," Max said.

"That's higher than anything we've ever seen before," Geoffrey echoed.

"I know," McKomic said. "That's freaking awesome."

"The energy and density distribution are similar to Earth's," Max said.

"What does that mean?" Yvette said.

Geoffrey continued entering code and said, "Spartan 007S transmission spectrum allows us to assess the finest details on planets than any space telescope before. With that much power, we can map the bio- and techno-signatures of Aoratosia by measuring the luminosity levels on Aoratosia based on the atmospheric density."

Yvette nodded.

Geoffrey said, "The electromagnetic spectrum observed by the telescope using multispectral analysis of Aoratosia, the planet's characteristics are relayed as colors—red for heat, blue, water. You get the point. That way we can make analogies between Earth and Aoratosia."

Geoffrey pointed at the amorphous kaleidoscopic streaks of green, red, blue, brown, and yellow.

"Sort of like a heat map," Yvette said.

"Correct," Geoffrey said.

"So there should be life, right?" Doc said.

Geoffrey showed the spectrum of Earth and Aoratosia juxtaposed against each other.

"The planet's bio-signature is similar to Earth's," Geoffrey said. "There's oxygen, carbon dioxide, methane, ozone, water, and other typical life gases."

"Look at the carbon dioxide, helium, methane, and nitrogen levels," McKomic said. "They are super high."

"Which is strange," Geoffrey said.

"Yeah," McKomic said. "That's typical of gas giants like Jupiter."

Doc said, "We are detecting traces of water too, which is rare."

"How can you tell?" Yvette said.

"By these swirls," Pete said, pointing to the dense, concentrated brownish-red cloud-like wave that covered almost half of the map. "I've never seen anything like that before."

"So?"

"That's promising. It can still be habitable."

"But if there is life, say, plants, shouldn't we be seeing green?"

"That's right," Max said. "But what if plants on Aoratosia use a different pigment other than chlorophyll for photosynthesis or what-ever process they use for energy metabolism?"

"That's possible. I think the life gases are our main bet right now."

Geoffrey grabbed the image and threw it with his hand motion onto the big screen besides Earth's heat map. He juxtaposed the two images.

"As you can see, Aoratosia is about half the size of Earth. There are also traces of excess hydrogen and helium typical of large planets," Max said, pointing at the screen.

"How did we miss this for so long? We have spent centuries

looking all over the place, but there it is right in our faces," Geoffrey said.

"There is nothing new under the sun, son," Doc said, with a smile on his face.

Max smiled, remembering how Aunt Dori used to say the same thing.

"Does the planet have an atmosphere?" Doc said.

"We are still working on it, but a dense composition of industrial gases, I would guess," Geoffrey said.

"How do you mean?"

"In an area like Aoratosia, radiation is isotropic, but we have been able to discriminate among sources of radiation using our radiation detectors."

"Interesting," McKomic still looked confused. "How?"

"You see, matter and antimatter, things like positrons, electrons, and neutrinos, for instance, collide and annihilate to produce energy, and that energy is then detected through our special computers. That's why you see these energy variations."

"How did you do that?"

"We have tomographic algorithms built in the system which allows us to scan all the points on Aoratosia," Geoffrey said. "The software then analyzes the data points into a pseudo color spectrum which can be mapped to the international standard. We can also do some adjustments and play around with the data to get a better simulation of Aoratosia's characteristics in real and virtual time."

"So some of it is arbitrary?"

"Yes. It is. It's hard to pinpoint which of the signal is noise and which is not. So we set a threshold for what is likely to be the real thing."

"In simpler terms, please?" Max said.

"Don't worry, you'll get it once we start the analysis. It's all about probabilities," Geoffrey said.

"That's an amazing image there."

"Spartan 007S has amazing quantum efficiency, man," Geoffrey said. "Especially in low-light-level imaging. This is the most insane space baby ever made."

"You can see the pattern, almost similar."

"We still cannot tell for sure if there is life."

"No, we cannot be certain," he said. "However, based on what we already know about Earth, the data suggest Aoratosia's conditions are almost similar to ours, meaning there is a possibility for life there."

"Where there's water, there's likely life, right?" Doc said.

"Probably; depends on the temperature,"

Max nodded understandingly.

"Can we be sure what we see from the colors is water?" McKomic said.

"If all the laws of chemistry apply on Aoratosia, sure," Geoffrey said.

"Sir, the results from KIT from the chem lab came in," Pete said.

"Let's see them."

"Yes, sir."

They waited for the results to process.

KIT was a built-in module fitted into the Spartan 007S telescope. Functionally, KIT identified different elements by estimating their properties based on their appearance on the transmission spectrum to calculate their molecular weight, density, water content, half-life, and even boiling or melting point, using all the elements found on Earth as a reference.

After a few seconds, the results from KIT popped up on the screen and Pete opened the tab. The results confirmed the presence of water, carbon, and oxygen, although at significantly lower concentrations than on Earth. The results also confirmed the high levels of ammonia, nitrogen, methane, sulfur dioxide, and carbon dioxide.

"Same as our previous conclusion," Doc said. "Higher levels of industrial gases."

"The Aoratosians are industrialized; they even emit higher levels of poisonous gases than we do?" Yvette said.

"Perhaps more industrialized than Earth," Geoffrey said.

"Or it might be the environment is naturally highly dynamic."

"That's true," Yvette said. "But Aoratosia is relatively smaller than Earth and has less gravitational force, which would suggest that time there moves faster than our time if it follows the laws of relativity. In that case, people there would be way ahead of us."

"On the contrary, the compound effect of both gravity and magnetic force from Aoratosia's core might result in a pull four times greater than our gravity. In that case time would pass more slowly, and Aoratosians would be living way behind us technology-wise," Max said.

"I hope that's true," Geoffrey said.

"If your hypothesis is true, that would mean all water would be ice because of the immense pull from the core despite the high temperatures."

"That would not support life."

"It would," he said. "We might find some bacteria and other primitive lifeforms. We've discovered bacteria that live in boiling hot springs and in deep seas and ice cores. So, it's probable."

"Are we saying there are people there?"

"If Aoratosia were separated from Earth, I'd think so."

"The rendering does show a biosignature that's conducive for life."

"I'm still not convinced," McKomic said.

"How so?" Geoffrey said.

"Think of any nightmarish space environment, then multiply that by ten. That's Aoratosia for you," McKomic said.

Everyone nodded.

"Well, KIT results also show insane levels of microwave radiation," McKomic said. "All the shitload of nitrogen and hydrogen gets turned into ammonia under such high pressure and temperature conditions. And that turns the whole planet into a massive magnetron or a ticking bomb."

"That's a valid point," Doc said. "The massive heat produced by the asteroid smashed matter into electrons and hydrogen atoms, turning the whole planet into a giant microwave oven."

"And that could also be a result of Jupiter's intense magnetic field which might create electron currents to produce microwave radiation," Max said.

"And all that microwave radiation can cause all the plant and animal molecules to vibrate, heat up, and eventually, kaboom!" McKomic said.

"That explains the barren topography," Doc said.

"So the planet should be inhabitable then?" Geoffrey said.

"I don't know," McKomic said. "If there are humans or live organisms there, they have to be advanced morphants or mutants."

"I see your point," Geoffrey said.

"Why?" Max said.

"The microwave radiation levels are too high for life," McKomic said.

"Any normal human would not survive," Yvette said. "The gravitation and magnetic effect would definitely overwhelm the human body. Tissues and organs would automatically start failing due to wear and tear and then crumble."

"Or they might be a species of small humps or dwarfs to minimize gravity's effects."

"Maybe. We don't know that yet."

"Even if we sent people there, all the blood would concentrate in the legs and they will eventually die of fatal strokes and seizures due to a shortage of blood in the brain."

"That's the tough question," McKomic said. "With such conditions, the planet would be unstable. Its atmosphere is in a state of constant flux. How can we prepare for that?"

Doc said, "We need to take that into consideration where and how the ship will land in a possibly unstable environment like Aoratosia."

"Good point."

"We have a suit, right?" Geoffrey said, looking at McKomic.

"Correct. The main threat we have is massive magnetism and radiation. We already have a prototype suit in development that can withstand those extreme conditions over extended periods. So astronauts will be able to roam around and study Aoratosia in the suits with ease.

"The point remains that the planet may be uninhabitable for humans."

"Technically, yes," Max said. "I'd expect it to be devoid of life, but you never know with nature." He stepped closer to the whiteboard and sketched.

Everyone waited impatiently.

Max studied the sketch more and said, "Wait. Microwave currents are usually directed in linear dynamic like this," Max said, pointing along the densitometry image. "So it can also be possible that life and diverse biology in some of these cavities and pockets might have survived."

"Genius!" Geoffrey said. "That makes a lot of sense."

"Also, the shockwave from the asteroid hit may not have had enough energy to vaporize all life," Yvette said.

"We can't conclude that yet," McKomic said. "How can the people survive?"

"How was the radiation environment on Aoratosia overcome?"

"As McKomic pointed out, they may develop some teratogenic characteristics that allow them to live under the harsh conditions of high levels of atmospheric toxicity and intense magnetic fields."

"That's possible. Assimilation and deposition of metals and toxic gases in their bodies over generations could alter their entire genome," Max said. "We might be talking human morphants and mutants."

"Like people with huge lower bodies, thick metallic skins and extra limbs," Geoffrey said.

"Maybe."

"And that would explain why our radio signals cannot locate them in the images. Brilliant!" Geoffrey said.

"That doesn't make sense," Yvette said.

"If that's right, we'd be detecting the beings like any other mineral or metal."

"Possibly."

"So maybe those are live organisms. Look how they are spread out, sort of a pattern, like a large, scattered settlement," Doc said.

"Could be," Geoffrey said.

"I have an idea," Pete said. "We can use thermal imaging to capture the heat released by the beings. Heatwaves move as waves and particles, so we might be able to capture the heat they release."

"That's true," Doc said.

Geoffrey worked on his keyboard more, and after a few seconds, the red dots turned into red and green colors.

"It worked," he said. "The colors show the regions of higher energy and lower energy on their bodies. And look, some of them seem to be moving," he said, with a broad smile on his face.

"Can we tell what they are?" McKomic said, looking intently at the image.

"No sir, I don't think so. Our technology can't do that yet."

"At least we know there is a possibility of industrialized beings on the planet," McKomic said, with a sigh. "Good job, people. I'm sure the White House will be pleased."

The monitor beeped twice, and the mechanical animated voice said, "Initiating return phase in one minute."

"Rotation complete," the voice said.

The control room was abuzz with excitement. Geoffrey removed his huge spectacles and jumped up and down, hugging Max. "We did it! You did it!" he shouted.

Doc had tears of joy in his eyes. There were high-fives and laughter. Max hugged Doc, then Yvette, Reverend Kay, and many others who were there. Even McKomic showed a broad smile on his face, with his hands clasped behind his head in relief.

"We've done it!" he said. "We have found Earth's sister!"

McKomic and Doc exited towards his office to relay the report to the president. They returned a few minutes later with broad smiles.

"We did it, ladies and gentlemen," Doc said. "The president sounded ecstatic about our findings, so let's keep our fingers crossed that Congress will feel the same."

"Now it's time for a celebration," Doc said. "If anyone wants to go home, you can, anytime."

"What's next now?" Geoffrey said.

"Party. Go home. Take a break and wait for the results on Monday morning. Good job, everyone."

Champagne was promptly brought from the cafeteria and everyone celebrated.

"To Aoratosia!" McKomic said, raising his champagne flute. Glasses clinked throughout the room.

"To Aoratosia!" everyone cheered back in unison.

Doc put his arm around Max's shoulders and started humming

quietly. Everyone stopped to listen to him, glasses in hands. McKomic joined in, snapping his fingers and tapping his right foot, and one by one, everyone joined in the humming. Max did not know the song, but the rhythm flowed over him and he was humming, too. Others were stomping their feet and drumming the tables, producing a beat. The young and the old—as one. It was the NASA anthem. Everyone started singing, hand in hand, quietly and gradually getting louder and faster:

> *Started with a dream,*
> > *Staring in the sky,*
> > *Now we go,*
> > *As we go,*
> > *We ascend,*
> > *Through the stars,*
> > *Beyond the galaxy!*

It was a spirit of triumph. It was a spirit of accomplishment. They sang, danced, and gleefully popped bottles of champagne. They felt they had already stamped their way to Aoratosia.

Max hung around for the cocktail reception. More and more Spartan Enterprises employees flocked into the hall, engulfed in noise.

Midway through the reception, Max approached Yvette in the wine queue.

"Hey, Yvette. I need you to do something for me."

"It depends on what it is."

"I saw that geology blast tracer device. That's from your department, right?"

"Yes. Our department recently got it. Expensive piece."

"I guessed so. Can you sample what material this necklace is made of?"

"I could. Why?"

"I want to know what it is made of."

"The device is expensive to use."

"Oh."

"I'm kidding. I can run it through tomorrow."

"That's fine. Whenever you've time."

"I have to go into the lab tonight to check on my tissue culture. I might be able to check it during one of my incubation times."

"Great."

Max checked his phone.

"I gotta run. The Metrolink will be here soon."

"O.K. I'll let you know how it goes."

"Awesome."

Max gulped the champagne and shared some pleasantries with Doc and others on his way out.

The train arrived early that day. Max was worn out, and he retired to bed immediately when he reached his apartment. Max lay supine on the bed, thinking about Aoratosia. What were the inhabitants like? Were they monsters or humans like us? He thought of Alonna, and he missed her. He thought of Aunt Dori. He was smiling at the ceiling, knowing how blessed he was to be part of the Folksay family. This team. He wanted to call but felt too sluggish to move.

CHAPTER FIFTEEN

335 2nd Street, Houston

THE ALARM MADE its jarring noise four times.

Max rolled over and slapped the snooze button, disappointed that he had forgotten to turn off the alarm as he always did on weekends. He hated the ringtone. It was too loud. The loud sound always freaked him out.

A streak of sunshine slapped onto his eyes through the window blinders.

"Morning already!" he grumbled, burying his head under the sheets.

It was already 8:00 in the morning. Max twitched and turned, asking the heavens for more sleep. He knew then that he was not going to church that morning. He tried to turn with difficulty. The jeans! How the hell had he forgotten to remove his jeans and socks? His neck and back were hurting slightly. *The couch!* he thought. He threw off the bedsheets and lay on the bed facing up. He felt an expectant, smug, clown-like excitement. Oklahoma! Still quite buzzed from the previous day's event, he wiped sleep from his eyes and stretched, feeling the soreness clench his muscles. A crunchy and painful sensation shot in his throat when he tried to swallow saliva. Haziness. A stomach rumble. Nausea. Ouch, damned hangover! He wished he hadn't drunk alcohol. He silently promised he would never be coaxed to drink again.

He remembered why he had set the alarm in the first place. He reached over to his phone on the bedside lampstand. There were two missed calls and a voicemail from Yvette. Max decided to call her back later.

Max jumped out of bed and called the University of Texas Travel Agency and fortunately, was able to secure a seat for an 8:00 p.m. flight to Oklahoma City.

Max yawned and stretched a great deal. He retrieved two aspirin capsules from the bedside drawer and chugged them with one glassful of cold water, which momentarily gave him a brain-freeze, causing him to wince. He needed a long hot shower. Max frowned at his reflection in the long mirror on the back of his bathroom door. He felt that he had lost a few pounds in the past 48 hours. *Damn!* He turned on the water to warm up before he stepped in; when he did, he jerked up, screaming, "Dammit!" The water had suddenly switched from optimum warm to searingly hot. The shower in his apartment had a tendency to randomly change from warm to hot then unexpectedly to ice-cold. He had reported the issue to the property manager, but so far there had been no action. He had been too busy to follow up on the request. After the shower, Max called the super shuttle to schedule a ride to the William P. Hobby Airport. His stomach was bloated and grumbling, so he did not feel like eating any oatmeal and peanut butter, his usual breakfast. Instead, he snatched a leftover cold and crusted peanut butter-and-jelly sandwich in the refrigerator, and probiotic yogurt. That usually did the job soothing his occasional stomach discomfort.

Although still shaken from yesterday's events, he felt some febrile excitement. He had some clothes in Stratford, so Max felt no need to pack any. As for toiletries, he could use some of Aunt Dori's; she always had plenty stocked up.

He had a few hours to kill. After packing up his laptop, and a few of the latest issues of science magazines, Max stopped by the laboratory to check on his transgenic experimental mice. The experimental compound seemed to be doing wonders; the mutant mice were recovering well. He had not had the opportunity to notify Doc of the results since he had been away for the past week. When Doc was at the lab, he spent most of his time writing grants and catering to some of his department's administrative duties. The mice with M.S. seemed to be recovering well, and Max was pleased with the results. Max imaged the mice, measured the alertness and weight, and recorded the preliminary results in his notebook as usual. Doc expected every intern to submit a report of their findings every fortnight. The lab was deserted; none of the other interns or postdocs were there—nothing new, mostly when the boss was not around.

He took out his phone and called Yvette. The phone rang once.

"Hey, Max."

"Hey. Were you staring at your phone or what?"

Yvette chuckled. "I had just finished talking to my dad when you called."

"Sorry I wasn't able to return your call sooner."

"No problem. I wanted to show you the results from the necklace before I head out."

"You got anything for me?"

"Are you on campus?"

"Yeah."

"Can you come to Thenus? You have to see this in person."

"I'm on my way. I'll be there in a few minutes."

"See you."

Max sprang out of the Epictetus building and jogged the few blocks towards the Thenus building.

Yvette was sitting on a desk, scrutinizing some sheets of paper.

"That was quick," she said.

"I was excited. And I had to see it."

"Here, see," Yvette said, handing Max a copy of the printout. "I've never seen anything like this before."

"What do you mean?"

"I checked the mineral database for all known elements and some proposed ones. I couldn't find it. It's not even on the periodic table, possibly heavier than anything we know. And the material is super magnetic. Like nothing I've ever seen—probably 40-50 times than Earth's strongest magnets."

"That's interesting."

"It is," Yvette said. "The element is not even on the periodic table."

"Is that why it's encased in plywood?" Max said.

"I guess so. You knew that, didn't you?"

"No, not really. I had my suspicions. Yesterday during the Aoratosia viewing, it felt as if my energy was being drawn away when we were focused on the planet."

"That's weird and strange. But I noticed you were drinking kind of a lot of coffee."

"That too," Max said. "When I left for the restroom, the necklace was lit up. It freaked the hell out of me."

"Does it light often?"

"It lights up sometimes," Max said. "Don't know how it works, though. Thought it was some energy stone. Because of the luminescence."

"Do you think it's a device, a bomb?"

"I don't think so. It doesn't have any moving parts. It's been in the family for a while. My uncle gave it to me."

"We should tell someone, maybe Doc."

"I think we should wait," Max said. "We need to learn more about it."

"What should we call it?"

"Elixirium," Yvette said.

"I like it."

"Where did it come from?"

"I've no idea. It was a gift from my uncle."

"Where did your uncle get it?" Yvette said.

"He traveled all over. Maybe he made it."

"I see."

"You don't think the energy-draining thing is weird, do you?" Max said.

"Kinda, but I've seen super weird stuff before."

"What else did you find?" Max said.

"There is another thing," Yvette said. "I tested the age of the mineral using hydration method of dating minerals, well, basically based on how minerals lose moisture. My results suggest this mineral is billions of years old."

"That's out of the ordinary."

"Also, if you look closely, you can see the edges of the stone are designed in such a way to fit into something. Like a jigsaw puzzle piece."

Max scrutinized the necklace. "A key maybe?"

"I don't know."

"This is freaking me out more," Max said. "And exciting also."

"We might be onto something unprecedented."

"Looks like it," Max said, checking his phone. "Thanks, Yvette."

"I will keep you posted if I find anything else."

"Sounds good."

Geoffrey entered the room. Max and Yvette filled him in on the details. "Seems like it was communicating with Aoratosia. Like Aoratosia was sucking the energy out of the body, producing that blue light."

"Was that a weapon?" Geoffrey said.

"Let's not rush there yet."

"I'm starting to wonder that maybe we have just exposed ourselves to Aoratosians."

"How do you mean?"

"By connecting our satellite and telescope to Aoratosia, we might have somehow created a direct energy connection between them and us. They could feel the necklace."

"Might be, but if the necklace was already here, doesn't that mean they already know we exist and our location. Maybe they have been here before."

"I don't know."

"The alien sightings recorded before," Geoffrey said.

"How does a necklace respond to the whole planet?"

"This is speculative," Yvette said. "We don't know what these beings are capable of."

"Maybe they already know everything that we do and everything we were doing?"

"That's far-fetched. It's only a stone," Max said.

Max left the lab and went back to his apartment.

Max's phone rang.

"Hello," Max said.

"Sir, the shuttle is here," the concierge said.

"I'll be right there."

It was close to six in the evening. What was intended as a 20-minute power nap had turned into a two-hour sleep. Max hurriedly washed his face and crosschecked the contents in his backpack. He rushed down the stairs into the lobby, grabbed a copy of the *Houston County Daily Newspaper* at the newsstand, and hurried outside.

"Hobby Airport?" the shuttle driver said. His appearance and accent suggested he was Middle Eastern.

"Yes, sir," Max said. "Got a flight in 30 minutes."

"We'll be there in no time," the man said.

"Great."

"How're you doing this evening, sir?" the driver said, a broad smile across his face.

"I'm doing pretty good. How're you doing?" Max said.

"Very well, sir. Business is slow today."

"Oh, is it the same most Saturdays?"

"Sometimes," the driver said. "Do you have any more luggage?"

"No, that's it."

"All right. Let's get you to the airport," the driver said, shutting the van door behind Max.

There were six other people in the shuttle. The shuttle left the campus onto the main street. Max perused the newspaper. Despite the advancement in technology, newspapers had not shown any sign of dwindling in popularity. Many people still subscribed and purchased newspapers. Reading the newspaper was even perceived to be an economic status symbol. The headline read: "SOMETHING COOKING AT SPARTAN ENTERPRISES!" on the top of the page, with a large photo of the limo with lights covering almost half of the page, twice as much space as the story itself. The story included testimonials and opinions from pundits and views from the locals who were anxious to see what was going on. On the left was a small gruesome picture with a small headline: "Terrorist Bombings in Somalia Kill 200." Below that, "Husband Runs Amok, Slays Wife" the story of a man who had tattooed a message on the chest of his cheating wife using a hot iron after stabbing her to death. Max flipped the pages through the lifestyle column, then the business section. He browsed the stock market and other financial articles. The sports section was covered with reviews from analysts about the upcoming Longhorns and Sooners preseason showcase football game set for early August. The editor was trying to comfort the passionate Longhorn fans that there was still a long series ahead despite last season's beatdown, emphasizing some major plays, players, and changes that needed to be addressed by their new head coach. Results from the Olympics and the upcoming schedule were on the next two pages. Max passed over the classifieds section and glanced past the obituaries. Nothing else interested him. The shuttle reached the airport.

The check-in was quick, and moments later, Max was relaxing on the plane for his 35-minute flight to Oklahoma City. He was glad to have been, by chance, upgraded to a first-class seat to fill the spaces. This was his first time sitting in that section. Max enjoyed the attention from the flight attendant and ate everything that was offered. The flight attendant brought red wine; he drank it. She brought Coke; he drank it. She brought some chips; he ate them. Max rather liked the feeling of being in first class, experiencing what he had never experienced before. He felt he belonged there. He had flown only in the economy section all his life, the few times he had flown. Max realized that all along he had thought of himself as belonging only to that section. He embraced today's first-class opportunity.

He overheard someone speaking on the phone in thick Russian. He scrutinized the lady on the phone, trying to match the voice to the face. He recognized his college professor, the French teacher from Russia, who drawled while she taught French. She sat on the opposite seat.

"Hello, Dr. Tsocov!"

"Hi," she said, with an inquisitive look in her eyes, trying hard to recall him. "I remember you. Remind me of your name again."

"Max."

"Oh, Max Folksay. I knew it. How're you?"

"I'm great. How are you doing?"

"I'm doing well. You look great! What are you doing now?"

"Thank you! You, too. I'm at FIST. Studying biophysics!" Max said, with an air of pride.

"Graduate school?"

"Yes. I started a few months ago."

"That's nice. I'm excited to hear that."

"Thank you! Are you still at North Central?"

"Yes, I'm still there."

"That's nice."

There was a brief pause.

"So, where are you going?"

"Heading home for the weekend. It's been a while."

"Good. It's good to take breaks once in a while."

"Yes, it is. Where are you going?"

"I just got back from Russia. The semester starts next week!"

"I almost forgot. We don't have breaks in my program, so I kinda lose track of time."

She laughed.

"That's true. Good to see you again, Max."

"Good to see you, too!"

She opened her laptop and started typing. Max relaxed and gazed through the window.

The airplane touched down at Will Rogers International Airport close to 9:30 p.m. Dr. Tsocov asked for Max's business card, but Max explained he had none. Her driver showed up, and she left. Max took a Lyft to Stratford. The cab meandered out of the parking lot, passed a few cars waiting at the pick-up terminal, and then leveled into the dimly-lit street out of the airport area.

Max opened the cab window and glued his eyes on the Devon Energy Tower, immersed in a massive cumulonimbus cloud that made its colorful pinnacle appear to be floating on the cloud. It was a pretty view. He pulled the fresh air in. Oklahoma always made him feel at home. He missed the friendly people—his family, and everything about Oklahoma.

MAX WAS DELIGHTED to be back in Oklahoma. He welcomed the moist atmosphere with a deep breath. Slightly less humid and hot than Houston. It was past 10:00 p.m. when he finally got home. He was exhausted and had many things to tell Aunt Dori and Alonna. This was the only time he had been away from home for a long time since his summer mission trip to Papua New Guinea after his junior year of college.

As he approached the front porch, he struggled to maintain his composure, trying to absorb all that had happened in the previous few days. It had started drizzling, and Max flicked water droplets off his hair and shook off his coat and shoes before entering the door. Max pinched his cheek in a bid to let go of his thoughts. Trouble hung in the air. How was Alonna supposed to believe him? He knew he could not stand lying to Alonna to her face. Was he going to tell her the truth? The reality of facing his fiancée seemed more challenging than he had thought. He was in a dilemma: either to choose to tell the truth to Alonna or lie and keep the truth to himself. He knew the latter would be futile in front of Alonna. Alonna was naturally confrontational and had an uncanny ability to ferret information out of people—possibly a trait she had inherited from her legendary lawyer father. Maybe that is what made her a great nurse. For the two and half years Alonna and Max had been dating, she seemed to have mastered all his facial expressions—she could tell when he was lying or when he was sad. Max hoped his story would be genuine as it was.

Max stealthily unlocked the front door and tiptoed into the living room to avoid disturbing Aunt Dori. Being an M.S. patient, Aunt Dori had been complaining about being woken up in the night or early in the morning. The doctor had said she needed all the sleep she could get. Often times she had called Max to complain about Alonna waking her up early in the morning while taking showers before school.

"Is that you, Max?" Alonna shouted from her room.

"Yes, it's me."

She came out and hugged Max.

"Wow! You look gorgeous," Max said, marveling at her magenta-laced white chemise.

Alonna looked up and met Max's gaze. "Thank you," she said. "You look great—and grown up."

She caressed his two-day-old stubble.

They laughed.

"Well, thank you!"

"I missed you so much, Max," she said, in a soft whisper

"I missed you too, Alonna," Max said, his lips lightly touching Alonna's daringly.

She jumped onto the couch backward, pulling Max on top of her. Max remained on top of her. *Oh, how he missed holding her!* Alonna locked her legs around Max's waist. She kissed him, all the time examining his eyes. Max seemed perplexed.

"Are you O.K.?" she said.

"Yes," Max said. "Have you been—?"

"Drinking? Just a little wine," she said.

"I could tell."

"One glass. I've been studying too much for my previous exam and I wanted to clear off some stress, and here you are. Good fortune for me."

"Me too, I'd say," Max said, breathing on her neck. "You smell good."

"Thanks! You too, silly boy," she said, tapping Max's lips with her forefinger.

"I tried calling you all day yesterday," she said.

"I know. I'm sorry, babe. I can explain."

"What's going on?"

"Something came up."

"And?" she said.

"We are going to wake up Aunt Dori," Max said.

"She won't," she said. "Don't worry, we won't. She actually sleeps with the TV on these days."

"Really?"

"Yes. She says it helps her sleep."

"That's weird," he said. "How did you figure that out?"

"It just happened."

"You're a genius!"

They giggled.

Max could feel his blood pressure rising throughout his body. His muscles tensed as his hot hands unbuttoned Alonna's chemise with careless ease. Alonna obliged. Alonna's breath was increasing as she clung around his neck. With each moan, he could feel his vow to chastity slipping away from the grasp of his willpower. His restraint was succumbing to Alonna's touch. At that moment, he felt complete infatuation. His brain raced, suddenly rejuvenated. Haywire. Autopilot. He wanted to stop it but couldn't. He wanted it. She wanted him. He softly ran his lips on her neck, caressed down her neck with his rough hands, with little light teasing bites, which she shuddered at and begged for more. He eased past the crescents of her collarbone and navigated down into the heavenly escarpment between her breasts, the laces on her nightgown tickling his chin. Lavender smell. He wanted it all!

"I love you," Max whispered as he nuzzled softly into Alonna's left ear.

"I love you too," Alonna said, drowsily. "But not today; I'm tired."

"Are you kidding me?" Max almost yelled.

"Let's go to sleep," she said.

"What?"

"Gotcha! You thought today was your lucky day, huh?"

Max laughed. "So that was a test?"

"I wanted to see if you can restrain yourself."

"Come on. You got me. I'm glad it was. Otherwise, it could have been another story."

"Don't worry, goofball. You will get it soon."

"I know, I know."

They laughed.

"I've got to get up early for work tomorrow. Let's talk at lunch."

She kissed him.

Max brought some cushions from the bedroom and squeezed next to Alonna on the couch.

CHAPTER SIXTEEN

Stratford, Oklahoma

MAX WOKE UP AT MIDDAY. His back felt much better. Abstaining from sex made him miss Alonna more and he waited for the day he could finally make love to her. And that energy seemed to fuel him to be a better man. Today, he was going to ask Alonna about their impending wedding. Thank God their families still upheld the traditional way of wedding planning. Max liked the idea that the bride's family did most of the planning. He was ready to be her husband. Everything that had transpired in the previous few days made him realize the importance of an intimate relationship and how things can change at any time. He felt he would be a coward if something happened before he was married to Alonna. He felt incomplete now. At that moment, he wanted a family, he wanted kids, he wanted a dog, and he wanted a large house for him, Alonna, Aunt Dori, and their children. *But not quite yet.*

Max sauntered into the kitchen. Alonna had left warm oatmeal in the warmer. There was a note on the table that read, "Hayday at 1. In class all morning." Max knew what it meant. He had seen many sticky notes like this before. When he checked his phone in the living room charging, there was another such note. Alonna wanted to make sure Max got the message. Aunt Dori was still asleep. Her door was slightly open and Max could hear the morning TV news. Max puttered around the house before eventually deciding to vacuum the carpet to clear his mind. He had a few hours to kill before lunch. Shortly after turning on the vacuum cleaner, Aunt Dori called.

"Alonna! I need help!"

Max ran to Aunt Dori's room.

"Max! Look who's here," Aunt Dori said, smiling. She seemed to be in high spirits. "You're home. I didn't know you were here."

"Hi, Aunt Dori," Max said, hugging her.

"Hi Max. It's good to see you. When did you get here?"

"Late last night."

"I see."

"You were already asleep, and I didn't want to bother you."

"I'm glad you're back."

"Good to see you, too." Max walked over and embraced her.

"Did you want help?"

"I can't find my exercise putty. The doctor said I should exercise my fingers and hands every morning for 30 minutes," she said. "I've been rummaging through the bedsheets looking around desperately everywhere. It's frustrating."

"Oh, it probably fell somewhere on the sheets or under the bed."

"I always lose it."

"It's O.K. It happens to all of us. I'm sure it's somewhere."

Max looked for the putty. After few minutes of looking, he found it next to Aunt Dori's pillowcase.

"There it is."

"Oh! I always forget where I've put it. I'm sorry, honey. I looked all over the place, and it was right there."

"You're welcome."

Aunt Dori looked sternly at Max.

"So tell me, how is research treating you?" she said. "That's a nice badge. Where did you get that?"

"It's from school—a reward," Max said. "I wanted to show it to you."

"Thank you. That's sweet of you."

"And please don't post it on the Internet."

They laughed.

"I won't," she said.

Max talked while checking the Christmas movies piled on the TV stand.

"Nice collection," he said.

"Yup. Every day is Christmas for me."

They laughed.

"That's a good way of saying it."

"It is. That's the truth anyways for me."

Max nodded, absorbing Aunt Dori's statement.

"So how's everything in Houston?" she said, breaking the brief silence.

"It's great! Busy, but good."

"Great! I'm glad you're doing well and enjoying it."

"How about you? How're you doing with your therapy?"

"I'm doing great. Improving little by little."

There was a brief silence while Aunt Dori opened the putty container.

"Now that I think of it, Titus had a badge like the one you have," she said.

"He did?"

"I'm positive I've seen it before."

Max's face lit up. "I knew it! I knew I had seen this badge before somewhere."

"Yup. It was your uncle's."

"Where is it now?"

"I probably threw it in one of my odds-and-ends toolboxes. You can look through the house if you want."

"I will."

"One more thing," Aunt Dori said. "Your uncle left you something in the shop that I meant to give to you."

"What is it?"

"Help me onto my wheelchair."

"Where are you going?"

"You don't mind taking a walk to the shop, do you?"

"Not at all," Max said.

"Let's go."

"You haven't eaten or brushed your teeth yet."

"I'll do it later. It's only going to be a few minutes."

"Fine."

Max helped her onto the wheelchair and pushed the wheelchair with a smile.

The area around the backyard was untidy. Tall grass surrounded the house. Kaitlyn, Aunt Dori's daughter, had promised to take care of the house as often as possible. They lived in a mobile home on the property a few yards from Aunt Dori. Kaitlyn was a hairdresser. Her husband, Gary, was a self-taught mechanic, who made ends meet by hopping from piece job to piece job. They both did nothing to maintain the ranch. They were seldom at their home, with long stretches where they would not live there at all. Max wished he could be around to help at the ranch. Moving away from Stratford had not done him any good in accomplishing that goal.

Max pushed the wheelchair past the storm shelter towards the shade. The narrow path was littered with weeds and leaves. A few geese loitered around the pond overlooking the backyard.

Max unlatched and swung the large door open, which groaned against rust-coated hinges. The black-locust wooden threshold gave in as he stepped on it, leaving Max startled.

"Oh, leave it," Aunt Dori said. "Be careful. This shop is too old."

Max carefully walked over the rustic timber floor creaking.

"Someone ought to work on these things."

"They never bother to fix anything, let alone the shop."

"And they live here for free."

Boom! Bang! Something fell from the ceiling. Max froze. His heart was pounding.

"What was that?" Max said. His eyes searched the room for the object that had hit the wooden floor.

Aunt Dori was relaxed. "C'mon now. Don't be a wuss," she said. "It's probably one of my Christmas decoration boxes or nativity sets that slipped off."

"I think so."

Max felt the coarse, crispy planked wall for the switch and flipped the dust-ridden switch on. After a few seconds, the bulb flickered then shone. The bulb produced faint light, barely enough to illuminate the room. Max opened the wood-braced windows, freeing dust motes into the air.

Max sneezed. "Damn!"

The room was large, with yellow insulation foam barely clinging to the wooden trusses under the roof. *Good memories.* The sunlight formed patches of light through the windows, where it polarized with the dusty air and tons of spider web threads that stretched across the room. A box had fallen from the ceiling. Max brushed off the cobwebs and dust with the broom. Fishing rods, spades, shovels, and electrical cables hung on the wall. Two bags of fodder, expired. A big plastic trash can on the corner. There was also a riding lawn mower and a stack of hay bales in one corner, long-since designated for Good Friday, Christmas, and Easter parades. A big carpentry table spanned the room's entire length, with an electric saw mounted on it. A few tool-boxes sat on the shelves and everything else was neatly hung and sorted on the walls. The room was warm and humid, instantaneously eliciting a sickly feeling in Max's stomach.

"This was Titus' shop," she said. "Where he stored all his physics and astronomy equipment."

"I know. I have been here a few times before. Long ago."

"I remember."

"Man, this room is definitely haunted," Max said, looking around.

Aunt Dori laughed. "Let's find out."

"When did someone last use this place?" Max said.

"Six years ago, I think," she said, in a melancholy voice as if she missed something or someone from the old days. "It still feels like yesterday."

"Are you O.K.?" Max said.

"I'm fine. Just having a moment there."

"All right."

"Don't worry about me," she said. "It's that this place makes me feel like Titus is alive."

"I agree."

"Your uncle used to spend loads of time in here after his discharge from the air force, and I would come to see him sometimes. He was changed then."

Max massaged her shoulders.

"I'm sorry to bring back the sad memories."

"He wanted to stay home and spent as much time he could with me and the grandkids, somehow making up for the many months he would spend away from us. When he gave up, nobody cared to carry on looking after this place. And sadly, none of our daughters were into science.

"I tried keeping the place presentable whenever I could," she added. "But with my condition, I could not manage anymore, and I gave up. Plus, since Gary and Kaitlyn moved over, I thought they would at least clean the place, especially since they live here for free."

Max and Aunt Dori entered Uncle Titus' study in one corner. It was an average-sized inner shop room, about 27 square meters. A dust-ridden wooden desk and chair stood in one corner. A dusty shelf sat below the windowsill, stuffed with thick dusty volumes—physics, philosophy, geology, and many other similar subjects. Max marveled at the dusty telescope, with the initials T.F. inscribed on its neck, standing behind the door facing the window. He remembered the first time he had used it with Uncle Titus. He smiled. Apart from these, there was not much in the room.

"This is amazing! I remember the first time I used this," Max said.

"That used to be your favorite thing in the shop."

"Really?"

"Of course. Then you grew up and went to college."

"I've always wondered. Did you and Uncle Titus ever discuss science?"

"Sometimes," she said. "That's what he mainly talked about every night."

"Don't tell me that was your pillow talk?"

Tellingly, Aunt Dori laughed. "I was married to a genius; what would you expect? Sometimes I thought he loved physics more than me."

They both laughed.

"Man, Uncle Titus was possessed. This is unbelievable!" Max said.

"It is."

"What did he use all this stuff for?"

"In his last days, he claimed he had found a way to communicate with beings from another planet."

"I remember hearing him say that a couple times. What happened to all that?"

"I don't know, really," she said. "I always gave your uncle a hard time, that if he couldn't do anything then he should stop yapping about it." Aunt Dori laughed, then continued: "That got him fired up. Unfortunately, he got worse and worse, and his illness finally got the best of him."

"Why didn't he inform the air force where he worked?" Max said.

"The air force?" Aunt Dori said, and paused for a few seconds, and laughed impishly. "With the record of everyone working in his field losing their minds after their term, it was difficult for anyone to believe him. They thought he was just as unhinged. I mean, he tried. It didn't work I guess."

"That's not fair," Max said.

"It isn't. But that's how life works sometimes. Boom, and he was gone before he could present his ideas to the government."

Max remained silent.

"They discharged him when he became obsessed, and at first, he would spend hours and hours in here developing models. Sometimes I'd have to bring him food to get him to eat or leave the meal at the door. I wanted to stop him, but I couldn't. That was the first time in years I had seen him so passionate about something since his discharge after the pneumonia diagnosis. After a few months, he became less and less involved in his project. I guess the stress and the disease took a toll on him, and he succumbed."

Tears were soaking Max's eyes.

"He used to take me to the park and the library a lot before he died, and played soccer with me. How come he never mentioned this to me?" Max said.

"Yes, he loved you, and he didn't want you to worry. He knew you would understand at the right time."

Max nodded, trying desperately to hold back the tears. "I know."

"Your uncle, before he passed, made me promise that I would give you this when the time was right. Maybe that's why he left this for you."

"What is it?"

"Come on, I'll show you."

Aunt Dori rolled her wheelchair towards the west wall.

"Come over here," she said.

"What is it?" Max said.

"Help me flip this rug," she said.

"Leave it," Max said. "Let me do it. I don't want you to hurt your back bending over."

"O.K., macho man, go ahead. I wasn't always this fragile."

"You're still awesome."

"Trying to woo me," she said. "It's not going to work."

"Doesn't hurt to try, right?"

She smiled, and Max helped her reposition herself on the wheelchair.

"You're such a sweetheart, Max," she said.

Max hauled up the thick rubber carpeting, exposing the dark granite tiles. They were barely visible due to thick dark grit from dust accumulation over many years.

"Remove the tiles there," Aunt Dori said. "There should be a keyhole."

"All right."

Max pried four tiles, using a flathead screwdriver, along the wall's edge, leaving a hollow area.

Aunt Dori handed to Max a massive silver key that was wrapped in her handkerchief.

"Wait, is this the key that's always hanging on the bamboo hutch in the living room?"

"It is."

"So you kept it there? Weren't you worried someone was going to find it and use it?"

"No. Not really. Always keep the important things where everyone least expects them," she said. "Many people thought it was a souvenir."

"That's smart!"

Max hurriedly cleaned the keyhole. He struggled to slide the key into the slot, but it finally clicked. He turned the key clockwise then counterclockwise until the lock clicked. He pulled the tile out of place. A wave of deep, pungent stench, redolent of wet pine cedar, shot into Max's face causing him to choke and cough, and wipe his watery eyes.

"Man, what a smell," he said.

"Concrete."

There was a small hole, about 30 square centimeters.

Aunt Dori moved closer and handed Max a flashlight. There was a small silver box snug in the hole. He cleaned the handle with a cloth, retrieved the metal box and set it on the wooden table. He wiped the chest, all the time thinking about what was inside. It was lighter than he had anticipated. The initials "T.F." were inscribed on the side of the chest, and close to the base was engraved "Product of South Africa".

"South Africa?" Max said.

"He brought the chest from South Africa on one of his missions many years ago."

"That's a nice piece."

"It is," she said. "I think something happened there."

"Why so?"

"He changed," she said, pausing momentarily as if struck by acute nostalgia. She smiled blankly as tears swelled in the crescents of her eyes. "It all started after South Africa."

"What happened?"

"He was different when he came from his trip to Africa to investigate alleged UFO sightings in the Sahara desert. Recalled from retirement to lead a South African team to study extraterrestrial sightings. You know that your uncle was an air force astrophysicist tasked to monitor space and its operations with the Search for Extraterrestrial Intelligence, SETI. I told him not to go. He was never the same after he came back."

Max looked blankly at Aunt Dori in thought. "You have any idea of what happened there?"

"I think so, but you know your uncle. He never talked much about it apart from saying that he was going to help find a habitable planet."

"That's why he kept all those books and machines?"

"Yes. I think he left everything in that box."

"Should I open it?"

"Of course. Open it."

Max wiped the dust off the small, lacquered table and placed the metal box on it. He sat in the adjacent dusty chair by the wooden table, inserted the big key into the metal box, and carefully opened the lid.

"I don't understand. Why didn't he keep this in your safe at the bank?"

"I don't think I know the answer to that question."

Max opened the lid without saying anything.

Aunt Dori giggled.

"What's funny?" Max said.

"Titus was obsessed," she said. "He was convinced that we were not alone in the universe. To him, it felt like he had answers to centuries of terrestrial life mysteries."

"Amazing," Max said, sifting through the chest full of papers.

"I had never seen him that much obsessed," Aunt Dori said. "The only time he was that happy was when we got you and after that trip. He became even more engrossed in his studies. He was so adamant that there were other beings somewhere else. I never bought into his theories."

Max's hands trembled, opening a neatly folded laminated paper. He held the paper to the light.

"I'm glad you found this at last," Max read. "I knew you would find it one day. I'm sure Dori is with you. I love you, honey, and I always do."

Max paused for a moment, overcome with emotion. Aunt Dori sobbed. "Still feels like he is here with us," she said.

"It does," Max said. "How did he even know we would find this?"

"He knew a lot of things. He knew someone would, one day."

Max continued reading aloud.

"Son, people are different. You can never be me or someone else. People like different things. Have you ever wondered why we choose to do what we do? Why do some people choose to be doctors, nurses, teachers, soldiers? Maybe it's a calling—an act of bringing equilibrium to the universe—our own little universe in the bigger scheme of things. Why do we hate or love another person? Maybe it's for balance. And sometimes we are forced to open and embrace opportunities that are brought to us. Likewise, at times we have to let go of things we think we love to reach that balance. Fate deals you opportunities, and it's yours to choose. We are always fighting for approval. You never know that you are special until you start looking. If you're reading this, I know you've been looking.

"From the first day your aunt and I found you, we knew you were special," he continued. "You were fond of space navigation, and mathematics, and designing new things. You reminded me of myself. Your aunt is a very observant woman; she quickly realized your talents and took it upon herself to encourage you to pursue that—buying you toys and books to foster your skills. Your teachers complained that you were different and smarter than most students, that you lacked attention—oh, what's the word—hypomanic! But we always knew you were special.

"You might be wondering why I'm telling you this," he added, "but I want you to know that this world is connected like strings: Everything that happens, happens for a reason. Everything is put in place for a purpose, but you can only find the purpose if you are careful enough to look. Discern. Never stop seeking your rightful place in the universe. Your *raison d'etre*. If you find it, have the boldness to follow it relentlessly through, even when it makes no sense. I learned this the hard way! I believe that God created this world with every specific bit to fit a larger puzzle. Unfortunately, we have upset that balance for centuries and caused chaos. There is a Creator, son, a creator who cares about the universe—who marvelously designed connections in the universe most of us do not see. On Earth, we spend billions of dollars trying to fight the unknown, crippled by our selfishness, yet the truth lies there dormant, waiting to be unraveled by persistent minds, hungry but patient. I am troubled when we always think that some extraterrestrial life will invade our Earth, but nobody thinks what those other beings think of us. If God created other beings on other planets, then he has a reason for that, and that's not for mankind to calculate God's mind. The brevity of our existence. What then?

"I am sure you already have the necklace. These are the gifts I am leaving to you, son. Treasure them; I think with time you'll understand their value. I love you! Pass my love to Dorinda."

By this time, both Aunt Dori and Max were crying.

Max emptied the chest. There were a couple of notebooks scribbled with sketches and calculations. He found the BBA badge underneath.

Max sat sobbing quietly, holding his necklace.

"There it is," Aunt Dori said.

"That explains everything! This whole thing—I mean, the dreams, the nightmares, the necklace, and my obsession with astrophysics that I've had for many years. And the algorithm is true." He started laughing loudly. "It's true," he said.

"O.K. I'm lost," Aunt Dori said.

"Yesterday, I felt like my power was being sucked out of me when we identified Aoratosia. When I removed the necklace, it stopped. It was like I was in harmony with the planet, like it was communicating with me. I'm starting to think this has all been planned. Do you think my dreams and all have anything to do with what Uncle Titus was talking about?"

"Maybe or maybe not."

"What should I do?"

"How could I know? He trusted you. Your uncle didn't even tell me. I think it's your call. I say follow your heart."

"I don't understand; why me?" Max said.

"Titus knew you were the right person the minute you started going to school. He came home one day and gave this to me, and three days later, he passed away."

"He knew?"

"He did," she said and paused, taken aback. "Don't ask me how."

Max hesitated for a moment.

"I wanted to tell you I applied for a chance to be part of a mission to Aoratosia."

"To where?"

"It's a long story. You remember the side project I worked on all along. The government has agreed to fund a mission to that planet. I might go if I am selected. I'm not sure yet."

"That's exciting!"

"Thanks. I hope I'll be selected."

"I hope you are, if that's what you want."

"I think it would be a great adventure."

"I'm sure if Titus were here, he would say the same. That's all he ever wanted, but never got the chance. Who doesn't want to represent their country, let alone their planet?" she said. "Your uncle would be very proud of you." She squeezed Max's hand. "That's great news, Max. Congratulations."

"Thanks, Aunt Dori."

Max checked his watch.

"We gotta be going back. I've got lunch with Alonna at noon."

"You'd better hurry."

Max pushed the wheelchair towards the house.

"How am I going to tell Alonna?"

"You might as well, or she will find out soon herself. And that won't be very good."

"How did you feel when you found out that Uncle Titus was part of BBA?"

"I was upset at first for him not trusting me. But I knew that was his purpose. And I still loved him. I understood he did that to protect me."

"So, what should I do?"

"My advice, you go ahead and tell her. What's the worst that could happen? Swear her to secrecy."

"Nothing bad would happen, I guess."

There was a brief pause.

"I'll tell her today."

"Good."

They reached the house and Max rolled the wheelchair up the front porch ramp.

"Can you mow the grass before you go back?" Aunt Dori said.

"Sure," Max said. "It'll probably be in the afternoon after lunch with Alonna."

"That's fine. You can do it anytime."

"Do you want the food now, before I leave?"

"Don't worry, I'll get it myself after cleaning my teeth."

"You sure?"

"Yup."

"Alonna left everything ready in the warmer. The fruits are packed in the fridge. Call me if you need anything."

"Thanks, Max. You're a sweetheart."

"I'll bring you some chicken-fried steak if you want."

"Great. Thanks."

"Can I take your car?"

"Of course. The keys are on the table."

Max hugged Aunt Dori and kissed her on the forehead. "You're awesome."

"You'd better hurry before I change my mind."

Max snatched the keys and left.

He called Alonna to let her know he was on his way to the restaurant. The phone rang once.

"Hey," she said. "I was about ready to call you."

"I'm on my way," Max said.

"Good," she said. "I'm heading over right now."

"O.K. See you in a bit."

MAX ARRIVED at the restaurant 10 minutes early. He sat at a dimly-lit corner table facing the exit. He breathed in the barbecue-saturated air and looked around, cherishing the moments he had spent in this place. Alonna and Max had sat in this spot countless times since their first date. They always got the same food every time—whole-grain toast, pickled cucumber wedges, onions, barbecued ribs, and green beans. The place was unusually empty for lunchtime, as far as he could remember. About a dozen people were sparsely dining around the restaurant. A few cars went past the drive-through and disappeared onto Harrison Avenue. Max nibbled on the sour-sweet pickles, contemplating the best way he would break the news to Alonna.

The first encounter in his room. The mission trip. The stories. The adventures together. The necklace gift. Was that all a setup? Max thought. Max was perplexed. His mind was in a whirlwind, and he felt a little bit angry with Uncle Titus. For some strange reason, he also felt sorry for him—that he owed Uncle Titus something, that he needed to do a favor for him.

By the time Alonna got to Hayday Pig, Max had already finished his first saucerful of pickles.

Max kissed Alonna and drew the chair for her.

"I'm famished," she said.

"I've already ordered," Max said.

"Great. What are we having?"

"Light rib dinner with double green beans portion for the sides for both of us."

"Perfect."

The waiter brought the glasses of water. Max thanked him and they were momentarily silent.

"So," Max said. "How was work?"

"Busy. Glad today is a half-day," she said. "We had six vasectomies today."

They laughed.

Max sat back and smiled. "That's interesting. Does it happen often?"

"No, today was unusual."

"Good. Otherwise I'd be worried."

"Me too," she said. "And how has your day been?"

"It's been great!" Max said. "I actually woke up around 9:30. Felt good. Got to chat with Aunt Dori for a while."

"Feels good sleeping in, huh? How is Aunt Dori?"

"It does. Aunt Dori was in good spirits today. We even took a stroll around the ranch."

"Really? Thanks for doing that. She loves being outside."

"I guess then she was in good spirits."

"She was. I think she enjoyed it."

"I know she did."

"How long is your time off?" Alonna said.

"I am off until Wednesday," Max said.

"Awesome. Three long days to hang out with you."

"Yup," he said, handing her the pickle sauce.

She puckered her forehead.

"Wait," she said. "I didn't know interns could get that many days off?"

"Now you know."

"And the other interns too?"

"I'm not sure. I only know myself."

"You're a very hard worker; maybe that's why they feel you deserve some time off."

"I guess so," Max said. "That's why I wasn't able to call you for the past 36 hours."

"I thought so. That must have been very important, to make you miss my race and not return my calls," she smirked teasingly.

"It was out of my control," Max said. "I apologize."

"It's not a big deal," she said.

The waiter called Max's name. Max excused himself and left to collect the food from the counter.

He was glad to get that break from the discussion, but he knew the interrogation was not over. Alonna had an impressive sixth sense; he liked that. She had a strong personality which, aside from an ability to manipulate people if she chose to, it helped her be a good influencer—a trait that made her a successful nurse, being able to coax her patients into holding on, even the most difficult of patients. To him, it sometimes came across as nagging. Max had not convinced her to believe that mere lab mice had stopped him from attending the rodeo. He saw that in her keen eyes.

He brought back a tray loaded with food and passed some to Alonna.

Max gobbled down the ribs. The barbecue sauce soaked his fingers, which he licked off.

"This is super good," she said.

"Man, I miss this place," Max said.

"Me, too," Alonna said.

"I can't believe I haven't eaten here in 30 days."

"I know! Right?" she said. "Time moves fast."

They continued eating silently.

"So, is it your M.S. research?" Alonna said.

"Yes," Max said, avoiding direct eye contact with Alonna's piercing eyes.

"Babe, what's going on? You are not telling me something," Alonna said.

"Um, everything is fine," Max said, attempting a grin.

"You are not O.K. I can see something is bothering you," she said, with an intense glare in her eyes. "I know you always look me in the eye when we are talking, but not now. You're not my real Max."

Max shrunk in his seat, managing an apologetic stare at Alonna. The trap was sprung, and he knew he was not getting out of it. Alonna tended to have a persistent temperament: not a mere sense of perfectionism, but what seemed like a powerful sixth sense. She knew the right spots to tackle in people, especially him. This sometimes turned overbearing and resulted in arguments. When she started probing, Max knew she would never quit until she felt convinced. She had a knack for making him divulge all his secrets.

Max despised lying, and worse, lying to his fiancée. How could she trust him if he lied to her on the verge of their wedding day? Max vacillated about whether to tell Alonna. He was still hesitant to tell Alonna all about Big Brains America. He tried to change the subject to no avail. She would not give up.

"For your own protection, I think it's best I do not tell you," he said.

"Protect me from what?" she said.

Max gazed into Alonna's eyes, trying to predict her reaction, and said, "I worked with the Secret Service this weekend."

"Interesting," she said, seemingly unshaken. "You could have said that a long time ago."

"It slipped my mind."

Alonna lowered her head closer to Max, and in a hushed voice, she said, "What do you think will happen to me if something happens to you?"

"I'm sorry."

"I hope you told them about your project. What did you do?" she said.

"I told them," Max said. Then Max told her a truncated version of his adventures in Texas. He was surprised that Alonna was not surprised. She applauded him.

"That's insidious," Alonna said after Max recounted Wattenberg's humanoid presentation.

"I was thinking, 'Are these folks serious?'" Max said. "I, too couldn't believe what I was hearing."

When he was done, Alonna's eyes were wide open.

"I'm not a very good storyteller," Max said.

"That was fair enough," she said.

"I should have told you from the beginning."

"You could have," Alonna said.

"I know. I apologize," Max said.

"That's great," she said. "Isn't that what you wanted all along?" Alonna thanked Max for trusting her and kissed him. She promised to tell no one.

"Look what I found this morning," Max said, placing the BBA badges on the table.

Alonna's furrowed her forehead confused. "What is that?"

"This my badge, and this is Uncle Titus's," Max said. "Identical."

"I can see that, but what does that have to do with anything?"

"He was in the same program that I am in."

"That's good, right? You knew it, didn't you?"

"I knew he was in the air force, but not part of BBA."

"Why is this a big deal?" Alonna said.

"The badge is awarded to a few individuals in the program—more like a task force."

"The smart ones."

"Yeah, but he left me more. We found notes and sketches in the shop that he left for me. What is stranger is everything ties into what I've been doing all along. As if he knew what I was going to do."

"Maybe it's a coincidence. He was your guardian. Maybe he knew your interests."

"Could be, but I wasn't even doing physics that much then. I'm starting to feel that this badge and the sketches were all connected to me."

Max told Alonna about his conversation with Aunt Dori, about Uncle Titus and events from Science Park to the discovery of Aoratosia at Spartan Enterprises.

"That still doesn't show that he knew you were going to do this. I mean, it's not like he told you anything, right?"

"Right." Max paused for a moment. "And the necklace incident yesterday."

"You sure it wasn't because of exhaustion? From the way you said it, I think you worked too hard and were sleep-deprived for three days in a row. Plus, I know you don't eat when you get busy."

"Might be. Maybe I'm taking this too seriously."

"Relax for a while these few days you're here."

"You're right."

They finished eating.

Max's phone rang. They looked at each other. Max declined the call. He looked up and said, "We should do something fun."

"Let's get out of here," Yvette said.

"Anywhere in mind?" Max said.

"Wherever we decide."

"How about bowling?"

"Sounds good."

"Let's take my car," he said.

"Let's go."

The waiter brought the to-go chicken-fried steak and they left the restaurant with Alonna leaning on Max's shoulder. It was 1:45 p.m.

They laughed, and he squeezed her hand that was rested on his thigh. She drove smoothly down Harrison Avenue, turned right on MacArthur Boulevard, continued straight, then turned onto Airport Road, passing through the Bison football field where cars and buses were lined on each side of the street.

Max's phone rang again as the car engine roared to life. It was an unknown I.D. Alonna said, "Aren't you going to take that?"

"I probably shouldn't," he said and hung up the call.

The phone rang again.

"Who is it?" Alonna said.

"Unknown I.D."

"You should take it."

"Fine."

"Max," a voice echoed on the other end. "We need you at the central station. Can you be ready in a few minutes?"

"Wait, who is this?"

"It's Doc," The voice said. "A jet is on its way to pick you up in 15 minutes."

"Um," he said. "I just got home. Can I come tomorrow?"

"We don't have much time," Doc said. "You've been selected as part of the recruits for the mission. We are leaving for Central Africa today for training."

"Where?"

"The Democratic Republic of Congo."

"Did you say D.R.C.? I—"

"Yes. See you in a bit."

"Oh."

"Jet will be there in the strip in 15, so get yourself ready," Doc said. "Don't worry about packing anything; you will be wearing uniforms there."

"Yellow fever vaccination?" Max said.

"Don't worry, son," he said. "Our doctors have everything ready at hand. Everything you need."

"O.K., sir. I am on my way there."

"Thanks. See you."

The line went dead.

Alonna looked at Max with eyes that said "not now," and she looked slightly miffed by the phone call. She said, "Who was it?"

"I have to be back at work," he said. "A jet will be here to pick me up in 15 minutes."

"Why? That's too soon. Is everything O.K.?"

"Yes. I've been selected as part of the trainees for the mission to Aoratosia."

"Oh, great. Nobody else can do it?"

"I didn't know it was going to be this early."

"So what do you want to do now?"

"I have to go to the airstrip."

"When?"

"Today. In 15 minutes."

"You just got here."

"I know. I'm sorry. I hate this work sometimes."

"O.K.," she said. "I can drop you there."

"I'm sorry, baby."

"I hope it will not be like this when we're married," she said with a smile.

"I promise. It's only a few weeks until summer is over. Doc said I've been selected for the Aoratosia mission."

"That's awesome. I'm super happy for you."

"Really?" Max said. "I expected you to be upset."

"Why?"

"I don't know—all the plans we have—wedding, travel—everything will be paused. This is going to be huge, Alonna."

"I know."

"If you go with me on this one, I promise I'll make it up to you."

"I am sad because we didn't even get time to talk about the wedding plans, but that's your dream. I wouldn't want to live with you with resentments that you never did what you wanted to because of me. I'd rather have a happy Max."

"Thank you. I promise I'll make it up to you. What if I end up going on the mission?"

"It's fine. I'm guessing it'll only be a short time, right?"

"I think so."

"As long as you come back for the wedding."

They laughed. "I will."

"It's going to be O.K., I promise," Max said.

Alonna remained quiet, and a gentle smile slowly worked its way across her face.

"I think this is your passion," she said. "Do you remember the first time I came into your room? It was a mess—like, man—clothes, shoes, papers everywhere."

Max laughed. "I do. Thanks for lending me some of your organizational superpowers."

"And you said, 'It depends on how you look at it'," Alonna said.

"Until then, I always wondered why you'd never let me go into your room, yet when you came to our house, we would hang out in my room."

"It was weird," Max said. "I had all these improbable designs lying around. Crazy days. Truth is, I didn't want anyone telling me otherwise. When you are chasing something big, some people tend to bring you down. It was so real to me. I am glad you saw that, too."

"Of course."

"You're welcome. I always believed you could do anything."

"I know. Everyone thought I was a fruitcake, and I even felt the same at some point. Especially when I didn't get a temporary job after graduating. I sometimes thought I was wasting my time, but I loved it. Now I can appreciate it in retrospect. All that idle time after graduation. It actually gave me time to do work on the project."

"That's true."

"You're one of the few people who inspired me," Max said. "I still remember when you told me I should keep doing it so people like you can see it too. You seemed so sure I could do it."

They looked at each other silently, then Alonna giggled. "I guess I did. Thanks. You inspired me more. I have never seen someone so dedicated to their goal as you are, Max."

"Thanks."

"Everything is connected in a web. It's a web of string and numbers. Invisible numbers that only a few people can see. No idea comes from nowhere. There is an equation for every happening, action or event. Like the probability of your coming into my room. An algorithm can be developed to explain that, your behavior, intentions, actions. That's how people can control other people."

Max laughed. "That's poetic. Did you make that up?"

"You did," Alonna said. "You said that to me."

"I said that?"

"Yup. You did. That was kinda creepy! For a second, I changed from seeing this nerdy quiet guy to seeing a full-fledged weirdo."

"I had a point though."

"Maybe."

"That's funny. I can't believe you still remember that."

They laughed.

They reached the Stratford airstrip.

"We're here," Alonna said.

"Thanks, babe."

"Next time when you come home, I will turn that phone off!" she said.

Something beeped from Alonna's handbag. "Oh, my pager," she said, and dug it out.

"You have to go back to work?"

"Yes. We've got biopsy samples coming in at two. It wasn't confirmed, but they gave me a heads-up."

"We're in the same boat then."

"Looks like it. Our family in a nutshell."

"You can go. I'm sure the plane will be here soon."

"I can wait a few minutes."

"O.K."

Alonna dropped off Max outside of the gates by the deserted concessions house.

The blue and white small jet arrived a few minutes later. A pilot dressed in a white uniform stepped out and opened the door. Max said farewell to Alonna and promised to update her as soon as he could on how things were going. He greeted the pilot and thanked him under the noise of the jet engines. Max waved at Alonna as the jet taxied away.

The jet landed at the Spartan Enterprise Shuttleport 25 minutes later, southwest of Houston. There were good vibes throughout the plane. He was led to a gray aircraft that was already running. The name "Spartan Enterprises" stared from that plane's belly. Two pilots dressed in white and blue were standing at the doors. Max strode behind them. He did not know whether to be excited or to worry. He had never been in a supersonic jet before.

Doc, McKomic, and Reverend Kay were in the lounge section of the jet. The trio were joined by a group of other recruits, among them Geoffrey and Yvette. Max walked over and sat next to Geoffrey.

"You guys are in, too?" Max yelled under the noise of the jet engines.

"Yes," Geoffrey replied.

"How did they choose all these people?"

"A random selection process," Geoffrey said. "That's what Doc told me."

Doc was inspecting the aisles and counting everyone. He stopped when he got to Max and Geoffrey and smiled. "You found each other, huh? Look back there, Max," said Doc. "Your friend, the reporter from the *Tribune*. Alex Hunter."

"We're bringing the media?"

"Alex was playing reporter, to get the perks of a reporter. She's a whiz kid engineer and sociologist. Cordell gave her a job."

Max looked around, marveling. "How will they land this plane in the D.R.C.?"

"McKomic has a private shuttle landing pad there, in Kinshasa."

Max had many more questions for Doc but kept quiet. He knew this wasn't the right time—but he would ask. Later.

CHAPTER SEVENTEEN

Spartan Hypersonic Jet

MAX SAT NEXT to Geoffrey in the hypersonic shuttle. He was reeling with his newfound confidence from Uncle Titus' message. Like a prophecy coming to fruition. He closed his eyes to relax. The identification of Aoratosia, the engraved necklace, and the recent revelations about Uncle Titus gave him some solace and motivation, despite leaving many questions unanswered. He felt he was doing something —at least for Uncle Titus. This feeling filled him with an unexplainable jolt of excitement and, at the same time, anxiety about the whole odyssey. Being on the plane with Doc and McKomic, and the rest of the recruits, was surreal. There were good vibes throughout the plane, despite the general awareness that most of them would be returning home soon after failing training. Apart from all the facade, he knew deep down it was chaos. He knew everyone in the plane felt the same.

While scientists at NASA and Spartan Enterprises viewed this as another breakthrough in Project ASHE's planetary search efforts, the discovery of an Earth lookalike planet had sparked more concern than jubilation at the White House. The president, like most laypeople, was much more concerned and afraid. The finding was revealing the existential dread buried deep in any Earthling. The thought of having another Earth with people with advanced capabilities frightened her.

Dozens of thoughts lingered in everyone's head. Especially because of Aoratosia's proximity. What if Aoratosians had been watching Earth? What if they were more aggressive than Earthlings? The president feared failing to protect the world. The United States wanted to be on the always-ready side. This mission would be the greatest operation the Pentagon had ever carried out. The president had convened with her advisors, and after a long and tedious meeting she had finally relented, hesitantly ratifying the mission. The mention of a potential Russian element in the planet search was a rallying point for all on the House Committee on Science, Space, and Technology. Decisive action had to be taken now and before the Russians could win this race. The summarized file was faxed immediately to Doc.

The fax machine beeped twice, and copies printed. Max took the papers, handed them to Doc, and watched him peruse the files with a cold expression.

In the file was a detailed list of all the possible threats of this new planet. The first page summarized the meeting minutes. It showed all methods necessary and available to defend Earth in case of an attack and how to handle preemptive strikes: all the doom and gloom one would anticipate from such a civilization. There was a briefing of the council discussion. Doc skimmed the debate part. The council had argued about using nuclear weapons, atomic weapons. They had also weighed on the possibility of sending drones or of sending infected bats in drones, which would make it easier to locate the magnetic beings. A copy of the Space Exploration Amendment bill was attached on another sheet. Below the bill were signatures from all the Congress members, and President Blanchard.

"Looks like we are going to Aoratosia," Doc said with a smile, still leafing through the paper.

"That's great news," McKomic said.

There was a brief pause.

"Damn! That was a close margin," Doc said.

"What's the final tally for the vote?" McKomic said.

"154 for to 153 against."

McKomic quirked. "A win is a win. No one can stop project ASHE now."

"That's all that matters," Doc said. "Let's hope everything will flow as planned." Doc handed the sheets of paper to McKomic.

"It will," McKomic said. "The team has been able to make some tweaks on the ship, and the needed components, with the help of engineers from the Ames Research Center."

"That's great! So is it good to go?"

"It is. That's what Bosco said."

"Great!"

The phone rang.

"We have a call from the White House," McKomic said.

"Let it through," Doc said.

Everyone was hushed.

"Madam President," McKomic said.

"Tony, I'm guessing you already received the parcel," the president said.

"Yes. That's good news. Thank you for pushing this through."

"Thank me when this mission is complete. Thank Tony for nagging me."

"All right, Madam President."

"Make this happen."

"You bet."

The video feed died.

The anxious masses were pushing even harder towards destroying the supposed humanoids, based on recent sightings in the Amazon. President Blanchard hoped that a successful mission to Aoratosia would help shift the public focus, allowing her enough time to make plans to take decisive action regarding the humanoids and maybe more time for Dr. Scrivner and the missing anthropologists to resurface from the Amazon jungle.

Max had been sitting quietly listening to the conversation.

"Why are we going to Congo?" Max said.

"That's where NASA's National Magnetron facility is located, and where you'll do your training," Doc said.

His answer brought interest from the rest of the recruits.

"I've heard it's the largest in the world," Geoffrey said.

"It is!" Doc said. "The place was once a civil-war wasteland, but

NASA transformed it into a world-class research center. Since then, we've been experimenting on animals, plants, model ships, simulations, and drones for future space exploration to magnetic planets like Jupiter."

"And a lot of doomsday kind of crap as well," McKomic said.

"That, too," Doc said.

"They also do flu vaccines, right?" Yvette said.

Doc looked at McKomic before replying.

"They have a famed BL4 Biodefense lab," he said. "They do all kinds of biodefense research as well."

McKomic laughed.

"You never know everything the government does," McKomic said, with an odd quirk. "I'm sure when you do, you'll be dead."

"How come you use the facilities?" Max said.

"We have a partnership with NASA."

"That's cool," Max said. "How do you get the equipment to Kaligari?"

"Everything is built in Texas, then shipped," McKomic said.

Max nodded.

The plane shook mildly as they passed some turbulence.

"The eddy currents are high this time of the year," Doc said.

"Are we still over the ocean?" Max said.

"No, it's Lake Victoria."

Max nodded, looking out through the small window. "That was fast."

"That's the beauty of the hypersonic shuttles," McKomic said. "I hope we can ramp up production and make it affordable to the masses."

"That would be cool," Max said.

"Ever been to Africa before?" Doc said.

"I was born in Malawi," Max said. "At least that's what my parents tell me."

"Oh, O.K."

"I have," Yvette said. Geoffrey nodded yes too.

"Which part of Africa have you been to?"

"South Africa, Zimbabwe, Morocco, and Egypt," Geoffrey said.

"That was when I was in junior high. Used to travel a lot with my parents."

"Your parents still travel a lot?"

"They do. Every six months or so they go somewhere. My dad has some businesses in Cape Town and all over Africa."

"Nice," Doc said. "You'll like the D.R.C. The weather is perfect."

"I lived in Madagascar for a few years on a foreign exchange program. Best time ever," Yvette said. "Picked up some French as well. You remember that, Doc?"

"I do. Your mom and I were worried to death."

"You were always worried."

They laughed.

Shortly after, the pilot announced they were beginning their descent into the Kinshasa International Airport. Everyone hastened to fasten their seat belts.

CHAPTER EIGHTEEN
Kinshasa

THE SHUTTLE TOUCHED down onto Kinshasa International Airport at 1:00 p.m. The weather in Kinshasa was delightfully breezy and cheerful. Doc was right; it felt like home. The airport looked nothing like the stereotypical substandard African jungle that the western media portrayed. There was freshness. Max faintly remembered the smell— the trees, noise, liveliness, and smoke. He could feel shadows of every memory he had fought to suppress for many years. Nothing good, nothing worthy of remembering, not from this place. He had been young back then. He could remember the hundreds of impoverished faces behind the fence. Hoping for a lucky day to get asylum somewhere safe. He remembered that fence long gone from his memory, buried deep, recalled only in bits frightening enough to be true. *I owe it to these people!* Max thought. He vowed silently that he was going to succeed no matter what. For those faces!

Five white Land Cruisers waited outside the arrivals terminal, engines already running. The drivers, in khakis, stood by the sides of the cars and greeted them while holding the doors open. Geoffrey, Yvette and Doc joined Max in the same vehicle. Within a few seconds later, they hit the road and the airport was out of sight.

Through the one-way view window, the world looked different. Pedestrians lingered on the sidewalks where vendors were busy trading their merchandise on makeshift wooden stands. A group of children lolled on the light-green turf, suddenly alerted by the passing motorcade. A soccer game was ensuing on an almost bare field nearby, boys and girls playing barefoot. They looked happy, seeming not too worried about what was going on in the rest of the world.

Four police motorcycles led the way in front, and four others trailed behind. Police officers stood at every intersection, flagging down oncoming traffic as the motorcade whizzed past the intersections without stopping. The crossroads had no traffic lights. The lanes, barely a single car's width, were unmarked, which added to the chaotic driving and constant honking. It had to be done instinctively to share the road with cars going the other direction, in such a way that one side of the vehicle leaned off the paved surface onto the gravel to allow an oncoming vehicle to pass. The crowds along the way looked on in amazement, curious about who had come to their country.

As they continued farther away from the airport, the infrastructure changed. They passed ghostly, high-rise buildings with occasional patches of renovated efforts reminiscent of the country's dystopian past of greed, corruption, civil wars, and western exploitation. People sat at leisure on the frail balconies and windowless rooms of the dilapidated graffiti-ridden buildings that lined the streets, a reminder of the difficult times past of war and exploitation. Even centuries after, the colonial shadow of Leopold of Belgium still lingered over the resource-rich country.

Max wondered how such a poor country in a continent with no major heavy ammunition factory managed to amass some of the world's deadliest weapons. As an act of friendship, the D.R.C. president ensured that American officials who visited the country were escorted safely because, even though the war was over, they remained wary of attacks.

The SUV bumped over a few potholes and turned onto a narrow gravel road. The cars negotiated the winding road, which shot nearly straight over the hill before vanishing into the Kaligari forest. The huge

teak and mahogany trees shot past. The path finally leveled and
reverted into a wider asphalt surface that wended into a wide-open
area fortressed by a tall razor-wired stone wall. A huge, conspicuous
red sign stared from the fence. It read: "Danger! Haute Tension!" with
a lightning zigzag sign below and a skull and crossed bones. Below,
the same warning was written in English, in small bock letters.

The driver tried to initiate a conversation, but he could see none of
them understood what he was saying.

"Parlez-vous français?"

"No," Doc said.

Max looked at Yvette, but she had her earphones on.

The car stopped in front of giant metal gates. The area was well
guarded by armed soldiers, both in American and Congolese combat
uniforms. The driver flashed an I.D. at the sensor mounted on the side
of the gate. Someone opened a small metal window on the gate and
talked back and forth with the driver in French. After a few exchanges,
about 30 seconds, the gate opened with a screech and the five cruisers
rolled into the fortress. They parked in an open paved area.

"*Merci!*" Doc said to the driver.

The tall driver smiled back and cordially said, "*De rien!*" He kept
smiling and said nothing more.

They quickly left the cars and headed inside. Passing through two
glass doors, they scanned their passcards and finally reached the lobby,
where they were received by a clean-shaven man in a white lab coat
and green tailored scrubs.

"Welcome to Kaligari!" he said.

The man shook Doc and McKomic's hands. His name was Bosco.

Bosco had been waiting. His small head was perched between his
prominent ears on his tall, slender frame. One would think a light
breeze would topple him. His long, stilt-like legs, coffee-dark skin,
pronounced cheekbones, jutting chin, and bone-chilling stare from
sunken eyes lent him the air of a Masai warrior.

Bosco had been on several missions before, Doc had said. Max
nodded, assessing Bosco. He did not look that old. Maybe pushing 50.
The only betrayal was his graying hair. But his body was slender and

chiseled, with arms roped with toned muscles and protruding veins. A body that disguised sheer strength. Skinny, in a skinny-strong way.

He had a deep voice and spoke English so rapidly that his Adam's apple danced with each word. At first hearing, you would think the accent was Scottish, and it took a bit of getting used to. Turned out Bosco was born in New Zealand to Kenyan immigrants, moved to Ireland for his master's degree, then moved to Germany for his engineering doctorate, ending up in the US for his post-doctoral fellowship at MIT. He never went back. As Doc had explained, that is where NASA snatched him. He had been one of its engineers and astronauts for nearly two decades before he abruptly decided to retire. He had vowed to stay away from space travel and had apparently declined NASA's repeated offers for him to participate in any space mission strategies, but fate had followed him. McKomic managed after many attempts to coax Bosco to come out of retirement to train the recruits because of his invaluable experience. And now he was in the D.R.C. McKomic had convinced him he would be doing a great service to the next generation.

Doc introduced all the recruits, one by one. Bosco nodded each time.

"This way," Bosco said. He led them through a turnstile.

"Are you ready to begin?" Bosco said.

"Yes, super excited," one of the tall recruits said.

Bosco stopped and glared at the recruit.

"It's 'Yes, sir!' when I ask you a question. I'm not here to be your buddy."

The recruit wilted under Bosco's glare.

"Now listen, privates," Bosco said. "What you're about to embark on is a war. You'll be intruders, and intruders, if not careful, get killed. So, if you came here thinking this was going to be a safari vacation, you are wrong. This is a military training camp. You are all cadets, and I will drill the hell out of you to make sure you understand. Is that clear?"

The recruits nodded.

"I will call you by your name when I want to," he said. "For now, I will call all of you privates. So whenever you hear the word 'Private', know that I'm talking to you. I usually motion to the one I'm talking to."

Yvette tittered and, in a clear undertone, said, "What a jerk!"

"That's his modus operandi," Doc whispered. "Don't worry, you will get used to it."

Yvette pursed her lips.

CHAPTER NINETEEN
Kaligari, D.R.C.

Bosco scanned his I.D. on the wall card reader. The turnstile clicked before each of them went through, one at a time. They strode behind Bosco into a hallway that led into a dimly-lit expansive room lined floor to ceiling with cages reeking of animal stench. The vivarium was lined with caged bats, chicken, dogs, rabbits, and primates.

On the left side of the entrance was a plaque carved into the wall explaining the lab's history.

The BL4 lab in the Congo had been built in the 20th century when the US was fighting the Ebola epidemic that had ravaged that region of West Africa for many years. After the pandemic, the US government had decided to continue using the facility for further research rather than let the facility rot. The US agreed with the Congolese government to own the 10,000 hectares of land that surrounded the lab in the middle of the Kaligari forest as payment for D.R.C.'s debts over the years. Because these debts continued to exist due to corruption in the Congolese government and endless civil wars, America had owned the area for over a century.

The BL4 lab was renowned to the world as the annual flu vaccine production site. This made sense; billions of people needed flu shots every year, which provided a good reason for the lab to stay. However, like any other developed nation, the US found this the ideal site to develop its biodefense. Superpower nations tended to bully less-developed countries by using them as sites for weapons stockpiling and as wastelands. The poor nations needed money, and the developed nations needed to safeguard their powers. A win-win, depending on one's vantage point.

One of the baboons lashed at Max, leaving a streak on his jacket. Everyone froze.

"What the heck!?" Max yelled.

"Oh," Bosco said. "Don't walk close to the cages. It's one of the core instincts you should have to survive and succeed on this mission. Carelessness will kill you. Think, control your consciousness, your self-awareness, teaching it to respect and obey you."

Everyone looked at him; no one responded to his comment. None of the recruits understood what he meant. They were already developing an increasing dislike for Bosco. They continued to the middle of the hallway. Bosco led them to a room lined with blue protective dust coats, bonnets, rubber booties, and polished wooden lockers.

"All right, everyone," Bosco said. "Grab one. The size is on the label at the top."

The recruits scrambled to put on the coats and slid the elastic rubber booties over their shoes.

"This is a requirement. In case of emergency," Bosco said. "Any metal should be put in the lockers over there. Does anyone have a metal implant?"

They all shook their heads.

"Good," Bosco said. "Otherwise, I'd have wanted to know how you were accepted for this program. Leave any metal objects out here; they will cause problems with the machine."

Bosco assessed the recruits. When he was satisfied, he led everyone out.

They finally reached the elevator and crammed in. Bosco scanned his I.D. card again.

"How many floors down?" Yvette said.

Bosco grinned at Yvette. "We're almost there."

"The elevator is not moving," Max whispered.

He reached forward and pressed the basement B button.

Bosco smiled. "Good catch, Mr. Folksay. Remember, be aware of your surroundings."

Then the loud elevator chimed, and the doors opened into the flight simulation control overlooking a wide mechanical area with dozens of engineers in white lab coats. The site was ringed with gray and white walls about 200 feet on each side made a large hollow giant squared hangar, guarded by a thick, rigid translucent plastic barrier from the platform where they were standing. There were a few chairs behind them, and Doc sat on one of the chairs.

"Is this the magnetron?" Geoffrey said.

"Yes, Mr. Foster," Bosco said. "I like to call it the hoverground. The top and bottom are sealed with two meters of lead and iron embedded within the walls. This will be your playground for the next few weeks."

Everyone smiled. Even Bosco showed a twitch on the side of his mouth, giving him a redeeming characteristic.

"Wow!" Yvette said.

"It's amazing," Bosco said. "We can simulate Aoratosia's geography from here. It's not 100 percent correct, but it suffices for our purpose. Top-notch technologies for all our space travel drills. Can be tested under perceived and calculated Aoratosian conditions to mimic Aoratosia's geography. We recently added earthquakes and cosmic radiation simulators too."

"Cosmic radiation, really?" Yvette said.

"Yes," Bosco said.

There was a brief silence.

"I've heard you have been on a space mission before?"

"Yes, I have," Bosco said.

"How was it?" they said in unison.

"Overwhelming but great," he said. "There's no feeling like it. No words to describe it. The enchanting feeling of not knowing what to expect is superb. You can only understand it once you get there in person."

As he spoke, Bosco pressed his face onto the retina scan unit. The sealed barricade opened, and they stepped into the magnetron via a staircase on the wall below the platform. A tray emerged from the wall at the bottom of the stairs. They climbed on, and Bosco hovered it forward.

"Let me give you a quick tour. I know you all are jet-lagged, so it'll be quick. Feel free to ask questions."

As they approached the center of the magnetron, several storage lifts emerged from the wall.

"That's the ship. To the left you have the aerogliders and farther you have the sleek suits," McKomic said, pointing at the empty tray.

"Where is the ship?" Max said.

"On the shelf."

Everyone stared at the shelf.

"That shelf is empty!" Max said. The recruits murmured in awe.

"No, it's there. The ship is there," McKomic said.

"Where?"

"Right there; can't you see it?" Everyone was grinning, almost as if McKomic was out of his mind. Maybe this was one of his ploys to mess with their minds.

McKomic climbed into the larger concrete port, opened an invisible door, and climbed into the ship, vanishing when he closed the door. After a few seconds, he opened the invisible door and stepped out. Everyone was in awe.

"Wow, this is super cool. An invisible mode!" Geoffrey said.

"That's right! We can sneak around anywhere in this baby," McKomic said.

"Wow, this is even cooler than I anticipated!" Geoffrey said. "Can the ship travel in the invisible mode?"

"Yes, of course. The only problem with using the invisible mode is power. In invisible mode, the ship consumes double the amount of power compared to normal mode operation."

"So the invisible mode is for emergency situations?" Geoffrey said.

"That's right for now. Only when really needed. As time progresses, we will make one that can efficiently travel in invisible mode."

"How's that even possible?" Max said.

"Electronics! It's all electronics tethered into the frame, pre-programmed," one of the recruits said.

"Right," McKomic said. "The outside of the ship's body is embedded with stimuli-responsive color-changing photonic crystals—precision sensors. I know; it's a mouthful. We call them PCs. PCs can adapt and camouflage to mirror the ship's surroundings. Same applies for the aerogliders and the spacesuits."

"Wow."

McKomic turned on the remote control, and the whole lustrous capsule came into view. The spacecraft was shaped like a cocoon resting on a sturdy iron grid. A central axis line streamed around the ship's frame, bisecting the body. The name "SPARTAN ENTERPRISES" stood boldly on the ship's outside, all the way from her nose and over the side doors. Information about the ship played on a screen embedded in the wall.

"This looks almost like Zelda," Geoffrey said, looking at Bosco.

"Yes," Bosco said. "The platform is the same. But everything has been upgraded—the command, communications, life support systems, the chassis. Tougher and more durable than its predecessor for sure."

The ship was a modification of Zelda, the spacecraft used by Bosco and his crew on their tragic attempt to land on Mars. Most of the crew perished. Bosco was the only one who survived to return.

Bosco continued. "Radiation assessment has shown the presence of high energy galactic cosmic rays, X-rays, microwave radiation, and solar particles, not to mention high pressures powerful enough to cause death by blowing up all human cells within a few hours."

"Now before y'all freak out," McKomic said, "the spacecraft has been designed to counteract such conditions."

"How?" Max said.

"The body is made of a lightweight silica and Inconel," McKomic said. "And a graphene, asbestos, and aluminum composite lining capable of withstanding temperatures as high as 4000 degrees Celsius, the immense pressure generated at warp speeds from the teleporter, and the belt of intense radiation surrounding Jupiter's magnetosphere."

"How did you get all that stuff in this thing?" Alex said.

McKomic laughed. "That's why I have smart people around me. The walls are also lined with a 20-inch layer of liquid cladding to withstand both cold and hot temperatures and to block deadly radiation. There's also a retractable shield to further block excess radiation storms, which could potentially melt the ship in space at such warp speeds."

"The cladding also insulates," Bosco said. "The ship was designed to withstand the fluctuating space subzero and high temperatures generated by the ship's ultra-speed."

"How long does the journey take to reach Aoratosia?"

Bosco said, "Five hours. According to our projections. Most of that time is wasted meandering around electric currents in Jupiter's magnetosphere before landing on Aoratosia."

"That's what the shields are for," Alex said.

"Correct," McKomic said. "The shields counteract the excess magnetic fields and can be activated at an appropriate distance to Jupiter's magnetosphere to reduce waste of fuel and energy."

Bosco climbed into the spacecraft.

"Once on Aoratosia, the ship can transform into various shapes and sizes depending on the situation, for speed or breaking through barriers," Bosco said through the loudspeaker. As he spoke, everything happened at unprecedented speed. The ship transformed into a flat fighter-jet-like form. He explained as the ship wriggled into a bulldozer shape with a large rack on the front bumper. It then twisted into a square-domed structure, and soft classical music played. "Now you are home," he said.

"Wow, that's fast," Geoffrey said.

"Four seconds for each transformation."

"That's insane!"

"It's not quite where I want it to be yet," McKomic said. "We're getting there."

"How does the ship power itself?" Alex said.

"There is a small nuclear-fission reactor at the base which powers all electronics and other functions."

"That small nuclear power plant can power the ship for 25 years nonstop," McKomic said. "As far as lift-off and cruising, the ship has three engines using oxygen, hydrogen, and kerosene. The fuel power is only needed for the first and second stages."

One of the boys, the tallest recruit, interjected. "You have mentioned a couple times about warp speeds. Can you explain more?"

"Good question, Basil. That's actually what I was about to show you. Anyone here know how warp speed works?"

The recruits looked at each other and shook their heads.

"All right," Bosco said, switching on the console on the wall.

"Have any of you ever heard of Saucepan?"

Everyone nodded.

The video started playing.

Saucepan was a whimsical name McKomic coined based on the high energy produced by the device, enough energy to fry a portion of an entire moon into oblivion. But Saucepan was not really a giant frying pan. The device consisted of four high arched laser-emitting plates that were connected to a pivoted axle, each with a radius of 100 meters. The device operated on a constant flow of liquid nitrogen to cool it off. Spartan had built the facility in the Sahara desert. When the mega-electric motor rotated at superspeed during launch time, the beam plates emitted high-energy lasers to form a vortex that spiraled into space. The direction and strength of the vortex could be manipulated by computer programs. The energy vortex from Saucepan collided at a constriction point called the teleporter ring, causing a distortion in space-time, forming a portal which allowed objects to move at the warp speeds to pre-programmed destinations.

"Anyone know how it works?"

"I know it involves high-energy emission and warping of space-time," Max said.

"Yes, the ship uses laser propulsion to teleport."

"Right," Bosco said. He looked at McKomic.

McKomic smiled. "In simpler terms, yes." McKomic cleared his throat and continued, "Saucepan is a high-energy technology developed by Spartan Enterprises. The project was started by NASA, but they kind of pushed it around until we took over about ten years ago. We wanted to find a way to scour space faster and more efficiently. We wanted to send humans on trips to Mars and beyond. And the only way to do that was to develop Saucepan. We are the only company to warp microbes, rodents, and plants to Mars using Saucepan."

"I remember hearing that on the news my junior year in college," Geoffrey said.

"Yup; the project faced great opposition," McKomic said.

"As most of you might remember, building Saucepan was a challenge. Even the proposition raised hell with the public, environmentalists, cynics, and political bureaucracies who capitalized on the public outcry to advance their careers. Most people thought we were playing with fire and believed the machine would suck up the whole Earth or blow the planet into smithereens. Some theories even came up, but NASA finally prevailed," Doc said.

"How did you convince the public?" Alex asked.

McKomic giggled. "Some ingenious public relations, demonstrations, lots of lobbying, some luck, and honestly, some balls of steel."

Everyone laughed.

Doc gazed on. "We are always afraid of the unknown, but yet we have to confront that fear to bring about breakthroughs. That's what we did. NASA stayed on the project but nearly gave up on it until McKomic came along and resurrected it. From the first time I saw him and his vision, I knew he was the guy. He sparked a renaissance in spacefaring. So I thought, why not join him, right? That's been my dream for as long as I can remember. Which is why I'm still here today."

Doc patted McKomic on the shoulder.

"So how does Saucepan work?" Max said.

McKomic pointed to the illustration playing on the screen. "The four pans emit high energy."

"Is that why you called it Saucepan?"

"That's right," McKomic said. "With the right atmospheric conditions, that energy can be transferred into space. Basically cooking space."

"Second law of thermodynamics!" Max said.

"Correct! What does it say?"

"Energy can neither be created nor destroyed but can only be transferred from one medium to another," Alex said.

"That's correct. Simple principle, but it controls everything alive. And not easy to create," Bosco said, eyeing the group intently. "Energy can't be formed or destroyed, so we had to devise a proper outlet to harness it. In principle, all the energy from the pans is transferred into space as a vortex, which then distorts space-time, creates a portal, and warping occurs."

"On a larger scale, the universe is isotropic and homogenous. But there are occasional episodes of imbalance which give rise to phenomena like loopholes, cyclones on a smaller scale. That's basically the concept behind Saucepan and this whole project.

"The pads rotate at ultra-speed, which allows for the formation of an infinite ion-electric vortex that propels within the vortex at warp speeds."

"Like a loophole?" Max said.

"Yes."

"How?"

"Inside the vortex is constant low pressure, which equals no resistance, which results in warp speed. This energy is directed into infinite space. This distorts space-time allowing anything that enters into the portal to travel at speeds greater than light. And using our computer programs, we can direct the vortex towards a destination in our solar system."

The video played on the screen.

"The precision sensors help keep the ship inside en route at warp speeds."

"How do you get it to come back?"

"Good question. That's the beauty of AI. The teleport channel is directed to Aoratosia's surface. To return, we simply reverse the direction of motion of the pads. And with precision time and estimations, we can allow the cargo to reach Earth at reasonable speeds."

"Are we the first to test this?" Yvette said.

"We tested it to Mars about ten years ago." McKomic paused, then added, "but this will be the first time it will go so far and fast with real people."

"Why wait for ten years?" Max said.

"Building this thing is not a joke," he said. "A single mission can cost up to the gross domestic product of Texas. Well, maybe not that much. You get the point. This structure is expensive."

Doc interjected: "As you can imagine, this contraption raised hell from the public, which stagnated almost all Project ASHE major operations and developments. So for the past decade, the project has been surviving on private donations."

McKomic laughed it off. "I can remember when investors slammed Saucepan as a hoax. Some were even convinced it would blow up."

"Now it's paying off exponentially," Max said.

"I don't understand politicians," McKomic said. "Small minds, narcissistic, yet don't get it. Sending cargo to the space station was only a warmup for us. The big boys go to Mars and far beyond our planet. It's always interesting meeting some of these crackheads who believed we would not pull the project up. It pisses me off that even to this point, some still don't buy into the idea that Project ASHE is not going back."

Doc said, "This is a chance to prove to the world that Project ASHE was not a gimmick to bilk taxpayers of money."

Everyone nodded, touched by the way McKomic spoke. He was the man, and it showed in the way he spoke.

"As you can see from below," Bosco explained, "we have designed super propulsion systems never done before; this will allow the ship to travel at warp speeds. Unlike its predecessor, this baby has four engines and one solid-fuel booster and only needs two stage separations before plunging into the portal created by Saucepan."

"How's that even possible?" Max said.

"It's very possible. The teleporter ring is like a spiraling cylindrical hollow tube into space made by bombarding and harnessing high-energy particles and redirecting the energy from the Saucepan. Anything that gets in that space gets warped into infinite space."

Everyone remained quiet.

"Like an artificial loophole," Geoffrey said. "It happens all the time in nature, cyclones, tornadoes, and all those claims of people disappearing and never to be seen again."

"Exactly! Just on a mega scale."

"You said infinite space; how does the ship get to Aoratosia? I would think it would keep going," Yvette said.

"You people have a lot of good questions!" McKomic said. "In response to your question, the ship is programmed to have enough momentum to reach Aoratosia. It's basically like tossing a projectile from point A to B. Does that make sense? Even though I'm pretty certain, you can't be precisely 100 percent guaranteed everything will work exactly as expected."

"So there is a possibility of being warped into infinity?" Alex said.

Bosco sneered. "Yes, possibly. A very slim chance of that happening, however."

The candidates looked at each other, but no one said anything. Bosco seemed to enjoy the panic in the candidates.

"All right," Bosco said. "It's less likely. Again, nothing is guaranteed. Space changes continually, and our predictions may not exactly mirror the conditions."

"How could astronauts endure those warp speeds?"

"Great question. I will show you when we get there. We have designed a suit that allows the human body to withstand supersonic travel. All right, everyone, you can go through and check out the inside of the ship. Don't touch anything yet."

The recruits filed into the ship.

The capsule looked much bigger on the inside than outside. A prominent immersive control screen overlooked the dashboard. The control cabin had four chairs, two on each side of the cramped passageway to counteract and balance the ship's centrifugal motion and distribute the teleportation energy. These chairs had gravity sensors and were self-adjustable depending on the position of the ship in the air. The dashboard was cluttered with an unnerving glut of buttons, joysticks, levers, and gears below the big screens. The Spartan Enterprises logo streaked across the dashboard. The front of each chair was equipped with a head camera and virtual goggles, which Bosco explained allowed the crew to experience the ship's ultra-speed and motion in real time, sort of like a movie experience, real-life fantasy adapted from each one's life experiences. He said the device was able to skew the mental faculty of perceiving space and time, which was necessary for the trip.

"Which is another reason why we cannot send drones. To control the ship, a conscious human being has to be in control!" Bosco said.

A narrow passageway led to a research chamber directly connected to the control room. The back cabin had five berths to sleep on, two on each wall and one at its end. They descended a narrow set of stairs to the lower deck which led to a refreshments room and kitchen, and a small exercise room. There was a medical room and, at the far end, an artillery room with magnetochrome pulse guns (MPGs), designed to work under magnetic conditions, and all kinds of ammunition strapped on shelves.

"Why is it so cold?" Max said.

"It's chilly in here, isn't it?" McKomic said. "That's why I call this baby Coldbox! That's the optimum temperature required to function."

"Won't radiation or heat break the windows?" John, one of the candidates, a tall fellow, said.

"It would, but all the windows and glasses are beryllium coated, which improves their thermal stability. It's built to withstand even Jupiter's nastiest sand cyclones."

The next device on the other shelf looked like a wheel-less motorcycle. There were only four of the vehicles. Bosco introduced them as aerogliders. Bosco walked toward one, and when he was within three meters, the butterfly doors opened. He sat down and punched a few keys. Four automatic seatbelts snapped in place.

"How does the aeroglider work?"

"It uses magnetic levitation," Bosco said.

"This is really cool!" Geoffrey said.

"So the levitation allows the aeroglider to suspend in the air?" Max said.

"Precisely."

"How does it move?" Alex said.

"The structure is dipped in the front, which allows a forward thrust by pseudo levitation. More of the engine load is in the front with two propellers, one in front and another at the back, covered by copper and iron coils. The structural differences allow the aeroglider to move one way or the other."

"I see," Geoffrey said. "So the base delivers magnetic pulses from the huge iron and copper coils on the bottom, which could be adjusted for direction change and propulsion and speed."

"That's right! The coils also produce the electricity needed for the aeroglider controls to function."

"Simple Lenz's Law!" Geoffrey said.

"That's right, Mr. Foster. Seems like you paid attention in your physics class." Everyone chuckled.

Bosco continued. "An exterior magnetic field causes the supercon-ductor to produce an eddy current that induces an opposite effect, and the aeroglider shoots forward by repelling the external magnetic field."

"Wow," Geoffrey said, smiling.

"How do you control it? I'd imagine it would topple over?"

"Good question, Mr. Folksay. The concept is the machine is directly connected to your brain. This aeroglider is activated when you are within three meters."

Bosco pressed on the handles. "The handles contain automated deep print sensors which connect you to the aeroglider. Waves from your brain relay information about your position and speed and provide a feedback loop that allows the aeroglider to adjust continu-ously as you move along by adjusting one or more of the base's elec-tromagnets. So always remember, the machine is a part of you when you're driving it.

"A magnetic plug is attached along the spine at the end of the sleek suit, which locks into the aeroglider, and subsequently pressurizes the suit to form a rigid exoskeleton and stabilizes the driver in all the swooping and sudden maneuvers the machine is capable of undertak-ing. I'll show you the suit in a minute."

"That's pretty cool," Max said. "Do we have any contingency plans in case the systems do not work?"

"Good question," McKomic said, flipping through the slide show on the information screen. "Our scientists have thoroughly tested all the equipment here, so we would expect nothing to go wrong. Just in case, we have the emergency hydraulic system, which allows the aerogliders to function and stay airborne for 12 hours, but this uses excess power and energy and reduces the battery's lifespan. You have all the communication, shields, and equipment you need in case of an emergency."

Max nodded.

"And there is a supplementary nitrous oxide tank loaded on the front. Should you need it," Doc said.

"We have that, too," McKomic said.

"I would think magnetic interaction would interfere with the system," Alex said, rubbing her chin.

"That shouldn't be a problem. Our engineers took that into consideration: either way, high or low pressure, magnetic fields. Every piece of equipment is built to withstand that. Plus, Coldbox is the administrator, so you can upload and upgrade new software to the aerogliders and suits remotely."

"Meaning we can fix the suits or aerogliders from the ship?" Alex said.

"Correct."

Alex nodded.

"Why are there only four seats?"

"Because only four of you are going."

There was a brief contemplative silence.

"Any more questions?"

They all shook their heads. Bosco pressed a key on the remote, and the pad drifted to the next display.

"Now, here is my favorite," Bosco said enthusiastically. "The sleek suit!"

A dozen of the suits, tagged with a replica of the American flag and the Spartan Enterprises logo on the right breast, hung on a shelf in the glassed incubator. Each suit was equipped with two magnetochrome pulse guns, one strapped to each hip.

Another video played next to the glass door.

Bosco continued, "As I said before, the aeroglider and suit work as one unit. The ring on the suit's spine snaps into the back of the seat during operation, creating a single unit."

"Each suit is personalized for each crew member," McKomic said.

"The suits are programmed so that each member can use only their suit and no one else's. The suit works in coordination with the limbic system, allowing split-second responses from the driver—like a whole-body plastic surgery—an extension of the body, except with wiring all across it."

"It creates a machine-human interface, allowing the machine to work as a natural exoskeleton?" Geoffrey said.

"Yes," Bosco said.

"How does it withstand the Aoratosian conditions?" Alex said.

"That's my favorite part. The suit's artificial intelligence can adapt to its environment; for instance, it can camouflage or disappear. All the controls are in the Life Support System unit (LSS) which provides both fresh air, constant atmospheric pressure, is impervious to radiation, and is heat-proof. The sleek suit can be used both in and outside the spaceship. Let me show you."

More information played on the screen describing the suit.

The sleek suit fabric was comprised of a lightweight magneto-phobic bilayer, designed with an inert material able to shield and reduce the amount of radiation by 90 percent. They were light and body-hugging. After the suits were on, they would not be removed until after the mission, when Spartan Enterprises engineers would reset the suit program. The outside of the suit was constructed using a supple superconducting material bi-layered to form a magnetophobic sheath. This flexible bilayer allowed the suit to have a soft exoskeleton able to fluctuate between a north and south pole in response to an external magnetic field, enabling the inside to remain homeostatic and unchanged.

"The same principle as the hydrophobic effect observed in lipids and oils and phospholipid bilayer in our human cell membranes," McKomic said. "Except that on the suit, the magnetic heads and tails are made from micro-superconducting diamagnetic molecules on the suit's exterior to produce a magnetophobic effect. They can change orientation in response to a magnetic stimulus in less than a millisecond."

An illustration played on the screen. The suit could respond to different conditions by rearranging these micro-magnetic molecules to allow desirable interaction. Along the suit's spine was a thin 400V lithium battery pack powered by a series of embedded micro solar panels. The battery was used to power the suit and power the magnetochrome pulse guns.

"The suit has self-sterilizing capabilities as well," McKomic said.

"Is that necessary?"

"It is. The planetary protection office won't authorize the mission until their required sterilization standards are met."

"Oh, O.K."

"I think we learned enough for today," Bosco said.

McKomic punched a key on the remote, and the tray transported them back out of the magnetron. Bosco went on to recite the rules for the upcoming weeks, and the recruits were dismissed.

"I know this is a lot to learn in a few hours, but you'll get it soon enough. You'll be playing with these every day," Bosco said. "We meet at 5:00 a.m. tomorrow morning."

McKomic and Doc exchanged their well wishes. Bosco, McKomic, and Doc took the elevator up.

A guard arrived and escorted the recruits to their quarters on the west wing above the magnetron. Their luggage was already there. It was a big room with several sleeping pods arranged into a triangle in the same large room.

"Did he say 5:00 a.m.?" Yvette said, pacing next to Max.

"Right," Max said.

"I'll be damned," she said. "That's—"

A crackling in the speakers interrupted her, followed by a female voice.

"Ladies and gentlemen," the voice said. "The lights will be switched off in five minutes. Good night!"

The recruits hurried to ready themselves for sleep.

From the small pod, Max observed the lights changing into crimson red and lime green. The artificial lights were tuned to mimic the predicted Aoratosian day and night patterns, he guessed.

Max stayed supine for a long time starring into the blank ceiling. He was going to make the most of it. *For Uncle Titus! For Aunt Dori! For Alonna! I will succeed*, Max thought. He smiled as sleep overtook him.

CHAPTER TWENTY

Kaligari Magnetron

MAX SCRAMBLED up in the middle of the night, awakened by the blaring siren and the incessant red emergency light.

"Radiation alert! Radiation alert! Evacuate the area!" the mechanical voice warned again and again.

He shook both Yvette and Geoffrey, who were still asleep.

"What—what is it?" Geoffrey said, still dazed.

"Come on, wake up!"

They both sprang from their beds. The other recruits were up, too.

"What's going on?" Yvette said.

"Do you hear the alarm?" Max said. "We need to get off!"

"What the heck is happening?"

Alex jumped off the pod. "Let me see what's out there."

"No, don't open the door," Max said, pulling Alex back.

"Why? We have to get out of here somehow!"

"Yeah, but we need to find a better way."

"What better way?"

"We have to choose one."

By this time, everyone in the room was up, some scrambling to put on their day clothes.

"Do you think the magnetron just blew up?"

"I hope not."

"Maybe they are only messing with us."

"Whatever it is, we have to shield ourselves."

Max was already putting on his shoes, Yvette as well. They sprang towards the exits, where Max suddenly screeched to a halt, blocking Geoffrey, who almost flew over the edge, and part of his glove was smoldering from the radiation. Max managed to remove the glove and threw it into space where it burned up in a flash.

"Shoot! What the heck is this?" Geoffrey said.

"I have no freaking idea," Yvette said.

"We can't go over there. It's all contaminated."

"Radiation," Geoffrey said. "This is awesome!"

Everyone looked at him, prompting him to shut up.

Alex was looking through the small binoculars on her wristwatch.

"What do you see?" Max said.

"Nothing, only some mountains far off," he said, handing the watch to Max.

Their building stood on an elevated ramp covered by dense smog. Far off were shadows that looked like clusters of mountains and glens faintly visible in the distance under the half-moon. The platform shook vigorously. The front side of the concrete broke off the wall. They rushed back and forth along the steep edges. The quarters shifted and vibrated in a disorienting way. A wave of freezing cold air swept in.

"Damn. We gotta block that hole."

"We don't have time. This thing is falling apart," Max said. "We gotta find a way out now!"

They went back into their room and scrambled to find an exit. After a few minutes of fruitless scrambling, Max stood up and said, "Where are the sleek suits? We gotta find the suits!" he shouted.

"We don't even know how to use them!"

"We'll find a way!" he said. "You remember Bosco said we should trust our instincts."

"He said we should not touch anything."

"Screw that! Unless you want to die here. I'm getting out!"

"The suits are downstairs in the casing," Yvette said.

Max jumped off and ran down the stairs.

"We can't go down there," called Yvette. "The lower ramp may be already be compromised."

"We'll find out," Max called. "Are you coming along?"

"Are you sure about this?" Yvette said, edging down the staircase.

"I'm getting out of here," Max said. "You can come with me if you want." Max handed them their suits.

Max, Yvette, and Alex tussled with the suits, with repeated trial and error, clicking and undoing before eventually getting them to work. Max shot through the ceiling on the first attempt. They were finally able to activate the MPB suits. Max pressed the red activation button, and the suit snapped and compressed tightly to the skin.

"How did you do it?"

"It tells you what to do!"

"All right, let's go!" Max said.

Max extended the tip of his suit glove at the edge of the unstable ramp into the radiation fog. Nothing happened.

"I think we are good," he said. "Ready?"

The others nodded.

He stepped into the fog, staying on the leeward side of the ramp.

Yvette followed hesitantly, and so did Geoffrey. Fortunately, the ground was firm.

"Hurry up!"

They air-walked towards the mountains. A giant lizard sprang from the ground and swallowed the recruit still waiting on the edge, afraid to walk into the radiation fog. Halfway along the walk, a huge red-hot ball hit the ramp, blowing it to smithereens, and with it several more recruits. Max tried to run toward them, but Geoffrey and the others held him back. They ran to the other side while the monstrous lizards attacked. As they got closer and closer, the mountains were transforming into stairs, around images of a screen. They climbed up the stairs and staggered up the barricade. There were only seven of them. Everything cleared up, and the makeshift landscape retracted into the walls.

"I'll be damned; this is all a hoax!" Geoffrey said.

"I don't think so," Max said. "Did you see what happened to my glove back there? That was real."

"And the strange creature, and all that stuff. It really ate that guy!"

"It did."

"That was messed up!"

"It's a simulation," Yvette said.

"Like Bosco said earlier."

"I didn't think simulations would be so real?"

"Like a freaking life-size reality game."

"3D to a whole new level. This is real!"

"I hope that's what it was. What happened to the others?"

"I don't know. Carlos and Mike decided to stay back."

Shortly after, Bosco entered the room and everyone froze. They immediately scrambled into a single file.

"Fellows, you are up so early!" he said.

"Man, what was—" Max said, catching his breath.

No one answered, even though the crew wanted an explanation.

"So you made it past the first training exercise," Bosco said. "Sorry for the impromptu first day of training. I would like to go over the details, but we got no time for that."

Flustered, everyone remained quiet.

"Who ordered you to get off the ramp and to put on the suits?" he said.

Bosco paced back and forth scrutinizing the recruits. They remained silent.

Max cleared his throat and said, "I did. It was my fault, sir."

Bosco paced to face Max and looked him directly in the eyes.

"Why is it your fault?"

"It was my idea, sir. I started the suits."

"Does that make it your fault? Did your friends stop you?"

"They tried, sir."

"Oh, did they?"

"Yes, sir!"

"Then why did you carry on?"

"We had no choice. The whole ramp was falling apart, and we couldn't get off the ramp into the radiation. We had to find a way out. Someone had to do something, so I went for the suits. I trusted my gut."

Bosco clapped his hands in a somewhat sneering manner, scrutinizing everyone.

"Yvette, why did you listen to Max? Why did you get off the ramp?"

"We had no choice, sir! The suits were the only way out," she said.

"You did not answer my question. I asked, 'Why did you listen to Max?'"

Max glanced at Yvette appreciatively.

"I trusted Max's judgment."

"Good job, Mr. Folksay. That's leadership. You saw a problem, and you acted. You saved your crew. You will need that skill on Aoratosia," Bosco said, a tinge of acknowledgment softening his stern face.

Max remained quiet, unsure of what to say.

"Congratulations. You passed the test."

"This was a test?"

"Yes," Bosco said.

"Like anything else, it's a video game. You're in the game, and I am in charge of moving the pieces around. Think of it like that. This whole complex here is a simulation that can be manipulated to mimic any mission we design. In your case, we mimicked Aoratosia. Congratulations to all of you standing here. You passed your first training exercise."

"How?"

"AI. That's why it's called the magnetron. We can manipulate matter within these walls to any forms that we want based on algorithms we input."

"You can do that?" Geoffrey said.

"Basically transferring energy from one form to another, and vice versa. And it's true, we are the only ones who can do this on Earth.

"Three of you have already given up. Gone!" he said. "I was watching from the control room, and I'm impressed at how you cooperated, being able to get together. Now, I know most of you are wondering where the other three went. Home! They failed and are done! More of you will join them soon!"

The recruits remained silent. They did not like the sound of Bosco's statement.

"When you are out there, you don't know what's waiting for you—
I know you're all saying, 'We're scientists, and there's nothing to worry
about,' but trust me, there is a lot to worry about. You don't know
what's waiting for you out there, wild animals, cannibals. I don't
know, anything bad you can think of. Or maybe the opposite is true,
which would be nice. In either case, you need to work together. If you
stick together, you can accomplish this mission. If you don't, then we
are all doomed."

Bosco turned on the projector screen on the wall and replayed what
had happened.

"Panic is deadly. Some of you ran into the radiation. And died.
Some decided to stay behind. And died. The point is you have to work
together. The team has to be compatible, and you'll develop that. An
essential part of any mission is chemistry and the ability to think as a
team. I'm impressed most of you passed the first lesson."

Faint smiles among the recruits.

"So the others are coming back?"

"They are done," Bosco said. "There are no second chances on this
one. The ship only takes four people, and only four of you will remain
at the end of this training. If less, then so be it. I would rather have one
strong person than a bunch of wusses!

"This is not one of your science projects or some hiking trip with
your buddies. You are invading a planet. Most of you will quit, guaranteed! You're not guaranteed to come back. So if any of you want to
back out now, this is your chance."

No one moved.

Bosco continued, "I hope you all understand. No human has ever
done what you're about to attempt. There's a chance of not coming
back, dead or alive, of never being seen again," he said, and paused to
make sure the message sank in. "My job, our job, is to make sure that
doesn't happen, by any means possible. You're all young and can do
something else with your life. This is your chance to balk and leave if
you are scared. No one will judge you. There will be more nights like
today here. And a chance to be remembered in history."

The candidates remained silent, muscles tensed.

Bosco paused for a while, popping gum into his mouth. He stood in front of Geoffrey.

"Why are you here?"

"Sir. To train, sir!"

"Is that what this is?"

"Yes, sir!"

"Why are you not playing video games at home?"

"Sir, this is all I ever wanted!"

"Really?"

"Yes, sir!"

"Good. You'll need all that motivation to get through training! Trust me, it's not going to be fun."

"Yes, sir!"

Bosco moved to the girl standing next to Geoffrey, Sarah.

"That's not the way you wear the suit. But not bad for a first day."

Sarah stood mute. After a few moments, she could not take any more of the tension. She set her mouth and silently left the line, picked up her stuff, and left the room.

"Any of you want to follow her?"

No one moved.

Geoffrey instructed the remaining recruits to remove the suits and rack them in the incubator.

"Everyone, follow me!" Bosco said.

Bosco exited the playground through the west entrance's heavy metal doors and climbed up the staircase. They passed a few offices before reaching Dr. Cluck's office.

They entered Dr. Cluck's office and occupied all the chairs in the waiting room. A few minutes later, an old man in an unbuttoned white lab coat, with a heavy limp, entered. Dr. Cluck was a jolly man, probably in his late 60s, the facility's head physician.

"Today is a good day," Dr. Cluck said with an enigmatic smile. "I've waited ages for this."

Dr. Cluck greeted everyone with a firm handshake. He opened the exam room door and let everyone in.

"Good morning, Doc," a mechanical voice said from behind the door.

"Hey, Ulysses."

"Everyone, welcome to the newest addition to the team," Doc said. He pointed to the shiny metallic cuboid droid with a large screen on its belly. The bot produced some clicking sound, wheeled to the center of the room, and said, "Hi, everyone. My name is Ulysses. It is nice to meet you."

"Nice to meet you too," Max said.

"Smartass," Geoffrey said.

"I do not like foul language, Mr. Foster," Ulysses said. "You can call me doctor."

"The robo doctor," Yvette said.

"I do not like that name, Ms. Yates. Call me 'doctor'," Ulysses said.

"That will work," Yvette said.

Everyone laughed while Ulysses looked puzzled.

"Did you create him?" Geoffrey said.

"He has been in the works for a decade now," Dr. Cluck said. "Ulysses is two years old. I actually did most of the initial programming," he said. "Ulysses is like an accessory. A medical reference kit. Basically, a medical database, with some ability to interact with humans and diagnose diseases and emotions and offer treatment recommendations."

"That's awesome!"

"It is, isn't it, Ulysses?"

"It is awesome, indeed, Dr. Cluck."

Everyone laughed.

"Ulysses helps me with medicine. He can cure most of the health conditions. And his intelligence is increasing with all the patients I treat."

"I'm starting to like this place," Geoffrey said, beaming.

"That's good, because Ulysses is the newest member of the team," Bosco said.

Dr. Cluck opened the Styrofoam box he brought into the room. "All right, let's get started."

One by one, Dr. Cluck went about applying an ointment across the area under each recruit's right ear with a swab, much to the amusement of the recruits, most of whom dodged his first attempt to do so.

"Don't worry," he said. "It's sterilization ointment."

Everyone sat in the chairs lining the front of the examination room opposite Dr. Cluck's desk. Bosco stood leaning on the wall next to the desk. On the other portion of the extended room was an examination chair, machines, and some other medical paraphernalia. Dr. Cluck brought a plastic casing to his desk and retrieved a small package.

"All right, ladies and gentlemen, I present to you the lucky stone," Dr. Cluck said. "This is an otic microchip. Anyone ever heard of this?"

No one answered.

"I thought so. It's recent technology. The chip helps improve coordination and balance," he said. "It works by interrupting the brain's impulses sent from the utricle in your ear to the cerebellum. It's been clinically tested to treat balance and coordination."

"What is it made of? Metal?" Geoffrey said.

"No, it's made from otoliths from a rare deep-sea fish species, with a hint of silicone coating. So far, as far as we know, that's the only known creature with the capability to defy gravity and pressure changes.

"Humans can flourish in any condition given enough time," Dr. Cluck said. "Since we don't have eons to adapt, what we have done here is induce the process faster and in a reversible way."

Bosco jumped in and said, "The microchip is designed to counteract Aoratosia's magnetic field by changing direction with reference to the magnetic field around it." He pointed to the illustration. "Whereas the natural rods function like this, the movement of the microchip gives the brain information about the body's perspective in space, thereby deceiving the coordination parts of the brain as if the person were on Earth under normal gravity and pressure."

"Well said," Dr. Cluck said. "The chip has a different specific gravity than the rest of the body, and its vibrations in response to a magnetic field are out of phase with those of the body. Its position allows it to emit pulses to counteract any variations. In doing so, it affects how the brain perceives balance. This helps prevent the feeling of disorientation, or lightheadedness if you will, that might occur whenever a human being is subjected to this amount of gravitational pull."

"That's really cool!" Geoffrey said.

"So how does the chip function on humans?" Max said.

"Good question. That's exactly where I was going next," Dr. Cluck said. He explained using the animated video on the screen.

"Same way. The chip is implanted in the area below the utricle. It acts like a gravitational sensor that monitors field changes in space and sends frequencies to the brain that maintain balance and coordination. It shifts depending on your position to prevent nausea and lightheadedness by counteracting external vibrations including magnetic fields, which you will likely experience on Aoratosia.

"I'm going to implant the microchip just under your vestibules, that area I swabbed. It's not as bad as it looks, as you shall see," he said, holding the drill with a long flat needle with his shaky hands, like a possessed executioner, which left cold sweat on many of the recruits. They wondered how he was even able to use that needle. Most of them were contemplating whether or not to go through the seemingly traumatizing ordeal. All of a sudden, the cooperative recruits turned cold at the thought of having the implant. Remembering Bosco's gut-chilling threats from a few minutes earlier, everyone hated Dr. Cluck at that moment—his smile, his large brown glasses, the sunken eyes, and the long white coat—like a punisher after the apocalypse.

"How safe is this thing?" Alex said.

"Safe. Clinical trials in humans have succeeded."

He looked at Alex, who still looked unconvinced.

"We've also tested the chip in rodents and primates—monkeys and chimps, and they seemed to operate fine under extreme gravitational and magnetic conditions, similar to what we're expecting on this mission. Here's a demonstration video."

"So we're sort of part a clinical trial?"

"Not really. This is the real deal. It's not medication, so it doesn't affect anything."

Everyone was still not convinced.

"Have you looked into what happens after using the chip?" Max said. "Say adjusting to your old environment after prolonged use of the chip in another environment. The long-term effects?"

"Yes. The baboons exhibit normal function, and they adjust to their old environments as if nothing ever changed. The human sensory system is similar to a baboon's, so it should work the same."

Dr. Cluck showed them a live two-minute video from one of the cages containing baboons in a highly magnetic and gravitational field. The primates hopped and chattered like those under normal conditions.

"Positive?" Alex said.

"So far, yes. But you cannot guarantee what will eventually happen in individuals."

"Guys, I feel bad about this," one of the recruits, John, said. He dropped his notepad and left the room.

"Let him go," Bosco said.

Dr. Cluck smiled and continued. "One more thing: The chip is also programmed to allow us to track each one of you."

"So for balance and tracking?" Alex said.

"Correct."

"Now, if you don't have any more questions, let's begin. Who wants to volunteer first?"

"I will," Max said, without thinking.

They lined up for the treatment. Max sat on the examination chair. Three leather straps wound around his body, one above the ankles, one above the knees, and another around his trunk. Two rubber pads clamped his head and neck, in a position to make sure the incision was made in the right place. The doctor felt the under-ear area by hand palpations, marked it with a sharpie, and inserted the needle. He seemed to know every part of the neck. Max wanted to ask him how many times he had done this, but the local anesthesia from the swab had kicked in.

He watched the doctor's shaky, shriveled hands holding his ear. He focused on the bald scalp sparsely spotted with patches of thin gray hair, the few strands of hair clinging to his bare scalp, above focused eyes—his voice blubbering like a psychopath's on a binge spree, ready to perform a forbidden ablation ritual. Max felt a pinch as the doctor made the small incision with the surgical blade over his numbed flesh. He gnashed his teeth as Dr. Cluck drilled the square needle into his skin, and the ordeal was over.

"Done!" Dr. Cluck said, wiping the area with an alcohol swab and bandaging it.

"Great!" Max said. "That wasn't as bad as I thought it would be."

"Yup, it's not bad."

Despite his outwardly weary body, Dr. Cluck did the job with impeccable smoothness. It left Max wondering how many people the doctor had poked with that same machine. He could barely feel the incision. Next, it was Geoffrey, Alex, and two others.

Yvette was at the back of the queue, pale. Max walked over to her.

"It's really not that bad," Max said, rubbing the puncture on his neck.

"I hate needles!"

"How did you get that tattoo?"

"That was at prom. I was wasted. When I woke up the next morning, it was there."

"Bad girl!"

They laughed. "A misstep, I guess," she said.

Her turn to step on the examination chair came up. Yvette's face flushed.

"Relax. Take a deep breath," Max said, smiling reassuringly.

Yvette inhaled and exhaled deeply.

"You can do it. It will be over before you know it. You ran a marathon, remember?"

"Like you've done it before?" she said.

"If I can take it, you can. The baboons can take it."

"Right!"

Yvette smiled, her face loosening. She stepped onto the strapped chair platform and closed her eyes. From the moment Dr. Cluck touched her neck, Yvette erupted into an anxious continuous laugh that left everyone fearing she was going to choke herself. Dr. Cluck had to shake her to stop her when the procedure was done.

The cafeteria siren rang, and they were dismissed.

"Eat more, whatever you want; today is your last day to eat that food in a while," Bosco said as they headed up the stairs.

The cafeteria was packed. Max had never seen so many white and blue coats in one place. The recruits sat in one corner and enjoyed plates full of pot roast, fried rice, and broccoli.

∾

THE NEXT EIGHT weeks flew by, the recruits coping with the intricacies of preparing for the mission. Each passing day was proudly making American history. The mission was showing no signs of stopping. Bosco was right; the group had whittled down to four. Only Max, Geoffrey, Yvette, and Alex were left, and they encouraged each other to stay together and hold up.

In the following weeks, they spent 14 hours every day practicing a host of maneuvers and drills that Bosco thought were necessary for their survival on Aoratosia. These included experiencing weightlessness, emergency response drills, combat, communication, and control tactics, with occasional number solving and puzzles. Sometimes they would trek and jog to the top of Mount Kaligari. This training was supplemented with high-altitude simulators in the magnetron facility every day during the drills. Max had clearly emerged as the leader, so that at times Bosco would call on to Max to get the others to act. Max had been reluctant at first, but Bosco reminded him of the importance of having a leader on a team. The team depended on him.

The training included various exercises to create a bond among the crew. A big chunk of that time was with their mind coach, Kai-Eliud. He preferred both names, as he said, his friends had always called him by the two names growing up, and it was weird hearing only Kai. After hours and hours of mind reprogramming, breathing to achieve a unique sense of consciousness and awareness, they were ready. The routine was the same for days. It was judo drills, shooting, and meditation; judo, shooting, and meditation again. Kai-Eliud, the hired monk, spent hours and hours teaching them how to focus and harness the energy around them—to control their energy and thoughts and avoid distractions. Kai-Eliud said this was the most important thing.

"The only thing that matters is your mind," Kai-Eliud would say in his graceful but powerful Vietnamese accent. "Focus. The rest is noise."

"Master the simple things," he said. "We, ourselves, are what we fear the most."

They repeated these sometimes monotonous, procedures for weeks. The training, the simulations, meditation, and mindfulness all chiseled their emotions to that still calmness, steel strength—a compass, an ideal that Kai-Eliud claimed was the only essential to this mission's success. This introspection went on for weeks until the drills were second nature.

The procedures required great precision and brilliance. After weeks of conditioning, Aoratosia was real, they could feel her, and they were ready—no more fear. It was scarier getting out into the world again, even more than going on the mission.

As weeks and weeks wore on, they were emerging from the chrysalis of shock from the brutal training. The training became more fun as they pushed further and further. Even Bosco's exacting attitude towards the trainees was waning as time went by. They were forming a biunivocal relationship—the crew and him. A great dyad. Bosco was smiling more often.

"I've been thinking," Bosco said, one morning during a water break when he unexpectedly brought water for everyone. "It's a good thing we are in the same reality; otherwise I would lose my mind. I keep thinking of all the possibilities out there."

He paused, staring blankly into the air.

"Your team has a chance to change the world and the history of mankind. To do what my team and I were not able to do."

His face turned pale. None of the crew said anything. Max finally said, "Are you all right, sir?"

"I'm fine," he said. "I was afraid you would fail, but you proved me wrong. Your training is done. I think you're ready. Your shuttle is coming to get you tomorrow."

"Tomorrow?"

"Yes!"

Everyone stood startled, wondering what was on Bosco's mind.

Bosco took his tablet and threw an image onto the TV in the breakroom.

"A report came in last night from our analytics department

confirming the launch window for the day after tomorrow. They have confirmed the teleporter wave will be stable for approximately three days, and they said it will take 12 hours' round trip to Aoratosia."

He waited to see the reaction of the crew. Everyone looked confused, as if they had not known that this day was coming. Max broke the silence, wiping sweat from his forehead with his t-shirt.

"So if we take 12 hours total of flight to and from, that leaves 60 hours for us to explore."

"And to collect as much data, artifacts and evidence as we can!" Yvette interjected.

"That's right," Bosco said. "Everything we trained for."

"That should be do-able," Geoffrey said.

"Yes," Alex said. "But we don't know exactly what's there. We're assuming it will be smooth."

"Come on; we practiced for this. We're one. We can do anything!" Max said.

"We can do this!" Geoffrey said, a smile visible under his now thick beard, grown long enough to graze his t-shirt. Geoffrey had made a bet to himself to keep his beard and observe the difference before and after the Aoratosia mission. "Woohoo!"

Bosco smiled slightly.

Everyone was excited, but the thought of leaving the facility was dreadful. It had become a home to them for the past eight weeks. They were afraid to go into the world. Afraid to be strangers somewhere else. Max was storing up many stories to tell Alonna.

"You have the opportunity to restore the faith and trust of the American people's ability to conquer the universe," Bosco said.

There was a brief silence.

"What happened on that mission?" Yvette said.

"What mission?" Bosco said, looking at Yvette.

"Zelda."

"Oh, that one. That was a hell of a mission. It paved the way to all this we're doing now," Bosco said, staring into the distance, his face pale. He said nothing more. His countenance said it all. None of the crew bothered to press him. There was no need for that. They knew this was a sensitive subject. After all, the media and conspirators had published their own versions of the story.

The Zelda mission to Mars had tested the public's trust and resulted in the stifling of funding for any future Project ASHE endeavors. After the trip, Bosco had left NASA and completely withdrawn from anything to do with spacefaring. Maybe guilt or resentment, or remorse. He believed he could have saved his crew. He had failed. However, McKomic had managed to persuade Bosco to work for him on a new exciting project—project ASHE, as the chief engineer. That's how Bosco started working at Spartan Enterprises in Kaligari. To him, this was a powerful incentive and a second chance to redeem himself. He was not going to fail. He believed that was his life purpose.

Even though the Zelda mission had failed, as Bosco felt it had, many people considered it a steppingstone in space exploration. He was relentless in making sure his team had not perished in vain. After joining Spartan Enterprises he had worked relentlessly to develop Zelda in the hope that one day he would be able to accomplish what they had started, and clear his crew's names. After the news of Aoratosia, it didn't take much for McKomic to convince him to join. In some way, he had personally volunteered to train the crew. He had experience; he knew what his team had lacked—the caveats that played a vital part in their mission's failure. He wanted to make sure that none of those mistakes ever happened again.

"I think you all are ready!" Bosco said.

He stood up and took badges from his handbag. He pinned the Captain badge on Max's suit. And tagged officer badges on Yvette, Geoffrey, and Alex. Yvette was the chief researcher; Geoffrey, the pilot in command and engineer; and Alex, the chief engineer.

"Captain!" Bosco said, saluting Max.

Max laughed, as did the rest of the crew. Everyone was excited.

"Teamwork, trust, and compatibility. Always remember that!" Bosco said.

"Now, there's only one issue left," Geoffrey said.

"Which is?" Bosco said.

"What should be our crew name?" Geoffrey said.

"I don't know. You decide."

"The Teleporter Crew!" Geoffrey said.

"That sounds so mainstream," Yvette said.

"How about The Pioneer Crew?" Geoffrey tried again.

"I don't like that one," Alex shot in.

"The Quadruplets!" Yvette retorted.

"No way. Not gonna work," Geoffrey said.

"Coldbox," Max said softly.

"Say what?"

"Coldbox. That's it. We're Coldbox!"

"Coldbox? Why Coldbox? That sounds so boring and archaic," Yvette said.

"That's what McKomic calls the ship. Yvette, you're always complaining that it's cold inside the capsule. Plus, it's fresh," Max said.

"I kind of like the name. It's unexpected!" Geoffrey said.

"I second that," Alex said.

"All right, Coldbox it is," Yvette said.

Bosco was silent, smiled, and stood up.

"All right, Captain, officers! Playtime is over. Let's finish the remaining drills and get ready to take off," Bosco said, trying hard to remain serious.

They frowned and hurried to their designated training stations.

Later that day, the Coldbox stamp was made and plastered onto the area above the Spartan Enterprises logo adjacent to the front windshield.

The crew looked on, imagining what was about to come.

CHAPTER TWENTY-ONE

Kennedy Space Center Launch Complex 39A, Houston

THE LONG-AWAITED DAY ARRIVED. Max sat silently in the reflection room situated next to Conference Room 2. The press conference was to be held that afternoon at the central station. The past few days had been a rollercoaster of mixed emotions for Max as everyone worked assiduously toward departure. For the first time in his life, he felt butterflies in his stomach. He had lost his appetite. For the past few days, Max had relied on yogurt and apples, with peanut butter and jelly sandwiches—his appetite seemed to have deserted him. He could describe exactly what he felt. It was the thrill of restlessness, bewilderment, excitement, anxiousness, nervousness, fear—all in one. Of stepping into the unknown. His brain felt like a lightning rod, thousands of thoughts rumbling in and out of his head all at once. Meditation practice in Kaligari came in handy and was helpful. His brain wanted to think—scary, anxious thoughts. He could not let it.

He had barely slept the last couple of nights, often waking up two or three times per night after having nightmares about Aoratosia. He could not grasp that all the things he had dreamed of while working on Titus' project were finally coming to light. He would be on Aoratosia in a few hours. The NASA anthem's melody seeping through the hallway reminded him of why. He hummed the tune. It always made him feel better.

Yet despite all this, he felt energized.

Geoffrey entered the room. "Are you good, man?" Geoffrey said, slapping Max's shoulder.

"I'm fine," Max said, trying hard to mask his annoyance at Geoffrey interrupting his quiet moment. "What's up?"

"Your folks are here."

"Oh, man, time is flying! Thanks. They called me before they left the hotel." Max got up from the chair and stretched. "Your folks here too?"

"Nope, only me," Geoffrey said.

"But you told them, right?"

"No. They don't think I do anything special. My parents have never liked what I do. They think it's a waste of time."

"Really? Why?"

"My dad wanted me to inherit the family business. But I'm not into that stuff!"

"Your brothers and sisters?"

"I had a little brother," Geoffrey said. "He died when he was six. Since then, I barely talk to my parents."

"I'm sorry, man," Max said. "But be thankful that you still have them."

"I guess so. Good for you to see your folks here."

"It would've been nice if my mom and dad were here," Max said.

"I thought they were in the group," Geoffrey said, evidently surprised. "They are not coming, too?"

"No, I was adopted. Oh," Max said, catching himself. "Those are people from my church back home." He stared blankly into space before continuing. "I never knew my parents. My mom left me at the front of a missionary church. I am sure my father was some thug or the like. The lady in the wheelchair is my aunt. She and my Uncle Titus adopted me as their nephew despite criticism from their friends."

"I'm sorry, man," Geoffrey said. "I know you must miss your parents."

"I don't really miss them or care about them much," Max said. "I

240

had all the love any child could get from great guardians. What more could I ask for?"

Geoffrey nodded but did not say a word.

"I'm sure your family will be at least watching," Max said, patting Geoffrey on the shoulder.

"Thanks, man," Geoffrey said.

Max and Geoffrey entered the foyer, packed with people—relatives and well-wishers. Max stopped mid-step. He suddenly felt some nostalgia. *What am I going to tell them?* he thought. He had not seen Aunt Dori or Alonna in more than three months.

The launch was scheduled at 9:00 p.m. Max embraced Alonna and Aunt Dori, their eyes all filling with tears. Max spent the rest of the evening with them, trying to block all the ensuing tension before the launch, recounting his adventures in Kaligari. Many family members of the crew were there in the auditorium to provide emotional support before departure, to lend some strength and encouragement.

Max, Alonna, Aunt Dori, and some church members had lunch at the in-house cafeteria on the third floor. Soon after, Max ran off for a quick press conference. Most of the questions were directed at Max, as the captain of the team, and at one point he had to defer some to Geoffrey, Yvette, and Alex. He had no interest in any media hoopla. Still, he understood it was all part of the procedure—a public relations campaign for Project ASHE and a strategy to engage the support of the taxpayers.

As the day began to wane towards launch time, thousands and thousands of revelers thronged the streets to witness this once-in-a-lifetime launch. People stood all the way to the viewing pads outside the air force station. They were entertained by live countdown commentary on the jumbotron facing the viewing pads. Hundreds of millions of Americans were glued to their TVs awaiting the launch. Some of the local firms and schools had made the day a holiday as the city celebrated the ascension of the mission to Aoratosia.

∾

THE LAUNCH WAS BROADCAST on live national television and thousands of other streaming services. McKomic appeared live from Spartan Enterprises. On that day the TV station netted a record-breaking number of viewers for any event in media history. There was jubilation all across America.

"Good evening, America," McKomic began, in his familiar, simple, sheepish enunciation.

He wanted to be the one to personally announce the name "Coldbox."

McKomic applauded the American spirit of learning and adventure. He thanked the teachers, from kindergarten to higher education, who had continued to offer the best education in the world to American children. He also pointed out that better education was the foundation for America's growth to the top of the world and was the reason why America had stayed there, always attracting people from other nations who sought better education and freedom. He commended the scientists for their determination to explore the universe.

McKomic then commended his team at Spartan Enterprises, specifically Doc, who had been a mentor and inspiration. Calling it a concerted effort, he thanked NASA, President Blanchard, and her administration for their determination and efforts to pursue excellence and their exceptional service to the nation by supporting AI. McKomic also encouraged younger people in all areas of study to follow the example of the crew in pursuing their dreams. He said the team was a testimony to how dreams came true with persistence, no matter where one was from. Max was also the firsts astronaut to discover a planet and part of the youngest team to go on a space expedition of this magnitude. "I mean, who has ever been featured in ten high-impact scientific journals in the same week? That's wild! Even to me," McKomic said, chuckling.

The crowds responded with thunderous applause.

Lastly, McKomic thanked and introduced the remaining crew members. "Please welcome," he said grandly, "the Coldbox crew!"

McKomic thanked them for their brave efforts and willingness to explore uncharted airspace and wished all of them good luck. He thanked them for being Earthling ambassadors in another world. He said they represented the pride of America to the whole world who was witnessing this event. He hailed American pride. The crew walked across the stage amidst great fanfare. Fans clapped and cheered as if the launch validated their wildest space fantasies. McKomic concluded by challenging the American people to keep up their spirit by supporting "projects like these" and encouraging young people in the crowd.

"Lastly, this is about this team," he said, pointing to the crew. "They show us what our youth can accomplish with determination."

The crowds applauded loudly at the conclusion of McKomic's speech, followed by spontaneous singing of the Apollo anthem. Thousands of voices rose in unison across the viewing pad's expanse. It was surreal.

After McKomic's address, Max was dumbfounded to find his social-media following going from only 27 people to 50 million in a matter of an hour. He got some phone calls from well-wishers and from close relatives who informed him that the paparazzi were storming his undergraduate institution to get its take on Max. Several newspapers, including the *Houston Tribune* had released a front-page headline that read: "WHIZ KID FINDS SISTER EARTH"; "GENIUS OKLAHOMA KID LEADS DARING YOUNGEST TEAM INTO SPACE"; "OKLAHOMAN TO CHILL ON NEWLY-FOUND SISTER EARTH." The media and public frenzy elevated him to the level of a genius. These stories were filled with Max's background, all that the press could uncover from his college friends and purported long-lost friends who supposedly knew him years ago. Who does not like an underdog story? Whether fact or not, these stories and speculations fed the hungry public. Anything was possible! Max just wanted to leave Earth for a while already.

As the clock ticked towards 7:00 p.m., Aunt Dori and Alonna were invited for a light dinner with family members of the crew as they bid each other farewell. All the excitement that had engulfed them was creeping into sadness. They did not want to let each other go. The room was filled with melancholy and excitement as the family members offered their best wishes and farewell. Max hugged Aunt Dori. Reverend Kay asked Aunt Dori to pray for the crew and the mission. With the hands of friends and family interlocked, Aunt Dori thanked the Lord for planning this event and she said she knew the Lord had a plan and it was a plan for good, and not to harm Max and the rest of the crew. She prayed for safe sailing in the skies. Max felt motivated and refreshed after the prayer.

A huge "Amen" echoed across the hall at the conclusion.

"Thank you," Max said.

"You can't believe what happened in Stratford," Aunt Dori said with a broad smile. "The mayor declared it a half-day so that everyone can watch you. All your friends."

"That's nice of him to do that," Max said, smiling. Aunt Dori looked calm; she didn't seem the least bit worried. Max wondered if she even felt the intensity of the moment. He admired her courage.

"I am proud of you, son," she said, hugging Max tightly from her wheelchair. "I'm sure your uncle would be very proud of you. That's all he ever wanted."

"Thank you, Aunt Dori!" Max said.

Max then turned to Alonna. Saying goodbye was one of the things he had dreaded about the mission. She wrapped her hands around his shoulders. She looked tiny against the bulky flight suit Max was wearing.

"Promise me you'll come back soon!" Alonna said over the noise, tears filling her eyes.

"I will," said Max. After a few seconds of thoughtful silence, he said, "I will be back before you know it."

He smiled and kissed her gently. "For you."

She smiled.

"I know you will," she said. "I'm just scared."

"You and me both. It will be all right. It's only a few weeks."

"I'm going to miss you, Max."

He held her waist.

"I am going to miss you, too!"

The crew arrived at the airfield with great fanfare. Dozens of well-wishers packed the pavement leading to the launch site, shouting their farewells. There sat Coldbox, mounted on a massive rocket which stood many meters high off the launch pad. White smoke billowed from underneath the base gridiron. The bold red and blue "COLD-BOX" insignia smiled at the marveling crowds. It was victory. An American flag waved on top of the spaceship.

Max and Alonna stood a few yards from the ship's entrance as the clock wound down, neither wanting to let go of the other. Alonna dreaded the thought of missing Max. The ship's engines were already warming up and white smoke from the burning aluminum perchlorate and kerosene rose from the bottom of the rocket, engulfing them both, causing a transfiguration effect. The gale from the ship's engines ruffled Alonna's hair swiftly, causing it to stand vertically. The story later became the toast of the media as they developed some prince and princess stories out of the image.

"I am sorry, Ms. Price, but Max has to go now," said the guard, about to close the barricade nearest to the rocket.

"I have to go!" Max said, freeing himself from Alonna's hands on his shoulders. "I'll be back before long."

"Take this. I made a scrapbook for you," Alonna said. "I want you to record everything that happens there."

"Thanks, I will."

"I'll be waiting for you when you come back!" she said, darting backward.

"I love you," Max said.

"Go!" she said.

Max let go of Alonna's hand. The security guard snapped the "no crossing zone" orange barricade that separated the spectators from the takeoff zone. Max jogged to the ship. Security then escorted Alonna to a safer place where Aunt Dori and the rest of the specta-tors were gathered to view the launch. The diapers Max wore under the flight suit felt slightly uncomfortable as he jogged up the small stairs.

The crowds were now singing the Apollo anthem in unison. The jumbotron showed 20 minutes to go. The crowds counted down. Two large screens captured Coldbox, and the other one showed action from the Saucepan.

"Geoffrey, Geoffrey!" someone was shouting over the noise.

Geoffrey was standing at the spacecraft entry step. Geoffrey turned and noticed his mother shouting and crying. He jumped off the step and ran towards her. They hugged over the barricade.

"Mom! You came!" Geoffrey shouted, tears in his eyes.

"Yes, we did, son," she said. "How could we miss this?"

"And Dad too?!" Geoffrey said, in disbelief.

His dad arrived and hugged Geoffrey. "I'm proud of you, son."

"But how did you know?"

"We have been following your success since you designed that popular app."

"We were in the Bahamas on vacation when we saw it in the papers this morning. I told your father we had to come back immediately. I couldn't live with myself if you left the planet without saying goodbye."

"Thank you."

"No, thank *you*!" his mom said.

"Listen, son, I'm sorry for not believing in your capabilities," Geoffrey's father said. "It's been a hard time for all of us. But you have taught me that it's the best idea to pursue your dreams and not get caught up with what others want you to do. Look at what you have done here. You will be remembered forever. Your mom and I wanted to let you know that we are proud of you!"

"Thanks, Dad."

The voice from the jumbotron advised the crowds to stay behind the barricade and put on their noise cancellation headphones and polarized goggles.

Geoffrey's mom kissed him on the cheek. Numbers danced down on the jumbotron, with the crowd chanting as the countdown began: "Sixty. Fifty-nine. Fifty-eight—"

"I love you, son," Geoffrey's mother said. "Now go find this planet!"

Geoffrey hurried to the craft as more smoke billowed from under the ship and the engines revved even more loudly. The staircase retracted into the capsule. The hydraulic doors screamed into place, dissipating the noise from the crowds and the massive engines. Peace engulfed the capsule.

The crew waved at the crowd through the capsules' small

windows, then vanished into the interior control chamber to their respective seats. This was happening.

"Everyone ready?" Max said.

Everyone nodded.

"O.K., let's roll!" he said.

"Yes, sir," Geoffrey said, placing his headset. Max and Yvette sat next to him with Alex on the other side.

"One, two, over. Coldbox clear to ascend. One, two, are we clear?" Geoffrey repeated.

"Coldbox clear, over! You're clear!" a voice responded from the other end.

"Copy that," Max said.

"Status check," Geoffrey said. "Everything is good to go."

The automatic seat belts tightened on their bodies, followed by a powerful thunderous roar that shot the ship into the atmosphere. A dense whirlwind glare of cylindrical steam from the Saucepan shot into the sky, disappearing into the clouds. Thicker plumes bellowed under the launch gridiron as the counting wore down. Five, four, three, two, one. *Poof*. Coldbox was gone, leaving a cloud of smoke trailing behind her as she growled upwards towards the teleporter ring. Within 15 minutes, the crowd could see her no more, except for the trail of white smoke that marked her path. Alonna watched the ship recede until it was only the tip of the white streak in the sky. Soon she and everyone would be rushing to their TVs, to be updated with live images and messages from the crew members frequently throughout the journey.

"Ten thousand miles from the portal," Geoffrey said.

"Boost separation good! Rocket separation initiated!" Alex said. "Everybody prepare for transformation!"

Max pressed and turned the release gear knob next to his seat.

"Transformation activated!" he said.

The ship shook and whirled around as it transformed itself into a flat cocoon, releasing the rocket into blank space. Protective ammunition automatically assembled itself as programmed.

"Alex, activate shields."

"Yes, sir!" Alex said, turning on the electrostatic neutralizer shields.

Popping sounds crackled as the shields snapped in place, covering the capsule from front to the rear end exhaust.

"Shields intact!"

"Everyone sit tight," Geoffrey said. "Here we go! Impact in 60 seconds!"

"Let's do this!" Max shouted, showing a thumbs-up. Everyone reciprocated.

The ship burrowed into the teleporter ring. The spectators could only see a glare of staccato colors as the ship warped into space. There was jubilation at the Spartan Enterprises headquarters. Engineers and technicians high-fived each other. Doc and McKomic smiled; the first part was a success.

Drowsiness and serenity engulfed Max. He was back in time—the good old days.

Paleness. Whiteness. Colorfulness!

CHAPTER TWENTY-TWO

Aoratosia

THE SHIP BURROWED into Jupiter's magnetosphere. The obstacle detection system blared as the ship plunged into the clouds of smog blanketing Aoratosia's atmosphere, making it impossible to see outside of the spacecraft.

"Geoffrey, what's our status?" Max said.

"Shields. Check! Invisible mode. Check! Perimeter surveillance is good to go. Everything is set!" Geoffrey said.

"All right. Let's get this baby down!" Max said.

The spacecraft shook and rumbled, skirting through the surrounding magnetic field. The smog cleared out as Coldbox sailed down into Aoratosia's troposphere before shooting down towards the surface. Coldbox lurched heavily toward the ground, then steadied and slowly jolted to a halt, dropping the four shock-absorbing landing bars into the barren, rocky Aoratosia surface.

"Everyone good?" Max said.

"All good," Yvette said.

Exulting in the successful landing, the crew quickly set out to install probe AQ4. Everyone hurried to put their sleek suits on, anxious to explore their new surroundings. The blood-colored sun was lower in the sky, casting a peculiar tranquil red hue along the horizon. They had only a few minutes to get out and plant probe AQ4.

Geoffrey keyed the transmitter module. "Mission Control, do you copy?"

The encrypted signal was weak, and they waited a few minutes before a voice responded. The time lag considerably delayed communication with mission control.

The transponder squawked, dead silence, squawked again, then a breaking voice emerged from the transmitter. "Coldbox, copy that! What's your status?"

"Sharp! Coldbox landed. I repeat, Coldbox landed! Do you copy?"

"Copy that!" the voice said. Joyous chatter was heard in the background from the control station, many voices celebrating.

"Bounty?"

"Coldbox copy that." A voice came up again, after another five minutes: "Dispose the bounty!"

"Confirmed. Copy that, sharp!" he said.

Another wait.

"Copy that. Sleep time!" the voice said after a few seconds.

The radio crackled. Geoffrey dialed the transponder. No reply. Geoffrey disconnected the communication module to Earth, except for AQ4 live feed for security reasons, not wanting to expose Earth to Aoratosian beings.

They triangulated the area for a place to put the probe.

The crew was elated to finally reach Aoratosia. The enrapturing feeling of being on Aoratosia also brought fear, which was slowly transforming into a sense of foreboding. Everyone peeked out through the small windows into the bizarre landscape. They could hardly wait to leave. Clouds of dust and ash spurts engulfed the air surrounding the spacecraft. The outside was sluggish and hazy, reducing the visibility of the barren escarpment.

They expected aliens foraging the land—monsters and savages— but instead, everything was different. Inscrutable! There was no sign of life. The terrain was bizarrely bleak—the sterile craggy, scorched bone-dry landscape, the strange colors, the periodic electric sparks, the occasional giant plumes of steam and molten lava from the sparse fumaroles and volcanic cones. Yet, it was also serene in some kind of way. Everything was perfect in its form. The rock boulders, sand dunes, and the planet's aurora all merged perfectly. All captivating. How long had these structures taken to form?

"The cameras are in place, ready to scan the area," Geoffrey said.

A cluster of images streamed onto the central bubble hologram projection and the overhead screens in the control compartment.

The signal crackled and died.

"Geoffrey said, "Exactly as I thought."

"What is it?"

"I figured the interaction might be too much for our frequency, but no worries. We have a solution."

Geoffrey struck a few keys on the computer, and the images popped back again.

"Scanning the area. Nothing peculiar so far!"

"This is awesome!" Yvette said, snapping a picture with her camera.

The rest of the crew nodded.

"It looks like we landed in a hole," Alex said. "Look, everything is so rugged. See all this," Alex observed, pointing at the screen from the live video surveillance. "It feels like we are in a mine!"

Rugged, steep-sided hills punctuated the landing position and extended farther into the horizon.

"You're right," Yvette said. "I'd think this area was once a caldera or ghost crater of some sort. All these structures can only be formed by water, which means this area was once covered by water."

"Probably unstable," Alex said.

"Yup," Yvette said.

"What do you think happened to the water?" Geoffrey said. "It's so dry!"

"Evaporated," Max said, who had returned from the back room carrying a heavy bag. "I'd imagine being scorched by the massive heat from the asteroid."

"Maybe."

"Yet it looks beautiful and strange!" Yvette said.

The crimson light from the sun shed on the far horizon various colors over the bare ground.

"Look at the beautiful colors over there," Yvette said, sighing.

"It's chemical iridescence," Geoffrey said. "I suppose there are lots of metals and chemicals on the ground surface."

"And light-absorbing gases in the atmosphere can cause interference too," Max said. "Some radiation interference."

"Or could be particles from the sun interacting with Aoratosia's magnetic field," Alex said.

"As we predicted," Geoffrey said.

"One thing down," Alex said.

"Man, I can't seem to detect a single living thing. Nothing moving!" Geoffrey said.

"Let's get ready," Max said. "Yvette and Alex, you're coming with me."

"Can I go today?" Geoffrey said. "Tomorrow will be a big day and I have to stay here anyways for the rest of the expedition. At least I can say I stepped on Aoratosia. I can't go back to Earth without ever setting foot on this planet."

"O.K.," Max said. "Who wants to stay behind?"

"I will stay," Alex said. "Not sure how I'll operate the computers like you, though."

"Thanks," Geoffrey said. "You'll be fine. Plus, you've got Ulysses here to give you advice."

Ulysses made a squeaky sound of approval and said, "Anytime!"

"O.K., let's get ready."

Alex continued examining the surrounding for the next ten minutes, looking for a high point, while Yvette, Geoffrey, and Max prepared to leave the ship. There was still no sign of life—no plants, no animals, nothing!

"Let's see if we can find the highest point closest to the ship," Max said.

"Copy that!" Alex said. "I'm on it."

"All right!" Max said, "Time to go plant this baby."

Max loaded AQ4 onto his aeroglider, and waited as Yvette and Geoffrey mounted theirs.

AQ4 was outfitted with a camera and a radar system which would allow them to map, collect data, and study Aoratosia. Aoratosia Quest 4, short-termed AQ4, was a fourth-generation interspace communication data probe developed to be planted on Aoratosia, the fourth model in the power satellite lineup developed by Spartan Enterprises. The first did not work. The second was sent to Mars and recently exploded in orbit. The third was on Mars, relaying information back to Spartan Enterprises. AQ4 was the only way of communicating and sending data to Earth.

"I found a spot!" Alex shouted. "Not far!"

"That should be a nice vantage point," Max said. "Let's go!" The hydraulic doors opened with a hiss.

The thick heavy air from the dense smog and hot steam ejections made it challenging to aeroglide at first while they adjusted to Aoratosia's atmosphere. They hovered over kaleidoscopic magma ponds and navigated around the sparse hot steam ejections and small plumes of volcanic ash. The ground was barren and greenish. It was dark now. The infra-red night mode on the visor made everything greenish. It was difficult to tell which way was east or west.

The feeling of walking, well, air-walking on Aoratosia was overwhelming. Max had imagined what this place would look like for a long time, but he had never dreamt of walking on Aoratosia.

Alex watched the video feed, seeing a rocky hill about 40 meters higher than the ship's position. On top of the hill was a conical stone tower, with a sharp spire structure that looked like a hollow metal pole. Its end was attached to a coiled snake-shaped sculpture that became visible as Geoffrey's video zoomed in. The feature was about 150 meters tall.

"See if you can zoom into that," Max said.

Yvette's and Alex's gazes were now also fixed on the screen.

"Is that a fort?"

"Looks like a watchtower. Probably man-made," Alex said.

"We don't know that yet," Max said.

"Strange. Look at the structure on the top," Yvette said.

"Let's see," Geoffrey said, moving the camera control.

"Not sure what that is, either. Gothic design, maybe?"

"Similar to that."

Instantaneously, the top of the coiled structure sparked.

"Did you see the spark?" Yvette said, startled.

"I saw it. We gotta be careful out here," Max said.

Max stared at the image. *Fortress? Maybe not. Why that structure on the top? Necropolis? Looks like it.*

"Looks like an obelisk of some sort. Like the ones used by kingdoms a long time ago to map their conquests."

"Yes, it does!" Yvette said, zooming the image closely.

"Or maybe a necropolis," Max said. "Wait, that thing looks like a snake or dragon structure on top."

He paused the video.

Alex zoomed in on the frame. "It does!" she said.

"This freaks me out," Yvette said.

"Wait!" Geoffrey said. "It looks like the logo for our health department."

"I have always wondered where the caduceus came from," Max said.

"Snakes on a stick have been believed to possess vast medicinal powers from medieval times," Alex said.

Geoffrey said, "In the Bible, Moses created a snake on a pole so that anyone who looked at the snake would not die after being ill. I always thought that's where it came from."

"Probably," Yvette said. "So you think the beings here are some supernatural beings who look at this hill to be made well?" Yvette said.

"Or ancient kingdoms who looked up to the snake statue, I mean, if your suggestions are true."

"We don't know that yet," Alex said.

The snake structure was surrounded by a symmetrical stone fence, composed of only rocks without mortar.

"Probably sacred masonry geometry," Max said. "Anybody have a feeling that might be a religious monument?"

"I don't like that feeling, man," Geoffrey said. "We might have just offered ourselves up for sacrifice. I have heard this kind of stuff has powers to attract humans for sacrifice."

"Brace yourself, for thou art in holy land!" Geoffrey said, smiling, exaggerating the statement with his hands. Everybody giggled.

"I have heard the same thing about the Washington Monument," Yvette said.

"Me too. Mind-bending stuff. Same thing about the Stonehenge and Easter Island, too."

"Superstition! I don't believe in that crap," Alex said. "Some useful purpose must have inspired those who designed the structures," Alex said.

"Maybe visions were given to the architects."

"It would be nice if we could interview the designers about how they came up with ideas."

"They might not even know where the ideas came from."

"Maybe the two planets still communicate even after all this time," Yvette said. "Like two lost twins, no matter what happens they always connect when they meet."

"The universe works in mysterious ways," Alex said.

Yvette glanced at Max and Geoffrey. Max felt around in his pocket.

"All right, Alex," Max digressed. "How big is this structure?"

Alex entered some formulas on her computer, then said impishly, "About 120 cubic megalithic yards, I would say."

"Can you please say what we can all understand?" Yvette said.

"Oh, just trying to be archaic," Geoffrey said.

Alex said, "About 68.5 cubic meters from the base to the top where the sculpture starts, and 20 meters total height."

"That shouldn't be too bad."

"All right, let's keep moving. We have what we want," Max said.

"Don't you think it's too dangerous when the moon is the only light?" Yvette said, eyes filled with anxiety.

"There is only one way to find out. We should be fine," Max said, patting her on the shoulder before sealing his own helmet.

"They chose us for a reason," Geoffrey said. "We have a whole planet waiting for us to explore. Alex, how are the life-support systems?"

Alex typed on the keyboard. "The sleek suits are powered up, about two hours Life Support System, magnetophobic effect activated, radiation and pressure stable, shields activated, self-sterilization activated, and automatic armor ready!"

"That's plenty!" Max said. "Let's roll! And, remember, don't eat dirt!" Max said, snapping the opaque visor over his pressure helmet.

Everyone giggled. They nodded, and Yvette managed to say, "Got ya, Captain!"

"This is beautiful!" Yvette sighed.

"Yes, it is," Max said. "Somehow the terrain looks exactly as Earth's!"

"We should, uh—"

"What is it?" Max said, noticing Yvette had stopped.

"Did you hear that?" she said.

"All I can hear is lava shooting out of the ground," Geoffrey said.

"No, I heard something different."

"You sure?" Max said.

"You know my senses are impeccable."

"Are you sure you're not making this up?" Geoffrey said. "You may be getting paranoid. I think we all are."

Yvette gave Geoffrey the look.

"I'm sure it's nothing," Max said. "Let's collect some soil samples. Do you see this, Alex?" Max said, directing his head camera to a specific spot on the ground.

"Got it," Alex said. "I am working on a match right now."

They waited while Yvette drilled into the ground and collected a fistful of the sample into her side aerogel pouch. She sifted sand under the moonlight. The soil was crumbly with a few remnants of what seemed like petrified mollusks here and there. She forwarded the images and data to Alex for analysis.

"Hey Alex," she said. "I am sending some soil sample images now."

"Got them," Alex said.

They proceeded farther down the stretch, capturing more images.

Max ran his gaze across the horizon. *Were there any people in these barren lands? Were there any beings? What if they were watching us?* Yet, there were no signs of life. Max had always dreamt of meeting an alien. He had dreamt of a being with a strange face, wings, and talking in a foreign language—some unfamiliar sound, for that matter! Or some metallic being with superpowers, evil, and living in a barren land. With an artificial droid voice. Well, not here, in this still and tranquil yet lifeless expanse of land. A shiver raced down his body.

Max paused, thinking of what Kai-Eliud, the monk, had said. *After all, we are all cyborgs. Mortal machines. We are all searching that something deep down, call it a calling, that most of us spend our lifetimes fearing to encounter. Yet, it's the very thing that will make us alive. Maybe our selves are what we fear the most.*

"Hey, look! Rising! All four Galilean moons! That's Io, Europa, Ganymede, and Callisto," Yvette said, interrupting Max's reverie. She enjoyed flaunting her geophysical knowledge.

"How do you know all of them by name?" Max said.

"I paid attention in class," Yvette said.

They laughed.

"That's interesting," Max said. "Perfectly lined up."

Jupiter's four moons were lined over dark gray-bluish cumulonimbus clouds. A halo surrounded Jupiter's Europa with resplendent brightness, giving the dark clouds a grayish incandescent tint. The moons' linear orientation across the sky to the snake hill spire carried a peculiar feeling, as if directing the crew to the hill.

"It would be cool if we could see the other 59 of Jupiter's moons."

"Most of them are too small to see through the smog. Others may be on the other side of Aoratosia at this time," Yvette said.

They aeroglided to the hill under the moonlight. The tall conical tower became more evident as they inched closer. It was made from four massive boulders of flat rock, joined on top into a single point. There was no mortar binding them. The coiled snake-like structure wound around a pole extending from the spire of the boulders into the sky.

Two minutes later, they reached the bottom of the hill. They parked the aerogliders and began the steep ascent.

Climbing the crag was simple. The rubber gloves on the sleek suits made it easier to maneuver with less work. The crew noticed four other hill summits, all with the same snake-pole structures. There were various natural structures far off, including massive balancing rock boulders and cliffs.

"This reminds me of Arizona, or Utah," Geoffrey said.

"It does," Max said, securing a nice view by holding onto a gap between the rocks with one hand.

"Except you don't see sand dunes in Arizona," Yvette said.

"Come on, guys," Geoffrey said. "It still is a pretty close analogy."

"Look how calm it feels out there," Yvette said.

"I think the wind blasts in waves once in a while to form these structures," Geoffrey said.

"Guys, do you hear that?" Max said. "A sort of roaring?"

"I told you I heard something," Yvette said.

They paused.

A frightening loud screech came from inside the hill.

"Can you hear that, Geoffrey?" Max said.

"Yeah. I don't know what it is, though. It's coming from the other hill on our left."

"We'll find out. Stay flat to the rocks."

"Aaah!" Yvette screamed as Max barely finished the sentence. She lost her grip on the rock and slipped off the ledge. Max caught her hand before she plunged down. She was breathing hard. A black bird whizzed across from the rock crevice above their heads. Within a split second, a thunderous wave of birds whirred past the cliff and wheeled into the sky before veering away in a single transverse wave motion, fading into the crimson-stained horizon.

Geoffrey's gun was already drawn, anticipating an encounter.

"Those were birds!" Geoffrey said.

"There's freaking life!" Max said, struggling to pull Yvette up.

Geoffrey rolled over and helped Max. The three laid flat against the rocks until the birds were gone. Yvette's heart was still pounding, and she covered her face, breathing heavily but slowly.

"Dang, that was close!" Yvette said. She took a long, deep sigh.

"Nice reflexes, Max," Geoffrey said.

"Is everyone O.K.?" Alex said.

"Fine," Max said. "Just an unexpected noise."

"How is Yvette?" Alex said.

"Fine," Yvette said, gasping. "Man, that was close. Thank you."

"You're welcome!" Geoffrey said. "Man, that scared the crap out of me."

"All of us," Max said.

They lay flat for a few moments listening for more sounds.

"Let's keep moving," Max said. They clambered up to the top of the hill and lay on the flat surface.

"Stay as flat to the rocks as possible."

"Alex, did you get any images of the birds?" Max said.

"Yes, and audio, and I am on it now," she said.

"How much time do we have left on life support?" Yvette said.

"One and a half hours," Alex said. "Still plenty."

"Thanks!"

"I got a hit," Alex said.

She forwarded the results to their headsets.

"The camera captured blurred images of the birds, but I refined the image," Alex said.

As they proceeded up the cliff, the image appeared inside their facemasks.

"They look like swifts or swallows," Yvette said.

"Makes sense," Max said. "They tend to live on rock boulders in colonies."

"But when I ran the data for a match, I did not find any matches from our *Aves* database," Alex said.

"That's exactly what I was thinking!" Geoffrey said.

"Can you narrow the search by habitation?" Yvette said.

"Still no hits," Alex said.

"Maybe we identified a new species," Geoffrey said.

"Maybe," Yvette said. "Can I see the image of an Earth sparrow? I want to see them side by side."

"To you now," Alex said.

The image appeared on the facemask screen. Yvette scrutinized and juxtaposed the images. Evidently, there were similarities between the Aoratosia night birds and Earth swallows and swifts. It was a black bird about a firefinch's size, but with a long, slender forked tail.

"At least they do not have teeth," Geoffrey interrupted. "Thank goodness they are not vampire bats."

"It has features of both a swift and a swallow, including the forked tail," Yvette said. "And because they lived together, it supports the idea of communal roosting behavior common in both swift and swallow families."

"What do you conclude?" Max said.

"This is an ancestor to both swifts and swallows," she said. "Convergent theory can explain how swallows and swifts can evolve from the same ancestor."

"Or the other way around," Max said.

"True," Yvette said. "Or just a trait shift. Everything looks similar to a sparrow."

"But why haven't they evolved here like on Earth?" Alex said.

"Many factors may be responsible for that. The environmental conditions for one. Diet and other factors may account for that too."

"Wait a second," Max said. "Swallows and swifts feed on insects, so this may suggest there are insects somewhere close."

"Yes!" Yvette said, smiling. "And the insects feed on vegetation, which could be somewhere on this planet."

"Amazing!" Geoffrey said.

"But who knows? These birds travel very fast," Alex said. "They might be feeding very far from here and choose to roost here because there are few predators."

"That's a possibility," Max said.

"We now know there might be plants and insects here. That's all that matters," Yvette said.

"All right. You have one hour fifteen minutes," Alex said. "Remember the AQ4, people."

"Almost there," Max said.

They hastily assembled AQ4 on the summit of the hill. The rock gave way against the drill-head. Sparks spurted out against the drill. Jupiter's moons provided sufficient lighting. Doing things in the dark offered a safer and comfortable environment despite the faint sound from the drill head as it crashed through the rock. The crew preferred to work in natural light. After a few Earthling minutes, the probe was ready.

Geoffrey powered AQ4 on, then entered a few numbers on his handheld device. They waited for a few seconds.

"Alex, do you copy?" Geoffrey said. "I finished priming AQ4."

"Loud and clear! Tracing the data input now," Alex said. "Tracing, imaging, and motion-sensing also activated. Everything is good to go. It should be able to relay images to Coldbox now."

"What range do we have?" Max asked Alex.

"I activated the coordinates; we should be able to monitor the radar system within a 100-mile radius from our location," said Alex.

"Good," Max said. "We're heading back now."

"We should check out that structure there," Geoffrey said, coaxingly. "Let's see what was making those sounds."

"Can we do that, Alex?"

"You have plenty of time."

They walked cautiously towards the spiraling snake column sculpture. The structure was made of mortar-less rock boulders. They drilled a hole for a micro camera to explore the hollow interior. Max hand-controlled the camera using a joystick. Careful not to hit the walls, Max guided the micro camera into the slit. A live feed of the inside appeared on their facemask screens.

"Can you see the feed?" Max said.

"Yes," Alex said.

The inside of the hollow shaft was filled with running turbines and gears, almost forming a mega carburetor made from rock boulders. The top consisted of a jet, which ejected a gas into the turbines. Below were pistons running and another jet providing a liquid flow, which egressed the compartment through a narrow canal and disappeared into the ground. On the far left were huge reservoirs connected to aqueducts leading to the outside of the chamber. Max directed the micro camera into one of the collecting pools to collect data.

"Did you get that?"

"Yes," Alex said. "I am working on it."

"Careful, all. This is unique," Geoffrey said. "What is this thing?"

"Trying to find out," Alex said.

Max stretched his hand and mistakenly moved the camera, which snapped and crushed between the giant gears.

"Oh, snap!" Max said.

"Uh-oh!" Yvette said.

"A million-dollar device, gone," Geoffrey said.

The video feed died. Yvette stared at Max.

"My bad, guys!"

"It happens," Yvette said. "Good thing we got most of what we need to analyze the structure."

"You must head back now," Alex urged.

They packed their belongings and quickly descended the hill. They jumped on the aerogliders and drifted towards the other hill to look for the source of the roaring sounds.

"You have 45 minutes left," Alex said.

"That's plenty," Max said.

They were startled by hovering of wings followed by munching and mooing sounds, a roar, but cut into forced, short, repeated bursts of air out of the lungs. Immediately a massive bird with two dangling legs hovered over them and disappeared on top of the nearby hill.

"Was that a dragon?" Geoffrey said.

"No, Geoffrey. It's not a dragon," Alex said. "You believe that crap?"

"It sure looked like one," Yvette said.

"That's a folktale," Max said. "Those things never existed."

"Don't be so sure," Geoffrey said. "You never know what to expect in a strange land. I am scanning the footage from AQ4 to see if we captured it."

There was a brief silence.

"I got it!" Geoffrey said, exhilarated. "I'm sending it now."

The video popped on the head screens. This time they had stopped the aerogliders and hid behind one of the extended rocks.

"That's a pterosaur!" Yvette said, "Look at the ornate crest."

"How do you know that?" Max said.

"The elaborate frill around its neck, and on the wings and tail. That's gotta be it. I had a collection of dinosaurs as a kid, and the pterosaur was my favorite. I vividly remember that."

"You are right. I looked up similarities with our known dinosaur records, and it matches the pterosaur perfectly," said Alex.

"That's cool!"

The noise from the hill was increasing. After a few seconds, six of the winged reptiles emerged from the hole and flew overhead in circles.

"I think we have disturbed them. I read somewhere that they have a good sense of smell," Yvette said.

"They are sniffing around."

"Be careful. They're carnivorous," Alex said.

The three lay flat on the rock and whispered.

"What are they doing here?"

"Probably roosting season," Yvette said. "You see, they are in twos."

"How do they survive extreme hot temperatures?" Max said.

"They have thick scales to retain water, which cools them off," Yvette said.

Right then, one of the pterosaurs emerged from behind a promontory of rocks and flew towards them. It flew high, surveying the area, and then suddenly descended like a bullet towards them. There was nowhere to hide. They lay flat in the grooves of the crag. The pterosaur attacked and pecked Geoffrey out of the groove, making even louder sounds. The other birds shot towards them, screaming. Max immediately flashed his flashlight and lunged towards the winged reptile, momentarily blinding it. It let go of Geoffrey, letting out a hoarse sound, then lunged towards Max. Max ran down towards more rocks.

"Go!" Max yelled at Yvette and Geoffrey.

The winged reptile picked up the chase again, this time towards Max with the flashlight. Max dove to the side into a crevice between two large rocks, wedging himself into the narrow space beneath the rock overhang. He shrieked at the pain in his chest, unable to move. The bird dashed and squatted over the rocks pecking its beak between the rocks. Max struggled to move. He was stuck. The winged reptile tried helplessly sticking in its long-pointed bill, its hacksaw-sharp teeth a few inches from shredding Max's head. It snarled, its round oversized eyes even more determined, its wedge-like long teeth chipping bits of the rocks with each attempted blow. The pterosaur produced sounds, splattering and dripping its slimy drool from its bill onto Max's helmet. The drool soaked over Max's facemask, and some almost dripped into his earpiece. The other pterosaurs from the rest of the pack were now roaring more loudly, but none got close, as if they were mere spectators, maybe afraid of the animal with the prey—probably the alpha. The animal continued scratching the rocks with its giant talons, and the rocks moved slightly.

Another pterosaur approached, most likely bored by how long it was taking the other to get at their meal. The alpha pachyderm vehemently lunged towards the other, and they squared off. The skirmish was filled with biting, roaring, sharp cries, and humping. Max realized his opportunity, pulled himself out of the rocks and ran towards the aerogliders, where Geoffrey and Yvette were hiding, at the hill's base. They could still hear the roaring of the dinosaurs in the distance.

Before they mounted the aerogliders, Yvette took a saliva sample from Max's helmet and sent it to Alex. Then they flew.

"Guys, I got the DNA sequence results," Alex said.

"That was quick. What did you find?" Yvette said.

"The genetic profile matches that of pterosaur remains excavated on Earth from our ancient DNA database. Specifically, the Pterodactyls family of dinosaurs."

"We were right then."

"Yes," Alex said. "But I also found some differences in the epigenome. I'm forwarding the results to your headsets."

"This is unreal!" Yvette said. "The genome between the two is identical, but the epigenome is different. The Earth pterosaurs and Aoratosia pterosaurs are the same species but may have had different fates."

"How so?"

"We can look at the chemical changes to the DNA and compare the two DNA sets. The superficial modifications to the DNA can switch genes on and off. As you can see, unlike the Aoratosia pterosaur, the Earth dinosaur epigenome shows a lot of methylation compared to the Aoratosia one."

"Is that important?"

"That can explain why Earth dinosaurs went extinct," Yvette said. "Methylation turns off genes, and—"

"Could an entire species be wiped out by changes in the epigenome?"

"That's possible. If the genes turned off are for fertility, then, yes, I can see a species going extinct."

"But what would cause such a change?" Max said.

"The environment can be a huge factor," Yvette said

"An asteroid can definitely do that," Geoffrey said. "The sudden temperature increase could have changed the epigenetic code of Earth dinosaurs, shutting off genes that were important for survival."

"Precisely," Yvette said.

Max nodded but still looked unconvinced. "What about other catastrophic events after the asteroid hit? The environment or climate changes, like the ice age, glacial cycles, plate tectonics."

"You're right," Yvette said. "That could have caused that as well. We are only throwing ideas around right now. But all those are possibilities if the time frame matches."

"I still don't get it," Alex said. "Why would the pterosaurs survive here when the impact was on Aoratosia, not Earth?"

"You're right, Alex. That doesn't make sense," Max said.

"Wait," Geoffrey said. "Unless the pterosaurs never belonged on Earth. Can't you see?" Everyone was listening. Geoffrey went on, relishing the attention. "We find a few fossils on Earth but never actually see dinosaurs. Got here, saw dinosaurs in person. I'm starting to think maybe dinosaurs were just visitors to Earth. After the separation, those that stayed there went extinct because of the climate change."

"That would mean the climate between the two sister planets was different?"

"It's not that hard to fathom."

"That actually makes some sense," Yvette said. "The oldest excavated dinosaurs in the national genomic library have the same profile as Aoratosian dinosaurs."

"That can't be right! That would imply that the separation caused the extinction of dinosaurs."

"It's possible!"

"Then that changes everything!"

"And we have always believed otherwise," Alex said.

"We believe in a lot of things," Geoffrey said.

"It makes sense," Yvette said. "Last year's fossil record excavated in the Western Sahara showed that the first dinosaurs had existed many years before the Mesozoic period, way earlier than we had initially estimated. Which correlates with the time the algorithm predicted the separation occurred."

"You might be right, there," Max said.

"Meaning dinosaurs were alien to Earth?" Alex said.

"Maybe. It's a theory," Geoffrey said.

"It will change history," Yvette said.

"Genius," Max said. "But that would mean we have been learning lies for centuries."

"It's science, baby," Geoffrey said. "That's how it works. Ideas evolve. Old ones get scrapped all the time, replaced by new ones."

"I like this trip already!"

"Me, too," Yvette and Alex said in unison.

By this time they sailed the aerogliders within sight of the spacecraft.

"Look!" Yvette said. "Is that a plant?"

Everyone stopped their aerogliders and looked in the direction Yvette was pointing.

"I think so," Max said.

"Where?" Alex said.

Geoffrey moved his camera around.

"There!" Alex said. "See if you can zoom in on that?"

Geoffrey zoomed the camera.

"Is that a cactus?" Yvette said, edging closer to the screen.

"Looks like it is!" Geoffrey said.

"Those features are exactly the same as some kind of cactus," Yvette said. "It does look like a cactus."

Everyone could not hold their excitement. *Plants on Aoratosia.* More smiles. The cactus-plant merged from the cracks at the bottom of a hill, shielded from wind and sun.

"More life!" Max said.

"We should get a sample of the cactus for analysis," Yvette said.

"You sure about this?" Max said.

"C'mon! I'll do it," Geoffrey insisted, already jumping off the aeroglider, with his jackknife in hand.

"Be quick," Max said.

"Be careful," Yvette said.

"I got this!"

Geoffrey approached the cactus. He squatted with his back toward Max and Yvette and stuck the knife into the cactus.

A shrill cry emanated from Geoffrey's direction.

"What the heck is that?" Yvette said.

"This thing! This!" Geoffrey stammered. Before he could finish the sentence, the cactus creature sprang up from the ground and glued itself to Geoffrey's helmet, emitting a loud shriek, its huge eyes changing color. The cactus kept expanding, morphing into a balloon-like blob covering Geoffrey's head. Geoffrey staggered, his arms wrapped around the creature, unable to see, all the time stabbing with his jackknife. The creature was almost engulfing Geoffrey. Max withdrew his MPG and fired, careful not to shoot Geoffrey. The bullet ricocheted off its skin. The cactus was almost cutting into Geoffrey's oxygen pipe.

"Stop moving around!" Yvette said.

"I can't! I'm stuck!" Geoffrey yelled helplessly.

"Aim for its eye!" Alex yelled.

"Stand still, Geoffrey," Max said, steadying his gun.

But Geoffrey could not. Dazed, he winced, flailing his hands and trying to free himself from the blob.

"*Pht!*" Max shot again. This time the ghastly creature emitted a deafening scream.

Yvette and Max fired at the cactus creature, which eventually fell down, with slimy fluorescent green-blueish exudate oozing from its corpse. They stomped it until it lay motionless. Max slashed it open with one blow using the jackknife and pulled Geoffrey's head free. He chopped off the creature's feeding tentacles emanating from deep in its oral cavity. They were glued firmly onto Geoffrey's helmet, some of them almost piercing the eye mask.

Geoffrey lay flat on the ground gasping for air, his sleek suit covered in the milky greenish slime and prickly glochids.

"Come on, Geoffrey," Yvette said.

"We're out of time," Max said. "Let's go. There might be more of them coming after that cry."

Geoffrey staggered and steadied himself towards his aeroglider. Max and Yvette helped Geoffrey onto his aeroglider.

"You think you can ride?" Yvette said.

"I can. Let's go!" he said, still dazed.

"Watch your step. There may be more!" They sped off.

"What was that?" Yvette said, while they were aerogliding.

"I have no freaking idea!" Max said. "The thing erupted from the rocks and expanded like—man!"

"A cactus monster," Yvette said.

"How the heck does it survive here?" Max said.

"Looks like a symbiont of both a cactus and an animal. The best of both worlds. Feeds on inorganic chemicals and minerals here, probably. A lithotroph of some kind," Yvette said.

"But those organisms are supposed to be microscopic."

"On Earth, yes. But that looked like an advanced life form. A symbiont. Hell, that's the only way something can survive in this area."

"Cactus and animal symbiont?"

"Possibly. That's the only reason I can think of."

"Or just a plant," Yvette said.

"Plant? With all that movement?"

"We've pitcher plants on Earth that eat whole mice and rats. There may be bigger species that eat bigger animals."

"That's scary," Max said.

"Alex, make sure Ulysses is ready!" Max said.

"Got it!"

"Sensor software updating," Ulysses' mechanized voice said.

"I feel lightheaded," Geoffrey said.

"Hang on, almost there," Max said, as they made a beeline for the ship.

CHAPTER TWENTY-THREE

Coldbox

THEY GOT BACK with only two minutes left on the suits' life-support systems. Geoffrey leaned on the aeroglider and relied on autopilot to get to the ship. Alex and Yvette helped Geoffrey through the high-pressure decontamination chamber.

Geoffrey felt his head begin to feel lighter yet. "I need to sit down!"

"Hang on. We are almost done—"

Before Max could finish, Geoffrey collapsed to the floor.

"Alex, is there a way to hurry decontamination?" Max said.

"I'm afraid not. We don't want any contamination from outside," Alex said.

"Damn that. Geoffrey just passed out," Max said.

"Let me expedite some stages," Alex said.

Yvette held Geoffrey's motionless body, checking for a pulse. He was still breathing.

"You are good to go," Alex finally said, after what felt like an eternity.

Max and Yvette hurried him into the examination room. Alex and Ulysses were already waiting.

"He's unconscious!" Max said. "Hurry!"

They placed Geoffrey on the examination bed. Ulysses scanned

Geoffrey's body from head to toe with the red laser on the retractable module emanating from his trunk.

"What happened?" Ulysses said.

"He was attacked by a cactus," Max said.

"Cactus? That's a plant, Mr. Folksay," Ulysses said.

"Yes it is!" Yvette said.

"Seems like Mr. Foster suffered an infarction, in other words, an acute heart failure," Ulysses said.

"How did that happen?" Alex said.

"Mr. Foster suffered a leakage in his suit oxygen tubing. And that lack of atmospheric pressure caused bubbles to form in the blood, which caused the heart to fail."

"Can we fix it?" Max said.

"Yes, Mr. Folksay. I can mend it quickly."

"All right, let's do it. What can we help with?"

"Is he going to be O.K.?" Yvette said.

"Oh yes, Ms. Yates," Ulysses said. "He will be fine. Some rest should help. He should be fine in a few minutes once we flush out the air bubbles. I need to open his vein to drain some blood and allow the bubbles to move, and we have to do it quickly before they get to his brain."

"O.K., Ulysses. You know what to do," Max said.

Max and Yvette held Geoffrey down while Ulysses made an incision on Geoffrey's neck, and a jet of blood sprayed out onto the plastic covering the area. He then closed the opening with a tissue adhesive, then placed a bandage over the small wound. Ulysses elevated the bed to a steep incline, and hooked drips containing Geoffrey's blood type into his arm.

"What's that for?" Max said.

"This should allow the blood to push through the heart," Ulysses said.

They all nodded.

"Will he be well soon?" Yvette said.

"Oh yes, Ms. Yates," Ulysses said. "He will be up soon."

They sat around the bed quietly, listening to the faint beep on the

EKG. After exactly five minutes, the beeping of the EKG grew rapid and louder.

"He is breathing!" Yvette said. She got up and held his hand.

Geoffrey coughed and faintly opened his eyes. "What happened?" he said in a feeble voice.

"Rest and we can talk later," Max said.

Geoffrey went to sleep.

"Alex, is the perimeter surveillance up?" Max said.

"Yes. I activated the surveillance and motion sensors."

"Great. Let's keep our eyes peeled."

"He is stabilized now," Ulysses said.

The crew left the room and gathered in the control room with the chairs transformed into a lounge.

YVETTE SAT cross-legged on the lounger, squeezing a cup of hot chocolate with both hands. "That was quite a day!" she said.

"What a way to start," Alex said.

"Alex, anything new on the data?" Max said.

"Still running," Alex said. "We should be getting a ton of results in a few minutes."

Max nodded.

"What do you think that snake structure was?" Alex said.

"At first, I thought it was a megalithic monument," Yvette said. "Maybe a temple? But I don't think so anymore."

"Me either, after seeing what's inside. It's a machine."

"But how would someone get massive rock slates like that to the top of that steep mountain?" Alex said. "We didn't see any cranes and excavators lying around."

"That's the key question," Max said.

Alex punched the keyboard. "I'm running the footage on the software. Let's see if we can salvage anything helpful."

"Good."

"Where do you think those channels are going?" Alex said.

Max and Yvette clustered around Alex watching the screen. Alex played the video up to the point when the micro-camera crashed.

"Can't tell. Doesn't seem like there is any open water or irrigation around here as far as we can scan," Max said.

"Doesn't that seem strange to you? There is no freaking water here."

"There may be aqueducts taking the water somewhere?"

"I was thinking we can find a way to follow those aqueducts. Maybe it will lead us somewhere," Alex said.

"That's a good plan," Max said. "But how would we get in? The area is packed with gears. Plus, there sure won't be communication signals down there."

"I think we should start our search on the surface," Yvette said. "Then we do the aqueducts after."

"I agree," Max said. "I was thinking we could start here tomorrow."

He opened a separate page showing a series of black and white satellite images of Aoratosia's surface which Coldbox had captured during the descent while mapping for the best autonomous landing area. The photos were blurry but still provided a good outline of Aoratosia. Max pointed to an area highlighted with meandering lines.

"Why do you think we should head north?" Alex said.

"The landscape is different than anywhere else on these images. I bet we will find something there," Max said.

"That's the same direction the birds went, right?"

"Right," Max said.

"O.K.," Alex said.

"We sleep now, and tomorrow we head out to check out the dyke," Max said. "Hey Alex, did you find anything interesting in the soil samples?"

"Yes, we got a hit!" Alex said.

"Go on," Yvette said.

"The soil analysis is finished," Alex said, after a few seconds, pulling a paper from the mass spectrometer. She handed the pages to Max and Yvette.

"Anything interesting?" Max said.

"Yes," Yvette said. "The soil contains large traces of stishovite, silica, uranium, clay, and some mercury and shows high water concentration trapped in the rocks."

"That explains everything," Max said. "Stishovite can only be formed under high pressure and intense temperatures."

"An asteroid hit could be the only source of that amount of energy required for that reaction," Yvette said. "This might be indeed a meteor lake."

"That means we possibly landed at the impact point."

"And the uranium, too!" Yvette said, smiling. "After an impact, it leaves clouds of uranium dust that eventually deposit in the ground."

"That's true," Max said.

"Guess what else is enriched?" Yvette said, looking at Max.

"What?"

"Elixirium!"

"What is elixirium?" Alex said.

Max and Yvette exchanged glances.

"It's a chemical that I recently discovered on Max's necklace," Yvette said.

"Wait. Explain," Alex said.

Max removed the necklace and showed it to Alex.

"So you're telling me Max has a necklace made from an element we don't have on Earth," Alex said.

"Yes," Yvette said.

"How did you know it's elixirium?" Max said.

"I remember the infra-red spectrum. It was unique, like nothing I've seen before," Yvette said. "Highly magnetic."

"This is creepy!" Alex said.

"It is," Max said. "Hopefully we get some answers soon."

"We will look more into it when we get back home," Yvette said.

The spectrometer chimed. Alex opened the results.

"Guys, this is unbelievable!" Alex exclaimed.

"What is it?" Max said.

"The gas from the jet is carbon dioxide. There was no other match," Alex said. "And here is what doesn't make sense—the liquid in the reservoirs matched a simple sugar with a structure like this. The IR spectrum is very similar to glucose."

She displayed the chemical structure on the screen.

"So you are saying that machine uses carbon dioxide to produce a simple sugar?" Yvette said.

"That's what the data says," Alex said.

"Is anybody thinking what I am thinking?" Max said.

Everyone looked at Max.

"Aoratosia is maybe a self-sustaining bio-container," Max said.

"Explain what you mean," Yvette said.

"Look, the carbon dioxide, the monosaccharide; can't you see it?" Max said. "I think this machine is doing artificial photosynthesis."

"Basically, scavenging and cleaning the air," Yvette said.

"We have been trying to develop that technology on Earth for decades," Alex said.

"Exactly. I think this is the same concept except on a grand scale," Max said.

"So the liquid below was water, probably underground water. This is exciting," Yvette said.

"And scary too," Alex said. There was a brief eerie silence.

"Makes you wonder what else Aoratosians are capable of, if it is what we think it is."

"They can sequester water from the rocks and minerals and carbon dioxide from the air," Max said.

"That explains the tall structures into the clouds," Yvette said. "The machine extracts carbon dioxide from the dense cloud atmosphere and uses it to produce fuel."

"Man, we might be about to encounter some of the smartest beings in the universe," Max said.

"That explains why the air below the atmosphere is clear and probably clean," Yvette said.

"Tons of carbon dioxide from the volcanoes," Alex said.

"Sunlight?" Yvette.

"Maybe there is no need. I don't see any way they could see sufficient sunlight here," Max said.

"I have seen things like that before," Geoffrey said, from the background. They turned to find Geoffrey leaning against the wall, still pale.

"Geoffrey! You're supposed to be—" Yvette said.

"Resting? I know. But we have only one day, so I can't waste hours sleeping. I may be out of breath for a bit, but my blathering might help."

"O.K.," Max said. "If you say so."

"What were you saying, Geoffrey?" asked Alex.

"The structure with the spiral is a power generator, with turbines that use heat from the Aoratosia's core to produce energy or power. And they can do that because of elixirium. Those are not ordinary rocks. Elixirium is stronger than steel and resistant to high temperature."

"So, not the sun?"

"Probably not," Geoffrey said.

"But it wasn't hot up there?" Yvette said.

"Right," Geoffrey said. "It's an intricate system. They harness heat from the volcano to power the gears; they harness carbon dioxide and produce sugar, water from the rocks, like a water mine. That water is used for cooling the system. No energy is lost. It's a self-sustaining system."

"Man, that would mean Aoratosians have created their own biosphere," Yvette said, wide-eyed.

"I am getting excited about meeting these beings," Geoffrey said. "We may borrow some of their ideas to save our planet from the accumulating industrial gases. Can you imagine?"

"That would be awesome!" Yvette and Max said simultaneously.

"I'm starting to wonder. What if Aoratosians have more dimensions than ours?"

"That would be epic," Alex said. "We would get to experience that too."

"I'd like to see what my beard would look like in another dimension," Geoffrey said, caressing his beard.

They laughed.

"Guys, what exactly was that out there?" Geoffrey said, looking at the distorted image from his helmet's video.

"We are still waiting for the results," Alex said.

"Yvette and I thought it was a mutant cactus. That's the only plausible explanation. It hibernates in the ground and protrudes its sprout as bait for wildlife," said Max.

"We have protean plants and creatures like that on Earth too, like the snap trap," Geoffrey said.

"This had eyes on it," Alex said. "Look at these. It could freaking expand!"

"Like a freaking jelly balloon on steroids," Geoffrey said.

"Jumping and crying, too. That shriek was scary," Yvette said.

Everyone laughed.

"There might be more of those out there. We must keep our eyes open," Max said.

The machine beeped. Everyone looked at the monitor as the results displayed.

"You won't believe this," Geoffrey said. "Morphological analysis shows 70 percent physical similarity to that of cacti on Earth."

Geoffrey swiped the results to the big central screen.

"That's amazing!" Yvette said. "But our cacti don't move and attack people."

"We don't have cacti that both inflate and are carnivorous," Alex said.

"That leaves 30 percent non-similarity. I'm doing a rerun on the fluid in case I missed something."

"So we were almost correct then," Alex said.

"The genome is very different," Geoffrey said.

"That's possible," Yvette said. "We do have cryptic species on Earth: animals that are phenotypically identical but different genetically."

"So it's still a cactus then," Alex said.

"I think so," Yvette said.

"That's interesting," Max said. "Anything else?"

"A unique thing," Alex said. "It's got cryptic epigenetic markers. I couldn't get a hit from our database to map it out."

"That may answer our question," Yvette said. "Different epigenetic modifications can lead to a totally different creature regardless of similarities in the DNA."

"And also some mutations can completely change protein function even if the amino acid sequences look similar. And you end up with same species of animals with different behaviors."

"Which means it is a cactus," Max said. "But several generations divergent from our Earth cactus. That makes sense in an environment like this planet."

"Here's what more interesting," Geoffrey said. "Records from the Botanica Encyclopedia from the National Museum of Science in New York show that this type of plant is native to the Sahara."

"That is interesting," Yvette said.

"And exciting!" Max said. "We are getting answers very fast."

"I still can't get how the plant creature can survive in a hostile environment like this. It may feed on animals, but it looks like there aren't many here."

"They can extract water locked up in the hydrated minerals," Geoffrey said. "Remember we saw high traces of water in the rock samples."

"So you are saying the plant creature has a way of extracting that water."

"That's possible. I don't know how."

"But that's still not a convincing explanation why it can survive here," Alex said.

"Another possibility is that this creature feeds on hydrogen sulfide from the hydrothermal vents all over the volcanos on this planet," Max said.

"We have creatures like that back home too. Deep-sea mussels and giant tube worms live deep in the ocean and feed on bacteria, which feed on hydrogen sulfide as well," Yvette said.

"But we didn't detect any bacteria in the soil samples?" Alex said.

"Not yet," Max said.

"We might have to collect samples at the thermal vents directly," Yvette said.

"Maybe," Max said.

"So this thing can be anything or a combination of all those?"

"Precisely. A carnisulfovore!" Geoffrey said impishly.

Everyone burst into laughter.

"That works!" Max said.

"Genius!" Alex said.

"Ulysses, you got all this?" Max said.

"Right on, sir," Ulysses said in the background. "Everything is transcribed and secure."

"Good."

The radar detector bleeped.

"What is it, Alex?" Max said.

"Can't tell exactly," she said. "But the radar is detecting all kinds of sounds."

"Approaching us?" Max said.

"I don't know."

"Can you locate the origin of the sounds?" Max said.

"My monitor shows various peaks of increasing and decreasing frequencies, making me think the source is out of the 100-mile radius covered by AQ4."

"That's interesting," Yvette said. "I hope it's not more cactus creatures coming toward us." She could see dread creeping into the other crewmates' faces.

"Whatever it is," Max said, "the source of the sound might be very far from here. The dense microwave radiation here may cause the interaction with sound, which results in a radar effect that makes sound travel faster than normal over long distances."

"I didn't think of that," Geoffrey said.

"Meaning these sounds are maybe 200 or more miles away," Yvette said.

"Or even more," Max said. "The system can't predict that."

The sound increased and subsided in waves until it finally faded.

"O.K., let's keep watch for any changes," Max said.

"All right, good work, team," Max said. "We have a long day ahead of us. Now let's get some rest."

It was late into the night when they retired. They had discovered their first findings and pondered how they would transform Earth, politically and economically, if they could replicate any of this technology. Their findings today alone could literally reshape history.

Max tried to sleep, but somehow the thoughts of Aoratosians kept whirling in his head. The cactus experience frightened him: *What kind of beings were here? How would they talk to them? What's the proper etiquette here? Were they people like us or savages? Do they greet strangers nicely, like us?* he thought. His mind would not stop. He wished he could call home, which was prohibited. He had many things to tell Alonna and Aunt Dori. He withdrew the mini-scrapbook from his satchel, offered some gratitude, and recorded the day's events. He lay down facing the small window beside his bunk bed and gazed out into the quietness of the Aoratosian night. Max watched the Frisbee-sized moon sailing in the night sky. He perched his small 24-hour hourglass on the headboard and watched the sand drop slowly, occasionally dancing to the continual vibrations of the ship from the ground tremors. He felt O.K. so far; no motion sickness. Soon he would be home. He thought of Alonna and drifted with that thought into a deep, deep sleep.

CHAPTER TWENTY-FOUR

Area of Interest, Aoratosia

MAX GOT up at the earliest daybreak, euphoric for the day ahead. His body felt sluggish from the time change. He peeked through the tiny window above his bunk. All the haziness had cleared from the previous night's sky, and everything felt still and strange. The blood-red sun was visible, barely kissing the azure sky. It was confusing trying to determine which way was east given where the sun was. He flipped the compass on his wristwatch and acknowledged the position of the sun. A significant amount of sand had already slipped to the bottom of the 24-hour glass. There was no one else in the room, but there was a clinking, beeping sound from the corner as Ulysses rolled into the cabin.

"Good morning, Mr. Folksay," Ulysses said.

"Ulysses! I thought you were off," Max said.

"Off?" Ulysses said, squiggling, his tiny head screen moving side to side. "Yes, I was. Mr. Foster did turn me on."

Max nodded.

"I feel like I have slept a lifetime," Max said.

"It was only two hours," Ulysses said.

"Two hours?"

"Yes, Mr. Folksay," Ulysses said. "Nights on Aoratosia are very short, about two hours compared to that of Earth time, but the para-doxical space-time lapse makes it feel longer."

Max wiped his eyes, yawning. "It's definitely messing up my circa-dian rhythm."

"But the days are ridiculously long," Ulysses said.

"That's good for us," Max said. "I certainly don't need any more hibernation. That's more time for us to explore."

He walked toward the kitchen, where Yvette and Alex were sitting at the table.

"What's up, fellas?"

"Good morning!" Yvette said.

Max retrieved a protein smoothie from the fridge and joined them.

"Where's Geoffrey?" he said.

"He is in there, isn't he?" Yvette said.

"No. Only me!"

"Really. I thought he was."

"Maybe he went to the control room."

"I think so. Let's go check."

They left the lounge towards the control room.

"Where's Geoffrey?" Max said, looking at Ulysses.

"He's undergoing ice therapy," Ulysses said.

"Ice therapy? Where?" Max said.

"In the tub."

"Are you joking?"

Ulysses squiggled. "Mr. Foster is experiencing hypersensitivity anaphylactic shock. What you call an allergic reaction. His body temperature is above normal." The information about the diagnosis ran on Ulysses' trunk as he spoke.

"So the cactus creature was poisonous?" Max said.

"I believe so, Mr. Folksay. But Mr. Foster will be fine after a few hours," Ulysses said.

"Is it safe to get close to him?" Yvette said.

"Yes. It's not contagious," Ulysses said.

The crewmates hurried to the bathroom. Geoffrey lay in the tub filled with ice cubes.

"Man, you look like an oak on steroids," Yvette said.

"I know," Geoffrey said. "That cactus being really got on me. I feel like a specimen now."

Geoffrey touched his swollen face, eyes like tiny slits barely visible as Geoffrey struggled to open them. Almost unidentifiable. He mumbled some words in a funny mechanical voice, moving the ballooned lips that looked as if they might fall off. His computer was beside the tub.

Everyone laughed at the tragicomic scene.

"I'm glad it was me out there last night," he said. "I was gonna stay behind today anyways."

"You don't look so good. Anything we can do for you?" Max said.

"Not really. The doctor here said it will subside in a few hours. It's getting better now," Geoffrey said, looking at Ulysses.

"O.K. We are going to plan for today."

"I'm in," Geoffrey said, covering himself with a white robe.

They sat around the tub while Max went over the plan for the day.

"I wish we could just fly Coldbox there," Yvette said.

"That would be nice," Max said. "But it would be too conspicuous. Plus the ship has to port at the exact pre-mapped coordinates, otherwise we miss the teleporter."

"We are taking the aerogliders for easy maneuvering," Max said.

"I can control from here," Geoffrey said.

"Great," Max said. "You sure you got this?"

"Ulysses will help, right, buddy?" Geoffrey said.

Ulysses beeped. "I'll make sure you don't fall asleep, Mr. Foster."

Everyone laughed.

"The weather is beautiful today, but it's gonna be super-hot," Max said, looking at his tablet. "Let's get this done as fast as we can."

"You've 36 hours," Geoffrey said. "You have to be back before that time since the teleporter ring will be opening around the same time."

"That should do it."

"How ironic. We spent months training but only get two days to actually execute. We gotta do everything quickly," Alex said.

"That's why they say plan well, execute faster," Max said.

"True, time is not our friend. Let's roll," Alex said.

They hastily put on the sleek suits and loaded the rest of the equipment for the day. They prepared bowls of oatmeal, peanut butter, and milk and packed gear for the day. Max watched Yvette nibbling at her special gluten-free bars.

"Does it even work?" Max said.

"Yes," she said. "It does. I feel great these days."

Max laughed mockingly. "From a nutritionist?"

"No, I experimented on my own."

"I might need to do that at some point."

"You should."

Alex said, "Since we came here, our wind meter has recorded approximately zero wind flow. This place smells like death. There is no wind at all."

"I wouldn't be surprised if all this has not been altered for thousands of years," Yvette said.

"Standing on the sands of time," Geoffrey said. "Bring me some grains of sand for luck to take back home with me."

Everyone laughed.

"Are you ready?" Geoffrey said.

Max, Alex, and Yvette said yes.

"Everything looks good," Geoffrey said. "LSS positive for 36 hours, ammunition fully charged, and additional supplies all ready. Looks like you are ready to roll."

"Sharp," Alex said. "Let's do this. We are heading out."

Geoffrey punched a few keys on the tablet, and the hydraulic door slowly decompressed. Max, Alex, and Yvette hovered out.

THE CREW, feeling greatly elated, rode the aerogliders over the stark landscape, dust billowing behind them as they vanished farther and farther into the horizon.

They whooshed and meandered through narrow slits with a few bumps, spinning and sliding through the ridges and sand dunes. Sometimes the slits in the gorges were so narrow and clogged with rock pillars they forced the crew to ride in a vertical single file. They were all thankful for autopilot. An hour into the journey, they reached where the passageway split into a fork and chose to go to the right together. They rode for miles and miles with nothing of interest in sight. The desert went on forever—not a single life form.

"Woohoo!" Max said, while revving past a sand dune. "That's what I call aerogliding."

Yvette slowed down. "Guys, I think we're lost," Yvette said.

"You're on the right track!" Geoffrey said.

"Man, we've been riding for an hour and haven't seen anything that looks alive."

Max looked down at the navigation pane. "The radar detector still shows that direction."

"I hope it's right," Yvette said.

"I was hoping to see something by now," Alex said. "We have covered over 300 miles."

"We are getting close," Max said. "The life detector is beeping more frequently now."

"It's probably over the hills," Geoffrey said.

"Copy that!" Max said. "Guys, be extra careful here! Stay alert. We don't know what's on the other side."

Yvette and Alex nodded.

They slowed down as they approached the base of the hill.

"You wait here," Max said. "I'll go up and see what's on the other side. Cover me just in case."

"Copy that!"

Yvette and Alex situated their aerogliders in combat mode. Max hovered towards the hills and parked near the top. The life detector was beeping more and more as he approached the hilltop.

"Can someone turn that thing off?" Max said. "It's getting on my nerves."

Alex grinned and muted the detector.

"Be careful. We don't know what's on the other side of the hill," Geoffrey said.

Max furtively approached the top, crawling on all fours. He lay flat on the ground with his binoculars overlooking the other side of the hill. He remained quiet for a long time.

The others waited patiently.

"What is it? Yvette said.

"Whoa!" Max said.

"What's there, Max?" Alex said.

"Man, you were right! What is this place?!" Max said.

"What's up there?" Alex said.

Max did not answer for a few seconds.

"Guys, you gotta see this!" Max said, waving them over.

Yvette and Alex parked their aerogliders and hurried up the hill to where Max was lying. On top of the mountain, the desert gave way to a wide peninsula teeming with wildlife and vegetation.

"This is beautiful!" Yvette said.

"Geoffrey, do you see this?" Max said.

"I do. Wow! Can't believe my eyes!"

"Why is everything so purple?" Alex said.

"I think the plants here reflect the color purple while on Earth they reflect green."

"But why?"

"I don't know," Max said. "Might be that instead of chlorophyll, which is green, the plants here use a different pigment for photosynthesis, or whatever process they use to produce food."

"That explains what we saw earlier on the biosignature map of Aoratosia."

"Yes."

"This is magical," Yvette sighed. "I have never seen a place like this before."

"We're in paradise," Geoffrey said.

"We might be in heaven," Alex said.

"I wouldn't disagree with you!" Max said.

Max plucked a leaf from a shrub adjacent to them and forward the information to Geoffrey. They marveled at the sight.

Below the mountain range lay a vast peninsula. A river of crystalline blue water snaked down the middle of the valley and vanished into the forest. An expanse of sprawling purple vegetation edged the river on either side. The rising sun gave breath to the picturesque landscape. Wildlife wandered beyond the river. Mammals including gazelles, bucks, impalas, kudus, zebras, and many other herbivores roamed and bellowed along the stretch of the meadow in packs, enjoying the fresh, dew-rich, early-morning graze harmoniously. The purple grass formed a violet carpet along the base of the mountain range. About 400 yards ahead was a purple forest enveloped by dense fog. Patches of land were covered in thickets of yellow, white, pink, and purple flowers and shrubs.

The flowering plants gave the scenery divine tranquility. It was beautiful, as if purposefully designed by some great nature architect. Ladybugs flew by and flapped over the bright flowers close to where the crew hid. All kinds of colorful birds, including parrots and sunbirds, were clustered over the trees, basking in the morning sun, singing, welcoming the new Aoratosia day. They sang various melodies that brought life to the plateau. Small sunbirds hovered adjacent to the crew over the vivid purple and yellow flowers on the small shrubs, collecting nectar. A quartet of robins scratched the ground nearby, undisturbed by their presence. A gray-brownish eagle snatched a fish from one of the ponds along the river on the far right. The fish struggled helplessly before the predator disappeared over the forest.

"Wow!" Max said.

"That was unfortunate," Yvette said. No one else commented.

A company of gray and blue parrots scratched the ground close to them, swallowing roots, insects, and worms. Yvette moved, startling the birds. The rest of them flew and landed a few yards away, leaving one struggling to fly.

"I think it's injured," Yvette said. She walked over and picked up the bird. "What's up, little guy?"

"Waa cha kai!" the parrot in Yvette's hand said, bobbing its head. And the whole flock started singing the words "Waa cha kai, Waa cha kai!" The sound went throughout the plain like a wave as the birds responded to each other.

"Wow!" Yvette said. "They can speak!"

"I guess so," Max said.

"They kinda freak me out though," Alex said.

"Why?" Yvette said. "Parrots do that."

"What kind of parrot is this?" Alex said.

Max studied the bird and said, "I don't know, some kinda parakeet, similar to the African gray parrot."

"That's the Einstein of the parrot world," Geoffrey said.

Everyone laughed.

"I've heard that before," Max said.

"His leg is broken. I gotta fix it," Yvette said.

Yvette withdrew her first aid kit. She quickly glued a stick on the wing, wrapped it with dissolvable tape, and released the bird. The parrot did not want to leave and stayed on Yvette's hand.

"I'll call him Hubert," Yvette said.

"Why Hubert?" Max said.

"I don't know. I think it's cute, a cute name for a parrot."

Max cleared his throat and said in a coarse voice, trying to pet the bird, he said, "Hubert!"

As soon as Max finished speaking, the bird's ears rose, and he jumped up and down and pecked Max's hand.

"Damn!" Max said. "That was uncalled for."

Everyone laughed.

"See, he doesn't like you, or you making fun of him," Yvette said.

The whimsy parrot trilled, "Waa cha kai! Waa cha kai!"

Baboons and monkeys continuously chattered in the distant forest. There were other massive mammals clustered along the river.

"Dinosaurs!" Yvette said

"Looks like it," Alex said. "Look, there are elephants too, on the other side."

"I don't think those are elephants," Yvette said, scanning closely in her headset binoculars. "The tusks are too long and bent more than the elephants we have on Earth."

"What do you think those are?"

"Woolly mammoths!" Yvette said, looking into the binoculars. "So much fur."

"This is amazing. I have never seen anything as beautiful as this," Alex said.

"Let's go down there," Max said.

"You think it's a good idea?" Yvette said.

"Let's find out."

Max planted a small signal transmitter on the hill.

"Geoffrey, you got this?"

"Yes. I have the video."

"Awesome," Max said, climbing onto his aeroglider.

The aerogliders wouldn't start. Alex cranked hers four times, but it would not start.

"Something is wrong," Max said. "Mine won't start either."

"Mine, too!"

"How come mine is still working?" Yvette said, revving her aeroglider down. Soon after she reached Max and Alex, her aeroglider engine stopped.

"This is awkward," Yvette said.

"This is serious, man," Alex said. "If it's dead, how will we get back to the ship?"

"Hey, Geoffrey," Max said. "Any idea what's going on?"

"I am trying the best I can to see any malfunctions, but everything looks fine," he said. "I do have a hypothesis, though. Can you move one of the gliders back to the sand and try to start it?"

"Sure."

They pushed Alex's aeroglider to bare ground, and when she tried again, it started.

"Now fly it over the grass."

A few inches in, it blipped, rattled, and died again. Yvette moved hers as well, and it instantaneously met the same fate.

"I know what it is," Geoffrey said. "The aerogliders are designed to levitate against a magnetic field. And it looks like the area with plants has zero magnetic fields."

"How is that even possible?" Yvette said.

"It's a simple principle of magnetism. If you sprinkle iron filings across from a magnetic point, they spread away in ripples or ridges along the magnetic field lines. That might be the same principle here: vegetation is growing in areas of no magnetic field."

"Just as it is possible to experience zero gravity on Earth in some areas," Alex said.

"Yes. Sort of."

"I have produced simulated ground motion from using data from

AQ4, and I was able to model the behavioral history of Aoratosia from the asteroid impact point," Geoffrey said. "The magnetic field patterns show that the planet has two parallel fault lines, magnetic source points, which may be a possible cause for the zero magnetism. And it's where you are right now."

"So there are two magnetic core sources?" Max said.

"Most likely."

"Like a south and north pole?" Yvette said.

"Or east and west pole!" Geoffrey said. "It's all semantics."

"Can we figure out the latitude?" Max said.

"It's tough but possible."

"If we can figure that out, we will be able to tell where we are on Aoratosia," Yvette said.

"How do you mean?" Alex said.

"We can adjust our compasses relative to the magnetic poles."

"I see."

"Or this might be destructive interference," Max said. "What if the magnetic fields from the two poles of Aoratosia are in antiphase to each other so that when they intersect, they cancel each other? And plant life exists in those areas."

"Might be," Geoffrey said.

"I see what you're saying. Two fault lines may collide, producing an equipotential environment—a greenbelt of some sort," Max said.

"But why only this place?"

"It's a big planet," Max said. "We have only looked less than 300 miles radius. Maybe each destructive and constructive zone is that big, not even including the destruction caused by the asteroid. So there may be many other pockets with life here. The planet has pockets of green and barren lands."

"Possibly."

"We're probably in the same area and space, but another dimension or realm," Alex said. "Who knows, the Aoratosians may have discovered more dimensions than we have."

"Geoffrey, can you determine how long this portion of zero magnetism might be?"

"I can't tell," he said. "Like Max said, it might be a few to a hundred miles, we can only do that when we find the magnetic core source, and maybe we can construct models of the magnetic field, which we don't have time for right now."

"How long will that take?" Max said.

"I don't know," Geoffrey said. "It's a hypothesis, but we know now that this area has no magnetic field."

"All right, we stick to the plan?" Max said. "We'll go on all fours!"

On each aeroglider, four wheels dropped out, and they drove the aerogliders down the hill.

Everyone looked at Max.

"Who is ready for a hike?"

"I am," Alex said.

"Let's go. We don't have a choice anyway," Yvette said.

"Let's make camp and leave our aerogliders here," Max said. "Geoffrey, keep an eye on these." They parked the aerogliders a few feet from the river.

"Geoffrey, how long can our life support system last in these conditions?"

"A little over 24 hours," Geoffrey said. "You have to recharge before then."

"Good deal," Max said.

"The air analysis shows 10 percent oxygen," Yvette said. "Almost half that on Earth."

"I'd bet there is plenty of oxygen here to support life," Alex said. "Look at all these plants and animals."

Max punched a few dials on his LSS control unit. Air hissed from the release valve as the pressure helmet retracted quickly into the suit, exposing Max's bare face.

"Max, what are you doing?!" Yvette said.

Max smiled defiantly, disregarding protocol to keep the headset on at all times during the excursion.

"I'll be fine," he said. "Geoffrey, how are my vitals?"

"Everything looks fine so far," Geoffrey said.

Max removed the remainder of his head cover and took a deep breath. Everyone waited, expecting his face to wither and burst.

"Wow, this is refreshing!" Max said.

The divinely refreshing breeze wafted on his damp face, the ambient sweet scent captivating his nostrils. He enjoyed the thrill that came with it.

"Guys," he said. "This feels way better than in the helmet."

No sooner than he had finished the sentence than clicking sounds from Alex and Yvette's helmets filled the air as they snapped off their helmets.

"This feels wonderful," Yvette said. "I can smell the richness of the air."

"That means we can reset our compasses now. Using our decided south and north pole, it will be easier to find our way back here."

"Great idea."

They observed the animals over the hill for a while and then decided to descend.

"Let's move. We've already spent too much time here. Lock the aerogliders and carry as much equipment as you can for the next few hours," Max said. "We may stay on the other side longer."

"Yes, sir!"

They descended towards the river and the dinosaurs. A jackrabbit abruptly sprinted in front of them. Alex withdrew her MPG and almost fired.

"Do you think it's safe for us to keep our helmets off?" Yvette said.

"Yes, I think it's fine," Geoffrey said. "I don't see any compromise so far. In fact, it seems all vital organ performances are improving, even better than inside the suit. I'll keep an eye on it."

"This is awesome," Yvette. "Who else gets to say I spent the summer on another planet?"

"With real dinosaurs," Geoffrey said.

Max led the way past a herd of dinosaurs grazing, maintaining a safe distance and using the shrubs as cover. The pachyderms looked undeterred by their presence.

"Someone told me dinosaurs have an amazing sense of smell," Alex said.

"That is true. Especially the T-Rex. It's been shown in several DNA studies," Yvette said.

"Glad the wind is blowing towards us!" Max said.

Max stopped abruptly. "Crap!" he said.

"What is it?"

"Don't move! Stay back!" Max's heart was thudding. Memories of the cactus creature flashed in his mind. There was no pain, but his leg was sinking into the damp ground.

Max steadied himself and looked around. "It's quicksand! Everybody stay back!"

Alex and Yvette froze and retreated cautiously over the grass. The mud had already engulfed Max's right leg to knee level.

"The rope," Yvette said.

Alex quickly retrieved a rope from her backpack, threw the other end to Max, and together they pulled Max from the quagmire. Max extracted his leg from the mud and wiped the black sludge off by dragging his boots on the grass.

"That was close!" Max said.

"I'm glad you caught that before we were all got stuck," Yvette said.

"How are we going to go to the other side?"

"We'll find another way to the other side."

"Watch your step and look out," he said. "We don't know what's out here or might be hiding in the water."

"As long as it's not alligators or anacondas, I'm fine with that," Yvette said.

"We follow the edge of the swamp and stay on dry ground as much as possible. Be careful where you step!" Max said.

They took more photos of the animals and collected more samples of the water, mud, and plants, and stalked the length of the swamp, searching for a better area for crossing the river. There were alligator-like creatures spread throughout the swamp, some seen only by their snouts protruding out of the water, accompanied by streams of bubbles on the water surface. A colorful amphibian rested on a small dry island in the middle of the stream. The creature resembled a large lizard with long whiskers. It vanished under the water when they got close. They passed three ponds and installed three floating hydrophone transmission devices to monitor the activity in the river.

"I got the feed," Geoffrey confirmed.

"Sharp!"

They meticulously circumvented the marshes to the other side of the river, swatting tiny flies clustered above their heads. They dropped small red flags on the track. Alex now led the way, prowling the dense weeds with her walking stick and using the stick to navigate through the bog. Within a few minutes, they reached the other side. They stood in a field amid woolly mammoths and dinosaurs. Trumpeting, mooing, wailing, and whooshing filled the air while the animals grazed, some breaking down tree branches, some nursing their young, rubbing necks, rolling on the ground, and chasing each other. Two pterosaurs flew by.

"This is wildlife," Yvette said.

"Don't even know if I should call it wildlife," Geoffrey said. "Because this is where it started, undisturbed by humans."

Yvette took pride in explaining the various creatures as best as she could. She had dreamt of doing since childhood, and her dream was now reality.

"Triceratops, zigongosaurus, stegosaurus, dilophosaurus, wuerhosaurus. This one—I forgot." Yvette went on and on, but no one was listening. She took her tablet to search.

"T-Rex!" Geoffrey said, exhilarated.

"I bet that's the only dinosaur you know," Yvette said.

"There is some truth in that," Geoffrey said. "But I'm saying beware of carnivorous dinosaurs. Remember the cactus?"

"I don't see any raptors," Yvette said.

"In the law of the wild, the predator never shares a habitat with its prey. It has to hunt the prey. The raptors may or may not be here. But whether they are here or not, let's be watchful for other animals too."

"That's a giant grizzly bear!" Alex said.

"It's not a bear. That's a giant ground sloth," Yvette said. "Look at the head."

A herd of woolly mammoths gathered close by. Max approached the large mammals, and they seemed undeterred. He observed their long, layered grayish-black fur with large flappy furred ears, and huge, curved tusks below the tiny eyes.

"These are bigger than the elephants we have on Earth," he said.

"Yes, they are," Yvette said. "Archeological records show that the average adult woolly mammoths were bigger."

The bull mammoth trumpeted and splashed a jet of water and mud through his trunk into the air.

"What is he trying to do?"

"I think he's letting us know that we are in his territory and cooling himself," Yvette said. Yvette studied the pachyderms through the binoculars. "It's probably a member of the mammoth family, as you can see by the long crooked tusks," she said. "And the number of enamel ridges on the molar teeth make me believe it's the same species. I forgot the genus."

"*Mammuthus!*" Geoffrey said.

"That sounds right," Yvette said. "How did you know?"

"I looked it up."

"It's like we're on prehistoric Earth—a time capsule," Alex said.

"Most of the extinct animals on Earth are available in large numbers here," Max said.

"They haven't evolved at all, or evolved more slowly," Yvette said.

"Did you know that time travels in a straight line and can be adjusted by gravity? For example, time almost comes to a complete halt when you get close to black holes with increasing gravity," Geoffrey said.

"And?" Alex said.

"So the compound effect of both gravitational force and magnetic force caused time to slow down more here?" Max said.

"Exactly," Geoffrey said.

"Which explains the lack of change in structures of these animals over thousands of years."

"That means Earth resembles future Aoratosia."

"Exactly," Yvette said. "We are living ahead of time."

"But that presupposes that there are intelligent creatures here."

"After what we saw last night, I would say yes," Alex said.

"Some of our features have assimilated over long periods."

"We will find out," Geoffrey said. "There is less competition, which might not force them to sieve the weak."

"Climatic reasons maybe," Yvette said.

"I still don't get why the animals didn't go extinct in the previous episodes of the ice age and the glacial cycles," Geoffrey said.

"Maybe it never happened here."

"Yes," Yvette said. "That doesn't make sense."

"Like we said, they probably they never belonged to Earth."

"Possibly. Maybe they were seasonal visitors," Yvette said. "I believe they were indigenous to Aoratosia. Seems so. All our observations so far indicate that way."

"It's all assumptions," Alex said. "I believe most of the extinction on Earth was due to human interference. We hunt for sport and we destroy habitats. It's still happening today. And these lands seem undisturbed by any human interference. That's helped preserve the animals' natural habitat."

"Maybe they happen to have better conservation strategies than we do," Geoffrey said.

"Who's 'they'?" Yvette said.

"The Aoratosians?"

"Yeah, right."

Max looked around in all directions. Yvette noticed him.

"What's wrong?" Yvette said.

"Nothing," Max said. "I have this weird feeling that we are being watched."

"Me, too," Yvette said. "But it's probably nothing."

"Let's move on!" Alex said.

The crew proceeded towards the forest, wondering what lay in the woods.

Yvette broke their silence. "This may be a door to our de-extinction efforts on Earth," she said.

"Imagine all the history and science we will learn from all this," Geoffrey said.

"I feel jealous of the children born from now on," Alex said. "They will get to know and experience the real dinosaurs, not models, and many other things we grew up believing to be fiction."

"It'll be a boring world," Max said.

"Trust me," Geoffrey said. "I would take that world anytime."

"On the contrary, it'll deprive children the pleasure of developing their imaginations. As a kid, I always had these fantasies of seeing dinosaurs and being part of them. It was so much fun, whatever form and shape they were."

"I doubt that," Alex said.

"It gave me superpowers!" Yvette said, smiling. "I always imagined myself as a flying dinosaur on another planet. I don't know why."

"Well," Geoffrey said. "I was more of a dragon-kid. Knight on a quest, saving the princess, blah, blah, blah. I loved being a knight fighting dragons with swords. I had full-sized rubber dragons and swords in my room."

"That explains your obsession with dragons," Max said.

Everyone laughed.

"Whatever! I love dragons."

"Did you have real swords?"

"Yeah," Geoffrey said. "I don't know why my dad bought me real swords."

"Real ones?"

"My dad collected swords. Most from ancient Japan."

"There won't be any of that here."

"There will be new things to dream about," Alex said, then said, "Do you hear that? Stomping of some sort coming from the grass."

The crew stopped and listened. The loud clapping sounds from the grass became louder and louder, approaching them.

Everyone scrambled and lay flat to the ground behind the bushes, magnetochrome pulse guns drawn.

After a few seconds, a large bird with long, skinny legs sprang across from the tall grass.

"A bird," Yvette whispered.

The crew waited for a few seconds while the tall bird continued stomping the ground and making the thudding sound. For a while, they couldn't see what was on the ground. Moments later, a huge snake rose and struck at the bird. The bird swiftly leaped to the side and pecked the snake with its sharp curved beak. The bird and the huge snake stared at each other, each sizing up the other. The snake shot forward, and each time the bird swiftly dodged it. After a few futile attempts, the snake yielded and slithered behind a thicket. The bird leaped onto a bush. Seconds later, the bird and the snake squared off again. The bird kept producing fierce clapping sounds with its wings and jumping on the snake. The snake struck a couple more times. Each time the bird expertly sprang out of reach. Finally, the bird pounced on the reptile's head and clamped it with its talons. It poked the snake's eyes with its beak. The snake writhed, and after a few minutes of twisting and coiling helplessly, it succumbed to the tall bird's clutch. The bird gripped the snake with its talons and disappeared into the forest.

"Wow, that was breathtaking!"

"Balance in the ecosystem, right?" Max said.

"That was a huge puff adder!"

Alex checked the muted life detector. It showed more life existed ahead of them, in the forest.

"Let's continue."

Yvette and Alex nodded, and they rose.

CHAPTER TWENTY-FIVE

Purple Forest, Aoratosia

THE EDGE of the tropical rain forest was clogged with undergrowth, animal bones, scattered debris. The ground was damp, and the air humid, thick with fog, and smelled of decomposing mulch. The forest floor was covered with dense foliage. Echoes from the huge droplets of dew pounding the mulch from the tree canopies filled the air, creating a local rainfall. Vines and ferns clung to the broad tree trunks and wound to the top.

Something is not right, Max thought, as hard as he tried to suppress the premonition. The forest felt forbidding.

"Let's stay close," Max said. "Yvette, what type of forest is this?"

"Temperate."

"That makes sense," Geoffrey said.

"Don't hurt anything," Yvette said. "Nature doesn't hurt you if you respect it."

They cautiously made their way into the forest in single file, shoving through heaps of mulch and dense, thick vines. Max was in the rear, Yvette in the middle, and Alex in the lead. Thick undergrowth became sparser as they walked farther into the forest, but the trees increased in height and girth. Dense fog whispered in the stygian, eerie stillness. The crunching sound of soggy mulch under their feet echoed through the hollow spaces between the giant tree trunks. It brought chills up Max's spine, which made him continually check all directions. The canopy of the forest was dense with leaves from the enormous trees. The wind howled above the tree canopies, producing a long, continuous whizzing soprano note as if welcoming the visitors into a hallowed forest. Birds perched on the giant tree canopies warbled, bringing the forest to life. Ape-like creatures and baboons swung through the trees. The sound faded as the crew went farther and farther into the woods.

Parrots, hoopoes, and other birds flew in circles close to the canopies. At one point, mockingbirds started a chorus, mimicking the crunching sound caused by the crew's feet on the mulch and twigs. The sound echoed.

"This is the biggest tree I've ever seen," Max said, looking up to the length of the tall trunk to the canopy, which momentarily made him dizzy. Max pinned a marker on one of the protruding roots and recorded "Big Tree" in his scrapbook.

The roots protruded from the ground, making it challenging to navigate. Occasionally a deer or a rabbit sprang out of a hollow rotten tree trunk, startled by the intruders. The crew passed blue duikers feeding on the shrubs that managed to grow in the deep shade. The crew took pictures and recorded everything that they encountered on the way.

"Watch out for snakes!" Alex said.

"And giant scorpions!" Geoffrey said.

"Most people who live on ranches say they see plenty of snakes, but I grew up on a ranch most of my life, and I've never been bitten by a snake. I think I only saw two rattlesnakes."

"Don't jinx it!" Alex said. "I was bitten twice."

"Guys, can we talk about something else?" Max said.

As they perused through the forest, they passed trees twisted around one another, some shaped like human beings.

"Look," Yvette said. "That tree looks like a woman."

"That's funny," Alex said.

"It's amazing how nature can shape things in such beautiful ways," Yvette said. "I saw one like that in Madagascar a few years ago."

They continued through the forest collecting samples, taking pictures and videos of the birds, reptiles, and small mammals that they encountered. They also used extra mini hydrophones and probes to relay information to probe AQ4.

Yvette stopped, resting her hands on her knees.

"Can we wait for a sec? I need to catch my breath!"

"It's muggy and the oxygen levels are low," Geoffrey said. "Also when the parrot is on your shoulder, it's extra weight."

"How long do you think we should keep going?" Yvette was feeling drenched after walking in the humid climate for two Earthly hours in the sleek suit. The sample pouches were getting heavy.

"We should probably be heading back soon," Alex said, swatting the tiny fruit flies clustered above her head.

"Max, did you put a torch in your pocket? There's light in your pocket!" Alex said.

Max looked down. "Oh, it's the necklace!"

He took it out from his pocket. The violet luminescence was bright.

"What's that about?" asked Yvette.

"I don't know."

"I think it's leading us somewhere!" Yvette said.

"What's this about?" asked Alex.

"We should keep going and see where it takes us," said Max.

"Guys, am I missing something?" Alex said.

"Alex, it's a long story. I'll explain when we get back to the ship."

Max walked back and forth. The luminescence increased as he walked westward.

"We'll go west!"

The light kept getting brighter and brighter. Then it faded.

"Let's back up. I think we missed the source somewhere."

They reached a hollow opening in the ground.

"What's this?" Max said.

"A water cave!" Yvette said.

"Guys, look at these," Yvette said, retreating.

"Skulls!" Alex said. "Animal maybe. Probably nothing."

"I hope you are not walking straight into a trap, offering an easy lunch for a giant ogre," Geoffrey said.

"We'll be fine," Max said.

"No," Yvette said. "There's no way in hell I am going in!"

"You are the explorer. What happened to the adventurous spirit?" Max said.

"I don't feel right about this. Where's the life detector? How do we know what's in there?"

"Let's explore and find out."

Yvette drew her magnetochrome pulse gun.

Soon after they entered the cave, Hubert fluttered his feathers and clung around Yvette's neck.

"What's wrong, boy?" Yvette said.

"He's probably just afraid of the dark," Max said.

Yvette looked at Max, then Alex, and squeezed closer to them. They all grasped their MPGs. Hubert warbled, flapped his wings and flew around. They tiptoed farther into the cave. A sinister aura surrounded them. It felt as if a force was drawing them farther inside.

"Trust me," Max said, his MPG cocked and ready. The light from the necklace was bright, making everything violet. Max tied the necklace chain around his wrist, using the necklace's light as a flashlight.

"O.K."

"Stay close to me and step where I step," Max said.

A water droplet splashed and echoed throughout and sent spurts of water that filled the whole passage with luminescent circular waves. The crew froze to the wall of the cave, pausing momentarily to adjust their eyes to the colorful reflection on the limestone and coquina rocks in the water.

They attached micro-cameras to the entryway and on the plant roots protruding from the cave ceiling.

The luminescent body of water was lit from an underground passage of turquoise water. A large black bird buzzed out of the cave.

"If a bird lives here, that means there aren't larger predators," Max said, in a low voice.

"Or maybe the birds are the predators," Geoffrey said.

"Like what?"

"Like vampire bats."

"They don't bite people."

"I know. I'm giving you a hard time."

"After what I've seen so far, anything is possible," Alex said.

A few steps forward was a semi-sunken cave. The cave was splendidly festooned with stalactites and stalagmites all gleaming under the flashlight. It was neither too hot nor too cold.

"Where exactly does all this water go?"

"I would imagine it comes out to the surface somewhere," Max said. "If we keep exploring the forest, we might see where it emerges to the surface."

Yvette whispered, "I have always admired underground diving. This is beautiful."

"Me, too! I'm doing that as soon as we get back home." Max said.

Their hushed voices echoed through the dark, endless underground cavern.

"I think this cave was once above the ground in the open air," Yvette said.

"How can you tell?"

"By the three air pockets. It must have subsided underground when sea levels rose after the

Ice Age." Yvette pointed to the faint streaks of light that squeezed through cracks in the cave ceiling, causing a glistening luster on the turquoise underground river surface and a stained-glass-like effect on the stalagmites.

"That's interesting!" Max said, moving forward.

The cave was getting darker and darker, and the light from their flashlights seemed much brighter. Hubert fluttered nearby.

"This must be the darkest I've ever seen," Max whispered.

"I bet without the light you can't even see your fingers."

"Is anyone getting the creeps?" Max said.

"I am," Yvette said. "I can feel my hair standing up on top of my head."

Max said, "Settle down. It's probably nothing. Oh. I feel something slithering in the water."

"It's our feet."

"Look over there!" Alex shouted.

Bright jewels shone under her flashlight beam. The three walked carefully to the spot.

"Hidden treasure?"

"Should get a few of these," Alex said.

"I don't think we should," Max said.

"They're only stones," Alex said, taking a laser cutter from her bag. One cut, and the stones wiggled.

"Something is not right. I feel lightheaded," Alex said.

"Might be the air in here," Max said.

"I think it's moving!" Yvette said.

The stones wiggled again, this time more vigorously.

Max noticed movement ahead. Something big had slightly moved on the wall. Max held his necklace in his hand and pointed forward.

"Stop!" Max whispered, abruptly stopping mid-stride.

Yvette and Alex froze. "What is it?" Yvette whispered.

"Listen, do you hear that?"

"Hear what?"

"I see it. Look up ahead!" he said firmly but softly, in a way that would not startle Yvette and Alex.

"What is that?" Alex said, trying to suppress her thudding heart.

Jewels glistened in the flashlight. The creature's head had been camouflaged against the wall. The glistening creature moved stealthily, entrapping them.

"I see it. Is that a giant—?" Alex said.

"Don't panic. Stay calm and step back!" Max said in a hushed voice. "Turn off your flashlights and back off."

They dragged their feet in reverse towards the exit. The cave was so black such that they had to hold onto each other's hands as they felt their way back.

"Guys, I think it sensed our retreat. It's increasing—"

The slithering was audible now. The whole cave floor seemed to be shifting.

Before Max could react, he found himself airborne, but only briefly before crashing into the cave wall. The air was knocked out of him. He reset his vision in time to dodge a blow from another hammer-like tentacle. He heard groaning sounds from Alex and Yvette. He ran a quick physical inspection of his vertebrae. *Legs moving.* Check. *Hands moving.* Check. *Head can turn sideways.* Double check. He sprang and hunched against the wall. Despite the blaring headache from head-butting the stalagmite, he was fine. *How was that possible after being hammered across the midsection by the monster's limb? Thank God for the sleek suit.* Reorienting himself, he aimed his flashlight in time to catch a glimpse of a tentacle about to hammer toward his midsection. He was meat. Except this time his reflexes kicked in. Max rolled to the left as the creature's limb thudded against the calcified wall, sending shrapnel flying and water splashing everywhere, knocking Max's flashlight into the water. No time to waste. "Run!" Max yelled.

Yvette and Alex, closer to the exit, moved quickly. The cave creature seemed focused on trapping Max against a wall of the cave, blocking all hope of escape. In the dark, Max could feel its massive body churning the water. But the monster's size could be a disadvantage, Max thought. He counted the seconds between each thud and mapped the pattern. *Three seconds each strike.* That was enough time to dash through, only if he knew where he was. He wished he still had his flashlight. The odds were against him. He might be throwing himself into the creature's wide-open jaws. A long shot, but what did he have to lose? He was toast either way. Better to die trying. His mind raced, all the months of training kicking in. He was small, up against a mountain—that was a plus, but if, and only if, he could squeeze past and outmaneuver the hammer. The monster seemed to sense his nerves. It bellowed until Max's head rang, and careened closer. If only Max could see how many hammer tentacles the creature had! This was not a fair fight. He was blind against the nocturnal creature. Suddenly he thought of Kai-Eliud, the monk in Kaligari. He had to depend on his senses now. Sound! Instinct!

From the cave's entrance, Max heard shots and saw flashes from a gun's muzzle. Apparently Yvette or Alex had taken off or lost the silencer. Bad move. The creature let out a thunderous roar that shook the ground. Max sensed the creature veering to the right, towards the exit, in the direction of the shots. This was Max's moment. Max jumped and hunched, all the while counting the seconds. He hesitated, ducked, and dove between each moving tentacle, then squeezed through a tiny slit of space between the creature and the wall and bolted towards the exit, where Alex was crouched hoping for a clear shot at the monster.

The creature flung out an appendage and hit Alex a glancing blow, stunning her momentarily, and the hammer-like end sent chunks of the cave wall flying.

Max grabbed Alex's hand and shoved her. "Come on! Let's go." They stormed out of and away from the cave.

The breath of the creature wafted after them. Stone crumbled as the huge creature moved forward toward daylight. Its fiery eyes shone like two embers from the empty dark space. Smoke billowed from its dilated nostrils. There was hell in its deep red eyes.

"Run!" Max shouted.

Suddenly they were transfixed by another roar. The monster emerged and was following them. Another deafening roar shook the ground and sent everything shattering.

"Run!" Max said.

Max's knees were buckling under him. His energy had escaped his muscles.

The creature erupted from the cave. Like a tornado, the beast coiled itself, stretched, towering as high as Mount Kilimanjaro, ready to impose on the intruders. It body resembled an underworld replica of a dragon and anaconda mutant. The ground shuddered, sending Max and Alex diving forward, sliding and falling.

"Pht! Pht!" Yvette, yards ahead of them, shot twice as the creature pursued Max and Alex.

"Stop!" Max shouted. "Don't shoot!"

But it was too late. Yvette struck the creature in the neck with the laser blade, sending its head tumbling to the ground.

"I got it!" Yvette said.

"Oh, shit. That thing is growing more heads," Max said.

"It's true!" Yvette said. "It is!"

"Like a freaking hydra!" Geoffrey said, in a voice between thrill and fear.

"Do something, man!" Alex said to Geoffrey.

"Get out of there now!" Geoffrey said. "And don't shoot. Otherwise it will only get bigger and more pissed off."

The creature's head cocked, then it let out another shriek that ricocheted through the forest, almost bursting Max's eardrums and momentarily disorienting him. Max crumbled to the ground, writhing in pain, covering his ears with his hands. He regained his balance and struggled up. His legs felt heavy and stiff. Alex pulled him by the armpits. With great effort, they lurched forward. The sound of breaking twigs and leaves and pounding of ground continued.

"Run!" Max said.

"Where?" Alex said, under her breath.

"Just run!"

Alex leaped up and ran ahead, zigzagging through the trees. The creature had now zeroed in on Max. It emitted another deafening scream from the projections below its dangling whiskers. Trees exploded and mulch erupted. Max ran, stumbled and collapsed behind a tree. The tree was vibrating, and thick branches fell within a few inches of him.

"Come on, Max!" Yvette called out.

Max gawked at the approaching creature, transfixed. After a few seconds, Max regained his senses and pulled himself up. He looked to his right, where Yvette was covering her ears, and Alex was beside her. They snapped their helmets back on. Max pressed the helmet switch on his LSS unit, and it did not respond. *Damn! Gotta deal with it without the helmet!*

"Geoffrey, what the heck is this thing?" Max said, under his breath.

"I'm working on it."

"Hurry up!"

"I'm on it!"

Max, panting, peeked from behind the tree. The creature was not there.

"It produces some kind of an echolocation, which causes other things to burst," Geoffrey said.

"Explain!"

"Basically, the creature is a massive sonar system. It releases massive sound waves, and that sonication causes atoms, molecules, in that range to vibrate."

"What's causing the disorientation?"

"I think whatever sound the creature produces is oversaturating your senses, causing a catatonic state—"

"Like a tranquilizer?" Yvette said.

"Something like that."

"Shhh!" Max whispered. He fumbled with his helmet and finally snapped it on.

The creature stopped and stretched its necks out, as if seeking them. Max held his breath and made himself small behind the tree trunk. He wrapped a hand around the glowing necklace in his pocket. The creature's new heads waggled back and forth, and its prehensile grasping limbs scratched the bark off nearby trees. Max could feel its penetrating breath percolating, and his thudding heart. A sword-like tongue flickered only a few inches from Max.

"The vibration can cause auditory cells to burst and increase blood pressure to the brain which will result in blood vessels rupturing and the brain bursting."

"Can barely hear you!"

"Exposure for a long time to the echolocation might cause blood vessels in the brain to desiccate into goo—and kaboom!"

"Did you see those trees exploding? This is not funny!" Yvette said.

Geoffrey did not answer for a moment.

"I apologize," Geoffrey finally said. "Can you use your wrist camera, so I can see the creature better?"

"Thanks, but no."

"It's good you put on your helmets. Stay low to the ground if possible. That should reduce the effect."

"How come the creature is protected from the sonication?"

"It appears the creature is deaf, which is why it cannot be affected by its sonication, or it has a protective coating. The eyes are vestigial structures. I think the creature can't see but has some heat-sensing receptors on the eye slits, the red marks, which seem to allow it to locate its prey by mapping energy changes in its surroundings."

"Some kind of cryptochrome mechanism? I didn't know that existed!" Yvette said.

"The creature uses the finger-like projections from its nostrils for vibration detection," said Geoffrey.

"Is that why it's not moving?" Max said. "Like a freaking video game waiting for a command!"

"That's why its head is bobbing. It's searching for any air disturbance. It can sense it. And uses the sonication to paralyze the prey. Thanks to the helmet, the air around you is uniform."

"Right. It—"

"That may be the only reason you three are still alive after going into that cave."

"How the hell are we getting out of here?"

"You should crawl away, staying away from its radar system. I mean flat on the ground."

"How far can it sense?"

"I can't tell. You need to get as far away from there as possible without disturbing the air."

"I told you we shouldn't have gone in there!" Yvette whispered. She was crawling low along the forest floor.

Max ignored her. There was no time for playing blaming games! It did not matter now. The three of them were still together and alive. They had to survive, together.

"All right. You heard Geoffrey. On my count of three, we start toward the bushes."

"The thing is right behind you! I think it's coming for your necklace!" Yvette said in a coarse hushed voice. "You gotta throw it away!"

"No. I'm sure it's leading us somewhere!"

"We'll be dead by then!"

"Three, two, one. Let's go!"

"Where?" Yvette said, helplessly.

The creature's two heads stealthily stalked them, one on each side of each tree trunk. Then the creature pounded on the tree trunk, emitting its shrieks before the tree crashed down.

Max clasped the necklace with both hands and lunged into the nearby bushes where Yvette and Alex waited.

"We go as far as we can until we are away from the creature."

Yvette and Alex nodded.

They crawled for several yards over twigs, mulch, and dirt.

Suddenly the creature erupted into the bushes, sensing the sound.

"Run!" Max yelled.

They dispersed in various directions. Max's heart was pounding as he gulped for every bit of air, running as fast as he could. He tripped on a piece of vine, sending his face into the mulch. He did not care. He did not even feel the gash on his forehead as he continued running, escaping the hammering tentacles of the huge creature. Lactic acid was starting to set his leg muscles on fire. His lungs were burning as if to scream their way out of his chest, but he would not let them. He struggled for air. His mouth and nose were not enough to quench his need for air. Alex and Yvette were nowhere in sight. He stumbled through the shrubs and undergrowth. There was only one way out—and he kept going.

He ran and ran until he could run no more. That's when he realized he was alone and had no idea where he was. Then he heard footfalls, yet there was no sign of the horrible creature, at least for now. Max looked back and saw Yvette, who was sweating and breathing hard.

"Where is Alex?" Max said.

"I thought she was with you."

"No. We've got to find her," Max said.

"How? Go back?"

They stood, hunched and gasping.

There was a whizzing sound above. The damned creature's shadow appeared above and shot down towards them, and it emitted the disorienting scream. Max and Yvette dove to one side and sprinted forward, ducking into the shrubs for cover. They ran and ran through the brush until they reached a waterfall.

The waterfall stood between granite reefs and a deep flaccid fjord. The gorge was covered in mist framed by a rainbow. The creature was approaching.

"We're trapped," Yvette said.

"We don't have a choice! We have to jump!"

"No way!" Yvette, "What if there are rocks down there?"

Max stood, breathing hard, for what seemed like forever, feeling every breath of the approaching creature. His whole body trembled. His legs were failing him. Suddenly he felt a surprising surge of energy —a burst of heat that shot from his pounding heart through his burning lungs, through his gut and into his legs. At that moment he realized he could fly, that they could fly—there was nothing stopping them. He grasped Yvette's hand and stepped closer to the edge of the bottomless chasm—their only way of surviving.

"We're jumping!"

"No!"

Max grabbed her hand as the creature's tentacles swiped the air only inches away.

"I'm not—that's—" Before Yvette could finish the statement, they plunged into the roaring white abyss. Yvette's scream faded as the roaring falls engulfed the two.

Their senses failed them.

CHAPTER TWENTY-SIX

Dyke 54, Aoratosia

ALEX HURRIED from the decontamination chamber into the main control chamber where Geoffrey sat staring at the monitors.

"Man, it's insane out there," Alex said.

Geoffrey ignored her.

Alex approached him and slapped him on the shoulder. "Tell me what's going on."

"We have a problem," Geoffrey said, keeping his gaze on the monitor.

"What is it?"

"I think we have lost Max and Yvette."

"Lost them?"

"Their trackers have disappeared."

"Are you sure it's not a glitch in the system?"

Geoffrey wiped his face with both hands. "It's not. I'm sure about it. I've rebooted the system and still nothing."

"Crap. What are we going to do?"

"We keep waiting. Maybe a tracker will come up."

"We have to do something."

"I know. But we have a bigger problem."

Geoffrey pointed to the squiggling seismometer.

Alex climbed the platform closer to the monitors. The ship shook, almost knocking Alex off her feet. She cursed, steadying herself against the wall. Ceramic cups on the coffee table smashed to the floor.

"Careful," Geoffrey said.

"Was that an earthquake?"

"I think the volcano is about to erupt."

"That's sooner than we thought."

"I have been surveying the area since morning. And the tremors are increasing every second."

"Just when I thought things couldn't get any worse."

Geoffrey typed on the keyboard for a moment.

"See this."

Alex watched the screen. "Are those plumes from the volcanic cones?"

"We are detecting increasing magma levels."

"When did it start?"

"The seismograph has been going bonkers since noon."

"Eight hours ago. That means magma is closer to the surface."

"The radar shows some areas in the lake have already bulged up a few millimeters."

Alex picked up binoculars and scanned the area.

"Oh my God! We should leave soon."

"Not without them! We're sticking to the protocol. Remember—no man stays behind. If they don't show, we stay too."

"Did you see what's out there?"

"We will wait. It's too early for the portal, anyway."

"The portal will open in less than an hour, and we have to decide soon. If we don't, we will get stuck here too."

Geoffrey looked straight into Alex's eyes. "Are you even listening to yourself? These are our teammates, our family. Maybe you don't care because you grew up without your family. All you care about is yourself!"

Alex's upper lip shook as she sputtered. "Do not even go there!"

Geoffrey recoiled. "I'm sorry. I overstepped. That was uncalled for."

"You bet it was. It's common sense. I am afraid we don't have a choice!"

"Yes, we have a choice! We wait for them!"

"If we stay here, everything we worked for dies with us. All the bags of samples. All the hard work. What about people on Earth waiting for us? I'm being realistic here."

"I know. But right now, it's us we have to worry about."

"If we leave, everyone back home has a chance of knowing what's here," she said. "If we stay, we perish and go down in history as failures. No one will ever know about us, and maybe no one will ever come here again. What's the use?"

"I get your point. But can you live with yourself knowing you could have waited? Not knowing what happened to your team? We are family."

"What do you suggest?"

"Let's wait a little longer."

"Agreed."

"Otherwise, I will go out and look for them," Geoffrey said.

"Where will you start if there's no signal?"

"You can leave, but I'm not leaving without them."

"I can't do that. If you stay, I'll stay."

"Good," Geoffrey said. "There should be something we can do. I know Max won't give up that easily."

Geoffrey analyzed the seismograph.

"Just as we predicted," he said. "These gravity waves create brutal storms. And one will be upon us any minute now."

They heard clattering from the containment area.

"What is that?" Alex said.

They looked at each other, stood, and drew their MPGs.

Alex approached the door and listened, her eyes growing wider. Geoffrey stood on the opposite side. The rattling continued, followed by a brief pause and then the sound of scratching on the door, which caused both Geoffrey and Alex to jump into firing position. Alex raised three fingers and counted down. On "one," they kicked the door open.

"Waa cha kai! Waa cha kai!" Hubert flapped his wings, hopping up and down.

"Hubert! You freaked the crap out of us!" Alex said, lowering her gun.

"Waa cha kai!"

Alex picked up Hubert and put him on her shoulder. "How did you get here?"

"Over there," Geoffrey said, pointing at an open sample bag with its contents strewn on the floor.

"Don't tell me he was in the bag the whole time."

"He was."

"That's pretty smart."

After putting back the items back, they secured the bag and closed the containment room door.

"Back to the issue at hand. Time is moving fast and we have to find a way to find Yvette and Max," Geoffrey said.

"I know," Alex said. "Think! Think! Think! Hubert!"

"What about Hubert? How does that help us leave this place alive?"

"We can use him to take our message to them."

"That's almost impossible," he said. "You can't expect him to learn and understand everything instantly."

"I'll try it," Alex said. "He is a parrot, isn't he?"

Alex ignored Geoffrey's smirk.

"What's up, guy?" she said, extending her hand. Hubert landed. She patted the bird, which quivered and flattened his feathers.

"I'm sorry, buddy," Alex said, petting his crest. Hubert was not having it, and flew into the kitchen.

"He is scared," Geoffrey said.

"He can feel the tremors."

"Waa cha kai!" Hubert warbled from the back of the kitchen where he was hiding.

Alex lured Hubert with a handful of freeze-dried blueberries. She picked up the parrot and patted him on the head. "You can go back to the forest now."

"Like he is going to understand you?" Geoffrey said.

"He will," Alex said.

Alex put Yvette's picture in front of Hubert. She repeated the same phrase and fed him more treats, letting him off from the tips of her fingers. She repeated the sequence several times.

Hubert lowered his shoulders, raising his head upright. He latched his talons onto the photo. He seemed to recognize Yvette's picture.

"Waa cha kai! Waa cha kai!" Hubert squawked.

"Yes, yes. I want you to find her." Alex pointed at the photo again.

Hubert flapped his wings. "Waa cha kai! Waa cha kai!"

The flapping got stronger. Then Hubert flew around the room in a frenzy.

Geoffrey looked at Alex. "I hope he understands what you told him."

"He does!" Alex said. "I could see it in his eyes! He will go."

"How do you know?"

"He's a bird. Birds have homing abilities. Open the chamber. Then open the door."

"I hope you're right," Geoffrey said, and opened the chamber.

"Go. Go," said Alex.

From the window they watched Hubert vanish into the horizon.

CHAPTER TWENTY-SEVEN

Unidentified Location, Aoratosia

MAX WOKE up to the sound of the river slapping against the rocks. He lay on his back on the riverbank, the lower half of his body partly buried in the sand beside a heap of twigs. He groaned, holding the side of his pulsating head. Everything was whirling around him. He struggled to open his eyelids and blinked for a while, adjusting to the bright sunlight. With great effort, he pulled himself out of the sand and sat leaning on a rotting log by the bank. His legs were numb. There was a jarring pain in his left arm, the one that was twisted awkwardly under his body. He delicately felt it and stretched it, trembling slightly. He grimaced. Not broken. That was a good sign. He looked around, shell-shocked. What happened? He brushed his head with his hand, shaking the sand off. He spat a mouthful of goo onto the ground.

Where am I? Max tried to talk, but the words barely came out. His throat felt too parched and sore. Still disoriented, he crawled and heaved himself forward, planted his face in the river, and slurped the frigid water. He watched as red drops of blood dissolved into the river from the cut on his forehead. Something pressed uncomfortably against his groin as he bent. He straightened his pants and emptied his pockets. His portable first-aid kit still hung at his waist. But how long had he been here? It couldn't be that long. The sun was farther across the sky. The LSS unit on his suit was dead. He remembered flashes of what had happened. There was no one in sight.

Then he saw a white cloth downstream. He wrestled himself to his feet.

"Yvette! Alex!" He could hardly hear his own voice.

He hobbled and fell down.

"Yvette! Alex!" he yelled with all his might.

Max unzipped the first-aid kit, searched through the contents, and found the epinephrine syringe nestled below the bandages and cotton swabs. He plunged the needle into his thigh and squeezed. Nothing.

He labored along the riverbank, looking desperately everywhere for any signs along the river. Each step felt slightly more painful. He grimaced and kept limping forward. Again and again he called out. No reply.

Max stumbled upon Yvette's coat. He buckled to the ground, wringing it and slamming his fists in the sand.

He looked to the sky and yelled. "No, no, no!"

His voice was coarse.

Then, a few yards, he noticed in the distance white, red, and blue. He limped, slowly increasing his pace, ignoring the excruciating pain from his shin. *The Flag!* Half-buried in the riverbank was the same rugged flag that had flown on top of Coldbox on her maiden voyage; the same flag the crew had waved on landing on Aoratosia. He fell on it and embraced it. Even though there was no one here, the cloth reminded him that hundreds of millions of people on Earth were with him. It was hope. He pulled the flag out from the sand. "I will not give up!" Max yelled, again falling down to his knees.

He could feel the drug kicking in. With a fortified resolve, he stood up, carefully strapped the flag around his shoulder, and continued down the stream. He was going to find the others no matter what.

He saw buzzards circling above the trees a few yards downstream. There had to be something there. Max limped along unsteadily towards the area. The injection was kicking in, numbing the pain. The sand, rocks, and shrubs blurred below him as he increased his pace. He tripped over a twig and landed in the shrubs. The pain seemed to have disappeared. His heart raced. His senses became sharper. The sight of the buzzards energized him. There was something there. Something! *An animal? Yvette?* That was his only target. And nothing could stop him. He ran brushing and leveling the undergrowth to the ground.

He cautiously inspected the area as he approached a pile of dried twigs, a half-rotten stick in his hand.

~

YVETTE LAY MOTIONLESS and face down in a ditch behind a pile of logs and twigs a few feet from the riverbank.

"Yvette! Yvette!" Max yelled. She did not answer.

He noticed the bloodstains on the edge of Yvette's suit. Yvette lay with her neck twisted to the side. Max looked at the motionless body, heart thudding, mapping his next move. His body flashed. His left hand reflexively reached for his waist to retrieve the live feed radio. *Damn! Gone!* It was only himself now. For a few moments, he looked around for anything he could use to get Yvette out of the hole.

Using the small lancet from the medical kit as a blade, Max struggled to cut a thick vine hanging from a nearby tree. He sliced layer by layer until he could break it. He was sweating profusely when he broke the vine, yet he didn't feel the least bit tired. He tied one end of the vine on the tree trunk, then threw the other end into the ditch. He descended into the hole, using the vine as leverage.

"I'm coming for you," Max said.

He checked Yvette's pulse. None. Her face was blue. He adjusted Yvette into a supine position, checked her tongue, and started CPR. Yvette did not move. After four repeated futile cycles, Max was getting frustrated and emotional.

"Yvette, come on, wake up!" he yelled, shaking the unconscious body and slapping her on the cheek. Still no response. He felt her pulse again; still nothing. *Calm down. Don't panic.* He took several deep breaths. The many months of training were paying off.

"Don't worry; I will take care of you," he whispered. "Come on, Yvette! You can do this!" he said, pressing the area around her heart even harder.

318

Max placed Yvette's body face down and thwacked it between her shoulder blades. He thwacked again and waited.

Yvette's chest heaved up. Max held her down. She coughed and vomited, taking long, painful gasps. Her labored breathing produced a choking sound as she fought to clear her airways. She gripped Max's hand and squeezed it; her eyes opened wide.

"You're alive!" Max said, heaving a sigh of relief. Max squeezed her hand back.

Max helped her sit upright. After a long pause of forced deep breathing, she feebly spoke.

"What happened?"

"I was afraid you were dead," Max said.

"What happened?"

"We drowned, and you ended up here. We jumped into some crazy deep waterfall, remember?"

"Why did we jump?" she said.

Max smirked, thinking Yvette was joking. Her face registered genuine curiosity.

"You don't remember?"

Yvette groaned, pulling herself closer to the tree trunk. "I remember us being on the ship at night discussing the findings, and Geoffrey was sick. But how did we get here? Where are Alex and Geoffrey?"

"I see. It's a long story. I've got to get you back to the ship to make sure you are O.K."

"All right. But I still don't understand why either of us is here."

"The quick answer is we were exploring and got attacked."

"By what?"

"I have seen nothing like it before. Hey." Max placed his hand on her shoulder. "You need to rest and recover. I will tell you about it later."

"I will. But where are the others?"

"We got chased by something, and we separated. Alex is maybe somewhere in the forest, and Geoffrey is still at the base."

Yvette winced in pain.

"Stay down. Here, let me help you!" Max said, lifting her carefully into a sitting position.

"Do you have some water?" Yvette said. "I'm parched."

"Hold on, let me see if I can get you some."

Max climbed out of the ditch. He cut one of the wide leaves and slashed a nearby vine. Water dripped from its stem into the leaf Max was holding. He descended and handed the leaf to Yvette.

Yvette looked at the folded leaf, bemused. "How did you know to do that?"

"A few minutes ago I cut a vine to come down here. There was a lot of water dripping."

"That's genius."

"And safer than the river water."

Yvette gulped all the water and burped.

"The water is refreshing," she said, forcing a feeble smile. "Thanks, Max," she said, and sighed.

Max nodded.

"Where are we?" she said.

"I'm not sure yet," Max said.

"How long have we been separated?" she said.

"Not sure. It could be few minutes or a couple hours. Hard to tell. I'd say a couple of Earth hours. Your LSS unit showed 12 hours left."

"That means we have been away for 24 hours?"

"Yes," Max said. He opened his LSS unit on his chest. "Mine won't start. The control unit is banged up. Must have been when the monster creature hit me. Saved my life. I'll have to wait until we get to the aerogliders to use the repair manual and troubleshoot."

"You will need the suit intact to get back," Yvette said.

"I know. Hopefully I can fix it."

"I hope we can get back out with enough LSS."

"That's why I turned yours off. You should use it only when needed. That will buy us some extra time."

Yvette nodded. "Do you think Geoffrey will come looking for us?"

"I doubt it. Where would he start? I have no idea how far downstream we are from where we left. We are stranded unless we find our own way back to the aerogliders. I don't know Alex's status either."

"I know Geoffrey can track us."

"Yeah. But he wasn't in good shape when we left. He will not leave the ship unattended."

"So you came back for me?" Yvette said.

"No, not really. I nearly drowned, too!"

"But you saved me!"

"I guess! I was wandering around until I saw buzzards circling in the sky above me."

"I owe you one big favor after this," she said, a smile tracing on her face. "So where is the ship?"

"That's what we have to find out."

Yvette nodded.

"So you remember the ship?" Max said.

"Yes. Last night, but nothing after that."

"I'm sure it will all come back after you get some rest."

Yvette looked at him. "What are we going to do now?"

"We need to find a safe place to crash before it gets dark."

"But where is it safe?"

Max looked at Yvette. "Let me think about it. We will figure something out."

"I will be happy once we are out of this place."

"I know. Me, too."

"We are stranded, aren't we?" Yvette said.

"No, we—we need to find a way back to the ship."

"Where do we start?"

"I'd say we start by getting out of this hole."

Max stood up and checked out all directions.

"You think you can stand up?" he said.

"Let me see."

She slowly stood up and immediately grimaced, holding her right thigh as she applied pressure on the leg. She wobbled before steadying herself. Max helped her sit down again.

"Take it easy. You lost so much blood!" Max said.

"O.K."

Max checked and felt the swollen leg, bending it up, down, left, and right. Yvette grimaced again.

"There are no broken bones," he said. "Only some torn tissue. We have to clean it soon. We don't want you going into septic shock. And to do that we have to get out to get enough water."

"Max, I can't."

"Let's try this." Max secured the vine around Yvette's waist, climbed out, and pulled her out after him.

"What happened to your necklace?" she asked.

Max felt around in his pocket, realizing for the first time that he did not have the necklace. "Probably somewhere at the bottom of the river."

He balanced Yvette by placing her arm on his shoulders. They shuffled through the woods along the river while staying away from the open banks. The sun was directly above them. They hoped by continuing to move, they would find a mark or a spot that would lead them back to the aerogliders.

"I can't go any farther, Max. My leg is killing me," she said. "You have to leave without me."

"That's not gonna happen!"

"You have to," she said. "I'm only slowing you down. And we are running out of time!"

"At least this way, we are together," he said. "It's better that way."

"Can we rest for a minute?" she said.

"Sure. There is a good spot over there."

They hobbled and sat down between two large protruding roots. Max checked their surroundings.

"I think we can rest here," he said.

He retrieved the morphine from the first-aid pack and administered some to Yvette. "This should help," Max said. "Let me look at that leg."

Max unzipped the lower leg of Yvette's suit, exposing the deep gash on her thigh.

"Ow!" she yelped as Max pulled out an embedded sliver of wood from her flesh. She looked away.

"Close your eyes. That might help." Max said.

Yvette took a slow, deep breath.

"Ouch." She gnashed her teeth.

"Relax," Max said. "Let me look at the wound."

"What's there?" Yvette said, trembling. "I can't look. I don't like blood."

"It's not too bad," Max said. "Needs some cleaning. Here. Put this between your teeth," Max said, handing Yvette a dried twig.

Yvette nodded feebly. She could barely move her legs. She closed her eyes.

Max flushed the excess blood with water. After that, he added some isopropyl alcohol, which made Yvette squeak in pain, clasping Max's hands and clenching the stick in her teeth. He applied some iodine and then applied twelve sutures to the wound. He overlaid it with some leaves and tore a piece of cloth from the flag. Max then bandaged it up.

"This should make it stay clean and somewhat better. You can remove that now."

Releasing the twig between her teeth, Yvette looked at her leg.

"That wasn't too bad," she whispered. "Where did you learn to dress wounds like that?"

"I paid attention in my anatomy class in college," Max smirked.

"Who would've guessed?" she smiled.

"I paid attention, unlike you."

They laughed.

"That's kinda true," Yvette said. "I can hardly remember a few things that I studied in college. I only crammed to ace the exams."

"We all did."

"I'm impressed you still remember some things."

"My aunt was also a nurse, and into herbal medicine, so I learned a few things growing up."

"She should be very proud of you."

"She is, and I can't wait to see her."

"When we get back, I would like to meet her and thank her for raising such a considerate young man and a good caregiver."

They remained silent for a while. Max shrugged and said, "Thanks."

Yvette smiled. "So why did you change to biophysics?"

"I wanted to go to medical school, but then I realized going to grad school will ensure I get paid while I do what I love, maybe change the world."

Yvette looked at Max as if reading his mind.

"That's always a good reason," she said.

"It's interesting because, for the first two years of undergrad, I was an art major, then I switched to biophysics."

"Why?"

"I don't know," Max said, contemplating. "The class was boring the hell out of me. I guess I've always loved doing the unexpected. I wanted to help Aunt Dori. I was having these vivid dreams about Aoratosia before I even started working on the sketches. I'd wake up at midnight fired up and make sketches and stuff like that only for myself. I told no one because even I thought it was insane. Until my girlfriend came to my room and challenged me to make it happen. I was reluctant at first, but she was super optimistic, so I eventually decided to go for it."

"To win her?"

"Mostly. But it also made me feel better doing it. I felt excited about life. Plus, she gave me an ultimatum to either complete it or stop talking about it."

"That's an interesting story. I'm glad they didn't diagnose you with ADHD," she said. "What did your teachers say?"

"Man. I've got a lot of funny stories."

"Tell me one!"

"During my freshman year, I went to talk to my physics professor and asked him if I could enroll in the second-semester physics, and you know what he said?"

"What did he say?"

"He said, 'You will not pass that class!' But then I reminded him this was my decision. No one had forced me, and I was willing to bear the consequences head-on."

They both laughed.

"I told him I'd pass the test," Max said. "He looked at me like I was nuts, then told me to let him know how I was doing after two weeks."

"What happened after two weeks?"

"Nothing. The strange thing is, I turned out to be one of his best students in the class. Even the professor was surprised that I was crushing it."

"I guess seeing and imagining things helps sometimes," Yvette said, smiling. "It's a special gift."

"I guess so. But I also had to bust my ass off to pass. I was stubborn."

"My dad always said nice things about you, how you were always coming up with brilliant ideas and ways to resolve situations. I can see that now," Yvette said.

"Really, that's cool of him to say that," Max said. "He always says the same things about you."

"Come on. I am his little girl. I'd say he doesn't have much of a choice."

Max nodded. "That's fair."

"He is a special dad."

"I know. He is a smart guy."

They sat in silence, leaning against one of the large mahogany roots.

"What about you? Why did you choose astrobiology?" Max said.

"I am fascinated by life," she said. "Funny thing is, I was a linguistics minor. Don't know why. As a little girl, I hated science. Ironically, I ended up being a scientist. Plus, being the daughter of a scientist made it easier, I guess."

"That's an impossible bar to beat," Max said.

"True. I had to beat him. I think I'm on my way."

They laughed.

"You are!" Max said. "Look at you, you're sitting on another planet."

"Somehow I always knew what I wanted to do, unlike you."

"I am glad you did. Otherwise, I might not have met you on this beautiful planet."

"Stranded!" she said.

"Talk about timing and serendipity."

"Fate!"

"You can call it that."

"Now you need to get some rest," Max said. He removed his jacket and laid it down as a pillow for Yvette.

"All right."

In no time she was fast asleep. Max stood to study the area surrounding them. He watched her chest rise and fall with each breath. He hoped they would make it out on time or alive.

YVETTE WOKE UP a few hours later. Max had finished sharpening some wooden poles he had collected.

"Good evening," Max said to Yvette, now standing next to him.

Yvette yawned. "How long have I been sleeping?"

"A couple earthly hours, I'd estimate," Max said.

"Hours?"

"You needed the rest."

"I guess. Thanks, Max."

"For what?"

"For taking care of me."

"Of course. We're a team, remember?"

Yvette nodded silently.

"That reminds me. I should dress the wound on your forehead," Yvette said, touching the tissue around the cut.

"It's fine right now. I can barely feel a thing."

"Please?" she insisted cordially.

"Don't worry, I will be fine," Max said. "We should make you better first, or if you insist, you can clean it when we get to the ship."

"Deal!"

"Deal! Let's see if you are strong enough to walk, maybe find us some food. How are you feeling?"

"I'm better. Help me a bit."

Max held Yvette's arm. She put it around Max's shoulders.

The sun was touching the westward canopies, and the creeping shadow over the forest made it even darker. Sounds from nocturnal creatures were coming to life.

"We should find a place to spend the night. Soon we won't be able to see where we are going."

"I found a place."

Yvette struggled to stay standing but immediately leaned on a tree trunk.

"I don't think I can walk right now."

"Can you try?"

"I can, but I will slow you down."

"That's fine. The sooner we move, the better. It's not safe being around here at night."

"Why? I haven't seen anything scary."

"I know. Only a hunch," Max said. "When I went to fetch water at the river, I saw a pack of grizzly bear-looking giants sniffing through the woods on the other side of the river. I saw other smaller animals lined up on the river, and from what I could tell, they were all predators. In those few minutes I saw two male foxes tearing at each other until one died and floated away down the river. Hyenas sniffed along, chasing down the river for the carcasses. I'd imagine eventually they will pick up our scent."

"What are you saying?"

"I saw some day-old animal tracks on this side of the bank while I surveyed the area when you were sleeping. So we'd better get away from here."

"What happened?"

"They saw me, and then suddenly they ran away down the river into the woods, as if they were running away."

"Why?"

"I don't know," Max said. "Some diversion, but I'm sure they will be back by nightfall." His hair stood on end as he said this.

"Do we have any food?"

"Yes, I kept some for you," Max said, handing her two raw mice pierced on a stick.

"Are those mice?" she said, scrutinizing the meal.

"Yes."

"Yikes!" Yvette said. "These are big. How did you catch them?"

"I set traps earlier while you were sleeping. It's easy to track mice because they make trails littered with droppings. Mice here have never really encountered humans, so it was easier than I thought. So with a flat rock, sticks, a vine, and Geoffrey's peanuts, I found dinner."

"That's creative but ruthless, Max," she said, flinching.

"I know, but that's the only way we were going to eat. We have no choice. We need the energy to be ready for the travel early tomorrow morning. You'd better start eating."

Yvette hesitated before biting into the rodent's raw flesh. She chewed for a while before swallowing. Max looked at her quietly.

"This is surprisingly good," she said.

"Told ya."

"Where did you learn that trick?" she said after she finished the first mouse.

"I have vague memories growing up in the Congo. I was probably five or six that time before I left, but I vividly remember my grandfather catching mice using a similar method."

Yvette nodded.

"I've never thought I'd be eating a mouse."

"Tastes like chicken," Max said with a smile. "A human being can eat anything as long as their consciousness tells them it's edible."

"I've eaten all kinds of insects before, but this is a first," Yvette said. "I think it's our culture. It almost feels like a taboo to eat a rodent, yet I'm sure our ancestors feasted on these."

"No doubt. My uncle used to catch frogs, and we ate frog legs sometimes—he said it was a long tradition for our family."

"It's a delicacy around the world. Like escargot!"

They sat briefly, remember life on Earth.

"I could have started a fire, but didn't want to attract any unnecessary attention."

"It's O.K. It's not that cold."

Yvette continued eating.

"This actually tastes much better than I imagined. A little jerky and rubbery!"

"The sun can do wonders."

"How?"

Max pointed up the tree. "I put it up there."

"You climbed the tree?"

"Sure. We did it all the time when I was a kid. I'm surprised the skill hasn't left me yet."

"I'm jealous."

"I have a feeling you could live just fine if we end up getting stranded."

Yvette finished eating, and Max led the way searching for a place to camp for the night.

The giant tree trunks, the protruding roots, undergrowth, and clinging vines turned the forest into a bewildering maze, making it almost impossible to find a way out. They stealthily navigated forward. Each step on the damp mulch felt eerie.

"I think we were here before," Yvette said, seeing freshly broken shrubs.

"It might not be us."

Yvette looked at him. "We are going around in circles."

"Right. I think so, too."

Yvette sat down. "What do we do?"

Max climbed up a tall tree and looked for the edges of the forest. An owl hooted in the distance.

"We'll sleep here," Max said. "In the tree."

"Sounds good to me," Yvette said.

Max broke off and sharpened two tree branches and strapped them onto his back. Using a vine, Max helped Yvette up the big tree. The tree trunk branched into three, forming a flat surface wide enough for two people to lie down and curl up at the point where they converged. Both Max and Yvette used vines to strap themselves to the boughs.

"I have never been a fan of sleeping like this. I can't sleep without something covering my body."

"I don't think I can either, but I will try while I keep watch."

"It's getting chilly," Yvette said.

"Once you're asleep, you'll be O.K."

"I hope that happens soon. My jaw is literally shaking."

"Here, let me—" Max said.

Yvette leaned in and wrapped her arms around Max before he could finish. As she spoke, her face was so close that he could feel her breath. Max glanced at Yvette. She was staring at him. Instantly their eyes locked. They looked into each other's eyes and stopped for a long time, as if seeking permission from each other or not knowing what to do next. Max felt a sudden rush of blood throughout his body, followed by a powerful urge to kiss her. His heart was thudding inside his chest as she drew closer and closer, their noses almost touching. He could not breathe. And then, with an air of alarm, Max shook himself.

"You should try to get some sleep," he said, biting his lips.

Yvette closed her eyes and frowned. "Yes, you're right."

Max wrapped his arms around Yvette and rubbed her shoulders.

"This feels much better," she said. "Can we stay like this forever?"

"That would be nice, wouldn't it? Heat transfer is always better between two people."

They cuddled each other. Max felt the hard bare surface of the sharpened sticks pressing against his shoulder, within easy reach should he need to strike intruders. Uncomfortable, but he ignored it. He squeezed Yvette more tightly.

She reciprocated. They cuddled in each other's arms, their pair of hearts beating to the rhythm of the nocturnal sounds.

"It's gonna be O.K.," Max whispered.

"I know," Yvette said. "We will make it."

Max stayed awake for a long time but, like a wave, sleep swept over him.

CHAPTER TWENTY-EIGHT

Unidentified location, Aoratosia

MAX FELT A CRASHING SOUND. *Bones. Twigs.* He reflexively reached for his magnetochrome pulse gun. It was gone. "Crap!" He clicked his tongue, remembering he had had it the day before. His heart was pounding. He slowed his breathing. After gaining his composure, he noticed Yvette was not there. He looked around and saw nothing. He listened and waited. The mulch crashed again; this time closer. He stealthily withdrew one of the sharpened poles from the strap. He paused and listened. The sound was coming from his right, behind the thick undergrowth. Max slid down the tree. He clenched the sharp spike as a shield and tiptoed toward the sound. Cold sweat trickled down his spine. His legs shook slightly as he crept closer and closer to the sound. He held the spike tighter and gritted his teeth. He burst into the bushes.

"Aah!" Yvette screamed, her own spike pointed towards Max.

"Yvette!" Max said. "It's you. What are you doing? I almost hurt you!"

"Max! You scared the shit out of me! You almost gave me a heart attack."

"You should never sneak away like that, not in this place. We don't even know what's out there. Next time tell me, please!"

"I'm sorry. It never crossed my mind. I wanted to be helpful."

"By getting yourself killed?"

"I know, that was kinda stupid. Thought, I'm a big girl and can help out. I'm not used to being babysat. I'm usually the one doing the caregiving."

"You could have woken me up."

"My bad."

"When I heard the sound and you were not there, I didn't know what to think. I thought it might be an animal. Especially after what I saw yesterday."

"I shouldn't have done that. Part of me wanted to tell you, but then again, you were sleeping so peacefully."

"What are you doing here this early, anyway?" Max said.

"I couldn't sleep anymore. Sleeping on the branch was super uncomfortable, so I decided to climb down to look around."

"How's the leg?"

"Hurts like hell," she said. "But I can put some weight on it now."

Max noticed that the swelling on Yvette's leg had visibly abated.

"Great."

"Look what I found," Yvette said. She handed Max one of the brown round objects she was holding.

"What is this?" Max said, examining the hard-shelled seed. His body began to relax a bit.

"It's a fruit."

"A fruit? What kind?" Max said.

"It tastes like a fruit."

"You ate one?!"

"Two. They're pretty good."

"How do you know it's edible and not poisonous?"

"A group of ladybirds and beetles were eating the fruit, so I figured it couldn't be poisonous."

Max shook the hard fruit.

"I have already eaten some, and I am not dead yet," Yvette said, smiling.

Max nodded. He studied the hard-shelled iridescent fruit.

"Crack it, and you can suck the seeds for the juice and tissue. I think you can also eat the seeds. But problems pooping are at your own discretion."

Max smashed the fruit against a tree. It cracked open, sending some brown juice all over his suit. Max shucked the hard shell using the hilt of his pocketknife. He sank his teeth into the caramel-colored fleshy contents. Thick juice oozed, escaping through the corners of his mouth, and meandered down his chin. He spit out the bare seeds. He gulped three more mouthfuls before wiping the dripping juice off his chin with the back of his hand.

After a few more mouthfuls and with an appreciative smile, he said, "This is really good!"

"I told you."

"Good job." Max pulled a breath of air. "I like the tingling aftertaste that's left on my tongue."

"There's more if you want."

"I will gladly take more."

Yvette handed him two more fruits.

"Being stranded here might not be that bad," Yvette said. "We can survive."

Max chuckled.

"We can ride some primitive horses, probably tame them. The forest supplies plenty of food."

Max laughed. "And we can start our own human colony."

"Right."

"That would be interesting. But not like this, unless we don't have a choice."

"I think I would be okay with a life like this," Yvette said.

"We'll get out of here," Max said.

"What's the plan now?"

"To keep moving and find the edge of the forest and the aeroglid-ers. We can salvage whatever is left and head back to the ship. I don't how much time we have before the ship returns to Earth," Max said, looking at the sun through the canopies. "O.K., we need to start moving. The earlier the better. How're you feeling?"

"I think I can manage."

"That's good news."

Max helped Yvette collect fruits from the ground. They returned to the tree camp and collected all the poles.

"Wait. Do you hear that?" she said.

"Hear what?"

"The birds! The song! It's Hubert!"

"You mean your friend the parrot."

"Let's move in that direction before the singing stops."

"You think he is looking for us?"

"Yes. I think we are close to the edge of the forest. Let's go."

"Waa Cha Kai!" Echoes percolated through the woods, increasing in intensity with each call.

"We are getting closer. Let's hurry."

"I can see more sunlight!" Yvette said.

"Yes, that's the edge," Max said.

As they trudged closer and closer, Hubert's call became more audible. They finally emerged the forest's edge into the grassland. Early-morning grazers and other animals were already there.

A group of parrots swooped above them. Hubert flew and perched on Yvette's shoulder. Yvette grabbed the picture dangling on Hubert's leg.

"My picture?!" Yvette said.

Max drew closer.

"That means Alex and Geoffrey are still alive," Max said, beaming. "They sent him with the message!"

"Yeah. Because I left this picture at the ship."

"Good, boy!" Yvette kissed Hubert. "You came back for us."

"Come on," Max said. "I know the way now."

He led them past the river towards the hill on the river's other side.

MAX AND ALEX pushed the aerogliders up the hill. Max pressed the start-up knob, hoping the engine would work. There was no response. When Yvette tried hers, the screen flickered and the engine came to life. A note from Alex was projected on the screen.

"Alex made it!" Yvette said.

Max tried to reset the transponder. The radio was not working. He walked up and down several times searching for a signal, to no avail.

"No bars."

"We're screwed."

"Maybe and maybe not," Max said. "Let's keep trying."

"You think that will work?"

"It should work. We really don't have a choice."

After a few futile efforts with the wires, the radio finally crackled.

Max keyed the mike. "Coldbox, do you copy?"

Max and Yvette waited impatiently for a response.

"Coldbox, do you copy, over?"

They waited more. A faint squawk emerged. "Copy that, Coldbox. What's your status? Max, thank god you made it. Where are you? Is Yvette with you?"

"Hi, Geoffrey," Yvette said into the microphone.

"Thank god you are alive after what Alex told me happened in the forest."

"Yes, we are all here. Will need some medical attention as soon as possible, but we are fine for now."

"We will be ready."

"Preparing to set out."

"What's your ETA?" Alex said.

"Two hours. Non-affirmative," Max said.

"That's good. Looks like we are going to have a sandstorm very soon."

"Do we have enough time?"

"I don't know. But you need to move now."

"I'm afraid we have a problem," Max said. "The actuator on my aeroglider is non-responsive. And my suit LSS unit is fried."

"Crap," Geoffrey said.

"Can you reset the gearbox remotely from the ship?" Max said.

"Yes. I am on it."

A few seconds later, Geoffrey said, "For some reason, I cannot override the command and reset your aeroglider."

"Crap!"

"But we can only reset and update the software from the ship," Yvette said.

"Correct," Geoffrey said. "It has never happened before in training."

Max and Yvette looked at each other. Max said, "To hell with the protocol. Let's do it the old-fashioned way."

"How do you know how to do that?" Yvette said.

"Bosco showed me once during training. Watch and learn."

Max stripped the hood off the gearbox. "I will jump-start mine using your gearbox, and let's pray that's sufficient to power mine up."

He tinkered with the wires, and the aeroglider screen lit up.

"Geoffrey, try again," Yvette said.

"I'm in. Wait a few seconds." He punched more keys.

"It's good to go," Geoffrey said. "I was able to program the aeroglider and override the settings, but the update is taking longer to reset the engine. Once that's done you should be able to reset your LSS unit."

"How long?"

"It's still buffering, so I am not sure."

"O.K., we will wait."

The radio crackled.

"Geoffrey, do you copy?"

There was no response. Max hurled the transponder into the dirt and kicked the base of the aeroglider. He locked his hands behind his head. "What do we do now?" he said.

"We wait," Yvette said.

Max sat on the aeroglider, eyes downcast.

"What is that?"

"The sand storm. Shit!" Max said.

The wind had picked up speed. The sky was getting darker.

"Yes," Yvette said. "Look toward the other side of the forest."

Max glared at the black cloud over the forest.

"You need to leave now," Max said.

"We can find somewhere to shelter," she said.

"Too late," he said. "Take most of the stuff. I will catch up with you."

"Dammit!"

"Yvette, I know you can do this."

"I'll try."

"How far is the storm?"

"About five minutes away," Yvette said, looking at her aeroglider screen.

"Yes, hurry!"

"What are you going to do?" Yvette said.

"You have to leave. I will stay and wait for the update to finish." Max said.

"No, we will stay together!" Yvette said. "I'm not leaving you here."

"But both of us can't go," Max said. "That means only one of us has the chance to leave this place." Max already cutting one of the electric wires from the control box of his aeroglider. The machine interface kept blinking, indicating an error. He commanded it to override the protocol. Next, he retrofitted the aeroglider, overriding the command into manual mode.

"I will try to control mine manually from now on."

"What if it doesn't work?"

"It will," he said. "Otherwise, I am screwed. I don't even know if the updating is still going."

"Max, I can't—"

The engines barked, cutting her off.

"Listen to me!" Max said. "You have to go. Our findings will be of no use if they perish with us here. Studying these fossils will help change the world and evolutionary history."

Max secured the cache of samples onto Yvette's aeroglider.

"You're good to go now!" he helped her onto the glider.

Yvette was sobbing.

"Take the epinephrine," Max said. He handed Yvette the adhesive patch, which she applied on her shoulder.

"I don't want to do this," she said.

"Neither do I, but this is the only choice we have."

Yvette embraced Max and kissed Max on the cheek, tears in her eyes.

"Hurry!" Max said.

"Max—"

Max ignored her. "If I'm not there in the next few hours, tell the others to leave."

"I couldn't."

"You can," he said. "Promise me you will."

Yvette breathed a deep sigh. "O.K."

"I will be there," Max said, not looking at Yvette but tampering with the wires in the gearbox. "Now go as fast as you can."

Yvette steered the aeroglider over the hill.

"Don't forget the nitrous oxide. You'll need it," Max shouted.

She turned around and watched from a distance as Max was engulfed by the storm. He wasn't looking at her now. Tears streamed down Yvette's cheeks.

She turned to face forward and sped away.

CHAPTER TWENTY-NINE

Coldbox

GEOFFREY KEYED THE TRANSPONDER. "Mission control, do you copy?"

After a long pause, a voice crackled back. "Roger that, Coldbox. The port is ready for you."

"We have two officers missing; still waiting for them," Alex said.

"Copy that," the voice said. "You've got 60. . . can't. . . on time."

"Mission control, come again," Alex said.

The transmitter crackled and died.

"Dang it. We lost them!" Geoffrey said.

"Control station. Do you copy? Control station, do you copy?!" Alex yelled into the transmitter, turning the dial on the receiver. "No response."

"Did he say we have 60 minutes?" he said.

"Yes, I think so."

"What do we do now?" Geoffrey said.

"I don't know. We wait and see."

"What's wrong with the transmission?" Yvette said.

"Too much interference with Jupiter's magnetic field. I can't think of anything else."

"The teleporter ring will be up in an hour! We need to get ready for takeoff."

Geoffrey adjusted the diaper under his suit with his hand before sitting.

Alex stood at the far-right window looking outside and yelled, "Wait! I see something."

"What is it?" Geoffrey said, leaping from his seat.

"In the distance—approaching." Alex handed the binoculars to Geoffrey.

"That's an aeroglider!" Geoffrey said.

He pulled up the facial recognition software panel, which identified Yvette.

"Where is Max?" Alex said.

"I don't see anyone else."

"There is motion behind her," he said, looking into the binoculars.

"What the heck is that?" Alex said.

"It's a sandstorm," Geoffrey said. "Yup, like I said before, these gravity waves create massive storms."

"How big is it?"

"A couple hundred knots. The radar can't measure that far."

"We have to leave very soon." Alex snatched his binoculars and scanned the area.

"How long is it going to take for the storm to get to us?"

"About 20 minutes, I'd guess."

By now Yvette was close.

"Let's get her inside," Geoffrey said.

Alex was already at the dock chamber by the time Geoffrey finished speaking. She heaved open the hydraulic pressure doors. The burst of hot air from outside caught Alex on the right side of her facemask. She grimaced.

"Alex, are you O.K.?" Geoffrey said over the intercom.

"It's only a graze."

Yvette maneuvered the aeroglider past the decontamination chamber into the dock chamber where Alex was waiting. They embraced. Geoffrey joined them.

"Oh, man, that looks bad," Geoffrey said, as he helped Alex remove Yvette's facemask and then the bandage on her leg. They helped her to the medical chamber.

"Where is Max?" Alex said.

"I'm sorry," Yvette said.

"Oh, man!" Alex said. "But thank God we got you!"

Everyone paused.

"How much hydrazine do we have left?" Yvette said.

"Enough to get away, but we have to leave soon. Otherwise we are stuck here," Geoffrey said.

"Can we wait for a few more minutes? I'm sure Max is coming," Yvette said. "Max made me promise that if he doesn't get here in 30 minutes, then we leave. We still have five minutes."

The ground shook.

"Geoffrey, fire the engine up," Alex said.

Geoffrey sat down next to the control panel.

"Good thinking. The storm will be here soon."

"We'll wait and see."

As he spoke, a figure emerged from the storm.

"Look, it's Max!" Alex said.

"It's him!" Geoffrey said, observing the I.D. panel. "Open the door!"

"I knew he would make it," Yvette said.

"Can you open the door?"

"When he gets close. We don't want to lose any more pressure and risk excessive contamination from outside."

Max's aeroglider was in sight now, approaching quickly. The miles clicked down on the tracker signal.

Geoffrey radioed. "Max, do you copy?"

There was no answer.

"His radio is not working."

"He messed up the wiring."

"I hope his safety latch is not jammed."

"I doubt it. He is not slowing down."

"Activating the emergency braking chutes! He is gonna hit us and blow us up!" Alex said.

"Got it," Geoffrey said.

"Open the door," Yvette said.

"Wait for it," Geoffrey said, eyeing the screen. "We're surrounded by a storm. Stuff will get in."

"We don't have a choice. Either we open the door, or we leave Max out. The latter is not an option."

"I got this," Geoffrey said. He placed his hand next to the remote-controlled door switch and waited. He counted as the aeroglider got closer and opened the door when the aeroglider was mere yards away. The chute inflated, covering the whole entrance. The aeroglider slammed into the inflated chute. The crash shook the ship and knocked Yvette and Alex to the floor. Geoffrey rushed to the control computer and quickly sealed the door.

"He's in!" he said. "Get him in his flight suit, now!"

Alex was already running to the docking chamber. Geoffrey followed and Yvette limped after him.

Max lay on the floor, under the chute. He struggled to move. Yvette unlocked Max's helmet. She checked his breathing; he was fine. She noticed blood trickling down his temple from the same cut he had sustained from the fall from the cliff. She motioned to Yvette and Geoffrey and they carried him to the medical examination room. Ulysses beeped and scanned Max from head to toe. The others secured Max to the examination table and hurried to the main control room to prepare for departure.

"What do you see, Ulysses?" Max said.

The bot beeped. "No concussion, Mr. Folksay. You're going to be O.K. It could have been worse if not for the parachute."

"That's good enough for me!" Max said. "Let me up so I can zip into my flight suit."

Max swallowed extra pain killers. He forced himself to his feet and headed to the control room.

Everyone was surprised to see him.

"I'm fine," Max said. "We have to get out of here now!"

Everyone hustled to their seats.

"Start the ship," Max roared. "Let's finish this."

"How are you feeling?" Alex said.

"Good. Better than I thought I would feel."

"How did you do it?" Yvette said.

"The magic of nitrous oxide!" Max said, with a reassuring smile. "I flew like a bullet. Yourself?"

"A little nauseated, but gaining myself."

"All right, all," Max said. "We'll talk more about this when we get home. Geoffrey, how much time do we have for the portal to open?"

"Ten minutes."

"All right, let's get this baby going," Max said, turning on the takeoff gears. He entered the portal coordinates and turned on the fuel pressure booster.

Everyone smiled.

"Let's roll."

"Oh, no!" Geoffrey immediately said.

"What is it?"

"The main thruster is not producing enough power."

"I think we have a clogged valve or something in the compartment," Yvette said. "We're not getting enough oxygen."

"Can we fix it?"

"Yes, but someone has to go out. The only way to do that is from the outside. That will help stabilize the pressure and allow us more time close to the ground."

"I can go out and fix it," Alex said.

"It's too dangerous," Max said.

"No one is going out now," Yvette said. "We don't have much time. The storm is intense."

"At the rate of the tremor, we won't have enough time to disentangle the engine from the valves."

"Our sensors predict an eruption at our current position any minute now," Geoffrey said.

"What choice do we have?" Yvette said.

"We can use the nitrous oxide boosters to force launch. The updraft might give us enough thrust to the ring."

"The valves are not opening. We can't do that. It will blow the pressure pumps and gears!" Alex said.

"We have to, one way or another."

"Did you say the updraft 'might' help us?"

"Yes!"

"Be specific."

"We have a 20 percent chance of reaching the ring if we can reach that mountain at maximum speed."

"That's something. That's enough for me," Max said.

The others nodded.

"All right, let's get this baby going."

"Yes, Captain."

Geoffrey turned on full throttle. The ship jolted and shook free from the ground. It finally steadied and dragged forward. The seat belts latched automatically.

"All right, crew, sit tight and enjoy the bumpy ride," Geoffrey said.

"Let's run her low up to that mountain. That will allow us to build enough momentum and power. With the help of that mountain or something with high altitude, we might be able to provide enough upward thrust. The updraft should be able to overcome the air current and shoot us up."

"It's gonna be tough with all the rock and boulders in the way," Alex said.

Geoffrey turned on the boosters. "Let's do it!"

"Guys, we trained for this!" Max said.

The storm was approaching, its magnitude casting a shadow over the sun. The ground trembled even more and the ship creaked even with the noise cancellation system. Shrapnel and debris clattered off the ship's exterior.

"Looks like we only have one way to go," Yvette said.

"Ready!" Max said.

The others nodded.

"We practiced for this. Remember your training. If we work together, we will get to that mountain," Max said, his vigor starting to return.

"We got this," Geoffrey said.

"We can do this!" Yvette said.

"Let's do it!" Alex said.

"All right. It's show time!" Max said, engaging the liftoff controls.

The spacecraft hovered over the molten surface, stirring up a trail of regolith behind it. The ship leapt off and shot forward. It was everything. Horsepower. Speed. Smoke!

"Hold on!" Geoffrey said.

The ship swerved sideways into the narrow passage. It vanished between two massive boulders, barely missing one that stood on the center of the passage, then burst into the opening where numerous paths merged. The ship slashed to the left, narrowly missing another giant boulder. It maneuvered past the narrow gorge and squeezed through three pillars before accelerating over plumes of volcanic ash.

"Thirty seconds to target!" Geoffrey said.

The pressure of the storm was sucking in the ship, with debris battering on all sides. Metal cranked, clanked, and hissed. Coldbox shook free and shot over the mountain as the dust from the storm grazed its hind panels, taking traces of dust with it. The updraft shot the ship towards Aoratosia's atmosphere, then zigzagged into Jupiter's magnetosphere. As the ship surged, the crew was jerked from side to side, and were glad they were strapped in their seats.

After a struggle, the ship stabilized and maintained its proper path and sped into space. Geoffrey managed the transponder. The connection to mission control was back on.

"Mission control, do you copy?"

"Copy that Coldbox, go on. The baby is connected. You're good to go. Copy that, Coldbox."

"We lost some of our normal functions. Prepare for an emergency landing," Geoffrey said.

"We've also got some injured personnel," Alex added.

"Copy that. The medical team will be waiting."

"Roger that."

Geoffrey shut the transponder off.

"We did it!" Alex said.

"Home sweet home, here we come!" Max said.

They watched as Coldbox spiraled into the teleporter ring. The ship vanished into the black space.

CHAPTER THIRTY

Mission Control, Spartan Enterprises HQ

THE RUSHED departure from Aoratosia wreaked havoc at headquarters. Anticipating the worst, emergency landing protocols were quickly enacted. Recovery teams stood by on a temporary base near Galveston.

"The ship is coming down fast," one of the engineers said.

McKomic paced the room, studying the shuttle's path, outlined on the bubble hologram. His mind raced, considering a thousand possible scenarios. A perfectly safe landing of a reusable shuttle was a result of a carefully calibrated reentry into the Earth's orbit, relying on countless hours of simulations conducted by supercomputers programmed with a near-endless number of equations. But even so, a slight glitch could lead to catastrophic consequences. Doc and McKomic knew that. This was one of those dreaded and remote outcomes. How could they have not anticipated this from all simulations? The possibility of an early reentry into Earth's orbit at an angle this steep had not been accounted for. And now they had the additional issue of a glitch in the computer system that knocked out all communication with the capsule! McKomic worried about how the capsule could withstand the heat.

"Any alternative method?" McKomic said.

"No, sir," one engineer said. "Everything seems to be malfunctioning."

"How certain are you of an impact?"

"One hundred percent, sir!"

Pete interjected: "Sir, the shuttle is going towards Europe, over the English Channel!"

"Where?" Doc hurried to Pete's monitor.

Pete pointed on the monitor. "Calais, London, or any of these cities within the highlighted area."

"How much area are we talking about?"

"Fifty square miles. With that speed and momentum, I'd say about most of the shoreline cities will be demolished."

McKomic paced back and forth across room, rubbing his scalp carelessly. He cursed. His lower lip quivered. He had been through trying times, but this one tested his stamina.

"We should contact the countries," Doc said.

McKomic nodded.

"Connect me to the British and French ambassadors and representatives of the other countries."

"On it, sir." One of the engineers said.

A few moments later, the English prime minister and French president were live on the panel. Calls came in from the Spanish and Portuguese presidents simultaneously. A few seconds later, calls from Switzerland, Germany, and Italy came in. McKomic had met some of the leaders several times when they negotiated on behalf of their countries to use Spartan Enterprises shuttles to send cargo to the space station.

"Ladies and gentlemen," McKomic said, "I think you all know why you're here."

They all nodded.

"I brought you here so you can tell your countries to stand down from attacking our shuttle."

"Have you got it under control?" the French president asked.

"But we are working on it."

The Frenchwoman lifted her hands in a sign of disbelief.

"And we are supposed to take your word for it," the English prime minister said.

"I understand all the frustration," McKomic said. "I have done

347

business with you all before. Have I ever failed to deliver on my promises? All I am asking is for more time and your word that none of your countries will do anything stupid."

"Get it under control," the German chancellor said. "If your ship reaches the atmosphere still on a trajectory that would crash into a populated area in our country, we won't hesitate to destroy it. We are not going to jeopardize thousands and thousands of lives to save a few on the ship. We are talking about thousands of people whose lives are at risk here."

"I'm aware of that," McKomic said.

"I will try to withhold aggressive force as long as I can," the English prime minister said.

The others nodded.

"Do you all give me your word?"

They all nodded.

Doc ended the live feed.

Instantaneously, a call from the White House came in. McKomic turned the live receiver on. The POTUS sat with her usual entourage packed around the situation room, including the air force and navy generals, all staring at the screen. She said only a few words.

"Cordell, tell me you got this under control," the president said.

"We will! We are fixing the problem as we speak," McKomic said.

"I believe you. There's a lot at stake here. I hope you get this under control as soon as possible."

"We are doing the best we can, and we will have the situation under control," McKomic said. "If it reaches the atmosphere, you can blast it up, but give us a chance until then."

"This is our mess, and we are the ones who need to clean it up," the president said. "I've already instructed our people at the Spangdahlem Base and commanded them to destroy the capsule if it gets too close."

"I understand," McKomic said.

Browsing the briefing file, one of the generals looked up and said, "If we let it descend more, it may be impossible to intercept the ship without destroying the city and surrounding areas. If it comes to it, we will blow up the ship."

"There are people on that ship, too. We can't just blow it up."

"We don't have any other choice!"

"Dammit, George! There are people and precious cargo on that ship! We do have a choice! I'll tell you when you should bring it down."

"O.K. Get this under control, will you?"

McKomic ignored him. He turned to Pete and whispered, "How much time do we have until it reaches our atmosphere?"

"Twenty minutes at most," Pete said.

"The ship is 20 minutes away from our atmosphere. Can you stand back that long?" McKomic said.

"Sure. Let me know as soon as anything changes."

"I will."

The call ended.

Despite the mounting pressure from the Capitol and the Europeans, McKomic had lost none of his composure. He answered the phone calls and directed everyone sharply but calmly. His voice underscored years of experience and his uncanny ability to handle challenging situations. McKomic remained stolid, despite the looming catastrophe. Maybe it was experience. His experience as an entrepreneur had instilled a stoic composure which made him impervious to irritation and fear.

He looked around the room. Everyone was staring at him. He knew the mission's success hung on him—every action he took from now on. With it came the blame, fallout, and everything else. McKomic ignored the tiny droplets of sweat glistening on his flushed forehead. No one knew what was going on in his head.

"Pete, show me the trajectory again," McKomic said.

"We have to find a way to stop it. There is nuclear material on that ship. We don't want the containment gasket exploding."

"How strong is it?"

"Can withstand about 10,000 pounds of force."

"That should be O.K."

"I don't want to take any chance of creating a nuclear hell," Doc said.

Meanwhile, the TV to the right was also tracking, showing images of the red fireball descending towards Earth. The media, those creeps, feasted on stories like these. He wondered when they had had time to assemble so-called experts in suits debating the issue and what the air force should do. Even the ones who had praised him a few hours before had now turned on him. The pundits said they foresaw this happening because of McKomic's carelessness. He knew the whole world was watching. He switched the TV off.

"Let's prepare for an emergency landing," McKomic said.

"Sir, we don't know where the shuttle will land. We have to evacuate the city."

"We don't have time," Doc said.

"Then we have to use the repeller," McKomic said.

The repeller was a magnetic mesh prototype developed by Spartan Enterprises for the Department of Defense. The device was intended to stop missiles and act as a safer, space-saving way of landing reusable capsules from the space station. The model used six high-powered drones, carefully calibrated to fly in a hexagonal formation and emit magnetic waves, forming a net capable of stopping rockets or missiles.

"But that's a prototype, sir. We still need more tests."

McKomic slapped the table.

"That's good enough. Right now, we don't have time," McKomic said, with an exasperated sniff. "I want all the drone drivers ready to go now. I will drive one myself."

Everyone in the room looked at him, but no one dared question his decision although they felt it could be a suicide mission.

"Connect me to Coldbox!" McKomic barked.

GEOFFREY OPENED HIS EYES. He felt his face. He was O.K. He stretched and reached for the central console. The screen was covered in blinding, flashing emergency lights. He pressed the systems-recovery knob, but there was no response.

"Shit!" he said.

"Coldbox," the transponder said.

He scrambled onto the mouthpiece, hands trembling.

"Mission control, do you copy?" Geoffrey said.

The radio squawked.

"Coldbox, copy. Come in!" a calm mechanical voice responded from the other side. "What's your status?"

"We hit a snag!" Geoffrey said, as the ship burrowed into Earth's stratosphere. "We are coming down fast."

"We see you. Just stay the course."

"Roger that."

Around the same time, one by one, the rest of the crew regained consciousness.

"What happened?" Alex said.

Without answering, everyone strapped on their life jackets and masks from under their seats. Max helped Yvette fasten her life vest and snapped himself back into his seat.

"We will be O.K.!" Yvette said, sitting very still.

"We'll be fine," Max said as the spacecraft shook and lurched.

The emergency siren blared: "Engine malfunction! Engine malfunction!"

"What was that?" Yvette said.

Geoffrey banged the keyboard and yelled, "We just blew the left engine."

"How?"

"We hit something."

"Crap. Can we fix it?"

"No, but we can try to stabilize using the other one," Max said. "We don't even need the power since we are descending."

"We do. That's the only way we can decelerate and land on the exact coordinates."

Max pressed the mike. "Mission control, we've lost an engine."

There was a long pause. The line crackled, and finally, a voice came through, "Copy that, let's see if we can help. Coldbox, do you copy?" Doc said. "You have to alter your route."

"We lost the left engine," Geoffrey said.

"There should be a contingency safety protocol," Doc said.

"There is," Max said.

The ship lurched, heaving Max back onto his seat. The transponder wire detached and slid below the deck.

"Coldbox. Come in!" Doc's voice said.

He repeated this several more times. There was no response. After a long pause he said, "Crap! We lost them!" Mission Control's emergency signal blared in the background.

"The braking engine is jammed!" Geoffrey said. "We're losing control."

"We're gonna have to go old-school. Release the deceleration parachutes," Max said.

"The emergency chute system is compromised, too. Not sure if the capsule can withstand that much heat."

"Really?"

"Not working. Its main control is fried!" Geoffrey punched a few buttons to no avail. "Can you shut down all the engines? I tried to disable everything, but it's all going haywire."

Max pulled himself up. "We need to shut down the other one!"

"That will send us into a red-hot cannonball. I doubt the capsule can withstand the heat."

"Shutdown is the only option, unless you have a better one. We'll try to fix it," Max said.

"No one has ever fixed anything in space moving at this speed," Yvette said.

"Doesn't mean it can't be done."

"Someone has to go to the engine room and fix it manually."

"How's that gonna help?"

"Stopping the other engine will steer the ship from its current trajectory. If I'm right, that should pull us toward the Gulf of Mexico."

"But is that even possible? No one has ever done that before."

"No."

The ship was descending fast and accelerating.

"Man, we're screwed," Geoffrey said.

"At least we'll die as heroes," Alex said.

"How much time do we have left until we hit Earth's atmosphere?" Max said.

"Eleven minutes!" Geoffrey said. "But it may change since we are picking up speed."

"O.K.!" Max said. "Open the engine room door! I am going back there!" he said, unlatching his seatbelt.

"You can't do that!" Geoffrey protested. "Max, this is madness. You can't expect me to—"

"Open the engine door, Geoffrey!" Max said.

"This is suicide!"

"Goddammit, Geoffrey! Open the damned door."

Yvette, Alex, and Geoffrey eyed Max.

"Damn it, Geoffrey! Open the door! I order you! We don't have time for quarreling about this. Either we go down, or we take action! I choose to take action!"

Everyone looked around. *Was this their farewell?* Geoffrey opened the door. Max fastened himself to the retractable rope on the rails on the side of the wall and floated out through the small door into the engine room.

"No need for emotional farewells. We'll make it!" he said, before shutting the door.

"I will walk you through it," Geoffrey said.

"Great."

Something in the engine room exploded.

"Max!" Alex said.

"Max!" Geoffrey shouted.

"You gotta come back in here!" Yvette said. There was no response on the intercom.

Everyone looked at each other as smoke diffused from the engine room, displacing all the oxygen in the control room.

"I love you guys!" Yvette whispered.

"No, don't say that. We'll be O.K.!" Alex said.

"No, this is not O.K.," Geoffrey said.

Yvette held Alex and Geoffrey's hands.

"Whatever happens," Yvette said, "This has been the best time of my life." A tear trickled down her cheek.

"I love you guys," Geoffrey said, choking.

"You are my family," said Alex.

"Twenty. Nineteen. Eighteen," the heartless mechanical voice continued, counting down the hundreds of miles towards Earth's atmosphere for what seemed like an eternity. Geoffrey, Yvette, and Alex sat rigid in their seats, still holding hands. They waited for an explosion. Nothing. They prayed silent prayers, squeezing each other's hands. Then the ship whiplashed, jerking the crew against the thrust of the westward engine, inflicting a momentary lapse in time. Darkness. This was the end! Everything stood still. And then, there was silence— silence that felt like forever.

CHAPTER THIRTY-ONE

Space

THE RADIO CRACKLED. Alex recovered first. Blurry blue light. She groaned, resetting her vision. She heard sounds of joy and celebration. Rather short-lived. Maybe she was in another realm, a realm of the dead. So much light. *Or maybe not!* She heard applause on the other side of the transponder. She could see the ocean now.

The radio crackled again. This time it was much more audible.

"Coldbox, you did it! You did it! Do you copy?"

Alex struggled to sit straight in her seat. She glanced right and left. Both Yvette and Geoffrey were starting to regain consciousness. She searched for the transponder, then saw it dangling on the floor with the detached cable.

"You did it! You did it!" the voices said.

Everyone at Mission Control was applauding.

"It worked!" Yvette said.

"I'm glad I put my diaper on!" Geoffrey said.

The others ignored him.

"Max! Where's Max?" Yvette said, struggling in her seat.

"Stay down!"

"Coldbox, prepare for an emergency landing. I want the area secured! No Russians!" McKomic barked on the other side.

"He did it! Max did it!" they shouted.

"Coldbox, prepare for an emergency landing!" the voice came again.

The ocean was now visible.

"It looks like we're going in for a splashdown. Alex, try the parachute and surface tension pads!"

"I'm trying!" Alex said. "It's not responding! Where is the dang knob?!"

"Right next to you. Kick it."

"Hang tight!" Alex kicked the lever with the sole of her boot several times. The sudden drag heaved the crew forward, then with a thud, it all went dark.

McKOMIC GRABBED his keys and sunglasses. "We can take my helicopter!"

"Make sure nothing goes to the media!" Doc barked into the phone. He was already at the heliport when he hung up. He jumped into the helicopter. McKomic hoovered the helicopter before Doc even finished fastening his seat belt.

"We should be there in a few minutes!"

"Where is your pilot?"

"He's home. I'll fly!"

"Very well."

Fifteen minutes later, the helicopter landed in Galveston, near the recovery base, a few miles from the Gulf of Mexico. Plumes of steam from the red-hot shuttle splashing into the ocean were still visible.

The team quickly secured the recovery zone. There was frenetic activity at the landing site. The response team, army, and gendarmerie were already there at the location. A swat car lingered by the bay. Two fighter jets whizzed past before making another sweep toward NASA. Four ambulances and a firetruck were on standby, lights blinking.

The crew were immediately extracted and medevacked into mobile quarantine boats and rushed to isolated medical examination rooms through pressurized air decontamination chambers on the bay. They were extensively evaluated and screened for contamination as a precautionary measure. Sea divers forklifted Coldbox from the bottom of the Gulf of Mexico. The charred capsule, together with the samples and recovered hardware, were thoroughly scanned before being brought inland as a general precaution and immediately quarantined from all unauthorized personnel. All machines and hardware on Coldbox were salvaged and thoroughly inspected before being brought into the main shop for testing and repair. The agency took precautions so not to risk anything. McKomic had been paranoid about it.

Doc hurried to the scene. Yvette and the rest of the crew were strapped to stretchers, with oxygen masks covering their mouths and noses, and being rushed from the decontamination tents to ambulances.

Doc screamed, trying to push through the guards. They restrained him.

"Sir, you cannot go in!"

"My daughter is in there!"

"I understand, sir. We have orders."

Doc paced back and forth, rubbing his temples. "Do you know anything? Are they O.K.? Is my daughter O.K.?"

"I don't know, sir," the officer said. "We have to wait for the medical teams to do their job."

Doc flashed his I.D. The officer apologized and motioned him through. Doc reached Yvette as she was being lifted into the ambulance.

"How is she?" he said, holding onto the stretcher.

"We can't say yet," one EMT said.

"But she kept saying the name 'Hubert'," the other EMT said. "That ring any bells?"

"No, none!"

The EMT shrugged. "That's weird."

"Hubert?" Doc said.

"I apologize, sir. No idea who or what that is? You can't get in here."

"I understand. Thank you!" Doc said.

The ambulance drove off. Doc left to make a call.

CHAPTER THIRTY-TWO

Texas Medical Center

DOC SPENT the next few hours in the hospital room with Yvette. He took no food, only coffee. He placed the charred journal on the nightstand beside Yvette. He watched as the EKG beeped to the feeble rising and falling of Yvette's chest. He prayed over her, although he knew she could not hear him. Two gavage tubes, one blue and one green, ran through her mouth and nose. He kissed her on the forehead and left the room for the lobby where everyone else was gathered, looking solemn. Geoffrey and Alex, who had miraculously survived with minor injuries, had just arrived. Reverend Kay and other acquaintances were waiting outside. Doc did not care to make any public statement and returned to sit by Yvette. McKomic was reading a magazine. Geoffrey was lying on a couch.

"I say you bring her the bird," said Geoffrey, and such was his authority as the pilot of the Coldbox mission that despite the hospital's rules it was swiftly done.

"Waa cha kai! Waa cha kai!" Hubert called.

Hubert, perched in a cage near Yvette's bed, flapped his wings.

This was the first time Hubert had talked.

Right then, Yvette opened her eyes and forced a cough.

"Get the doctor!" Doc said. Doc squeezed Yvette's hand. "You're awake!" Doc said. His mouth twitched as happy tears flooded his eyes. He let the tears drip down. Doc bent and kissed Yvette on the forehead and held her hand affectionately.

"Lie still, don't move."

Yvette turned her head wearily and shut her eyes. She seemed confused. Then Doc was standing beside her bed together with a few friends and relatives. She opened her eyes and tried to talk, but made no sense.

"Don't speak," Doc said.

Yvette shrugged, then mumbled in a soft voice, "What happened?"

"Don't worry about it," Doc said. "I will explain later. Rest now."

She looked at Hubert. "What's up, guy?" She struggled to move her hand to touch Hubert, but had heavy dripper tubes strapped on her arms.

"Waa cha kai!" Hubert said. Doc opened the cage. Hubert hopped up and down, rubbing his head on Yvette's cheek.

"I missed you so much, Hubert," Yvette said. Yvette looked up at Doc and smiled. "How did you—?"

"The doctors told me you kept screaming 'Hubert' when they rushed you in. Geoffrey and Alex said it was the parrot. Don't know how it survived."

"And how did you get him in here?"

"Some calls were made. When you were six, you used to say you wanted a parrot. And that you would name it Hubert."

"Oh, really? That's funny because I don't remember saying that. Thanks, Dad!"

"You're welcome. Honey, you need to rest."

"How did you even get him in here?"

"They smuggled him in," he said. "It doesn't hurt to break the protocol a few times."

Everyone laughed.

"Aw, Dad. You're the best!"

Yvette coughed.

Doc pressed the "call" button. A few seconds later, a nurse answered. Doc told her Yvette was awake and asked for the doctor.

The doctor entered shortly after. She checked Yvette's pulse and did some quick checks on Yvette, then administered some sleep medicine. She asked Doc to step outside with her.

"Is she O.K.?" Doc said.

"She is fine," the Doctor said with a smile. "She is a strong woman. All tests show negative. We didn't find any internal bleeding or organ damage either. Surprisingly, her vitals are improving dramatically. I am confident she will be out of here in a few days."

"Thank goodness."

"It's a miracle how any of them survived this ordeal."

Doc thanked her again, a smile on his face as he returned to the room.

"When can I go home?" Yvette said.

"Good news! The doctor said you will be able to go home in a few days."

Everyone cheered.

"Thank God."

"You'll need to do a few sessions to restore your memory."

Yvette frowned at him. "Where's Max?"

An eerie silence filled the room. Everyone's head was lowered, and no one replied.

"Honey—"

"He didn't make it, did he?"

Doc nodded. "Unfortunately, he didn't."

Tears trickled down Yvette's eye to her temples.

"Max passed away a few hours earlier tonight, despite efforts to revive him. He suffered pressure to his head and chest, which ruptured his right lung. By the time the medical crew got to him, it was too late."

"What happened?" Yvette said.

"You don't remember?"

"I don't remember anything after landing on Aoratosia."

"Like the doctor said, you need some rest. You will catch up to all the details when you fully recover."

"That's good. What happened to me?"

"You lost a lot of blood from your leg injury from Aoratosia. Fortunately, it wasn't infected."

Yvette closed her eyes in anguish. Then she fell asleep.

Doc got a soda at the vending machine and joined Reverend Kay and McKomic in the lobby.

"Have you checked the news lately?" Reverend Kay said. "This kid is a rock star. The crowd may demand to see him."

"I have never seen the public so hyped. They want him, and the media is making it worse. And who can blame them? If I were among them I would want it, too. I wish he was still alive!" Doc said.

"So what are we going to do?" McKomic said.

"Keep everything under wraps and wait," Doc said. "We stick to the plan as discussed earlier. The president will announce everything."

"The crowds are going to be brokenhearted when they get the news," Doc said.

"I suggest we inform the president first and let her deal with the crowd," Doc said. "She's good with people. I am sure she will find a way to tell the masses."

"Tony has a point. I think we should wait," McKomic said. "The welcome ceremony is in a few hours anyway."

"By the way, the press has been parked out front for hours. Are you going to brief them?" Reverend Kay said.

"I hate these guys!" McKomic said.

"It's protocol."

"Protocol sucks! Why not give us some damned alone time?" McKomic said.

"Maybe I should go ahead and brief them," Doc said.

"Let me do it," Reverend Kay said. "I deal with these kinds of things all the time. You're too invested in this. I am, too, but I think it would be better for me to disperse the crowd. I'm paid to deal with these situations."

"Thanks, Rev!"

Reverend Kay patted Doc on the shoulder and left the room.

CHAPTER THIRTY-THREE

Spartan Enterprises HQ

YVETTE FELT BETTER the next day. The doctor cleared her to go home on the condition that Yvette attend a series of follow-up psychiatric evaluations as part of the prescribed home care. She hated the visits and grudgingly attended these and other precautionary follow-ups. The control—she always wanted to be in control of herself, to be in control of her fate, but these sessions made her feel helpless. Against Doc's cautioning, she had returned to work. She insisted on being included in the team to solve the mystery.

Meanwhile, the Spartan Enterprises complex felt like a death procession. Daily chores resumed the next day, and the various departments worked on the samples brought from Aoratosia. The employees worked like hell. The goal was to understand Aoratosia as quickly as possible. All dominoes were falling into place. Congress had unanimously passed the Project ASHE bill, so Spartan Enterprises was flush with Uncle Sam's dollars. The public was thirsty for more details. McKomic knew this was great public relations and breaking news. The more mysterious, the better. Hence he urged the Spartan Enterprises team to leak information on portions of their findings to reporters. The non-classified stuff. It worked. The first announcement ranked as one of the most-watched segments in TV history. McKomic didn't stop there. He used his Twitter account to amplify the anticipation. He posted vague snippets, soil and rock-sample pictures, and sometimes truncated statements like "#New Life!!!" He let millions in the growing circle of McKomic aficionados interpret its meaning.

With the prospect of amassing great wealth on this new planet, many heavy hitters around the globe hoarded Spartan Enterprises stock. McKomic reveled watching the Spartan Enterprises stock skyrocket, making him the world's richest man. Pundits believed he was on the mark to be the first-ever trillionaire. And the idea of being self-made made even better TV. Everyone liked feel-good stories, stories of possibility, the underdog overcoming the odds. Yet despite all the elation, a vague feeling bothered McKomic. He always followed his instincts. He left the room to find Doc.

YVETTE LOOKED AT the clock with disdain. Time was flying, and there was so little time to do her research as she tried to squeeze in the daily routine. She left her workstation for the evaluation room. She had kept herself busy until the last minute to avoid thinking about the dreaded and inevitable psychoanalysis.

Doc was waiting at the entrance talking to Geoffrey and Alex, who had finished their sessions.

"Is this necessary, Doc?" she said. "I don't think I need a shrink anymore."

"It's part of the protocol," Doc said. "It will be over soon."

"If you say so."

She closed the door behind her. Dr. Wiens, her psychotherapist, was already in the room. He smiled at Yvette.

"Good afternoon, Ms. Yates," Dr. Wiens said. "How precise: Four o'clock sharp! I'm impressed."

"Good afternoon," Yvette said. "I hope my brain will produce a useful thought today."

"You've been doing great."

"Thanks."

"How are you feeling today?"

"I'm feeling good. How about you? How're you doing?" she said, looking sternly at him.

"I'm delighted. I'm doing fantastic, thank you. Are you ready to start today's adventure?"

"I am."

"We will use a fresh approach today rather than having you simply answering questions."

Yvette looked at him blankly.

"Are you familiar with peEEG?"

"That's where you map my brain activity, right?"

"Correct. It's the Perceived Electroencephalogram. The device you see here allows us to map your brain and produce associations between different parts of the brain to create a narrative. A circuit linking what the patient is saying and what they are thinking. It's one of the few out there so far. We recently started using it here in the US, but it's been approved in Europe for over a decade now. Well, does that make sense?"

"Sounds complicated."

"It is. But thankfully, the machine does that all for us."

"O.K."

"Do you have questions before we start?"

"No."

"O.K., then. You can lie down on the sofa, make yourself comfortable."

Yvette lay supine on the evaluation couch. Dr. Wiens moved the equipment cart closer to Yvette's sofa and straightened up a few things. He placed a helmet over Yvette's head and clipped on some electrodes. The cables connected to a monitor facing away from Yvette showing graphs with varying amplitudes tracking across the screen as Yvette talked. A second screen showed images of real-life objects based on Yvette's brain activity.

Dr. Wiens looked at the blank glass screen wall and nodded to the wall. He knew Doc was outside looking through the one-way glass at what was going on. On the other side, Doc nodded his approval, although he knew Dr. Wiens would not see him.

McKomic arrived, and they exchanged a few pleasantries. They waited in the observation room overlooking the makeshift psychotherapy room.

"Cordell," Doc said. "Do you think she will get her memory back?"

"Surely she will. She is a strong girl. Maybe she needs more time. But things will eventually come up."

"I hope so," Doc said. "She has these nightmares calling for Max. I don't think the pentobarbital prescriptions are working. She hardly ever sleeps at night without the medication. She's still a little confused. And it's getting me worried."

"Do you think it's the physical injury? Or the drug history?"

"Maybe post-traumatic stress. She continues to have these periodic violent convulsions and incomprehensible expressions. She sometimes is claustrophobic, afraid of the room, all the machines and the lights in her room. She insists on leaving the lights on."

Dr. Wiens stepped out of the examination room.

"Hey, Tony. Anything useful for me today?" he said.

"Nothing new," Doc said. "She's still in a confused state. She doesn't remember anything. All she ever remembers is Max's name, but apart from that, nothing else that happened during the trip and after. She keeps asking, 'Who is Max? Where is Max?' and questions like that."

"Could be because they were teammates."

"Yes. But it's bothering me."

"She doesn't know he is dead, does she?"

"She does," Doc said, pondering briefly. "But she still has nightmares about it."

"That's interesting," Wiens said. "I can use that angle to dig something up. I can use that information to channel her thoughts. She might remember more from that."

"Sorry I couldn't be of more help."

"That's better than nothing," Wiens said. "I think I have what I need to probe more." Dr. Wiens checked his wristwatch. "It's about time. Let me jump in."

"Good luck."

"She will be fine."

"I sure hope this is not permanent."

"She will get through it, Doc. I know she will." McKomic squeezed Doc's shoulder.

"I hope so."

"Give her a couple days."

Doc nodded his head without shifting his gaze from the glass wall.

While they were still talking, Dr. Wiens started asking Yvette some questions in a low, soft, and articulate voice.

"I want you to take deep breaths," he said, "and relax."

Yvette lay on the evaluation couch.

"Tell me about Max. Do you know Max?"

Yvette nodded.

"Did you have any romantic connection with Max?"

"No," she said.

"Do you love Max?"

Yvette opened her mouth to say something, but she did not say anything.

"Do you love Max?"

"Yes."

"Great. I want you to close your eyes and relax. Think of nothing else, but imagine you are floating in space with Max. Deep breath."

Yvette lay still, a smile showing on her face.

"What do you see?" he said.

"It's beautiful!" she softly sighed.

"Now imagine you are on another planet," he said, then paused for a few minutes. "Are you there?"

"Yes!"

"Can you describe what you see?"

"I see a beautiful sunset. It's rugged terrain. Everything is beautiful."

"Have you seen this before?"

"No."

"What else?"

"Animals—dinosaurs and woolly mammoths, and—" She shivered.

"Breathe deep and slowly," Wiens said. "You're O.K. Relax your shoulders."

He paused a few moments while Yvette settled down.

"What is it?" Wiens said.

"A monster comes and eats one of the dinosaurs. And it's chasing us."

"Us? Who is with you? Only you and Max?"

"Yes. No. Others!"

"O.K. Have you seen that place before?"

"No. Yes! I am walking on the planet with others from a ship." Yvette started wheezing.

"Relax and take deep breaths."

When Yvette's wheezing had subsided, Dr. Wiens continued.

"Do you recognize anyone with you?"

"No!" she said.

"Relax and look closely. Who is with you?"

"Max?"

"And who else?"

"Someone or something is carrying Max."

"Where?"

"Out of the ship. I have never seen this thing before."

"What happens next?"

"Wait, I can't talk," she exclaimed, breathing hard. "It's coming towards me. I can't run!"

Yvette's body shook.

"Run."

"I can't!"

"What happens next?"

"I—I see it. I can't!"

Yvette grappled with the words. Her body shook violently, her face turning red. She dug her fingers into the cushions. Her legs went limp.

"Yes, you can. What do you see?"

"I can't. I can't!" she screamed.

"You can!" Dr. Wiens said, his voice louder.

In the other room, Doc slammed his hand on the table and headed toward the door.

"He is pushing her too far," Doc said.

"Wait," McKomic said, restraining Doc with his hand. "He is a professional, and he knows what he is doing. Maybe that's our only chance of getting her to remember something."

"How long is this hypnosis going to last?"

"I understand your concern. I'd do the same thing if I were in your shoes. But you don't want to stop the session before it's finished, not at this point."

Doc wiped sweat from his brow. "I'm sorry about that."

"It's O.K. Take a break. I will update you."

Right then Yvette started screaming again.

"It's coming toward me!"

"Who is coming to you?"

Yvette shook, mute. Keeping his voice calm, Dr. Wiens continued.

"What else? What do you see?"

"He—it touches my face!" Yvette said. She trembled, sweating profusely.

"Where is Max?"

"He's gone!"

"What else?"

"I can't see anything."

"It's all right. Take deep breaths. Relax. You did very well. Now breathe and open your eyes."

Yvette sat up.

"Max, where is Max?" she said, with an expectant look. "They took him."

"Who are they?"

"Them. The beings I saw in my dream. I saw it. That one!" Yvette said, pointing at the second monitor screen. "That's it."

"Are you sure?"

"Yes, that's it."

"Thank you, Yvette," he said. "You've done wonderfully for today."

"May I go now?"

"You may. See you on Friday," Dr. Wiens smiled.

"O.K.!" She walked out of the room.

Doc was waiting outside. He hugged her.

"You did great today," he said.

She did not answer, but pouted.

"You must be hungry. Let's grab lunch," Doc said.

"Still don't even know why I still need a shrink."

"A few more visits, honey. That's all."

They exited for the elevator, leaving McKomic behind.

CHAPTER THIRTY-FOUR

Spartan Enterprises HQ

THE NEXT DAY STARTED WELL. Doc spent lunch thinking about the results from Yvette's evaluation. *What if what she said was true?* he thought. The thought made him restless.

Later, Doc went upstairs to the conference room, where he met with McKomic, Dr. Wiens, and Dr. Srinivasan, the neuroscientist, to discuss the crew's evaluations. After signing non-disclosure agreements, Doc opened the floor for discussion.

"What was the monster creature from Yvette's brain?" Doc said.

"Same as Alex and Geoffrey's descriptions," Dr. Wiens said.

"How do we know it was a snake creature?" McKomic said.

"This is what the machine recreated from Yvette's assessment." Wiens pulled up an image on the projector.

"Strange!" McKomic said. "How do we even know that Yvette's assertions ever happened?"

"She seemed adamant. As if she had seen that before."

"And you believe her? Maybe she saw it in some movie or something. Things like this don't exist."

"On Earth, no," Dr. Wiens said.

"Do you believe her?"

"Somewhat I do. That's what we have now, so I believe her."

"How are we going to prove whatever this thing is, it is real?"

"I don't know. But I think we have a good start."

"I am not so sure, but I think she saw what happened," Dr. Wiens said. "In all my years as a psychiatrist, I have never been wrong about my judgment on any of my patients."

"Wiens, anything new from the footages?" Doc said.

"Yes. I don't know if it's helpful. Anyway, since we will not leave any stones unturned, here is what we have found."

He showed Max and Yvette in the forest.

"Go on."

"They did not kiss," he said. "But a strange thing happens here. Watch!"

"What?"

"You see here, they get really close to the point of kissing, but you see Max is unmoved by passion. His eyes are wide, and he seems to be not responding. We all know that every man who gets that close to kissing a woman usually does it once or twice before he consciously remembers it's wrong and stops."

"I get that Yvette liked Max, still I don't get the point," McKomic said.

"Look at an earlier image of Max with his fiancée from implanted chip data in Stratford. His body responds to the feelings and passion, but not with Yvette. He acts so differently. Just the subtleties."

"What are you suggesting?" Doc said.

"I don't know yet, but my gut tells me something is askew."

"So, a hunch, basically?"

"Yes. That's what happens when you have spent so much time doing this."

"Thank you, Wiens," Doc said. He turned to Dr. Srinivasan.

"Srinivasan, do you have any updates for us?" Doc said.

Dr. Srinivasan pulled up a slide onto the projector.

"I have seen nothing like it in all my practice," Srinivasan said. "It's not an infection either."

"Then what?" Doc said.

"It's a strange form of amnesia," Srinivasan said, holding the peEEG scans to the light. "Her amygdala was affected. My team looked, and I looked at the frames myself. We think there is some inflammation in that area. Not sure if that is enough to produce any noticeable effects."

"Meaning she should be fine once the inflammation goes away, right?" Doc said.

"Yes, she should be. But this will take time. You know the brain is a privileged organ. No immune system there; well, at least that's what we used to think."

"So you think the inflammation is causing this?"

"Yes, blood work results came back showing high levels of inflammatory markers. But we need more time prodding and testing to see what it is to make a solid diagnosis."

He pulled up a separate slide.

"Using fluorescent imaging, we see severe inflammation around the amygdala. And right now, we believe that the inflammation might be causing the disconnect. She conjures flashes, random images, but she can't seem to connect them and organize her memory. That's why there's this staccato brainwave profile, but it's been improving over the past few days, and I'm sure we will see improvement over time."

"But what about all those things she was saying, if she can't remember?" Doc said.

"The issue is not her memory. She remembers. But she can't connect the two parts of her brain."

Doc nodded. "Why do you think so?"

"Studies have shown that some amnesia patients still possessed their image association part of the brain, even if they temporarily or permanently lose the connection between the auditory parts to the image parts. This device allows us to see the images directly from the visual association parts."

Srinivasan showed images from the peEEG image.

"What else could be the cause?"

"Could be a head injury, or something she saw," Srinivasan said.

"Or it might be the Mandela Effect," Dr. Wiens said.

"How so?"

"In my experiences, I have encountered a few patients who believe that they had a certain identity before the amnesia, which, of course, is not the reality. The brain can play tricks on you."

"That's possible," Doc said. "At this point we cannot rule anything out."

"The beauty of functional imaging is that it allows us to interpret waves from the brain and construct a picture of what our brain conceives in association with what we say," Dr. Srinivasan said. "Even though Yvette did not specify the monster, her brain already had the image. She is failing to associate what she is thinking with her speech."

"Anything we can do?" Doc said.

"Not really," Dr. Srinivasan said. "Only stick to steroids to speed up the healing, and play the waiting game. I think living at the house is helping too. Most of the old stuff will help bring her memory back."

While he was speaking, there was commotion in the corridor outside of the conference room. Everyone turned to see what was going on. A few seconds later, Geoffrey burst into the room, panting.

"Guys, you gotta come see this!" he said.

"What is it?" Doc said.

Geoffrey didn't bother answering. Everybody jumped to their feet and squeezed through the corridor. Yvette was summoned, and Pete the engineer, and several other team members all flocked into the control room and clustered around the massive screen mounted on the wall.

∾

"I THINK I FOUND SOMETHING!" Geoffrey said.

"What is it?" McKomic said.

Geoffrey pressed a few keys on the keyboard. "I'm getting a cryptic signal from Aoratosia."

Doc and McKomic exchanged anxious glances. "How?"

"AQ4. Wait for it."

"Can you put it on the screen?" McKomic said.

"Yes, sir!" one of Geoffrey's assistants said, while swiping his hand and dropping the image on the screen on the west wall. "There!" he said.

The screen was blank.

"Wait for it," Geoffrey said.

A faint tick-tocking sound came on soon after.

"These are radio signals intercepted by Spartan 3007S satellite from probe AQ4, which the launch team implanted on Aoratosia. The signals from the chip work only when someone is alive and sends beeping ticks. Here!" he said, turning up the volume on the monitor.

"Can't the rover send images?"

"It can, but the signal source has to be within range for AQ4 to image," McKomic said.

"What does that sound mean?" Wiens said.

"This sound means Max is alive, or at least something with blood, flesh, and the exact genetic makeup as Max has the microchip somewhere on Aoratosia."

Doc glanced at McKomic and Wiens, then at Yvette.

"How are you so sure?"

"When we designed the chip, we matched it to the DNA of every crew member, which means only one person can use it. It also designed that it only works in a living body," Geoffrey said.

"That's right," McKomic concurred.

"Can you tell who that is?"

"No, but it shows that someone from the crew is still alive at Aoratosia," he said.

"Or someone with the 100 percent exact DNA as Max."

There was a momentary silence.

"But every crew member got back, and only Max died."

"Yes, sir, but the satellite is telling me otherwise."

"Maybe it's an old message," Doc said.

"Possibly. I thought about that—that it may be a time lag."

"But?"

"I embedded this in real time, and I still find the signal. Mapping with the previous communication, the time lag is off a bit. Accounting for all possible interference, we should have received this message many hours ago if what you're saying is true."

"What are you suggesting?"

"Nothing. I thought it was strange and might be useful."

"You sure it's not a hoax?" Doc said.

"Our systems are the most secure on the globe. It would take a legion of hackers years to break into our systems." Geoffrey continued working on the computer.

"Then what is it?"

Geoffrey grinned. "I'm talking about earthly standards. Can't say the same for extraterrestrials."

He stopped when no one else laughed.

McKomic felt cold sweat soak his armpits. This was scarier and more confusing than he had expected. *What if one or more of the crew members were not who they appeared to be?* He suppressed the thought.

"We'd better find who is messing with us!" McKomic said.

"On it, boss," Geoffrey said.

"It could be Max. The signal signature is from his chip. We designed that chip specifically for him. We have designed our transmission system with a signature that allows us to identify our own communication. Several parameters verify each communication signal before we archive it. Like a human's genetic makeup and the ability to detect mutations and destroy infected cells. We have several signatures that our systems use to sift through incoming signals," McKomic said.

"Now I see why your system is hard to hack."

"Exactly."

"And the incoming signal has Max's signature."

"Can we locate the chip?" Yvette asked

"From the signal source to the probe, my guess would be Max is within a 100-mile radius of it," Geoffrey said. "The beeping increases as you get closer to the chip, and when at the right place, it changes to a sharp continuous sound. The signal was either sent strategically or by accident."

"Can we decode it?"

"My team is working on it as we speak."

"Maybe Max is telling us something," Yvette said.

Everyone glanced her way.

"Max is dead," said Wiens to Yvette, gently.

"But how—then—?"

"We will find that out," McKomic cut in. "Geoffrey, can you test the sound?"

"Yes, sir."

All eyes focused on the screen while Geoffrey showed his skills with the keyboard. The savant was sweating. He used his joysticks to navigate the whole screen. The cursor trotted back and forth on the black screen. It went clockwise, then counterclockwise, and in each movement emitting different sound intensities and occasional empty intervals.

"It's going to take a few minutes, maybe 15 at least," he said. "It would be hard scanning for a chip in a 100-mile radius, in an area with high electromagnetic fields that interact with the sound."

"Do the best you can," McKomic said.

After 16 minutes of on-and-off sounds, as the cursor went farther west; the beeping and frequency intensified. Then sound changed into a sharp sound.

"Got it!"

"How do you know it's him?"

"Dead people don't pose a threat to national security!" Geoffrey put in. "Unless they vote in the presidential elections. Oops, didn't mean to say that," Geoffrey said, and smiled.

"Is there a way to find an image?" Doc said.

"We can try," Geoffrey said. "We have done nothing like this before."

Geoffrey slid his chair to the left towards the keyboard and entered numerals.

"Can you use thermal imaging to detect the heat from the body?" Yvette interrupted, walking closer to Geoffrey. Everyone's gaze shifted to her.

"Yes, that's what we will do," Geoffrey said. A red and green image appeared on the screen. "That's it, lying down there."

"Wait, the chip just shifted," Yvette said.

"It did?"

"I saw that too."

"O.K. Go on."

Geoffrey rolled his chair back to his keyboard and punched a few more keys.

"I saw that," Pete said. "As if some external force moved it!"

"Right now the chip looks slanted and unstable. Under normal conditions on Aoratosia and from the being's position, the chip is vertical, counteracting magnetic field and gravity," Geoffrey said.

"So this means something is providing an exterior magnetic field from the side," Doc said.

"Yes, but not just one. My guess is two or more, because the chip is balanced from both torques on either side," Geoffrey said. "I can measure the slant angle on the chip and its torque. That will let us identify the positions of the other external forces and how much force they are exerting."

"And then we can even calculate their sizes and mass!" McKomic added.

"Correct," Geoffrey slid to the keyboard and typed.

"Looks like there is one close to the body's feet on the left and one next to his head," McKomic said.

Geoffrey moved the cursor of his joystick towards those distances. A reddish, blue-green image appeared. He pushed it to the other side, and a more intense reddish blue-green image appeared.

"We have our two Aoratosians. A male and a female, looks like," Yvette said.

"How can you tell?" McKomic said.

"I can tell by the intensity of the thermal images," she said. "Women release more body heat than men, and you can see from the images there is a contrast between the two. Now we can try to monitor their movements."

"Is there a way to tell what they are doing?"

"No sir," Geoffrey said. "But I will keep searching. Hopefully, we will get something. We are also tracking and retrieving any information recorded on the chip. However, I am not sure if that's going to work. I have never done anything like this, and the magnetic field interference might cause problems. We can measure the after-vibration to detect the sound from probe AQ4."

"They may have distorted the chip, too."

"See what you and your team can do," McKomic said.

Geoffrey's tech team typed furiously on their computers while everybody waited impatiently. No one left the room. They wanted to witness it all. At least there was some hope. They wanted to retell the stories to their children, grandchildren, and great-grandchildren—that they had been there.

CHAPTER THIRTY-FIVE

Spartan Enterprises HQ

A DISTINCT BROKEN sound hissed from the monitor, startling everyone. Geoffrey's team continued to punch the keys.

"Progress?" McKomic said.

"Yes, sir. I think so. We're getting some audio."

"Great!" Doc said.

"Get the translating team here!" McKomic said.

"There's no one in the office! It's Friday evening," Pete said. "Everyone has already left for the Memorial Day weekend."

"Get them back!" McKomic said, rattling on his phone. "I need everyone here."

"Yes, sir. I will call everyone in right away."

"I need them, like, yesterday!"

McKomic's bark was interrupted by a deep crackling voice coming from the monitor. The voice went on for a few seconds, then died.

Geoffrey shrugged and worked on his keyboard.

"Anything else?" McKomic said.

"No, sir," Geoffrey said. "The rest is blank."

"Did you record it?"

Geoffrey glanced at Pete, who immediately said "Yes." Pete went to his own station and replayed the message.

The strange voice spoke in clicking staccato sounds.

"Sounds like some ancient language," Yvette said. "Like a cryptic message."

"Joe; where is Joe? He is the ancient languages expert. Bring in Joe."

"Sir, he is on vacation."

"Vacation?"

"Yes, sir. You approved it."

"Call him."

"He is in Arkansas, and doesn't have network service."

"Goddammit! Are we still in the Stone Age? I need someone."

"Sir, Joe is the only one who can translate this kind of stuff."

"Get the translating team here now quickly wherever they are, and whatever they are doing!" McKomic ordered with a loud voice.

"Yes, sir!" the officer said.

The voice from the monitor warbled for 30 seconds, skipping, with some blank spaces.

Yvette leaned in towards Geoffrey's chair. "Wait. They sound like medley expressions!"

"Can you tell what they are saying?" Geoffrey said.

"Yes. I think I understand some phrases," she said. "It's almost similar to a language I heard somewhere in sub-Saharan Africa. Madagascar maybe."

"They speak French."

"They do, but they have their dialects as well. Yes. I don't remember where, but I can feel the language. I understand it."

"You sure about this, honey? We only lived there for six months," Doc said. "And that was 12 years ago."

Yvette nodded. "I'm sure."

"All right, Pete. Go on."

"Do you understand any of it?" Doc said.

Yvette ignored the question as she paid maximum attention.

"Can you replay that part, slowed down?"

Everyone looked puzzled. McKomic seemed to have forgotten the phone that was buzzing. He hung it up.

Pete replayed the voice, which sounded more like spitting saliva than words. The strange, coarser voice, filled with high and low pitches, said, *"Hoyu u vhonala unga rine na ngangomu."* The message crackled briefly, then it continued. *"Muchini washu womuvhona satshipida tshashu. Mufheni zwidzidzivhadzi zwokalulaho!"*

A smoother voice said, *"Rido wana zwine vhakhou ita fhano!"* almost as a command.

The signal died, and the screen went blank again, with only some buzzing and scratching heard.

Yvette stood quietly.

"You got anything? Geoffrey said.

"I think so," she said. "It sounds like Coptic language. Play it again, slowly."

This time Yvette jotted notes on the purple pad she grabbed from Geoffrey's desk. Everyone looked on. The short recording played to the end.

"Do you know what it means?" McKomic said, the phone still in his hands.

"'This one—This one looks like us—from, um, within. Our machines have recognized him as part of us'."

"This one looks like us from within. Our machines recognize him as part of us?" Geoffrey said.

"Yes. That's what it said. The first voice. That's the literal meaning!"

Everyone looked concerned and stupefied.

"And the second?" McKomic said.

"'Give him high doses of the drug. We will find out what they were doing here!' That's what the female voice said."

"That sounds like an interrogation!" Doc said.

"We don't know that. We heard only a snippet. Maybe it's something else. We cannot jump to conclusions without having the full context," said Wiens.

"Still makes no sense. All our body cameras do not show anyone else except for our crew," Geoffrey said.

"Sir," one technician yelled. "This might be nothing, but earlier, when I was looking at the footage from the body cameras, something showed on Max's feed. Probably nothing. But since you mentioned that, I thought I would share."

He shared his monitor screen onto the big screen.

"O.K., go on," McKomic said.

"This is the footage from a camera on Max while stranded in the forest. It starts with the crew, step by step, then goes into the water, but suddenly the video is blanked out by bright light at the same time for three seconds."

"Maybe it's the sun," McKomic said.

"I have been thinking about that. But I contrasted the light before the waterfall and after; doesn't match. You can see the actual light when Max passes out and floats to the top."

"And?"

"Something else caused that light," he said. "It wasn't the cave creature, because the time-frame doesn't match."

"I also saw the same thing," another technician said. She looked at Pete. "We retrieved the silicon dust embedded on the suits. I've also been trying to construct 3D contrast images from it. We're not done yet, but we saw the same thing. We traced the light source to see what had caused the light, but could not identify anything behind the light. Yvette's body camera doesn't show the light. Yvette was the only one left who did not remember what had happened. We are still working on it."

"Silicon dust?" Dr. Wiens said.

"Yeah," Geoffrey said. "It was a last-minute thing. Before the crew left, we embedded some silicon dust in the suits as an extra precaution."

"Oh, great. Now we have light to worry about."

"Might be a coincidence."

"Or the light source might have to do with the message. I know that sounds far-fetched."

"Excellent work; keep on it," said McKomic.

Momentarily everyone stood silent with their own uneasy thoughts. Had the whole expedition been unwise? What had they unleashed into the world?

It was close to 9:00 p.m. and President Blanchard would soon call for a briefing. McKomic thanked the team, and he and Yvette walked with Doc and Geoffrey and Wiens toward the conference room.

"Then whose body is at the Heroes' Acre?" Doc said.

"That's the question we have to answer, quickly," McKomic said.

"But the crew would have noticed it wasn't him."

"No. The way we left, we didn't have plenty of time to observe that. Plus, he could drive the aeroglider, which requires a DNA match to run."

"This is insane!"

"But the DNA test results confirm it was Max himself," McKomic said.

"Yes, that makes matters more intriguing! Might be a weapon."

Everyone was quiet, thinking.

"We don't know what these beings are capable of. They developed a machine that produces fuel from industrial gases and their own greenhouse planet. What else can these beings be capable of doing?" Geoffrey said.

There was an eerie silence.

"Maybe they created another Max form?" Dr. Wiens said. Everyone stared at him.

"A cyborg?" Doc said. "It'll be impossible to convince anyone of that."

"Is it?" McKomic said. "This stuff is everywhere in sci-fi movies. People will readily believe it."

"True. But not scientists. We need evidence."

"What the mind can conceive, it can accomplish. It's only a matter of choice, how and when," Wiens said.

"Gentlemen, I think we should exhume the body and have it reexamined," McKomic said.

"That's not happening. Have you seen the number of people that are visiting Max's resting place? It would be almost impossible to remove the body. Besides, the space museum is raking in tons of revenue from these visitors. They would be unwilling to disrupt that."

"I doubt they'll be cooperative."

"We'll go through the president."

"Not so soon. The president has plenty on her plate already. She has re-election to worry about. Until we have more evidence. Only then can we go."

"His family will not allow that."

"I will talk to them," Dr. Wiens said.

"And let's say we do. What are we going to tell them? We have already done all the tests necessary to I.D. the body. Necroscopy results show that it was Max. Do we have any specified tests for cyborgs— dead ones?"

"We can try to use non-scientific methods," said Wiens.

"What do you mean?"

"Birthmarks, subtle body malformations, other things. In ancient African culture, they used to use loved ones to identify deceased members in the mass army killings. I am sure even if these Aoratosia beings duplicated Max, they would certainly miss something that only someone very close to Max can identify."

"That's risky," McKomic said. "That would be difficult to do. And no relative would want to spend hours studying a grown man's corpse."

"That's our only hope for now unless anybody has a better solution," said Geoffrey.

Everyone was silent.

"We have to invite Max's aunt and his fiancée; they might identify something."

"When can that be done? We have a full schedule. By then, they will have gone back to Oklahoma."

"We will urge them to come back and verify the body for suspicious marks," McKomic said. He ordered his secretary to check on the status of Mrs. Folksay and Alonna and make an appointment with them. "But that will be our last resort. And next week. They are already going through enough."

"There are many ways to explain this," Geoffrey said, who had followed McKomic and Doc into the hallway. "I think we are all assuming a lot of things here. We still need to verify thoroughly again. I don't want to leave any loopholes."

McKomic shrugged. "Seems to me anyone who is doing this knew Yvette would be able to translate their language."

"Like a puzzle. Maybe someone is monitoring us."

"How do we know it's not a mere cyberattack from our enemies?" McKomic said.

"It's possible, but the person has to be from within us to crack the firewall."

"Possibly! But I'm a hacker, and I know nothing is 100 percent unhackable." McKomic looked around the room, considering who might be a suspect. "At this point I don't trust anyone."

"Are you saying," said Doc, "they have taken his mind and created another Max?"

"I guess. The chip could only work with Max."

"I hope not," Doc said. "But we have shown that only a minimal gene set number is required to create new life."

"Forty to 60 times that, you have a functional organism."

"You think they can do that?"

"I'm just saying. It's not that far-fetched, Doc."

"If Aoratosians have preternatural abilities to construct such technologies, what else are they capable of doing?"

"We don't know that. Actually, we didn't see any beings there except for animals and the giant snake-creature," said Geoffrey.

"I think we're overreacting to this. I stick to the notion that the message was delayed, and there is nothing to worry about."

"The time lag might have delayed the sound retrieval to our sensors. Like I said."

"It's possible. Apart from all that, the question remains who these beings with language capabilities are," Doc said.

"If there were people there, why did they not hijack the ship?"

Geoffrey looked at McKomic.

"Literally," McKomic corrected himself.

"It doesn't make sense. How could they set Max free?"

"Maybe they sent a decoy to get among us. Maybe they are calculating us, knowing every move that we will make next. We may have just given them access to Earth. An overt mission."

"Have we found out anything from Ulysses yet?"

"I meant to tell you earlier. We analyzed Ulysses' black box. Nothing strange, except for this point where there's white light. Don't know what it is."

"Moon, sun?"

"That's what we thought initially. But the variations. The rest of the footage shows consistent lighting patterns, except for this one point where it's so bright. Peculiar! But we tracked the time; it's 13:00, around the time Max returned to the ship. The moon and sun schedules don't match."

"I still don't understand."

"Me either. But maybe the light was from something else. Something they didn't see."

"But why not capture the whole ship?"

Geoffrey shrugged. "That's the billion-dollar question."

"Unless it was a ploy!"

"Maybe, maybe not. Maybe it's only light. Not aliens."

"What should we do?"

Doc folded his hands across his chest.

"Did anyone hear from the hospital whether the doctors retrieved the chip from Max's body?"

"No one thought of that."

"Geoffrey, put me through to the autopsy department. I want to see something. If they found the chip, then we have somewhere to start," said Doc.

"They said it was there."

"I know. But I've something in mind."

The phone rang twice. Geoffrey put it on the loudspeaker, then turned back to his own work. The secretary answered the phone and transferred the call to the head doctor of the autopsy department.

"Doc, what's up?" the doctor said.

"Hey, Stevens. I have a quick question."

"All right."

"Did you check everything on Max's body?"

"Yes, Doctor Yates, I believe we did, thoroughly."

"Did you find a chip in his ear?"

"A chip? Yes, we retrieved one. It's with the rest of his effects, for further examination."

"You are positive?"

"Sure. Everything we cut and remove is properly cataloged by the scribes. Let me see what we have here. We found it. Is everything all right? We made the postmortem based on our initial diagnosis of the cause of death. There was no question about what caused his death. Nothing peculiar showed on the radiograph."

"There has been a stir that Max may still be alive! We want to make sure we have the real Max."

"Excuse me, Doctor?"

"We found some info that suggests he may be alive. It's a theory."

"That can't be possible! I took charge of the postmortem, with a team of experts to make sure we did not miss anything," Stevens said.

"I know you did. There must be an explanation. Do you mind sending me the postmortem analysis report?"

"Doc, that's a—I can't! That's a HIPAA violation."

"I know that, and I'll keep it to myself."

"You promise? I'm putting my career on the line here."

"You have my word. I'm trying to see if I can connect some dots. I know it's probably a waste of time, but why not try? An extra set of eyes wouldn't hurt."

"All right, I am sending them to you."

"Thanks, Stevens. Hey, I know you did the best. I'll get back to you if I need anything."

"No problem!"

He hung up the phone.

"Great!"

Right then, Pete the forensic engineer rushed up, holding his pad.

"Come see this," he said, exhilarated. "We were able to recreate some footage from the remaining embedded programmed silicon dust on the sleek suits for some extra surveillance. Much of it is destroyed, but we salvaged what we could. My team was able to piece together the fragments into something that makes sense."

"Any success on the black box?" Doc said, waiting for the video to start.

"No. The core is fried, maybe beyond restoration. We'll keep trying," the engineer said.

He played the video on the monitor. It showed a video of Max, Yvette, and Alex running from the cave.

"Why don't they have their helmets?"

"I guess the air is normal."

"What is that shadow?"

"A dragon of some sort." The engineer paused and zoomed into its shadow. "Yes. We mapped the silhouette and created a rendering image," he said, juxtaposing the image and the shadow.

He played the whole video and replayed it again.

"Doc, isn't that almost like what Yvette described?" McKomic said.

"I guess she wasn't imagining things after all."

"Pause it there! That looks exactly like the structure that was on Max's necklace he used to wear," Doc said.

"It does. Do you think it means something?"

"I don't know."

The video kept playing, with screaming, shouting, and panting, and then there was a white light, and it died.

"Nothing?" McKomic said when the footage ended.

"Wait. Play it again," Doc said.

The engineer backed the recording up a few more seconds and replayed it at half speed.

"Stop it there," Doc said. "Do you see that?"

"See what?"

"The creature on Max's necklace," Doc said. "It's the same creature!"

"It does look like it."

"Why is it glowing?"

"Maybe a reflection from the sun?"

"No, the lighting is different."

"The light. Look at Max's shirt. It's glowing!"

"There's some blue incandescence on his chest."

"The necklace."

"What does that?"

"I don't know. But why is his necklace glowing light blue?"

"This whole thing doesn't make sense. Strange."

"That may be the same light we retrieved from Ulysses' black box."

"We have to ask the rest of the crew. Not now. Give them some time."

"What should we do?"

"Right now, we make sure nothing leaks to the media. That will make this thing explode, a mess that we are not ready for," McKomic said.

Everyone remained quiet.

Doc knew this was an important time—that any miscalculated move could spur panic in the agency. Hell, it could shake the whole country. The whole world. He had seen how the public was easily swayed by the media. He understood that any premature announcements could wreak havoc. The press would nail Spartan Enterprises. Heck, no one used their brains anymore. People believed what the media fed them. He hated how, as much as social media and the press elevated you to soaring heights of fame, they could bring you down to catastrophic depths in a single stroke, with a hashtag and a few syllables. Cancel culture! Doc looked at the engineer and patted him on the shoulder.

"Good job, Pete. But let's keep this in here for now until we're certain."

"Don't you think we should inform the White House?" Pete said.

"Hell, no!" McKomic said. "Who in their right mind is going to believe this? The president has other important things to do and focus on re-election and campaigning. News like this would torpedo her chances of winning the Republican nomination."

"That's true. Not everyone is excited about this program. We don't want to give any advantage to the opposition to denigrate the president's support."

"Her approval rating shot up today, and oh, we wouldn't want to jeopardize that," Doc said with a laugh.

The president at the moment was leading the polls after the previous night's debate, overtaking Senator Bloeg, who had dominated for seven straight weeks. She now led by double her opponents' votes combined. She was making good on her promises to both the Congress and the American public to bring change to the nation. The discovery of Aoratosia had catapulted her popularity rating. Her main opponent, Senator Bloeg, was on her tail, still bashing the administration for wasting resources on Project ASHE.

"We need to let everything settle down. All this euphoria can easily turn into a debacle we're not ready to deal with!"

Doc was quiet for a while, then said, "Yes, I say we sleep on it. I'll call the Reverend and see what he suggests."

Doc tried his best to remain calm. Much had happened today. He knew it was one thing to tell the president they had left an astronaut behind, and it was entirely another thing to explain the inexplicable. He hoped it was a glitch.

McKomic and Doc went back to their offices. There was more to do.

Another sleepless night.

CHAPTER THIRTY-SIX

Spartan Enterprises HQ

McKOMIC SAT IN HIS OFFICE, contemplating all that had happened. He perused Max's postmortem report and dawdled over his notes and mission reports the entire day, but could not focus. He closed his computer and lay down on the couch facing up. It was already past 9:30 p.m. when McKomic exited his office. He noticed the light in Doc's office was still on and dropped in to check on him.

"Doc, you're still here?"

"Yes, come in, Cordell. I didn't know you were still around."

Doc never bothered McKomic unless something was troubling him.

"O.K.?"

"Yup. Finishing checking the records. Working late tonight?"

"No. Just busy being busy. Trying to look through the reports. Maybe I can see what we missed."

"Have you checked the news?"

"No, why?"

McKomic turned on the TV.

They both looked on as the TV screen bloomed.

"New intel came in," McKomic said.

"Good news?"

"Mostly!"

"What is it?"

"Scrivner and his crew have resurfaced."

"When was this?"

"This evening!"

"Are you serious?" Doc said, getting up and walking to his desk.

"Hell, yeah! It's all over the news," McKomic said.

"How do we know it's not bullshit?"

"Our informants have confirmed that with the US Embassy in Brazil. Scrivner and his team are in the custody of the Brazilian Intelligence Agency as of now."

"I got a call from Stan earlier today that they were narrowing in on the missing anthropologists yesterday. Thought little of it. I guess I've been preoccupied."

"Someone leaked the news or a photo. That's big bucks for a story like this."

"That's insane. What are they saying?"

"The media thing. All speculation and gossip. No one knows the truth for now."

"I probably got a briefing as well." Doc typed on his laptop.

"Damn. I have 20 emails. Let's see. The report says the air force has spotted an underground structure where they believed Scrivner and his team were held hostage."

"Held hostage? By whom?"

"It's a Class 1 file. I'm not privy to those specifics. They're not sure who could have built the structure."

"That's nothing new. We know there are Mayan ruins all over the Amazon forest over the years."

"But this is different," Doc said, perusing the file.

"How so?"

"Lidar technology from the air force has identified a hole—underground fortress, the report says. A massive metal bunker buried underground but vanished."

"Mayan ruins?"

"No. More than that. Traces show more advanced material than what the Mayans used. And guess what it is? The same element as what Yvette told us was on Max's necklace."

"Elixirium?"

"Crap. I hope what I'm thinking is wrong."

"You're correct."

"But why now? The air force has been flying, shooting light beams all over the Amazon for years. Detected nothing serious."

"True. But the technology has been refined. Most of the data collected over the years have been of ancient ruins. Mapping and analyzing that amount of data takes a lot of time, even with our super-computers and complex algorithms. They assumed it was only another footprint from Mayan ruins."

"How did they change their mind?"

"It says here they received a report from the European Southern Observatory of an unidentified flying object zipping from the Amazon rainforest."

"O.K."

"Some locals confessed to seeing something as well."

"Aliens?"

"Possibly."

"Why would they lie low instead of attacking us?"

"Maybe spying and prospecting for our intelligence and resources."

"What date was this?"

"June twentieth."

"The same day we launched?"

"Exactly as I suspected."

"Which means if they were aliens, they were stranded and used our portal to leave the planet. When I thought it couldn't get any weirder!" McKomic said.

"I guess we will know more soon," Doc said, while he continued browsing his emails.

"Sounds like it's going to be one of those Area 51 kind of deals?"

Doc looked up and said, "This is a classified mission, and the government will not release unnecessary information until they are certain. They have fortified the site into a restricted area. The best engineers at SETI are still trying to decipher how such a voluminous structure had existed underground without distorting any part of the forest —like nothing was there. Under all those massive trees. Another angle is that the captors had obviously left those clues for us to find the scientists. But why? Where did they come from? Where did they go? It's a mystery."

"Do you think this has any connection with our Aoratosia mission?" McKomic said.

"Maybe, I don't know. As a scientist, I have never had many coincidences where I have to depend on guessing. It's all messed up right now."

"But this is hearsay so far!"

"We will know as soon as Scrivner speaks out."

Right then, the 10:00 p.m. breaking-news banner flashed on the screen. Behind it, a pale and ill-looking Scrivner and team stood glaring at the news cameras. Captions ran across the bottom of the screen.

"How the heck did the media get the info so fast?"

"I don't know, Cordell. They always do."

"Someone leaked the news."

"Of course."

"Bastards!"

"Well, good riddance. At least that will keep the media off our asses for a few days."

"I sure hope so."

"Me, too."

"So what else do we know about Scrivner and company?"

"According to the report, they should arrive in D.C. this weekend."

"Anything else?"

"Doesn't say much. Obviously a clandestine operation."

"Should've known. The CIA would want to keep this low profile."

"No doubt!"

McKomic stood. "I think I'm gonna head out. Wanna grab a beer down the street?"

"Sounds great," Doc said. "I can't seem to figure out why I am still here at this time on a Friday."

"There is a McNeice's right down the street where we can walk."

"Fantastic. Walking sounds good. I think I need the exercise."

Doc slid into his sport coat on and joined McKomic in the corridor.

"Long day tomorrow," McKomic said.

"I'm tired already."

"It's been an incredible week."

"After all that's happened," Doc said, "I feel like we are denying these young men and women a normal life. Do you think we are doing any good recruiting these young adults and setting them up for situations like this?"

"I don't know, Doc, but our hands are tied. Rules are rules."

"It's like we're preventing these young people from enjoying young adulthood. You know—tearing them away from their families."

"That's the price of progress."

"I believe that, too. But I wonder how many more we have to sacrifice now that we have samples from this new planet? This is only the beginning."

"As a scientist, you want none of this," McKomic said. "You want to do science."

"I can't stop thinking what might have gone wrong."

"I looked through all the designs and software patches myself several times; I can't see anything wrong. The chassis is fine. And so far nothing points to what happened during the ship's reentry."

"I hear you. You get to where you don't know what you think you know," Doc said. "It's a bittersweet crossroads."

"It's a pain in the ass."

"That's a better way of putting it."

"It's complicated to decipher when you are on the inside of things."

"I'm glad Friday always comes around."

"Yes!"

They exited the building and strolled down the bright street towards the bar. The lights smiled at them—staring at their bittersweet triumph. McKomic frowned. *All was not O.K. Why the hell was that light so bright?*

CHAPTER THIRTY-SEVEN

Houston Convention Center, Houston

McKOMIC ARRIVED at the stadium a few minutes before the event started. He breezed past dozens of police, army, and federal agents patrolling the site. There was a beehive of activity as crowds filled the streets and tailgated outside the stadium, celebrating. McKomic did not speak to anyone. Recent findings preoccupied his mind. McKomic still felt terrible. He thought he was responsible. Being the boss, he knew damned well he was. His sole mission was to find the glitch. He passed through the concession stands and descended into a tunnel leading to the base of the field, thankful no one noticed him. He walked over to the platform at the center of the field without looking into the stands. The chaos. *These reveling crowds, what do they know,* McKomic thought. He proceeded and sat next to Alonna and Aunt Dori behind the podium where relatives of the crew and other important officials sat waiting for the president's national address. Reverend Kay and Doc were sitting in the same row. Reverend Kay shook everyone's hand and kissed Aunt Dori on the cheek. Alonna sat next to Aunt Dori, holding her hand. Doc sat next to her with Yvette, Geoffrey, and Alex.

"He was a great kid," Reverend Kay said, sighing. Alonna looked on but said nothing.

The president's motorcade arrived at the complex after 3:00. The masses stood as soon as the president entered the field. She shook hands, signed a few posters, and waved at the crowd with a broad smile. She continued to her reserved seat next to Doc and McKomic. People brought their own chairs and scattered throughout the grounds and surrounding roads, blocking Main Street and the other streets near the stadium's big screen. Volunteers distributed water bottles throughout the crowds who sat in the scorching sun. Some waved their green "Blanchard" banners and tiny flags. They waved to the exhilarated crowd of enthusiasts that had spent many hours camping outside the stadium, awaiting the presidential address about the mission. Millions more at home were glued to their TVs for the live broadcast.

After several minutes of applause, the crowd hushed as a local band performed the national anthem. Then everyone sat. Houston's mayor gave the opening remarks and introduced President Blanchard. The president walked to the rostrum with a loud ovation from the appreciative masses.

After straightening up the microphone, she said, "Good evening, America!" looking out into the packed stadium. Her voice echoed through the stands. "Today is a great day! A great day for our nation! A great day for our planet! A great day for anyone alive, for those yet to be born, and for those before us. It is a great day, indeed!"

She paused, letting the applause from the crowds die away.

"I stand before you today, as before and always, proud to be an American!" The crowds cheered.

"A great leader once said, 'It always seems impossible until it's done,' and he was right. They say dreams come true, and they sure do. Today, we can all attest to that. We are all witnesses to this impressive feat in human history." She paused as the crowd cheered more loudly. "Today marks the day we have achieved the dreams of all the great minds who paved the way before us. We honor those who sacrificed to ensure we would get to celebrate a day like this, and I am fortunate to be part of it. We all are.

"A few years ago, a young man had a dream—a dream to send people to Mars!" She paused. "Trust me, there are a few things that you can tell me, and I laugh at them, as ludicrous. This was one of them. I said to myself, 'This man is deluded.' Everyone thought it was impossible to do that. And yet the young man persisted in his convictions. Man, I've got to tell you. He is the most stubborn human being I have ever met. I mean, in my line of work, I meet lots of them at different levels."

The crowd roared with laughter.

"I too was a naysayer at the beginning. The whole concept of warping people into space sounded far-fetched to me. You've got to remember this is the stuff you watch in science-fiction fantasy. But I'm a convert now. He proved me and many others wrong. I believe! We can do that which we think is impossible. He showed us what an ordinary mind can achieve—extraordinary, with the right persistence! And that young man, ladies and gentlemen, Cordell McKomic, is here with us today. I believe in you, sir!"

The president turned around, pointing her palm towards McKomic. The crowds applauded. McKomic nodded and smiled.

The president continued, "Fast-forward a few years later to a few months ago. His team embarked on the most ambitious mission in human history since the landing of humans on the moon, to a planet where no known human has ever set foot. Despite the challenges and all the odds stacked against them—they prevailed. They succeeded. That is why we are all here today. Today we celebrate a leap in the history of humankind. We celebrate these brave men and women as a testament that anything is possible. I know the rest of the world is watching and rejoicing with us."

She paused, letting the words sink in.

"The dawn of tomorrow is here. Our team of dedicated scientists and explorers have found a sanctuary. We stand proud today, announcing to the world that we have found Earth's sister planet. Yes, sister planet! Through our scientists' unwavering determination, we have discovered planet Aoratosia—a planet similar to ours in almost every aspect of its structure. We shall build the best hope for our people with whatever it takes. Think of the possibilities onward. As long as I am the president of the United States, I will do everything in my power to push things forward."

The crowds cheered.

"The American spirit has carried us far beyond what man deemed conceivable a few decades ago. What's impressive is that we've done it at more incredible speeds and in less time than ever considered achievable. To the moon, probes to space, probes to the sun, and animals to Mars. And today, we have once again made history.

"We have come a long way; no spaceship had taken a direct path to the gas planet. On top of that we have managed to shrink a six-year journey into a few hours. What's interesting is that none of these previous ships had ferried humans with them, only robots and drones. And now we have attempted Mars and beyond.

"President John F. Kennedy had a dream to land man on the moon, and today we have exceeded far beyond Apollo's dream. We stand singing the NASA anthem and waving the American flag higher, above all nations, far into the corners of the galaxy."

The president paused to allow a long ovation.

"We have stood unwavering in times of need and trouble. We've endured and eradicated challenging diseases and epidemics, prolonging lifespans, improving lifestyles, and diminishing terrorism. Our forefathers never backed down from any challenge. That's what made our country great. We have done them proud today. I know they are proud of us. They are proud of what our nation has become. That we have carried alive their dream of continuing to explore the universe and overcoming challenges head-on.

"And most of all, I would like to thank you, fellow Americans. You're the ones who continue to support our basic research to remain the leader in space exploration. And it is my hope that young people today realize that there is nothing impossible with determination."

The crowd applauded.

"I would like to thank our scientists, engineers, and entrepreneurs who toil every day to move our technology forward. Spartan Enterprises, Dr. Yates, McKomic—they epitomize thousands of other Americans and private businesses that keep our country a global leader.

"And ladies and gentlemen, on this special day I would like to congratulate our heroes, the courageous young men and women, or rather boys and girls, if I dare say," she said, smiling broadly. "These young people risked their lives taking us to places where no human has ever been. What's more American than that?"

The crowds cheered as an image appeared on the bubble projection on the right side of the stadium of the crew members of the Coldbox mission.

"Ladies and gentlemen, help me welcome our heroes!"

Yvette, Geoffrey, and Alex lined up on the platform.

"These young men and women are a genuine reflection of the American spirit. The spirit of adventure and the spirit of never giving up. The spirit of victory in uncertainty and discouragement." She paused. "It is sad that in times of jubilation like this, there are some who are missing, some who did not make it. Let us never forget that for all the freedoms we enjoy, some pay for it with their lives."

Silence befell the stadium.

"Ladies and gentlemen, join me in passing my deepest condolences to the Folksay family for the loss of their son on this mission. A fighter, that's what he was—that's what this family is. I met Max once, and I can tell you that's an accurate description. He never gave up, to the end."

The president turned and bowed her head towards Aunt Dori. The camera then focused on Aunt Dori and Alonna, to applause from the masses.

"As a mother myself, I cannot imagine losing my 22-year-old son," she said in a lower voice. "Max is a hero who died doing what he believed and loved, and we should honor him for that. We ask that his soul rest in peace. May he serve as a role model to our young people.

"Every war we have fought, every rocket we have developed, every menace we have overcome, signifies the true American spirit. Although painful, we have suffered a good loss. Today, our nation and the world grieve for our lost hero, Maxwell Folksay. I hope our hearts find catharsis in the warmth of the survivors and the promising discoveries Max died bringing to us. We owe this day to him. Though too short, I believe his life was well-lived. He is gone, but in our hearts he is with us. His spirit will inspire a generation of fearless young people, no matter what color, creed, or race: young people who will explore the ends of the galaxy. I believe this is what Max would want us to do. That's what this country stands for.

"May we take several moments of silence to honor Max?"

A headshot of Max appeared on the screen, followed by mugshots of his team on Aoratosia. Several images played the sequence of events from Max's childhood all the way to Max in a captain's suit next to the AQ4 rover on Aoratosia. A childhood photograph, a high-school photograph, then one taken with Max wearing the sleek suit. A "just a simple kid from rural Oklahoma" statement rolled below the images. Whoever had created the presentation had intended to elicit great emotion from the crowd. It worked. There was barely a dry eye when the presentation ended. An eerie silence swept through the crowd as everyone paid silent homage to Max.

The president continued.

"I know there is nothing we can do to adequately show our gratitude for what they have done for humankind, but at the very least we can honor them. And I today, as the president of the United States, bestow upon these young men and women, the Presidential Medals of Freedom—for their courage and excellence in serving our country and our planet."

The president then draped medals around the crew members as they passed by the podium. The crowds applauded. She pinned Max's medal on a folded American flag and handed it to Aunt Dori.

After honoring the heroes, the president returned to the podium to give her final remarks.

"These men and women have brought us information that we need to study our newfound sister planet. And we hope through the hard work of our scientists, we will know what lies on Aoratosia. With your vote, we can continue to build a new beginning together."

The crowds cheered.

"And let's not forget, we are entrepreneurs. And they are! We are all forging our way to a better tomorrow. You may feel you are not at the forefront, but you are! Without taxpayers' support—your money—none of these things would be possible.

"We're the only ones who can change the world's problems—the ones bold enough to dare. And that's what we are doing! Are we going to lose lives? Maybe, maybe not. That's how revolutions happen. That's how progress flourishes. We learn from each experience, and next time our results get even better. The first step is always the riskiest, but once you live through it, anything is possible. Because you know you can take anything that comes your way. There is a price for any progress, though it may leave bitter tastes in all our mouths. That's something we have to face. And let's not forget what Max died for.

"Good evening, America! And God bless these United States of America!"

President Blanchard left the podium to thunderous applause. She hugged Aunt Dori and Alonna, and shook hands with a few other dignitaries before disappearing behind the stage.

After the event, the crowd dispersed, all talking about the wonders of Aoratosia—wondering what more was there. Some pressed against the line of security police, wanting to shake the crew members' hands. At least the successful mission gave the crew's survivors some solace.

CHAPTER THIRTY-EIGHT

NASA, Houston

MAX'S INTERMENT was at the Pantheon the next evening. The Pantheon was an acre of land used as the resting place for famous astronauts, thus sometimes referred to as the NASA Heroes' Acre. The area served as a tourist site for those who wanted to pay tribute to aviation and space exploration legends. DNA tests and other tests confirmed Max had died of lung failure and hemorrhaging.

The day began with a fair breeze and scattered clouds, with a 20 percent chance of showers in the afternoon. The televised funeral procession began at 6:00 p.m. Everyone dressed in black. It drizzled, and the funeral home brought small black umbrellas for everyone. Several people accompanied Aunt Dori, including her two daughters, the Prices, and a few friends from First Baptist Church. Geoffrey, Alex, and Yvette stood next to them. Doc embraced Aunt Dori. He felt terrible for not being forthright with her. What would Titus think? But then, it was all speculation. Could he tell her what had happened? Or what he had just found out? No, not now! At least give her time to grieve Max, he thought. With that thought, Doc stood up to give his eulogy.

Doc gave a brief history of how he had known Aunt Dori and Titus. A history of Max's time at FIST—the lab, golf, and Spartan Enterprises.

How everything had moved so quickly. He expressed how everyone was going to miss Max—his outstanding character, creativity, and hard work.

"He reminded me of my old self. That fire. The relentlessness. That drive! I've known this family for many years. I was bunkmates with his Uncle Titus during the Gulf War. That guy had thick skin. He never gave up. He always seemed to think there was more to this life."

Doc looked at Aunt Dori, as if giving an apology for her husband's unfair treatment by the air force, which Doc had been powerless to change. A few days earlier, he had asked Aunt Dori if he might have Titus's body exhumed and transferred to the Heroes' Acre next to Max. Aunt Dori had refused, knowing how long it would take. And she felt it was unnecessary. She had reasoned that Titus' father owned a large piece of land in the Stratford cemetery for the family. She was sure Titus would not like being separated from his parents. It was a family sanctuary. She had agreed only to having a stone marker placed honoring his name at the Heroes' Acre, at Doc's insistence.

Doc wiped his eyes.

"Over the few months of working with Max," he continued. "I could see he was a chip off the old block, and knew Max was going to be great. I am proud of you, Max. And I know Titus is, as well."

McKomic spoke a few words. When he finished, Reverend Kay read from the Gospel of John, chapter 14, verses one through four. He encouraged Max's family not to worry because Max was with the Father in heaven. He had slipped into another life. After that, he asked everyone to bow their heads as he prayed.

"Dear Heavenly Father, thank you for loving us before we even knew you. Thank you for telling us there is nothing impossible and thank you for Mr. Folksay. We know, God, you have a plan for every-thing that is happening, and we ask that you reveal in our hearts, and open our eyes to see, your plan. We pray you will lead us to the right decisions. I pray you will comfort Mrs. Folksay and Ms. Price as they mourn for their loved one. We pray for wisdom and courage for all our employees and colleagues as we ponder Max's death. Let it give us hope that you are there for us. And let it be fuel to propel us forward to greater heights. For your glory and the prosperity of humanity. Amen."

The crowds echoed, "Amen!"

Alonna walked to the casket and leaned on it with both hands. No tears came from her eyes, as much as she wanted them to. She placed a red rose in Max's hands and stared at his face for a long time. She took the ring off, held it in her hand, and after a long meditation, slid it back on her finger. She felt in her heart that he was still alive, but his eyes did not open. Alonna's father came and consoled her while assisting her away from the casket.

Aunt Dori rolled her wheelchair towards the casket, glanced at Max's face, and smiled. She put a white rose on Max's chest.

Doc watched her. His stomach churned seeing her anguish. It was all his fault. He shouldn't have let Max go. He should have done more. It should have been him instead. But we all die at some point. Then he comforted himself at the thought that maybe this was the real Max. He had looked through the forensic report many times, and everything was consistent. The doctor had confirmed it as well. He tried to suppress the thoughts buzzing in his head. But he knew it wouldn't leave him. It would be a parasite eating at his consciousness for the rest of his life. The strange signal. He hoped it was a mere glitch and nothing out of the ordinary would come of it. Then again, you never knew in his line of work. They were learning new things about Aoratosia every day. If Max was alive, he would do what he could to find him!

"Doc," McKomic whispered, shaking Doc from his reverie. "You're next."

"Oh." Doc inched toward the casket, his legs like stumps.

The pallbearers lowered the casket into the open grave as a three-gun salute punctuated the moment. A violin played "Amazing Grace" in the background. A chalkstone bust of Max was erected at the base of the grave with the inscription "MAXWELL FOLKSAY. THE DREAMER! DISCOVERER OF AORATOSIA." The funeral party dispersed towards the main lobby, one by one, for the post-funeral meal of pot roast.

~

THEY DID NOT KNOW what to think, still in a haze. Aunt Dori sat quietly in her wheelchair. Was her nephew never to discover the cure for M.S. he had always wanted to? In her mind, Max was still alive somewhere, even though she did not know where. She did not feel any sadness, which was strange, but somehow felt compelled to believe he was alive somewhere. Maybe it was because the nerve damage was taking its toll, but she thought it was not. She had always felt some strangeness suffused the whole issue from the beginning. She believed Max was living in heaven with God. The assigned aide pushed her wheelchair past the cypress trees lining the cemetery's edge, to the car, and seated her.

Alonna climbed in beside Aunt Dori. She sat clutching Max's medal and the tattered scrapbook in her hands, holding them close to her heart. She flipped the cover page of the scrapbook, the first time she had had the courage to open it. She read the cursive sentences—in Max's hand. It read:

August 24.

To Alonna, with all my love. Can't wait to see you soon!

Alonna opened the limousine's window and looked outside. She let the wind dry the tears soaking her eyes. The world was crashing down around her. Somewhere in her fragile heart, she wanted to embrace Max as a hero, as everyone else was doing, but she felt angry that Max had failed to keep his promise. He had not come back to her! Somewhere beyond the clouds, she thought, Max's spirit endured and was watching over her. That comforted her. She thought even more about Max. How much she loved him. She thought of their first kiss. Of the things she had wanted to tell Max—and the wedding, the traveling, the kids, the big house. She wanted to hold him, to kiss him, to embrace him, and never let him go. Yvette had told her what had actually happened on Aoratosia. *Ugh. How can I be so naïve to believe something so preposterous?* she had thought. Oh. But she knew she did. She had her own suspicions. Her heart could not stop racing at the thought of an alternative ending, of all the what-ifs. Maybe Max was here!

Alonna turned to the last page. Just like that, Max's life had flashed by. She read the shaky handwritten note.

This, as before and for always, is why we do all the things that we do. For the people we love. To make them proud. This is for YOU Alonna! I love you. See you soon!

Max

She sighed, closed her eyes, feeling the touch of Max's lips wafting on her lips with the wind through the slightly open window. *I love you, Max, and forever will!*

Tomorrow will be Sunday. Another day! Another week!

AUTHOR'S NOTE

Thank you for joining me on the AORATOSIA journey. If you enjoyed INVISIBLE WITHIN, a review would be much appreciated as it helps other readers discover the story. You can visit your retailer's page by inserting www.jmanyanga.com into your browser.

Sign up at www.jmanyanga.com to be notified of giveaways, new releases, and updates as we journey through this epic journey of discovery together.

Made in the USA
Coppell, TX
21 April 2021